A Message

from

Cupid

A Message from Cupid

VICTORIA BARRETT
ELIZABETH BEVARLY
MARGARET BROWNLEY
EMILY CARMICHAEL

St. Martin's Paperbacks

A MESSAGE FROM CUPID

"Wheels of Love" copyright © 1998 by Emily Krokosz.
"Cupid's Arrow" copyright © 1998 by Vicki Hinze.
"Top Cat and Tales" copyright © 1998 by Elizabeth Bevarly.
"Winning Ticket" copyright © 1998 by Margaret Brownley.

ISBN: 0-312-96483-8

Printed in the United States of America

St. Martin's Paperbacks edition / February 1998

10 9 8 7 6 5 4 3 2 1

CONTENTS

Wheels of Love

EMILY CARMICHAEL

PROLOGUE

"*A* sad case. Very sad. Clearly in need of our attention. I can't imagine why this situation hasn't been addressed before now." Senior Agent Hearts glanced at the file on his white enamel desk, then irritably brushed an imagined speck of lint from his lapel. He'd worn his best suit today—a bright red double-breasted jacket tailored just so, with matching trousers pressed to a knife-edge crease. Both shirt and tie were snowy white, and tiny little red hearts dotted the tie with a sprinkle of stylish color. Hearts liked red. It suited both his job and his personality.

The young agent intern sitting across from him, on the other hand, dressed all in white except for narrow red piping on the sleeve of her blazer. Irredeemably plain, Hearts reflected—the manner of dress, not the intern. The intern was quite a looker, if one ignored her "save the world" expression and near military bearing. She scowled down at her copy of the file, mouth pursed in disapproval.

"Have you read the file, Agent Flowers?"

She looked up from her study. "Of course, sir. What I see here is a clear violation of the Rules of Love, chapter five, section two, paragraphs six-a and six-b."

"I am well aware of the perfect score you earned on your academy examination, Agent Flowers. There is no need for you to show off."

"I wasn't—"

"Of course you were," he said with a faint smile. "All interns feel the need to strut a bit on their first assignment. Understandable. The work we do is important and a bit daunting at times. Intimidating to those just embarking upon a career. But the best way to prove yourself, my dear, is by a good showing on your first assignment."

She gave him a look the very young reserve for those they consider old and stodgy.

"Shall we go over the strategy we will use in the battle to come?"

"By all means, sir."

"Good." Hearts closed the file on his desk, leaned back in his chair, and steepled his fingers beneath his chin. "The situation is a rather unusual one for this day and age. The couple in question don't have a clue about love, joy, or romance, and yet they are foolish enough to plan marriage. I suspect this ignorant pair doesn't even realize the number of laws they are breaking." Hearts shook his head sadly, then rose and crossed the pink carpet to stand before a baroque artist's rendition of two rather fleshy ladies seated in a bower. The ladies were attended by two pudgy little winged cupids with bows and arrows.

Contemplating the painting, Hearts frowned. "Convenience and necessity—two of the ugliest notions that ever attacked Cupid's realm. We had to put up with too much of that nonsense in the eighteenth and nineteenth centuries. The situation before that was bad as well, of course. Especially during the Middle Ages and the Renaissance, but I wasn't around to struggle with it then." He turned to give Flowers a look of warning. "No matter how old you believe I am, Agent Flowers, I am not quite that old."

"I never thought so, sir."

Hearts snorted, then perched himself on one corner of his desk. "For the most part, the twentieth century has grown beyond that sort of thing. Especially the United States. They worship romance. Their picture shows and plays are full of it. Television, novels, magazines, advertisements—they all are grounded in the idea of romance as the most important part of creation."

"Very erudite of them."

"Yes indeed. But some, unfortunately, are less erudite than others. Some have not yet learned the rules of the game. Though how they manage to remain so ignorant, I don't know."

"Unbelievable," Flowers agreed obediently.

"Our subjects in this case are two intelligent, educated people—Eric Neal and Mary Elizabeth Chambers. I believe the politically correct term for their malady would be 'romantically challenged.' More to the point, they are both dunces in the school of love, dithering dunderheads in matters of the heart, as well as a few more minor areas of life."

"Setting them straight is both our honor and our duty," Flowers declared.

"Yes, it is. This will be a very challenging assignment for your first time out of the academy, but challenge only makes us stronger."

Flowers rose, her face aglow with the glory of battling in Cupid's army. "I'll give it my all, sir. You can rely on me to do whatever necessary to bring these poor souls onto the straight and narrow path of love."

Hearts allowed himself a faintly amused smile. "I know you will, Agent Flowers."

"I'll go get my weapons. My bow is freshly oiled and my arrows sharp as the lightning's edge."

"Agent Flowers . . ."

Flowers stopped at Hearts's hesitant tone. "We are using the standard tools, aren't we?"

Hearts cleared his throat, feeling again the uneasiness he'd experienced when first reading the orders that had come down from the head office. "Not this time, Agent Flowers."

"What?"

"We're a modern agency now, you know. The boss went to one of those management seminars a while back, and he's very keen to try a new behind-the-scenes style." He handed

Flowers her copy of their orders and watched her expression go from uncertainty to consternation.

"Is this a joke?" she demanded.

Hearts sighed. "One thing you learn after a couple of centuries on the force, my dear. Cupid never jokes."

CHAPTER ONE

*E*ric Neal grinned hugely and enjoyed the feel of the muggy July air. There was nothing like the open road to make a man feel free—the wind in his hair at sixty-five miles per hour, the hum of the tires, the bugs in his teeth.

He laughed and shut his mouth abruptly as a fat bug splattered on the windshield, reminding him of the hazards of driving a convertible. He couldn't help the ridiculous good humor. The joy of leaving suburbia behind was so sharp, he wanted to sing out loud. For this short moment in his life, no responsibilities tied him down. No schedules regimented his time. No checklists or three-inch-thick manuals told him what to do and how to do it.

A four-day drive from Chicago to Phoenix lay ahead of him. His fellow pilots at Sunbelt Airways had gotten a lot of mileage from the joke of him driving to his new home instead of flying. Eric didn't mind being the butt of their humor. The bachelor party they'd thrown him had needed a bit of laughter to get off the ground.

Eric glanced upward at a jet contrail that crossed the hazy Illinois sky. Seeing the country from thirty thousand feet had its advantages, but right now, the cockpit of his little Austin-Healey was where he wanted to be. This road trip was an intermission from life, and he intended to savor every moment of it. He had left behind Chicago, the privileges of bachelorhood, and a clean-cut house in a clean-cut part of suburbia. He headed toward the Arizona desert, a house in a different suburbia, and a woman who would shortly stand with him at a church altar and change his life forever. Not that he had any doubts about marrying Mary Elizabeth. No indeed! He'd reached the time in life when marriage and family were right for him. He was thirty years old, had a good job, and was steadily climbing the ladder of his chosen profession. The singles scene had lost its appeal, if it had ever had one, and coming home to an empty house, an empty bed, and only the television to keep him company got more lonely every day.

For Eric Neal, the time was right for marriage. Very right, he assured himself. Supremely right.

But he still intended to enjoy every moment of the drive— just him and his Healey. He gave the dashboard a fond caress. What a deal he'd gotten on this car! From the first moment he'd seen it two days ago, he knew it had to be his. Maybe the yearning was a last spurt of defiance against his conservative, regimented world of regulations and checklists. Or maybe he simply recognized a classic when he saw it. Whichever, he'd had to have it. The Healey was perfect, gleaming with chrome and new paint. The engine purred like a contented tiger. Some might complain that the bright red paint and white leather exterior were a bit extreme. And the radio was a bit odd. It kept shifting frequencies from the country-western station he preferred to a station that played nothing but romantic mush.

But radios were easily fixed, and paint could be changed. None of those details mattered. Once in Phoenix, he might sell the car—or he might keep it as a reminder of the road not taken. But right now, as he rolled toward the Mississippi River, Iowa, and points west, he was going to enjoy it.

Hearts congratulated himself with smug satisfaction. He had his victim snared, netted, and hog-tied. Eric Neal had been a goner from the first moment he'd spied the sports car on the used-car lot—though a 1966 Austin-Healey could hardly be labeled "used car." A classic is what it was, and there was no way the poor sucker could help but take a closer look, never suspecting what awaited him behind the lure of the bait. Hearts had done a thorough background check on Mr. Neal. Some agents preferred just to leap into the fray and start causing a ruckus, but experience had taught Hearts that every piece of information about a potential victim was ammunition as valuable as another arrow in the quiver—as if they were still allowed to use the traditional arrows.

No matter. Hearts had been dubious, but he was finding that this new mode of operation had its advantages. What other job would transform an agent into such a prime example of automotive distinction? This disguise had the works! Fold-down top, radio, white leather upholstery, reclining seats (essential for any romantic relationship), shiny red paint (Hearts had insisted upon that), and classic spoked wheels. Hearts had tailored the Healey to be Eric Neal's dream car, except maybe for the color. Lord, but he loved this Neal fellow's taste in automobiles. His taste in music could be better, but no one could fault his taste in wheels. Oh yes!

A few miles farther west, another car sped along the same freeway through the muggy midwestern morning. In the passenger seat, Samantha Vargas looked up from her sketch, gazing out the window at the flat farmfields and picturesque barns of eastern Iowa. Jeff Connors had the gas pedal floored, but the fifteen-year-old Ford Escort stubbornly refused to go faster than 60 mph. Loaded down with two people, four bulging suitcases, five boxes of books, two ice chests filled with pop and beer, and one cat cage with resident cat, the car was feeling every one of its nearly two hundred thousand miles. Jeff, however, was a person who would rather leave the speed limit in the dust than drag along behind it. The situation was making him even more testy than he already was.

Samantha slid a glance toward her companion, then added a touch of pencil to her sketch, making the mulish set of her subject's mouth even more sullen. For a fast caricature done speeding along a bumpy freeway, the work wasn't bad, she reflected. A month ago Jeff's mood would have upset her. A

month ago she would have tried to josh him out of the dol-
drums. That was before he'd gotten himself fired from the play
he was working in and before he'd decided that drinking beer
and grousing about being ''unappreciated'' were more to the
point than looking for·another job. Now, after a month of
letting him sleep in her apartment, eat her food, and borrow
from her meager savings account, she didn't care how put out
he felt. She was just sorry that he was spoiling a perfectly
lovely day by oozing his sour mood all over the car.

''What're you drawing?'' Jeff demanded.

Sam tilted the sketch pad so he could see it.

He snorted derisively. ''That supposed to be me?''

''Does it look like you?''

''It's not very flattering.''

''It's just a cartoon.''

''Trust you to highlight all the worst things about me.''

Sam sighed and rolled her eyes. ''That's not what I did.
You're every bit as cranky as you look here.''

''Well, I have a right to be. Damn!·It's going to take us
forever to get to Los Angeles the way this piece of junk is
running. I told you it needs an engine job.''

''Like I can afford an engine job.''

''You found the money to buy that fancy kit of artsy stuff
that's taking up room in the back.''

''The cost isn't even in the same league.'' Sam didn't mention that Jeff was perfectly capable of doing the engine work
himself, and she had told him she could pay for the parts. But
he had been too busy drinking·with his theater friends and
complaining about the injustice of being out of work.

Sam turned back to her sketch and did her own bit of silent
grousing. Once again she had added another jerk to the long
line of jerks, conmen, and losers that constituted her romantic
history. At first Jeff Connors had appeared to be as close to
the man of her dreams as any man could get. He was attractive, smart, sensitive, considerate, and funny. She hadn't
minded that she usually paid the bill when they went to dinner
or a show. After all, he was a struggling actor trying to get
his start in Chicago, and everyone knew actors didn't make

much money. And if he occasionally drank too much or displayed a fit of temper—well, no one was perfect.

Sam had tried to be tolerant even when she had caught Jeff snorting coke. That had been only once, though, and he'd claimed he did it only to be "in" with the theater crowd. She should have given him the heave-ho right then, but she'd kept trying to make things work, until a badly timed drinking spree had cost Jeff his job, his good humor, and most of his charm. He'd needed her then, he claimed, and she'd never been one who could turn away a person in trouble, no matter that he'd brought the trouble on himself.

The trip to Los Angeles had been Jeff's idea, but Sam had allowed herself to get excited about a change of scenery and a whole new place full of new opportunities. She would get Jeff to Los Angeles—he couldn't afford to get himself there, being without a car and broke—and turn him loose on the unsuspecting California crowd. Then, Sam told herself, she could bow out and go her own way. She could put up with him for that long.

"I don't know why you had to bring that damned cat along," Jeff complained. "It makes me sneeze."

"Sassy's not an 'it.' She's a 'she.' And I brought her along because where I go, she goes, too. What was I supposed to do? Take her to the pound?"

"Why not? She's just a stray."

"She isn't a stray now. She's better company than some people I could name."

"Don't get all sanctimonious."

The subject of Jeff's complaint popped out of the open cage, arched in an elaborate feline stretch, then picked her way over the luggage and boxes to curl on the floorboards at Sam's feet. In spite of tattered ears and a scarred nose, she managed to give Jeff a queenly look that clearly conveyed her contempt. He returned the look full measure.

"She came up here just to piss me off."

"Don't be silly."

"I'm not being goddamned silly. She'd blow her hair my way if she could. By the time we get to L.A., I'll probably have a sinus infection, and then how am I going to audition for anything? I can't believe you think a damned cat is more important than me getting my life together."

Sam sighed. She couldn't believe that someone who would suck cocaine up his nose could object to a bit of cat hair in the same place. In sudden inspiration, she added a few pencil strokes to the sketch in her lap, and suddenly the pouting caricature was wearing a cat on his head, front paws dangling over his brow, one rear foot grabbing for a toehold on his ear. She grinned.

"That's not funny," Jeff growled.

"Oh, lighten up." She closed the sketch pad's cover. "You're just a grouch because your stomach's empty. There's a McDonald's at the next exit. Let's stop for lunch."

Eric climbed out of the Healey, looked around the crowded McDonald's parking lot, and stretched. He'd planned to get a hamburger in the drive-through, but the aches in his back and knees convinced him he needed a break. The Healey didn't have as much room as it had class, and Eric had to accordion himself to fit into the driver's seat—all six feet, 190 pounds of him. Getting in and out of the little car was as hard as fitting himself into the tiny Cessna 152 all those years ago when he was a student pilot.

He smiled at the memory. The hardest thing about learning to fly had been deciding what to do with his legs and elbows in the plane, not to mention that his flight instructor, a petite young woman who probably didn't weigh a hundred pounds soaking wet, had been forced to endure the thrust of his shoulders and knees overlapping hers. That had been real flying, the way they had bounced around the sky in that little single-engine two-seater. Remembering tugged at his heart with nostalgia.

Suddenly, as if summoned by his airborne thoughts, a bright yellow biplane appeared at treetop level across the freeway. The noise of traffic, the shrieks of children in the restaurant playground, the diesel belching of the semis in the gas station next door—all were drowned out by the throaty roar of a radial engine as the Stearman swooped close to the ground, trailing a white fog of crop spray, then pulled up just in time to miss the row of trees at the far end of the field.

Eric felt the old exultation rise into his chest and speed his heart. He'd flown a Stearman biplane one summer, doing exactly the job this plane was doing—dangerous, dirty, daredevil work. He'd both hated and loved it. Once the sound of that nine-cylinder radial engine got into your gut, it was hard to find a sweeter sound. The memory was still fresh in his senses. The swoops and turns, the feel of G-forces squashing him into the seat as he pulled up into a steep climb, the sense of once again having dodged the bullet of death every time he touched down safely on the home runway. Even the memory was exhilarating. That was flying. That was living.

Not that he wanted to do it again. He was one of the lucky few who had made aviation a secure, comfortable, safe, high-paying career. A man couldn't accomplish much toodling around the sky in a little single-engine Cessna, nor could he support a family on a flight instructor's pay or a crop duster's income. He was past that, and glad of it. But still he stood there in the hot Iowa sunshine, watching the yellow biplane make precisely flown passes over the beanfield. He stood there until the gutsy little plane pulled up for a final climb and disappeared into the muggy summer haze.

The restaurant was crowded and noisy, but Eric didn't mind. The squeals and laughter that came through the door of the enclosed playground made him smile. He hardly even noticed the clamor, concentrating instead on his hamburger and fries, until the tense-looking man and woman sitting at the table next to him set out to compete with the playground in noise level. When Eric had first sat down, the pair had been eating in silence, attention glued on their food to the absolute exclusion of each other. It would have been hard for any man, even a man a week away from his own wedding, not to notice the woman, with her pixie face, large green eyes, and flamboyant red curls. The color was a totally natural red, the curls artless and styled by the Iowa wind. Her companion was eye-catchingly handsome in a lantern-jawed, movie-star sort of way, but the good looks were spoiled by the sullen droop of his mouth and a hard edge in his eyes. He further demonstrated his sour nature when something the woman said inspired a heated reply, which was liberally spiced with terms that would have rated an R in any movie theater. Heads all around the restaurant turned toward the budding argument, then looked away in embarrassment.

Green-Eyes hissed at her companion to be quiet, to no avail.

"If I'd known you were gonna be such a bitch, I woulda taken the bus, goddammit! All you care about is yourself. You get to make the rules, and I get to do all the work. Is that it?"

The woman closed her eyes in frustration while color crawled up her face, making freckles stand out like beacons of embarrassment. "Jeff, we are in a public place."

"Screw the public place! A man gets a little down on his luck, and you make sure he gets screwed from every direction and every possible way. You fair-weather whores make me sick! Take and take and take. Everything's sweetness and light until money stops coming in, and then it's 'Good-bye, sucker!' and all I see is your ass going out the door. Whatever happened to 'stand by your man,' huh?"

"Sssssshhhh!" she hissed. "*Will* you keep it down?"

"Screw you!"

At other tables, people had their heads assiduously turned away from the conflict, pretending they didn't hear the loud display. Not Eric. Green-Eyes was a long way from cover-girl glamorous, but she certainly did hold a man's notice. Those eyes of hers had a humorous slant, as though she laughed a lot, when not engaged in public battles with her boyfriend. Her mouth was generous and sweetly curved, and the rest of her was sweetly curved as well. Eric might be on the brink of matrimony, but that didn't deaden the part of him that noticed such things.

Her lantern-jawed boyfriend, on the other hand, was a jerk,

Eric concluded. At least, he assumed the shaggy-haired, overly handsome jackass was her boyfriend. He wondered what she saw in him.

The tirade went on as the jerk ignored the girl's warnings to pipe down. The restaurant manager scowled and shifted from foot to foot behind the counter, obviously trying to decide if he should intervene, call the police, or just ignore the whole ruckus in hopes it would go away. Before he could make up his mind, the girl got up, dumped her half-eaten food into a trash container, and dug a set of car keys from her handbag.

"Are you coming, or walking?" she said into the sudden silence.

Her companion shot her a venomous look but pushed his chair back with a loud scrape and got up. He stomped out without bothering to clear away the remains of his meal. The girl sighed, cleaned up the mess, gave a little apologetic shrug that addressed the whole room, and hurried out. Eric watched through the window as they climbed into a 1980s-vintage Ford station wagon. Tires screeched as they drove away, and he could tell that words were flying fast and furious.

He wondered suddenly if those two loved each other. The more intense love became the more destructive it could be—or so wrote experts supposedly in the know. Eric and Mary Elizabeth had never exchanged an angry word, as far as he remembered. They'd known each other since he was eleven and she was nine, when she'd moved to the little Oklahoma town where Eric's widowed mother had gotten a job in the local grocery store. Eric had escorted her to the Harvest Moon Ball on their first date in junior high, and all through high school they'd gone steady. College had brought new experiences and new people to both of them, but after a few years of dating others, they had once again fallen into the comfortable, amiable relationship that was as strong on friendship as it was on romance, in no hurry for marriage or great passion while they both carved out their own niches in the world. Until lately, when Eric's thirtieth birthday had reminded them both that youth and opportunity for a family could very well pass them by.

Eric was sure he loved Mary Elizabeth Chambers as intensely as any other man loved his fiancée, but those feelings certainly didn't inspire him to talk to her as the jerk had talked to his girlfriend. Not that Mary Elizabeth would put up with it if he ever did. Their relationship was much too sensible for that kind of nonsense.

Once back on the road, Eric took his time along the highway. He was in no hurry, the afternoon was a pleasant one, and the passing farmlands and little Americana-style burgs put him in a lazy, dawdling mood. The Healey hummed along like the well-oiled machine it was, and Eric finally became accustomed to the combination jazz–soft rock the radio insisted upon playing. No schedules to keep. No harried flight attendants, overstressed air traffic controllers, or overcrowded passengers to deal with. Just him and his Healey, cruising along without a care in the world.

Yes indeed! There was nothing like the open road to make a man feel free—until the open road suddenly threw a curve his way. That curve took the form of a hitchhiker standing on the shoulder of the freeway, a small, forlorn figure that was little more than a blur as Eric whizzed by. He didn't stop, of course. No one in his right mind stopped for a hitchhiker, not in these times, when every stranger was a potential serial killer and a Good Samaritan could become a depressing statistic in the blink of an eye.

No, Eric was not the one who stopped. The Austin-Healey was. Just as they sped past the hitchhiker, the car's engine noise went from a hum to a pathetic wheeze, the speedometer needle fell toward zero, and even the radio seemed to give a plaintive whine. Eric had no choice but to pull over onto the shoulder. He cursed as he looked in the rearview mirror. Of course the hitchhiker assumed he was stopping for him—no, it was a her. Definitely a woman. As she hurried along the road toward him, she ran like a girl, slender legs kicking to the side, her bundles bouncing along with her. Under one arm she carried a carpetbag and an oversize tablet of some sort.

The other hand clung to a carrying cage from which issued squalls and hisses that could have been used as sound effects for any of several horror movies he could name.

"Oh, thank you!" she cried breathlessly as she trotted up to the Healey. "Thank you for stopping."

Eric had recognized her when she was still twenty yards away. She was the beleaguered girlfriend—the pixie with the laughing green eyes and sweet curves.

"I didn't think anyone would stop and I'd have to walk to the next rest stop and spend the night sleeping in the ladies' room. Or if someone stopped, he'd be a serial killer out on a spree. You're not a serial killer, are you?"

"Uh . . . no. Not at the moment."

She smiled. Eric had been right in his first impression. Her eyes positively sparkled with silent laughter.

"Of course you aren't. I should have had faith, you know? Things always turn out, one way or another. At least for me they do." She dropped her things, including a cage containing one very unhappy cat, onto the small backseat. "You're the fellow at the McDonald's back there, aren't you? You were sitting at the table next to me and Jeff. Oh God! You must think I'm some kind of weirdo, or at least an idiot. That scene was *so* embarrassing. Right out in front of everyone. I hate scenes. I really do. I don't mind a good shouting match now and then to clear the sludge from your soul, but in private is the only place to stage one of those."

She dropped her shapely backside into the passenger seat and looked at Eric expectantly. Eric couldn't help but notice how shapely that backside was, even if he was a man on his way to the marital altar.

"You were awfully nice to stop," she told him.

He didn't know quite how to tell her that he wasn't nice at all. His car simply wouldn't run. The truth was about to come out of his mouth when the engine roared to life, just as though he'd turned the key, which he hadn't. The radio crooned a Barry Manilow song that yodeled something about love being enough to get anyone through anything. Barry Manilow, for cripes' sake! Eric felt suddenly as though he were cruising very close to the Twilight Zone.

"Hot car," his passenger said, patting the white leather dashboard with an affectionate hand.

Eric thought he heard the Healey's horn toot proudly as the car started to roll, but he couldn't be sure.

CHAPTER TWO

Mary Elizabeth gave the scuffed-up nine-year-old her best smile and gently patted the Ace bandage she'd wrapped around his ankle. "Does that feel better now?"

The boy gave the bandage a dubious look. "I don't get a cast?"

His mother spoke up. "Your ankle's just sprained, Ralph, not broken."

"Are you sure?" Ralph asked, and looked at Mary Elizabeth instead of his mother. "It hurts a lot. Are you sure it's not busted?"

"*Broken*, dear," the mother corrected him. "*Busted* isn't a word, and using improper grammar gives people the impression that you're ignorant. You don't want that." She pursed her mouth and raised a brow, reminding Mary Elizabeth of a home-economics teacher she'd endured in junior high. The tone of voice was similar as well, except that Mrs. Leetham's concern had not been Mary Elizabeth's grammar, but her unfeminine disinterest in domesticity.

Mary Elizabeth gave Ralph an encouraging smile. "I know how much that ankle hurts, young man, and you've been very brave. When I was just a little older than you, I had a sprain like this, and I cried all the way to the doctor's office."

"Really?"

"Yes, really. Sprains hurt an awful lot. Do you want to look again at the picture Dr. Myers took of your ankle?"

Ralph said that he did, and Mary Elizabeth clipped the X-ray to the viewbox. Patiently she traced the shadow of bones in his ankle once more, reassuring him that they were all intact. When she had finished, Ralph heaved a disappointed sigh.

"A cast would've been cool. A bandage ain't nuthin'." He sent his mother an apologetic glance and corrected himself. "Isn't anything. The other kids can't sign it or . . . you know."

"I know," Mary Elizabeth agreed sympathetically. "But you'll have crutches."

"Really? I get ta be on crutches?"

"Yes indeed. We wouldn't want you putting weight on that ankle before it heals. Besides, you don't want to give your all in a soccer game and have nothing but a puny bandage to show for it."

"Cool!"

A nurse walked in as Mary Elizabeth helped the boy down from the table. "Mrs. Jennings, will you help Ralph over to where you can fit him with crutches?"

"Certainly, Dr. Chambers. My! What a nice bright bandage Doctor gave you. And crutches, too! Aren't you the lucky boy!" she chattered cheerfully while helping Ralph hobble down the hall.

Mary Elizabeth asked the mother to stay behind so she could go over what Ralph could and couldn't do while his ankle was healing. "I'm afraid he's out of soccer for a while," she told Mrs. Bingham.

"That's fine with me," the woman said with a grimace. "I wish I could think of an excuse to keep him out of sports once school starts again. Basketball, volleyball, baseball—he wants to do it all, but he's as clumsy as they come. That boy can find more ways to hurt himself than any child I know. What is this, the third time we've been in here this summer?"

"Kids should be made of rubber at this age. I wouldn't worry too much about it. Growth spurts often make a kid lose his coordination." Mary Elizabeth made a note on Ralph's record. "With so many children vegetating in front of a television or computer monitor, I'd be grateful he wants to be active."

"I suppose. Will he have to come back to be checked?"

"Not unless the ankle doesn't get better. Why don't you call in a week or so and let me know how he's doing?"

"I will. And thank you for working us in like this. You're so conscientious, Dr. Chambers, and my husband and I do appreciate it. I hope you aren't going to move after your wedding. I would hate to worry about finding another pediatrician right now."

"I wouldn't dream of moving away from Phoenix. I love it here." Mary Elizabeth slipped Ralph's record into the holder on the door and walked with Mrs. Bingham toward the reception area.

"How are your wedding plans coming?" the woman asked.

"The wedding's next Saturday." She sighed. "A week from tomorrow. Somehow that seems so close. Everything's set, I dearly hope."

Mrs. Bingham laughed. "You sound nervous, dear. Don't worry. Women were meant to be married, you know. It's just a shame that once you have children of your own, you'll have so much less time for ours."

"Don't worry about that. I have no intention of cutting back my practice. I believe a family and a career can exist side by side if one is willing to work at it."

Mrs. Bingham clucked her doubt. "Yes, so many women these days are trying to have both. But something always suffers, doesn't it?"

With a smile that struck Mary Elizabeth as patronizing, the older woman opened the door to the reception area and left her standing in the hallway. Mary Elizabeth's mouth pursed in exasperation as she stared at the closed door.

" 'Something always suffers, doesn't it?' " she muttered in an imitation of Mrs. Bingham's sanctimonious tone.

"What's that?"

In her aggravation, Mary Elizabeth hadn't heard Alan Reirdon's footsteps in the hall. He stopped beside her, head cocked in amusement, blue eyes dancing at her obvious vexation.

"Mrs. Bingham," Mary Elizabeth answered, as if that were enough of an explanation.

"Ah. Ralph at it again?"

"Ralph has a sprained ankle. His mother has an advanced case of the butt-in-where-you're-not-wanted virus."

"Sounds as if you need a cup of coffee."

"I really do." She glanced at her watch, sighed, and was about to admit the impossibility of taking a break when the receptionist stuck her head around the corner.

"Dr. Chambers, your eleven o'clock isn't here, and your eleven-fifteen called to cancel. Johnny Rivers's rash has disappeared, and his mom got him to admit he'd snuck some peanut butter, so that explains it."

Mary Elizabeth grinned. "Perfect timing. I think I will take time for a cup."

"And I'll join you," Alan said.

The office coffee lounge was one corner of a storage room, where a round Formica table, three plastic chairs, and a microwave shared space with janitorial supplies, stacks of toilet paper, examination gowns, disposable urine cups, office supplies, and glass-fronted cabinets housing everything from cotton swabs to disinfectants. A tiny refrigerator was crowded with the staff's lunches, cans of soda, and two pitchers of sun tea. The medical partnership of Drs. Reirdon, Chambers, Myers, and Targot—obstetrics and gynecology, pediatrics, radiology, and family practice, respectively—was still in the getting off the ground stage, and ample office space was merely a hope for the future. No one complained, though. Mary Elizabeth was supremely grateful she had been taken into a practice where not only the other physicians put the patients before profits, but the whole staff was of the same mind.

Alan poured them both cups of coffee, dumped a packet of sugar into Mary Elizabeth's, and handed it to her.

"Just the way I like it," Mary Elizabeth observed with a smile.

"At your service, Dr. Chambers." He dropped into the plastic chair opposite her. "Why the puckered brow, Mary Liz? Wedding jitters?"

"Nah!" she denied. "Just Mrs. Bingham and her ideas on

all and sundry. She was bemoaning the prospect of my cutting back practice once I have kids of my own, and when I disavowed any intention of doing any such thing, she wheeled out the lecture on children suffering from the neglect of working mothers.''

"Just close your ears. Sheila Bingham belongs to a church that's very vocal about mothers staying home, and all women are destined to be mothers, according to them. You and I both know that's not true.''

Mary Elizabeth smiled sheepishly. "Guess I'm just being sensitive.''

"You're entitled. Zero hour is next Saturday, right? All brides are expected to be nervous, edgy, given to bouts of tears, and generally hard to live with for at least a month before a wedding. If not more.''

"Am I that bad?''

"Just a little frazzled around the edges.''

"I'm really glad we're having a simple ceremony instead of one of those elaborate hooplas that take a year to plan and an army of caterers and consultants to orchestrate.'' She grimaced. "I do wish I weren't leaving for a whole week after the wedding. I feel as though I'm neglecting my patients.''

Alan chuckled. "You're covered, Mary Liz. You've briefed us all about every patient's history, problems, and the likelihood of any of them having a crisis while you're gone. So wipe that worried frown off your face. Eric would definitely not appreciate spending his honeymoon in Phoenix. In July, no less, with the weather wizards predicting hotter than usual temperatures for the next two weeks. It's a hundred and eighteen degrees in the shade right now.''

For a moment, Mary Elizabeth considered the possibilities. "It wouldn't be so bad. We'd have the pool.''

"He'd be in it alone, knowing you. Or he'd be enjoying the air-conditioned comfort of our waiting room while you hung around here treating Joey Murdock's ear infection or Bobby McNamara's mumps. Do you think Eric might enjoy entertaining himself on the junior jungle gym or reading old issues of *Family Circle* while his bride put in her usual twelve-hour day?''

Mary Elizabeth had to laugh at the picture Alan painted. How well he knew her! ''The only fellow I know who would put up with that kind of honeymoon is you, Alan. You put in longer hours than I do.''

''That comes from being a very dull sort of person with no hobbies or home life.''

Mary Elizabeth arched a skeptical brow. ''I happen to know that Colin Myers has been trying to lure you onto the golf course for the last year, and at least two ladies of my acquaintance would be eager to offer you all the home life you wanted.''

''You caught me,'' he admitted, then smiled. ''It's the patients, you know. Who would take golf or tennis or the theater over helping a new life come safely into this world? When my mother pesters me about grandchildren, I just point to all the baby pictures in my album.''

Mary Elizabeth felt his words resonate in her own heart. ''The patients *are* family, aren't they? Sometimes I feel as though every child I treat is my own, that I'm mother to a hundred kids already.''

''But you're going to have your own family. Isn't that what you want?''

''That's what Eric wants.''

Alan's gaze became uncomfortably penetrating. ''And you?''

Mary Elizabeth gave herself a mental shake. ''Me, too, of course.'' She sent him what she hoped was a confident, cocky grin. ''I want it all.''

They finished their coffee over discussion of Jonathan Frickle's possible diabetes and the heart problem of a baby Alan had delivered just two days prior. Walking back to her office, Mary Elizabeth wondered, not for the first time, why Alan Reirdon kept dodging marriage. In spite of what he said, she detected a hint of loneliness in his manner. He was certainly attractive, with his Nordic good looks and fit build. Better yet, he was one of the gentlest, most caring men Mary

Elizabeth had ever met. She always knew she could talk to him, whether about a patient or a personal matter. His humor was never-ending, his advice generally sound, and a smile was always ready on his face.

Probably Alan didn't have time to date or get married, Mary Elizabeth concluded, which brought her back to her own concerns about a full week away from her practice. She was being silly, and a stick-in-the-mud, and very selfish, she acknowledged. How was poor Eric ever going to put up with her?

At the thought of Eric, Mary Elizabeth smiled. She closed her office door behind her and allowed herself a moment to think of her fiancé. Eric had always made her feel secure. Her parents had divorced when she was in high school, and Eric had been there to hold her together. In college, when the premed curriculum had seemed so daunting, Eric's letters had given her the confidence to forge ahead, and in medical school his encouragement had made the pressure and the effort bearable. In college she had dated other men, but seldom did they understand her ambitions or problems. After medical school, it had seemed so natural to slip back into the comfortable routine of dating Eric—whenever their busy schedules and sometimes distant locations had permitted.

It had seemed natural, Mary Elizabeth reminded herself, because they really were meant to be together. At some point in life, one had to grow up. Dating had to become commitment, especially when the biological clock was ticking away, day after day, month after month. Every woman needed a husband and children, didn't she? And Mary Elizabeth had loved children as long as she could remember. She had known from her first year of college that she wanted to be a pediatrician, just as she'd known when she first met Eric Neal that he was going to be a permanent part of her life. She'd only been nine years old at the time, but truths like that didn't change.

Her intercom buzzed. "Dr. Chambers?" came the receptionist's voice.

"Yes?"

"Your one o'clock has been pushed back to one-thirty, and at three Mrs. Carruthers is bringing in all four kids instead of just Jody. They've all developed the same cough."

"All right. Thank you."

Mary Elizabeth looked at her watch and decided she had time to do a bit of Internet searching to find a paper she wanted to read on juvenile diabetes. She sat down, logged on the computer, and pushed thoughts of the wedding, of Eric's imminent arrival, and everything but Jon Frickle's diabetes out of her mind.

While the computer hummed away on its search, Mary Elizabeth thumbed through the Frickle file. Only a moment passed before the article she wanted flashed onto her screen. She scanned it, then reached over to switch on her printer. When she turned back, something entirely different filled the screen.

"What on earth?"

The Web site called itself "The Romance Pages" and offered book reviews—of romance novels, of course—information about romance authors, and a bulletin board for fans.

"Where'd my article go?" Mary Elizabeth complained to the computer, as if it could answer her. She sent her Web browser back a few steps until the diabetes article appeared once again, then told it to print. The printer came to life, and immediately the screen changed again. This time the computer brought up a magazine piece from *Cosmopolitan*, titled "Is Your Man a Doer or a Dud?"

"Good grief!" Mary Elizabeth resisted the urge to give the computer a kick. "Modern communication!" she mumbled sarcastically. "Isn't it great?"

Next came a Web site called "Romance Communications," which offered an entire romance novel on-line, as well as links to home pages of romance authors and other romantically oriented sites. Mary Elizabeth was tempted to ask the medical secretary if someone had fed her computer an aphrodisiac. Fortunately her diabetes article was still stored somewhere among Cupid's followers, for it was printing. There were other sources she wanted to access, though, and she would never get to them with a love-happy computer.

Suddenly she chuckled and shook her head. The reason for this was obvious. She punched a button on her intercom.

"Very funny, Arlene."

"What?"

"This is Dr. Chambers."

"Uh . . . yes, Dr. Chambers?"

"Nice joke. What did you do to my computer, and how fast can you put it right?"

"Dr. Chambers," the medical secretary said, offense ruffling her voice, "I didn't do anything to your computer. Is something wrong?"

Mary Elizabeth bit her lip. She'd been so sure this had to be some kind of prenuptial joke, and Arlene was the only one in the office who knew enough about computers to pull it off. "Really? You didn't do anything?"

"No, Doctor."

"The thing's going crazy. You wouldn't believe how."

This wasn't bad at all, Flowers admitted. At first she'd been horrified by the idea of hiding herself inside the circuits of a computer. She didn't even like computers. Until now. Now that she *was* a computer, she was discovering all sorts of creative ways not only to do her job, but to entertain herself as well. The Internet was a wondrous world of possibilities—Internet, undernet, usenet, worldnet, newsnet, this net and that net. All very confusing at first, but Flowers had lots of time to explore. The avenues and alleyways were endless, especially on the subject of love—and what subject could be more important than love? In her wanders Flowers found romance making progress in chat rooms and on bulletin boards, on-line dating services, and Web sites. Though some offerings reeked of the less-savory aspects of love, Flowers was delighted with most of her discoveries.

Of course, the computer and the Web offered more than romance to catch her fancy: games—though solitaire was not really fun when the program wouldn't allow cheating—articles, photographs, and so much more. The shopping opportunities were divine. Possession of a credit-card number could get anything you wanted, delivered right to your door. Wonderful!

Not that Flowers had neglected her job in favor of shopping and entertainment. The first thing she'd done after getting the feel of her capabilities was to access all data available on Mary Elizabeth Chambers. She had looked at everything from her grade-school files to her record at the hospital in Boston where she'd taken her pediatric residency. Flowers knew how much money Mary Elizabeth spent each year, where she spent it, and what she spent it on. She knew her medical history, financial history, educational history, and every other kind of history one could imagine.

The thorough research simply proved to Flowers how much she liked Mary Liz, as her friends called her. The subject was a rather intense woman, sometimes so wrapped up in her work that she seemed stiff and humorless to other people. Flowers knew better, though. At heart, Mary Elizabeth Chambers was a gentle woman who cared so much about others that the caring could dominate her entire being. She had a wealth of love inside her, and she deserved so much more than a convenient, friendly alliance with a man who made her feel secure. What this woman needed was a man who shared her caring, who loved her for her good heart and dedication, and who turned her on. Way on, Flowers decided. Forget friendly, and forget secure. Flowers intended to deliver Mary Elizabeth Chambers to a man who could get her hot and bothered.

During the four hours Samantha Vargas had been in his car, Eric had learned more about her than he knew about himself. Or so it seemed. He knew her opinions on everything from flea care products for cats to the last presidential election. He knew she liked jazz, classical, and country-western, didn't like hard rock, was addicted to both Diet Coke and Diet Pepsi, preferred "personism" to feminism, and thought the Chicago Bulls should can Dennis Rodman. He also learned why her jackass of a boyfriend had thrown her out of the car with nothing but her carpetbag and her cat.

"He started in on the beer," she explained. "He does that when he gets mad. And by the time he opened the third can, I'd gotten mad, too. I grabbed it out of his hand and emptied it out the window.'' She grimaced slightly and laughed, showing more charity toward the situation than Eric would have. "Jeff really has a temper when he's drinking. When he slammed on the brakes and started pushing me out the door, I figured my healthiest choice was to beat a retreat—at least until he cools off."

She dismissed her boyfriend with a rueful smile, then went on about how happy she was to be moving west, about how much she was looking forward to days upon days of sunshine, about the importance of natural light to boost a person's creativity, and about the role creativity played in emotional health.

"People should listen to their inner selves.'' She carelessly pushed back the wind-whipped red hair that was blowing around her eyes. "They get tied up by what happened yesterday, or what's going to happen tomorrow, or ten years from now. They worry about what people are going to think about them and if they're going to go bald or get fat or if they're going to get a raise this year, and they get so wound up in that sort of garbage that they can't hear their souls speak to them. You know what I mean?''

"Oh yeah. Definitely,'' Eric lied. The girl was unlike anyone he'd ever met—spontaneous, open, trusting, vulnerable. Too bad she had ended up with a jackass, but it was little wonder. She was a natural patsy, Eric concluded, and tried to make the thought a cynical one. He failed. For all that the nineties looked with favor upon worldly, savvy, give-'em-hell women, Samantha Vargas's artless innocence—and innocence was the best word he could think of to define her—was as charming as it was unusual. Her smile was genuine, her laughter unconstrained, her conversation as fresh, intelligent, and interesting as it was abundant.

Usually, chattering women made Eric crazy. Samantha Vargas just made him want to smile. She did talk a mile a minute, in bursts of information, opinions, anecdotes, and laughter. But her prattle didn't grate on his nerves. Eric found himself watching her mouth as she talked. It was a generous mouth. The fashion gurus would say it was too wide, no doubt, but

Eric thought the curve was just right—gentle, with a twist of humor at the corners. She had a beautiful smile—sometimes bright and quick, sometimes soft and slow. Given her situation, Eric admired the fact that she could smile at all. Her humor was unshakable, her laughter ever ready—laughter that was a flood of music erupting spontaneously from the heart, or so it sounded. The wind snatched it away almost before it reached Eric's ears, and he imagined it trailing behind the Healy in a glittering golden banner.

Eric chuckled at his own fancy. The open road always had a strange effect on him—and today it had his mind straying from its usual practical path and wandering into idiocy.

"What?" she demanded, smiling.

"Huh?"

"You laughed."

"Oh, yeah. Just thinking of how being on the road makes a person think and do things he wouldn't normally do."

A slow smile lit her face. "It does, doesn't it? I've never been out on the road like this. I like it. Why're you driving to Phoenix?"

He told her. She grinned broadly and declared that he'd just revived her faith in romance. She had to hear all about Mary Elizabeth, what she did, what he did, how they'd met, how he'd proposed, how many kids they were going to have, and how excited he was to be headed toward the woman he loved and a new life in a new place.

Her nosiness was so good-hearted that Eric couldn't be offended. When he asked about her family, she took her cat out of its cage and formally introduced them, as if the animal were a person in a little furry coat rather than a somewhat tattered feline.

"I have a cousin in L.A. Other than her, Sassy's my family," she said without an ounce of self-pity. "And a fine one she is, too." The little not-quite-Siamese sniffed the floormats and glared suspiciously at the dashboard. Something there fixed the cat's attention, though Eric couldn't see anything more interesting than a radio and a glove compartment.

"What's she giving the evil eye to?" he asked.

"Don't know. Cats can see things people can't, you know?" She slanted him an impish grin. "Maybe your car has gremlins."

"Or maybe your cat isn't playing with a full deck."

Sassy chose that moment to hiss impressively. Her eyes narrowed and whiskers bristled in an impressive display of tigerish ferocity. Eric hoped the beast was threatening the car and hadn't taken exception to his last remark.

"Settle down, you silly girl," Samantha said. "Or you'll go back into your cage."

The cat hissed again, sneezed, turned in disgruntled circles on the floorboards, then finally settled into a cream-colored coil at the girl's feet.

"Aren't you afraid she'll jump out?" Eric indicated the open air above their heads.

"Not Sassy. She knows where she belongs."

"She's luckier than most of us, then."

Samantha shot him a curious look, and Eric wondered where that comment had come from. He certainly hadn't intended to say anything so cynical. As if sensing his unease, she steered him to a safer subject by asking about his profession, which she seemed to find almost as enthralling as his love life.

"I have never been in a plane my entire life. Isn't that a crock? Men have flown to the moon and back, and I haven't even gotten off the ground."

"I hate to disappoint you, but these days flying isn't even as exciting as driving."

"Oh, I don't believe you! Even if you're in the cockpit with the sky all around you and all that power at your command?"

"A lot of the actual flying in the big jets is done by computers."

"Oh." The sound was heavy with disappointment. "Then why do you do it?"

Eric grinned. "Because Sunbelt pays me a fair amount of money."

"Oh."

The single word reeked of sympathy, which Eric thought

was odd indeed, because she was the one who, by her own admission, was presently without a job, without a boyfriend, without most of her belongings, and without transportation to her intended destination, which was a day's drive beyond where he had to stop. She had a strange turn of mind to be feeling sorry for him.

They settled into a comfortable silence as the miles passed beneath them. Every once in a while she made a comment on some passing town or farm. She liked picturesque barns, Eric discovered, and towns that looked as if they were still in the 1950s. She also had no inhibitions about singing along with music she liked—in quite a lovely voice. Mysteriously enough, the stubborn radio allowed her to switch to the stations she liked, while it still refused to cooperate with him. No doubt the car liked her taste in music more than it liked his. When he commented on that theory, she simply said, "Of course," smiled, and patted the Healey's dashboard affectionately. "I told you the car has gremlins, and they like me."

Eric could have sworn that the car purred at her caress, but it must have been an odd hum of the engine, or maybe the cat.

By the time they rolled through Omaha, the sun was a ball of blinding glory on the western horizon. Eric suggested they stop until they could once again see without squinting. He knew just the place for a good dinner.

The ladies' rest room of the Garden Cafe smelled of potpourri and soap. Samantha inhaled a lungful of the pleasant freshness as she closed the door behind her. After hours spent breathing fumes along the freeway, she needed this break. Not that she was complaining. That little Austin-Healey was a hoot, and Eric Neal—well, if she had dreamed up a handsome road warrior to rescue her from her current plight, it would have been him—eyes the color of fine whiskey, shoulders plenty broad enough to pillow a lover's head, and a smile that could send a girl's heart into overdrive. Not only was he good-looking, he was nice. Very nice. Either that or he was great at faking it. He had to have the tolerance of a saint to put up with a cat who shed hair all over his deluxe car and a scatterbrained woman who bombarded his ears with pointless chatter and nosy questions.

Why had she been such a chatterbox? Sam wondered in disgust. Eric Neal could care less about her problems, plans, ambitions, and opinions. Yet he listened in patience, without rolling his eyes or making one sarcastic remark—which would have been richly deserved, Samantha admitted. The man was a hero, and Samantha Vargas was . . . was . . . really a fright, Sam discovered as she looked at herself in the mirror. Convertibles were fun, but they were hell on a girl's looks. Her hair was a mess that could scare the whiskers off Sassy's face, and what little makeup she had applied that morning had been replaced by a layer of dust.

"Lovely! I meet Prince Valiant, and I look like Broom Hilda. Typical."

She splashed cold water on her face, ran damp fingers through the tangle of short, wavy hair, and dabbed some lip color on her dry lips.

"You're never going to make the cover of *Cosmo*," she told the girl in the mirror. The sun had dusted her cheeks with a swath of freckles, and her red hair looked magenta in the fluorescent light. Usually she wouldn't care. It was amazing what meeting a sexy man could do to a woman's priorities. Mother Nature really had programmed females well.

Not that it mattered. Sam's luck with men was running true to form. She was rescued by a knight in shining armor, only to find out this knight was on his way to some other lady fair. If the fantasy-come-true Mr. Neal had been available, that clean-cut, handsome exterior would have hidden a conman, drug dealer, or worse. Since she was old enough to consider boys something other than pests, Samantha Vargas had been on Cupid's blacklist.

Eric waited for her in a booth across from a display of fresh muffins, sticky buns, breads, and pies. In the booth next door, two teenagers dined on a juicy mushroom burger and a fruit plate that made Sam's mouth water.

"I'm hungry enough to order one of everything," Eric told her.

So was Sam, but her wallet contained only twenty dollars, and that had to last her until she could catch up to Jeff. She ordered a muffin and tea.

"Is that all you're going to eat?"

"I'm not very hungry," she lied.

Those fine whiskey eyes cut right through the lie. "I can stand you a bit of a loan if you need it."

"Oh no, I'm fine. Really."

Handsome, saintly, and generous, too. Of course he belonged to someone else. Sam wanted to kick something.

He didn't press the point but ordered a huge fruit salad and extra bread along with his chicken dinner. His eyes had been bigger than his stomach, he claimed when halfway through his chicken. She should help him out with the fruit and a chicken leg, and a roll as well. Sam was proud, but not that proud. She took him up on the offer.

At least she wouldn't have to worry about paying for a motel room that night, because Eric intended to drive straight through to Colorado. There she could catch up to Jeff, her car, and her possessions, meager though they might be. She was sure Jeff would wait for her at his brother's place in Denver's suburbs. His temper would have cooled, and what sense he had would have returned. Jeff might be a jerk, but he wouldn't really take her car. He wasn't that much of a jerk. She hoped.

Eric Neal was truly a pathetic case, Hearts decided. The man had a beautiful, grateful, lonely woman in his car, the night was primed for romance, and what did he intend to do? Drive all night, straight through to Denver, where he would reunite Samantha Vargas with her idiot boyfriend and then drive righteously on his way toward Phoenix, virtue intact.

That was what Eric Neal thought. Hearts had a vastly different plan, and since he was the one with the wheels, he was determined to call the shots. As they sped west through the night, he concocted his strategy. Forty minutes west of Lincoln, Nebraska, he found what he was looking for—York, a homey little town basking in July moonlight, nothing about but fields of corn and open plains, no distractions but the local youth softball leagues. And certainly no auto repair shops open this late on a Friday night.

He coughed.

"What was that?" Eric asked. There was a worried undertone to his question. Hearts smiled to himself. Eric Neal ought to be worried. He coughed again and added a wheeze for good measure.

"Oh, dear . . ." Samantha sighed.

Outwitting these two was really so simple, Hearts thought as he added an ominous rattle to the Healey's symptoms.

"There's an exit up ahead," Samantha said.

"We'd better take it. I don't see much of anything but a couple of motels, though."

The Healey sputtered feebly down the ramp. "There's a gas station over there." Sam pointed to the left. "Maybe they have a mechanic."

Hearts gave a fine performance of a car in its death throes as they turned onto the highway and headed for a Texaco station. He really was enjoying himself.

"It's closed," Eric said.

The only thing to do was coax the car into the nearest parking lot, which just happened to belong to a two-story motel very similar to a thousand others that were strung along the freeway from one coast to the other. Just as they pulled into a parking space, Hearts wheezed out his final mortal agony. It was all he could do to keep it from sounding like a snicker.

CHAPTER THREE

*M*ary Elizabeth's computer was behaving once more as a computer should—and just in time, for her presentation synopsis for the October pediatric conference had to be in the mail by tomorrow, and Arlene, their secretary, didn't have time to put it in the word processor in her computer.

Actually, the technician who had examined her computer that afternoon had found nothing wrong with it. He had simply shrugged. "Sometimes it seems as if things get possessed by an evil spirit now and then, or so it seems. You know, a poltergeist sort of thing."

Mary Elizabeth didn't care who possessed her fruitcake computer, as long as it would do what it was told to do, when it was told to do it. For the moment the machine was cooperative, innocently humming away on the desk while Mary Elizabeth dug through a pile of patient records and statistics and every now and then added a line to her text.

The office was very quiet, in contrast with the commotion during office hours, when the sometimes frenetic pace of the growing practice could make quiet thinking almost impossible. That was why Mary Elizabeth sat at her desk on a Friday evening, taking advantage of the opportunity to focus on her presentation without the constant interruptions of the workday. Two of the other doctors were here as well. Alan Reirdon was catching up on his professional reading, and Colin Myers was reviewing papers submitted for a journal he had been talked into editing.

Yes indeed. A quiet evening after the office was closed was the perfect time to work. The trouble was, Mary Elizabeth was having a hard time focusing on her project, a problem unusual for her. Her mind kept wandering to a novel she had started— a romance novel, of all things. She'd never read one before, had always dismissed them as hopeless drivel. But last evening UPS had dropped a package of six of the things on her doorstep. The invoice was from some Internet book club, and it showed that the order had been paid in full with her gold Visa card.

Mary Elizabeth had figured the package was a wedding joke from some prankster at the office—probably the same one who'd gotten to her computer. She'd fully intended to dump the books in the trash, but she hadn't, for some reason. They'd lain on her couch until bedtime, when she'd picked one up— just to look at the cover more closely—and had read a line or two on the first page. The first page had turned into the first chapter, then the second, and by three A.M. she'd finished one book and started another. Bits and pieces of both books kept popping into her mind now, destroying her concentration. Romantic scenes, lively dialogues, drama that had actually put a tear or two in her eyes. She could scarcely believe it, but she had stayed up until the wee hours of the morning to finish a romance novel.

And now she couldn't get the silly thing out of her mind.

"You have mail," the computer droned.

"I'll look at it later," Mary Elizabeth replied, as if the machine could understand. She made another attempt to focus on the data she had gathered. The project was one she had started when she was an intern and worked on throughout her residency, assisting a noted expert in the pediatric field. He had encouraged her for months to present her part of the project.

"You have mail," came a tinny-voiced reminder.

"Just save it, please." Mary Elizabeth grimaced. She was talking to a machine. Maybe she did need a vacation.

"You have mail."

"Oh, all right!" She brought up the intraoffice quick-mail program and read a memo from Alan Reirdon. He suggested meeting for dinner at a pizza joint around the corner.

"Pretty lame when you can't walk down the hall two doors and ask me in person," Mary Elizabeth muttered. But the prospect of talking with Alan over pepperoni and mushrooms was tempting. He probably wanted to discuss a case. Many patients in the practice used more than one physician, and many of Alan's obstetrics patients used her as a pediatrician.

When she got to Alan's office, he was gone, and a check of her watch revealed the time he'd suggested to meet her was five minutes ago. She returned to her own office, picked up her handbag, and turned off the monitor. "Okay, computer, you win. I should have read it when you first told me about it. Next time I'll give your electronic pestering more respect."

At Petroni's Pizza, Alan was waiting for her at a table sporting the traditional checkered tablecloth and dripping candle stuck in an empty wine bottle. His face brightened when he saw her.

"Sorry I'm late."

"Doesn't matter," he said. "This is a great idea. I'm famished."

"I am, too. I'm glad you thought of it."

Alan chuckled. "I like a woman who gives me credit for everything."

"What do you mean?"

"It wasn't my idea to come for pizza."

"It wasn't?" Mary Elizabeth asked cautiously.

"No. You sent me a quick mail. Remember?"

"I sent *you* a quick mail?"

He cocked his head. "This wedding business really *is* getting to you, isn't it?"

"I didn't send you a quick mail. You sent me one. I thought you probably wanted to discuss a case."

"No. I didn't send you a quick mail. Though I would've if I'd thought of it. I'm always up for pizza."

They exchanged puzzled looks. Incongruously, Mary Elizabeth suddenly thought that Alan Reirdon, with his spun-gold

hair and bedroom eyes, was very much like the picture she
imagined for the hero of that silly book she'd read. Bedroom
eyes? she chided herself. Where on earth had that come from?
She had never thought of Alan in a romantic manner. He was
a colleague. A friend. A good friend. He had always treated
Mary Elizabeth as a person more than a female, and he'd made
no secret about appreciating her professional skills and dedication. She felt more comfortable around Alan than anyone
else in her life, friend or associate—except for maybe Eric.
Of course she was very comfortable around Eric as well. After
all, she was going to marry Eric.

Then why was it her stomach had fluttered so when she'd
seen Alan waiting for her at the table? And why had she been
so ready to interrupt her work to join him for dinner? Could
it have been more than just the prospect of pizza?

"It doesn't matter who sent the quick mail," Alan said.
"Maybe I had a brain boner, and I just don't remember."

"Brain boner? Nice medical talk, Doctor."

"Right now I'm more interested in pizza than medicine,
Doctor." But his eyes said he was interested in more than just
pizza. Mary Elizabeth's stomach fluttered again, and she was
pretty sure the flutter wasn't a symptom of hunger.

"Pepperoni and mushroom?" she suggested.

"Add olives and you've got a deal."

"Of all the nights for that bucket of bolts to break down, it
had to choose a Friday night when a Junior World Series is
in town." Eric threw his suitcase on the double bed—the motel room's only bed—where Sam's carpetbag already sat.

"Don't call him a bucket of bolts," Sam cautioned with a
smile. "You can't expect something that cute to run well,
too."

"The Healey's a 'him,' is it? I thought it was a 'her.' "

"No. Definitely a him."

"Insisting on all that mushy music on the radio? Definitely
a her."

"Nope. Just a him with good taste."

Eric snorted and rubbed his backside. "Questionable taste

in music and a sick sense of humor." From the bedside table he picked up the dart that had punctured his posterior when he'd gotten out of the Healey. It might have been a standard missile plucked from a tavern's dartboard except that it was red and had white heart-shaped feathers, of all things. "If I catch the jokester who wedged this lethal weapon behind the seat cushion, I'll make him think twice before pulling such a stunt again."

"Probably one of the kids at McDonald's. Or maybe someone in the parking lot at the café."

"Wise-ass hoodlum."

She smiled sympathetically. "Hurts that much, does it?"

"Not really. It's the humiliation."

An awkward silence fell. The hour was late. They were both tired. And here they were, strangers, man and woman, one broken-down car, one room, one bed. With any other man, Sam might have made a breezy joke about the situation or laughed and taken a suggestive bounce on the bed to bring the tension out into the open and allow it to dissolve. But not with this man. The possibilities of the night were too warm in her mind. The tingle along her nerves when she looked at his mouth, his eyes, listened to his voice, made her too vulnerable. These sudden feelings were new to her. She always fell for the wrong man, but she seldom fell this fast.

They were busy not meeting each other's eyes when Eric tried to reassure her.

"Uh . . . Samantha, I don't want you to get the wrong idea. This really is the only room in town. I must have called eight other motels from the lobby phone."

"I didn't think for a minute that it was some depraved plot."

"Not that I think you're . . . you're . . . not worth a plot."

She smiled uncertainly.

"Oh, cripes! I didn't say that."

Sam laughed as he turned red. "There's really no problem, Eric." Except that she sensed a certain heat about him that had nothing to do with the inadequate air conditioner. She told herself it was her imagination. Eric Neal was driving west to be married to his childhood sweetheart. The glint in his eye had to be a reflection of the shimmer in her own.

"Well, of course there's not a problem," he confirmed, clearing his throat. "No problem at all."

"Except that I have only twenty dollars in cash. I'll have to send you my half of the room charge when I get settled in California."

"Don't worry about it. It was my car that broke down, after all."

"No, no. I don't like to be in debt. I'll think of some way to pay you, though it might not be in money." Even before the words were out she regretted them. "Shoot! I didn't mean that the way it sounded."

It was Eric's turn to laugh—an honest, wholesome gust of a laugh, and it cleared the air. "I didn't think it did, but a man can always hope." His raised his hand for peace as her mouth fell open. "Just kidding."

"I knew that."

"Maybe we'd better just turn in. Tomorrow we can get the Healey fixed and be on our way toward Denver. I'll . . . uh . . . I'll take the floor."

"Oh, no," Sam protested. "You're paying for the room. You should have the bed."

"Nope. This might be the nineties, but I'm not sleeping in a bed while a woman sleeps on the floor."

"Well, I'm not throwing you out of a bed that you paid good money for."

They silently took each other's measure. Sam hadn't known that chivalry still existed, and the vestige that faced her made her want to smile. At the same time, she didn't want Eric to think she was making fun of his gallantry.

"You're a very nice man, Eric Neal."

He actually blushed. "There's no use in sucking up. I'm still not letting a woman sleep on the floor."

She smiled and cocked her head. "Actually, you know, we're both adults. I'll bet we could both sleep on that bed without jumping each other. Don't you think?"

His expression grew still, as if he actually had to consider whether or not that was possible. "Probably," he finally conceded.

"Then it's settled. Who gets the bathroom first?"

Sam got the bathroom first. While a bath was running, she squeezed her carpetbag into the little cubicle with her, pulled out clean underwear, cotton shorts, and a large T-shirt that sported a languid-looking Garfield the Cat. She undressed behind the closed door, stuffed her dirty clothes into a corner, and sank gratefully into a tub full of steaming hot water. Not until she had rinsed the last soap from her skin did she realize the bath towels were beside the sink on the other side of the door.

"Idiot!" she groaned, and sank into the water, hiding her eyes behind dripping hands.

Eric took advantage of Samantha's absence to confront himself in the mirror. What he saw was similar to what he always saw in the mirror—brown eyes, slightly crooked nose, straight teeth, and an airline-approved haircut. Fit, conservative, a man who inspired passengers' confidence when he walked down the aisle of a Boeing 737. He was everything his wandering father had not been, which was just fine with Eric. He shared his father's love of flying, but that was where the similarity stopped. Eric would never drag his family from town to town, air show to air show, scraping a meager living from the kind of aviation that had gone the way of Amelia Earhart and five-cent plane rides from a farmer's cow pasture. Tom Neal had been cursed with the heart of a barnstormer during the birth of the space age, and his family had suffered the consequences. His son, Eric, knew that life was more than following a dream. Responsibility demanded sacrifices at times, and the man who stared at him from the mirror looked every bit a responsible, conservative fellow who had his feet squarely on the ground even when he was thirty thousand feet above it.

Tonight, however, Eric didn't feel as though his feet were quite so solid upon the ground. On the outside, he still appeared down-to-earth and sane, but inside, he was giddy, ebullient, frustrated, and randy as a pumped-up bull.

This had been coming ever since Samantha Vargas had

dropped her curvaceous little backside into his passenger seat. No, Eric admitted. Ever since he'd first laid eyes upon her in the McDonald's where she'd fought with her boyfriend. His dismal state had gotten sharply worse since they stopped for the night. His skin was hot and cold at the same time, his heart knocked against his rib cage in double time, and that part of his anatomy that had always had a mind of its own was going to show Samantha exactly what state he was in unless he got himself under control.

He scowled at the face in the mirror. "Just you level out, buddy boy. You're all but a married man, and that girl in there deserves better than this. So cool it!"

"Eric?" came a hesitant query from the bathroom. "Could you hand me a bath towel?"

He went from cold to hot to cold again. "Uh . . . yeah, sure."

The bathroom door opened a crack and a slender arm snaked out. Eric put a towel in the seeking hand while nobly looking the other way. His effort at gallantry came to naught as the mirror reflected a slice of white, smooth body and rounded breast before the arm retreated and the door closed. He groaned, close to physical pain. He actually felt woozy and wondered if there had been some insidious drug on the dart that had punctured his backside.

This was going to be one hell of a grim night.

By the time Sam emerged somewhat sheepishly from the bathroom, Eric was pawing casually through his suitcase, pretending to be cool and collected. He was neither, however, and the sight of a nymph emerging from the steam of the bathroom made him even less cool. What the hell was she thinking, wearing shorts that revealed those long, tanned legs and letting her hair go all wild, damp, and curly, like a dark red halo of flame? It was an open invitation for a man to comb through those curls with his fingers, to take her down on the bed and feel those gorgeous legs wrap around him and—

"I'm going down the hall to the vending machine," she said. "You want anything?"

He swallowed hard. Damn, but did he want something! "No, thanks. Don't forget the room key."

A cold shower made him feel better. He came out of the bathroom rubbing his wet hair with a towel, and his heart began to hammer again. Samantha had returned. She lounged in a chair by the little round Formica table, her legs propped on the other chair, tossing pretzel sticks into her mouth. Her head tilted back to display a long, silky-smooth neck. He stared. Her eyes met his and widened as they traveled down his bare chest to where a towel was wrapped low around his hips. A pretzel bounced off her mouth, her legs tangled in an effort to rearrange themselves, and she choked.

Distracted as he was, Eric continued to stare for a full ten seconds before he realized she was really choking. For the first time in his life, he put his airline-required emergency training to use as he grabbed her around her middle and applied pressure in a Heimlich maneuver. The pretzel flew across the room, and she sagged forward in his arms.

Eric was suddenly very aware of the heat of her through the thin cotton of her T-shirt, the firm roundness of her backside pressed against his groin. "Uh ... are you all right?"

Her body jerked convulsively, and for a dreadful moment he thought the choking had brought on some sort of attack. Then he heard her laugh. The only attack she suffered was a fit of giggles. It was contagious. Within seconds he too shook with laughter. Both weak with their mirth, they fell together on the bed, almost landing on top of Sassy, who jumped nimbly out of the way and gave them an offended glare. Eric would have released her, for propriety's sake, but one of his arms was wedged beneath her body. It seemed a long, searing while before her laughter subsided and she realized the awkwardness of their position on the bed.

"Oh, shoot! I'm sorry." She rolled off him, her face turning a red to match her hair. "I am such an idiot."

"No. I'm sorry. I ... uh ... shouldn't have been parading around in bare skin."

Her hands rose in a helpless gesture. "It's not as if you were flaunting a string bikini."

The very thought of a string bikini flooded Eric's mind with uncomfortable images, all of them involving Samantha Vargas. "Maybe we'd better just go to bed . . . go to sleep, I mean." He sighed. "You know what I mean."

She smiled. "I know what you mean."

Sassy jumped back on the bed, apparently satisfied that the wrestling match was over. Tail straight up and twitching, she stalked to the middle, sat on her haunches, and fixed them both with her challenging regard.

"I hope you're not allergic to cats," Samantha said.

"No. I can't say I've ever shared a bed with one, but there's a first time for everything."

He'd never shared a bed with someone quite like Samantha Vargas, either. As they crawled beneath the covers, the cat between them, he wondered if Sassy was prepared to be the girl's bodyguard.

Half the night passed, or so it seemed to Eric, until his restless brain, and other parts, settled down enough for him to fall asleep. He slept with his face nearly against the wall. Samantha faced the other way, teetering on the very edge of the bed. At least a foot of cold, empty space gaped between them—space guarded by a snoring cat—but Eric imagined he could feel the warmth of Samantha's body. He was aware of every tiny move she made, every breath she took—until finally weariness got the upper hand and he drifted into uneasy slumber. Somewhere in the timeless reaches of the night, he became aware of a light glowing by the table, and though he didn't turn to see, he knew also that Samantha was no longer stretched out beside him. He mumbled an incoherent question. A quiet voice told him to go back to sleep, and that's what he did.

When morning came, penetrating the inadequate window curtain with a gray light, Eric woke to find Samantha munching on a breakfast bar and watching him from a chair by the table. On top of the table, Sassy picked daintily at cat food in a plastic cup.

"Good morning," he groaned. His watch showed five-thirty. Now that he had daylight to see by, perhaps he could discover what was wrong with the Healey without calling in a mechanic and a tow truck.

"I have something for you," Samantha said.

Eric's heart jumped, along with other parts. He fiercely curbed the reaction. Whatever Samantha Vargas had for him, it certainly wasn't *that*.

"I hope it's a very strong cup of coffee." He climbed off the bed and ran fingers through his tousled hair.

"Nope. Sorry. But I do have this."

She offered him one of the big tablets she had carried along with her carpetbag. Her voice contained a note of uncertainty, and her expression echoed it. Eric looked down at the tablet and found a pen-and-ink sketch of a man standing beside a road, looking up as a biplane roared by overhead. The man was unmistakably Eric, and the plane was a very good rendering of the Stearman he had seen the day before. The sketch was so alive that it seemed to vibrate with the roar of the Stearman's radial engine.

"This is . . . this is incredible!" Eric declared.

A smile lit her face and glowed in her eyes.

"You're an artist! Cripes! You've really got talent!"

"Thank you. I saw you outside the McDonald's yesterday, looking up at that plane. I could tell it meant a lot to you, so . . ."

She had more than talent, Eric reflected. The longing on his face in the sketch exactly captured the moment's mood. How had she known, just from catching a glimpse of that scene? How had she known it meant so much to him? How did she break away from her own problems and cares to feel so completely with another person?

He looked away from the sketch and into her shining eyes. "This is wonderful. Thank you."

"I wanted to do something for you, because you've done so much for me." A mischievous grin curled her lips. "I said I'd find a way to repay you."

They shared the rest of the breakfast bars Sam carried in her carpetbag, washed them down with water from the tap, and talked about Samantha's art. He'd called her an artist, and that was how she thought of herself, she admitted, though she didn't earn a living with her art.

"I've worked everywhere from a lunch counter to a typing pool, and once I got a job sketching houses and landscaping for a real-estate firm. That was too boring, though. It seemed disloyal to the real art I feel inside of me. I know that sounds silly, but it's true. So I decided to earn the rent doing everyday sorts of things, and in my own private time do the kind of art that I could put my heart into. I came to understand that how you earn your living doesn't define who you are. I could work in a bank, or a restaurant, or drive a cab, and I would still be an artist, because that's who I am."

Eric chewed thoughtfully on his breakfast. "I never thought of it that way."

"That's because you're lucky enough to make a living doing what you love to do. You're so lucky. Flying must be wonderful."

"Yeah." He didn't want to disillusion her with the truth: there was flying, and then there was flying. If he could truly do what he loved for a living, he wouldn't be hauling cargos of sardine-packed businessmen and tourists from coast to coast at thirty-five thousand feet.

By a little after six, the day was light enough for Eric to peer into the Healey's engine. He was a fair mechanic, but nothing looked wrong to him. No drips, no loose wires, no burn spots, strange smells, or cracked hoses.

"Try to turn it over," he instructed Samantha, who sat in the driver's seat.

The engine roared to life, then settled into a happy hum.

"Well, I'll be shucked."

"You'll be what?" Samantha yelled over the sound of the engine.

"Never mind. I don't believe this freaky car. It's the second time it's done this."

Sam patted the dashboard. "Gremlins."

Eric just closed the hood and shook his head. Ten minutes later they were ready to go. Before Eric slid into the driver's seat, however, he gave the cushion a narrow-eyed look. Suspiciously he felt around the seat, seat back, and the crevice between the two.

"Looking for darts?" Samantha inquired, her eyes sparkling.

Eric smiled sheepishly as he slid behind the wheel. "I'm beginning to think this car has its own agenda."

Eight hours and over four hundred miles later, Samantha dropped into the passenger seat of the Healey, shut the door, and heaved a disgusted sigh.

"No luck, eh?" Eric asked.

"I should have known when I saw that my car wasn't in the driveway." She glared at the 1960s-vintage tract home, as if an intimidating look would make Jeff appear, along with her car and possessions. Nothing happened. The house, with its ratty lawn and overgrown bushes, still sat peacefully in the bright Denver sunshine. Jeff's brother hadn't heard from Jeff in a month, he claimed, and had no idea where he was. "Shoot! How much does a bus ticket from Denver to L.A. cost? I'll just go out there and stay with my cousin until I get my stuff back."

"You could ride out to Phoenix with me. It's closer to L.A. The bus is probably cheaper from there."

Maybe and maybe not, Samantha mused. But that was as good an excuse as any to spend a bit more time with her knight errant. She didn't want to think about the implications of her reluctance to part company. With another sigh, she gave in. "When I get a job in L.A., I'll send you money for half the expenses."

"You don't need to. That sketch you gave me is worth more than money."

His praise made her feel warm. Too warm. But it was a good feeling. "Okay, then. Arizona, here we come."

The Healey had other plans. Two hours later Eric and Sam walked out of Sergei's Transmission Shop, scrutinizing an estimate for a rebuilt transmission. The keys to Sergei's loaner car, a 1975 Volvo station wagon, dangled from Eric's hand.

"Two days! Goddammit! If the Healey weren't already dead, I'd kill it with my own two hands!"

Sam smiled. "That car does have his own agenda."

"Her own agenda. Only a female would be this difficult."

"You obviously haven't had the same experiences with men that I have."

That got a laugh from him. "I should hope not." His laughter twisted into a grimace. "My wedding is next Saturday."

"How long does it take to drive from here to Phoenix?"

"Two easy days. One really long one."

"You have plenty of time. Just call your fiancée and let her know what happened."

Eric intended to do that very thing, but he certainly wouldn't tell Mary Elizabeth he was stuck in Denver with a woman who sorely strained the seams of his self-control. Not that his relationship with Samantha Vargas wasn't entirely innocent or that he had anything to be ashamed of. Or that Mary Elizabeth would be jealous if he told her. Jealousy had never been an issue between them. Suddenly he wondered if it should have been—just a little bit of jealousy, a good-natured, understanding sort of jealousy. Was their trust in each other so complete, or did the lack of jealousy stem from a lack of real involvement?

Eric was ashamed of himself the moment the thought entered his head. Of course he was vitally involved with Mary Elizabeth. He was going to marry her, wasn't he?

They climbed into the Volvo, and Sam settled her sketching tablets, carpetbag, and Sassy's carrier in the backseat along with Eric's suitcases. Sassy seemed much happier with this car. She'd never quite given up hissing at the Healey.

"Don't look so glum," Sam advised Eric. "Just think of this as an opportunity—two whole days in beautiful Denver with nothing but time to spend."

"You have a unique philosophy," Eric grumbled.

Sam grinned unrepentantly. "I have been told that a time or two. But it's true, isn't it? You have two days. You can do anything you want. What would it be?"

Eric thought a moment, looking out the Volvo window at

summer clouds drifting in a startlingly blue sky. Then he smiled.

Next morning, a bright, cloudless Sunday, they sat on the taxiway at the end of Front Range Airport's runway 26. Eric saw Samantha suck in her breath as he held the brakes firm and advanced the Cessna 172's throttle to perform a pretakeoff engine run-up. He remembered his own reaction the first time he'd sat in a small aircraft waiting to take to the air. The engine had seemed ready to shake the little plane to pieces, but the instructor had sat calmly in his seat, checking magnetos, vacuum pressure, carburetor heat, and a host of other items that had meant absolutely nothing at the time. He'd been sixteen years old, and he had thought, that first time, that he was going to shit his shorts. Samantha was doing much better than he had.

"You okay?" he asked.

The only reason she could hear him over the engine noise was that the headsets allowed them to speak through the intercom. The headsets, as well as the Cessna, belonged to Eric's friend Casey Shepherd, a pilot who'd moved to Denver when he'd retired from Sunbelt Airways.

Samantha took several deep breaths before she was able to reply. "I'm okay."

"You ready to go?"

"You're the pilot. You tell me."

Eric grinned at her. "The left seat's the pilot's seat, and you're in it. I'm just along to give advice."

"Oh, shit."

It was the first time he'd ever heard her curse, but again, he could relate to the feeling. Maybe that was why he had always enjoyed instructing. It called back memories of that first terrifying, glorious moment of taking to the air with his hands on the controls. Even though he seldom taught anymore, he kept his instructor's certificate current. It was something from the past that he couldn't quite give up.

He helped Sam taxi onto the runway, showing her how to steer the plane with her feet. There wasn't a control tower at the little airport, so he announced on the radio to area air traffic that they were taking off.

"Feet off the brakes, throttle full forward," he told her.

Her eyes widened as the little plane started its takeoff roll.

"Check your speed. Check your rpm, engine instruments. All in the green?"

"Yeah," she said with a gulp.

"Ease back on the yoke now. . . . Easy does it. Right rudder. . . . Right, not left. . . . That's it. See how simple it is?"

The ground fell away beneath them as the little plane took smoothly to the air. A look of wonder replaced the wide-eyed terror on Sam's face, and Eric's heart beat faster, as it always did when he saw someone first discover the wonders of flight. Maybe with Samantha it beat just a little faster than usual, he admitted.

"Oh, my!" she breathed.

"A slow turn to the left, now. Left aileron, left rudder. . . . That's it. Push the nose down just a little."

"This is wonderful! I'm flying!"

Eric was flying as well, in a way he hadn't flown in a long time. He'd forgotten the exhilaration to be found in these little aluminum birds. No computers. No jet engines. No tons and tons of metal and wire lifting ponderously off the runway. Just fragile wings and a single little piston engine. This was flying.

They flew toward the foothills, where Eric took over the controls so Samantha could enjoy the scenery. The air was rough, as it almost always was this close to the mountains, but Sam didn't seem to mind. She was delighted by every bump, every turn and bank, climb, or descent. Her joy in the flight was contagious.

After a couple of circles above the Boulder flatirons and a cruise over Golden to see the Coors factory, they turned south toward Colorado Springs, where Pike's Peak rose in awesome splendor against the deep blue sky. Approaching the airport, Eric let Sam fly the plane under his watchful eye while he talked to air traffic control. Only at the last critical moment before touchdown did he take over. The glow in Sam's eyes told him he'd made a convert.

"How lucky Mary Elizabeth is!" Sam gushed over lunch at the airport restaurant. "She'll have her own built-in flight instructor."

Eric laughed ruefully. "Not Mary Liz. She's scared to death of small aircraft. Refuses to go up."

"Oh, surely if she ever flew in one, she'd be hooked."

Eric had given up that hope long ago. "Some people just don't like flying. The sensation scares them. And small planes are a lot worse than the big jets for that sort of thing."

"I'd want to be up there every day, if I could."

Eric told her about his long-discarded fantasy of owning and running his own flight school, where newcomers to aviation could experience every day the miracle that Sam had discovered that afternoon. He'd never told anyone else about that stupid ambition, because it was something he would never do. He had a great job, a high-paying and secure job. To give up such a job for something as impractical as a flight school would be just plain stupid.

"Why don't you do it?" Sam asked innocently.

Eric was honest. "Money. Security. General aviation is a lot riskier from the business end than the safety end. If you have a month of bad weather when your students can't fly, you can lose your shirt. You're dependent on fuel prices, insurance prices, maintenance prices, hangar fees. It's no way to build a secure future for a family."

Her smile told him she saw through his practicality. "But you would love it, wouldn't you? You're a great teacher. I can see that your heart is in it. Don't you think a wife and family would want a man to do what he was happy doing?"

"It's not that simple, Sam. My father did what he loved to do, and he dragged my mother and brother and me from air show to air show, Podunk airport to Podunk airport, until he finally plowed up a cornfield with an AT-6, leaving his widow and two kids fifty-one dollars and thirteen cents under the seat of our old Ford pickup. That's no way to treat a family."

"But you're not talking about quite the same thing, are you?"

He didn't want to think along such lines. It was too tempting. Her reasoning was simplistic, Eric told himself. She also had an uncanny sense of what made him tick.

"I don't think that very many people lie on their deathbeds being grateful for their dull but secure lives," Sam ventured. "I'd rather think back on the good times, the times I was true to my heart and did what I was meant to do."

That night in the motel room, Sam couldn't stop talking about their flight. They'd rented two rooms, of course, but somehow they had ended up in one—at least until time to actually go to bed. Eric lounged in a chair, where Sassy promptly staked a claim upon his lap and folded herself into a loaf-shaped lump of cat fur that refused to be budged. Sam sat cross-legged on the bed, long, bare legs drawing Eric's eyes more than he would have liked, but when his eyes moved to any other part of her, the effect on his equilibrium was the same.

"Sassy likes you," Sam said.

"I'm flattered," Eric replied dubiously.

"Sassy doesn't like just anyone. She absolutely hates Jeff."

"Well, I'm not Jeff."

Sam smiled. "No, you're certainly not."

Eric told himself he imagined the warmth in her tone, but he couldn't deny the heat of his reaction. He would have liked to think the attraction was merely physical. Lust he could understand and excuse. But Sam inspired more than his lust. Her animation lit his heart. Her smile made him want to smile. He felt sometimes that he could see into her soul, and what he found there was the other half of himself. Ridiculous. He hardly knew her. He loved Mary Elizabeth and was going to marry her in less than a week.

Nevertheless, a bond had formed between him and Samantha Vargas the like of which he had never experienced before. He didn't know what the hell he was going to do about it, but he'd better figure something out before they got to Phoenix.

CHAPTER FOUR

Lunch was becoming a habit, if something of less than a week's standing could be called a habit. Mary Elizabeth had always been too busy to make lunch an actual meal—the kind that involved sitting somewhere other than at one's desk and indulging in conversation along with the food. For as long as she'd known him, though, Alan Reirdon had always insisted on taking a lunch away from the clinic—even if it was a ten-minute visit to Taco Bell. He claimed that such a break was needed for a person to stay sane in the medical business. Mary Elizabeth was beginning to agree. She could get accustomed to such a luxury, especially if Alan Reirdon sat across the table from her, as he had for the last three days.

Mary Elizabeth felt guilty at the drift of her thoughts. Getting such pleasure from Alan's company seemed wrong. She was on the threshold of marriage to Eric Neal, yet since that impromptu dinner with Alan the previous Friday evening, she'd jumped at every chance to socialize with a man who should have been nothing more than her medical colleague. Since then they'd had coffee breaks together, drinks after work, one other dinner, and an almost daily lunch. Today was Wednesday, always a very busy day at the clinic. Since they were pressed for time, they had hurried down to the fast soup, salad, and sandwich joint next door to the clinic.

"You seem very lost in thought," Alan said.

Mary Elizabeth looked up from her salad, positive that fla-
grant guilt colored her face. "I was . . ."

"Don't tell me." Alan grimaced with mock disgust. "You
were thinking about Eric. Aim a woman toward a wedding
and she grows a one-track mind."

Mary Elizabeth wondered what Alan would think if she told
him her thoughts centered on him, not Eric.

"It's too bad he was delayed."

"Yes." She allowed irritation to put an edge on her voice.
"I don't know why he insisted on making the trip by car. He's
a pilot, for pity's sake! He could have hopped a jet for free."

"Maybe for someone in his line of work, seeing the country
from the ground is a treat."

"It'll be some treat if he's late to his own wedding."

"He'll be here. Any man who's headed for a wedding to
someone like you would move heaven and earth to be there."

Mary Elizabeth had to laugh. "Alan, you are a hopeless
romantic. Move heaven and earth indeed! I wouldn't have
guessed two weeks ago that such fanciful declarations lurked
beneath that competent, professional exterior."

Alan smiled wryly. "We've known each other for over two
years. It's taken you that long to discover what a poet I am?"
He hesitated, then continued. "Seriously, Mary Liz, I'm glad
we've spent some time together these last few days. I think a
lot of you, you know, not just as a colleague, but as a friend."

Mary Elizabeth's heart warmed. "I think a lot of you, too.
In fact, since I joined the practice, you've been my best friend.
You were always there there when I needed someone. Like
when little Jerry Corcoran died in the surgery I recommended.
I think I would have actually renounced medicine if you hadn't
given me a good shake or two."

"You wouldn't have. You're stronger than that. And the
support hasn't been one-sided, you know. Remember the law-
suit on the Stein baby? You backed me up—"

"I told the truth. Anyone would have done the same."

"Not so. A couple of others I could name were so anxious
to avoid being associated with that case, they practically turned
themselves inside-out for excuses not to testify."

"That tragedy was not your fault!" she said with remembered vehemence.

"And I remember crying on your shoulder the day my sister was killed in that car accident."

She looked away, embarrassed. "Any other shoulder would have done as well."

"Not so," he denied quietly.

Mary Elizabeth sat in silence, wondering how the conversation had taken such a personal turn. Over the past two years, she and Alan Reirdon had developed a special friendship, and perhaps something closer. Their relationship was going to change when she married. The thought made her sad. She'd never considered Alan as anything more than a friend, but now . . . ? Now she didn't know what to think. She felt bombarded with uncertainties and strange ideas—a computer behaving like an out-of-control matchmaker and an old friend looking at her with eyes that were suddenly more than friendly. Or maybe that look had always been in Alan's eyes, and she just hadn't seen it.

"I hope Eric appreciates you, Mary Liz."

She looked up, then glanced quickly away. "I'm sure he does."

"You're a very rare person, you know. An unselfish heart, a physician with more dedication than ambition. People like you don't come along very often."

Her eyes begged him to stop, and for a moment she saw such naked emotion on his face that her heart jumped in distress. Or was it distress? Emotions awash in confusion, she averted her gaze. "We should get back," she said into her salad. "I have Ronnie Wagner coming in at one."

"Ronnie Wagner, eh? You know Mrs. Wagner is trying to have another one?"

"She told me that last time Ronnie was in. Is she going to have as much trouble as she had with Ronnie?"

"Well . . ."

Safely back on a professional footing, they walked together to the corner, where a traffic light would allow them to cross the street to the clinic. Midday traffic was heavy, and horns blared when a minivan showed some hesitancy in grabbing the first chance to turn left.

"Amazing what the heat does to driver patience," Alan noted. "Even in air-conditioned cars."

The light turned orange. The minivan started to turn—right into the path of a pickup truck that had speeded up to run the light. The sickening thud of impact was followed by the screech of tortured metal and shattered glass.

"Oh, God! Oh, shit!" Mary Elizabeth's heart seemed to stop for an instant, then she ran forward. Instinct that had been honed by a thousand emergencies took over. Alan ran beside her, pulling out his cell phone to dial 911.

The intersection was in chaos. Steam rose from mangled engines, and sweet-smelling engine coolant spread in a green puddle onto the hot asphalt. Traffic gridlock was instant. People gaped. A few jumped out of their cars and ran toward the accident. Someone was screaming.

Mary Elizabeth could see one person in both vehicles. The driver of the truck was slumped over the steering wheel. The windshield was shattered and bloody where his head had impacted. The minivan driver was a woman, and it was from her that the screaming came.

"You take the truck," Mary Elizabeth told Alan. "I'll take the minivan."

Distant sirens wailed. Help was on the way. But there was no time to wait. Mary Elizabeth tried to open the driver's door of the minivan. It wouldn't budge. A man came up beside her to help. The door yielded.

As the door opened, the woman scrambled out on her own, wide-eyed and white-faced.

"Easy," Mary Elizabeth advised her. The victim didn't appear to be badly hurt. A cut above her temple sent runnels of scarlet down her face, and an awkwardly held arm might be broken. The air bag had saved her life. "Easy. Just lie down until—"

"My baby!" the woman shrieked. "My baby!"

Mary Elizabeth immediately switched her attention to the van. On the passenger side was an infant car seat. An air bag had inflated there as well, but air bags had been designed to save adult lives. To infants and small children, they could be deadly. She crawled into the twisted van to look. The child was a little girl, about eighteen months old. She was unconscious, and blood ran from her nose and mouth. The car seat had withstood the impact without damage, thanks to the air bag. The little girl had not. For a moment, a woman's horror threatened to overwhelm Mary Elizabeth's professional detachment. Then she was a physician again.

"Get the passenger door open," she called to the man who had helped her with the door. Then she called to Alan.

"Right here," he said a few seconds later from outside the car. His voice was calm, but the underlying tension told her that he, too, had seen the car seat. His steady hands grabbed her waist and helped her back out of the twisted wreck.

"The driver of the truck?" she asked.

"Dead. The mother's just cut up a bit, along with a broken wrist. A couple of ladies back there are helping her out."

"The little girl looks bad," Mary Elizabeth said. "I couldn't tell if she was breathing. We need to get her out of there fast."

Alan shoved a set of surgical gloves into her hands. He was already gloved.

"God, Alan! You carry gloves with you?"

"Never leave home without them," he quipped.

His foresight was fortunate. Any health professional knew the importance of protection against the diseases that blood— anyone's blood—could carry, and the baby was bleeding from both nose and mouth.

Three volunteers had managed to pry open the passenger door, which was incredibly mangled. Alan ducked into the car.

"Damn! Broken nose. Probable skull fracture. Concussion for sure. Maybe a neck injury as well. Broken arms. Ribs. Her color's not good." He took off his belt and secured the child's head to the car seat to prevent further injury to the neck. Then, ever so gently, he lifted the car seat and set it down well out of the way of the coolant that leaked from the vehicle. The mother descended upon them in a flurry of tears and weeping, crying the child's name.

"Melanie! Melanie! Oh, God! She's dead, isn't she? She's dead! I killed her! Melanie!"

She made a lunge for the child. Mary Elizabeth had to use all her strength to hold her back. "Melanie isn't dead, Mom. We're doctors. You've got to keep back just a bit so we can help her."

The mother dissolved in a fit of weeping, and one of the women who had been comforting her circled her shoulders with an arm.

"The ambulance is having trouble getting through the gridlock," someone said. "It's still two blocks back."

"She's turning blue," Mary Elizabeth noted. "The trachea's partially crushed. This can't wait."

In the distance, red and blue lights flashed in grotesque flamboyance, and a siren screamed an alarm. The ambulance wasn't moving, and although the paramedics were offloading their equipment, Mary Elizabeth feared they wouldn't arrive in time.

Alan cursed under his breath. "Stay here. I'll be back in ten seconds. Promise." He dashed toward the door of a restaurant. In only moments he returned and pressed a small, sharp paring knife into Mary Elizabeth's hand.

"There's a ballpoint pen in my handbag," she told him. Her fingers carefully palpated the child's throat, feeling the rings of cartilage that were the framework of the damaged trachea.

"I have a pen here." Alan took the pen apart and discarded the ink cylinder.

With a deft slice, Mary Elizabeth cut between the cartilage rings of the injured trachea, then quickly inserted the shell of the pen into the tiny slit. Air wheezed through the tube, and slowly the little girl's color pinkened. Mary Elizabeth allowed herself a breath of relief as a paramedic finally arrived. She was a woman Mary Elizabeth had met several times before.

"Dr. Chambers, Dr. Reirdon. Hi. Looks like you have things under control."

"Just barely," Alan admitted. "Let's get these people to the hospital."

They rode together in the ambulance, then waited while the little girl was taken to surgery. Two hours later the surgeon announced the child was in fair condition. The mother had been treated in the emergency room and sedated. She was alert enough, however, to shower Mary Elizabeth and Alan with effusive thanks.

"We didn't do anything a good paramedic couldn't have done," Mary Elizabeth told Alan as they collapsed in the deserted doctors' lounge.

"Don't sell us short," Alan said with a grin. "We were stupendous."

She smiled faintly. "Or at least competent."

"Quit being modest, Doctor. You did a hell of a job out there. Too bad the woman wasn't having a baby. I could have been a hero, too."

Mary Elizabeth chuckled and closed her eyes, letting the tension drain from her body. The adrenaline rush had faded long ago. When she opened her eyes, Alan stood in front of her, looking down at her face. Wordlessly he took her hands and pulled her to her feet.

Mary Elizabeth knew he was going to kiss her before he even made a move. She could easily have stopped him, but she didn't. A sudden lassitude kept her still and yielding as his mouth came toward hers.

As kisses went, Mary Elizabeth graded this one an E for both effort and excellence. It started out as a chaste, gentlemanly tribute but grew into a mutual devouring that ended only when they both needed to surface for air. The kiss was right in a way that Mary Elizabeth had never experienced. She wanted to melt into the man who held her in his arms, a man so in tune with her soul that it seemed only natural their bodies be joined as well.

Her world snapped back into focus as Alan set her away from him. Gasping for breath, Mary Elizabeth felt heat creep up her cheeks in tandem with the red that stained Alan's face.

"Mary Liz, I'm sorry. Damn! I'm sorry."

"No."

"I had no right."

In a moment of crystalline clarity, Mary Elizabeth knew she had come to one of those turning points that alter the course of a lifetime, a clear-cut either/or decision that permitted no maybe or perhaps. She could blame her behavior on the tension of the moment, the shared victory, the comradeship of fighting together for a child's life, but that excuse would be a crock, and they both knew it.

Unexpectedly, tears overflowed Mary Elizabeth's eyes. She couldn't honestly say if they were tears of happiness or misery. Her head dropped onto Alan's chest, and he rubbed her neck with one hand.

"Lord, oh Lord," she groaned. "What the hell am I going to do now?"

While Eric had always enjoyed the open road, car trips, like plane trips, were straight-line propositions for him: plot the most direct course and follow it. So why had he gotten off I-25 to give Sam a tour of Santa Fe? The freeway bypassed the historic town. There was no reason to stop, and every reason not to. They were behind schedule. Fixing the Healey had taken a day longer than estimated. Rain showers had made the day's drive slower than it could have been. And an accident had blocked the freeway just north of the New Mexico state line.

But now traffic was light and weather was fine, ideal conditions for making good time. Yet they took the Cerrillos Road exit into town. Not the Healey, but Eric was the guilty party this time. Even as he took the off ramp, he wondered at his own behavior. Was he reluctant to arrive in Phoenix and the commitment Phoenix represented? Had some of Samantha's spontaneity rubbed off on him? Or was he simply reaching for an excuse to spend more time with Sam? Eric didn't want to ponder the possibilities, for they all implied he should take a good, hard look at where his life was headed.

"Where are we going?" Sam asked.

"You can't drive through New Mexico without seeing Santa Fe."

"I thought you were in a hurry."

He grinned. "Just finding out if there might be something to this 'go for the gusto' philosophy of yours."

"Santa Fe's got gusto?" Sam cast a dubious glance at the jumble of motels, fast-food restaurants, and other miscellaneous businesses that lined their route. They had driven all morning through beautiful scenery, but the outskirts of Santa Fe would never qualify as tourist bait.

"Wait," Eric told her, his grin getting wider. "Just wait."

They took two rooms at the Days Inn, established Sassy on a comfortable bed in air-conditioned comfort, then continued toward the center of town, where the twentieth-century jumble gave way to history. Eric loved this town. Every time he drove down Cerrillos Road, he felt as though he were rolling back time to step into another century. He was gratified by Sam's awestruck silence as they crossed the Santa Fe River and turned onto Alameda Street. He parked in the first spot he found.

"Impressed?"

Sam's mouth was ajar as she took in the new jumble. Not twentieth-century tacky, as the outskirts had been, but a scene that called to mind conquistadores and Native American pueblos baking in the high desert sun. Narrow streets threaded through a jumble of adobe buildings that looked as though they'd stood for centuries. Some of them had. Within sight was the Cathedral of St. Francis of Assisi, built by the Spanish during the reign of the all-powerful Spanish empire.

"I'm totally impressed," Sam admitted, her voice reverent. "This is incredible."

"Wait until you see."

They walked toward the Plaza, which had been the center of Santa Fe's activities since the Spanish had first built on the site in the early 1600s. Eric instinctively held out his hand, and Sam took it. Half a block later they both became conscious, at the same time, that they were holding hands.

Eric jerked away with an apology. Sam didn't say anything,

simply sent him an enigmatic look that made him wonder what she was feeling. Reaching for her hand had been so natural that he'd scarcely been aware of doing it. All instinct, straight from the guts, not from the brain.

His guts, Eric suspected, were bent on turning his well-organized, responsible life upside-down. He didn't want to think about it.

The slight awkwardness that sprang up between them couldn't survive the wonder of Santa Fe, however. By the time they reached the Plaza, Sam was enraptured by the old buildings, expensive clothing, exquisite jewelry, and wonderful art on display. Eric was enthralled as well, but his fascination centered on Samantha. He'd been on the Plaza many times before, and though he was not immune to its appeal, he was even less immune to Samantha's charm. She was like a child in a candy store. The history exhibits in the Palace of Governors, which had housed rulers from Spain, Mexico, and the Confederacy as well as the United States, made her silent with wonder. The Native Americans outside the Palace, with their handcrafted jewelry laid out for sale, brought a delighted smile to her face. The sculpture and paintings displayed in shops lining the Plaza made her gasp with admiration, and she laughed at the prices of clothing and curios offered to the shoppers who thronged the sidewalks and streets.

Eric had never met anyone like Samantha Vargas. He wanted to bottle her infectious laughter so he could uncork the sound to cheer him whenever he was down. Her soft voice could go in the bottle as well, and the flash of her eyes, the gentle curve of her lips, the way she wrinkled her nose at the outrageous price tag on a simple cotton shift.

And just what the hell was he thinking? Eric chided himself as they completed their slow circuit of the Plaza. Mary Elizabeth had a beautiful smile and a nice laugh, not to mention many other totally admirable qualities. He'd loved her for years.

Was it possible that more than one kind of love existed? he wondered. One kind led to marriage and passion, another kind led to friendship? He felt as though he were on the edge of a cliff, looking down, not knowing which way to step to keep his balance.

Then Samantha's laugh broke his train of thought, and she turned to smile at him. Lord! He didn't want to think about it.

They ate lunch in a Mexican-food café a couple of blocks from the Plaza, where Sam squealed at the prices but melted in ecstasy over the food. Then she persuaded him to drive out Canyon Drive. They parked and climbed a hill that afforded a splendid view of town, and Sam went to work on her sketch pad. Eric sat and watched as her pencil captured the essence of the Santa Fe mystique, the meeting and linking of cultures—Spanish, Mexican, Native American, and Anglo; the contrast of commercialism and history, art and junk; the aura of rich history and the energy of present day.

"I'm being selfish," she admitted, looking up from her work. "You must be bored."

"I'm not bored." Who could be bored watching Samantha Vargas work? She put her soul into her pencil strokes. She captured the spirit of her subject and combined it with her own The result took his breath away. "Your work should be hanging in a gallery somewhere, you know that?"

She gave him a soft smile that was a work of art in itself. "Thank you, Eric."

"I mean it. You're very, very good."

She turned back to the sketch, but her face glowed with pleasure at his praise. "It's my dream to make a living doing this. Someday I'm going to get my degree in fine arts, and then study with someone who can help me become a real artist. I've got a little money put away in a savings account in Chicago, and little by little I add to it."

Eric had no doubt she would accomplish her goal. Freewheeling and carefree as she seemed, she was a person who would pursue a goal, slowly but surely, until she had what she wanted. She might take setbacks in stride and laugh at difficulties—as she had on this trip—but eventually she would get there.

Eric felt a great wave of longing to be there when Samantha

Vargas got what she wanted. To be there on the journey with her and watch out for her along the way. That certainly wasn't part of his plan, and it would never happen, but the need for it was almost physical pain.

Toward evening they drove back toward the Plaza. Eric dropped Samantha at the Museum of Fine Arts and went to park the Healey. The tourist season was in full swing, and parking spaces were at a premium. Twenty minutes later, and a good distance on the other side of the Plaza, he finally slipped the little car into a slot. As he turned off the engine, the glove compartment banged open.

"What now?" He'd come to think of the Healey as a fractious child or an evil spirit, depending upon what particular mischief it was dealing out at the time.

Unexplainably, the door of the glove compartment gave a tiny bounce, as if to attract his attention. He'd had too much sun, Eric decided. Or this car was something straight out of *The X-Files*. Gingerly he reached out to shut the door and saw one of Sam's smaller tablets hiding among the registration, bill of sale, title, and other paraphernalia he had shoved into the compartment. He was seized with an irresistible urge to snoop.

He pulled out the tablet. It was the one Sam usually carried in her shoulder bag. She was never without sketching materials, Eric had noticed. Even this smallish blank pad served as a platform to receive her impressions and emotions. He wondered why she didn't have it with her.

It was full; that was why. He leafed through the pages. Here was a little rendition of Sassy, staring out of the page with typical feline hauteur. There was a drawing of the Healey. She'd put a mischievous smile on the car's grille, and a few well-placed pencil strokes made the headlights appear to be twinkling eyes, one shut in an impertinent wink.

"She's got you pegged," he told the car.

The last page was what riveted his attention, though. It was a head study of Eric. He felt a rush of warmth when he looked at it. No one should be able to see into someone's soul and capture it on paper. The beginnings of creases about the eyes gave the impression of incipient laughter. The not-quite-smile that curved the lips bespoke both warmth and passion. The passion was a surprise. Eric considered himself a practical man, not a passionate one. Perhaps Samantha's own passion and *joie de vivre* colored what she perceived in him.

And if this sketch represented what Sam saw in him—Eric didn't really want to think about it. The drawing should have been nothing, the casual, quickly done work of a person who drew everything and anything that made an impression upon her. It shouldn't mean anything.

But it did mean something. It meant too much. Anyone looking at that little portrait would have sensed the feeling that went into every stroke of the pencil. If Eric was having trouble sorting out his emotions, apparently Sam was not, for they were crystal clear in every line, every shading on the paper. The woman who drew this face was more than infatuated, more than casually attracted. The woman who drew this face was . . . was . . . Eric cursed. He didn't want to think about it.

He quickly shoved the little tablet back into the glove compartment and slammed the door shut. Looking at those sketches was as bad as snooping in a diary. He didn't know what had come over him. And he very, very definitely didn't want to think about it.

They spent an hour at the Museum of Fine Arts, then went to dinner at La Fonda, the historic hotel on one corner of the Plaza.

"There's been an inn of some sort here since the seventeenth century," Eric read from a plaque in the hotel lobby as they were leaving. "They don't allow pets, though, so obviously we can't stay here."

Samantha forced down laughter as she noted the room price. "I'm in debt to you as it is. This place would extend the debt for about the next hundred years."

"No. This Santa Fe thing is definitely my treat. After all, it was my idea."

She started to argue, but he hurried her toward the car. "We need to get back to the motel. After all, Sassy hasn't been fed."

Sam surrendered with a lopsided smile. "You haven't heard the last from me."

"I'm counting on that."

Somewhere between the Plaza and the Days Inn, a gut-wrenching sadness stole up on Eric and sucked the warmth from the night. Tomorrow they would arrive in Phoenix. Tonight was the last time he would see the moonlight in Sam's windblown fiery hair, the last time he would hear her say good night to his car—a peculiarity of hers that always made him smile. Worse, it was the last time she would say good night to him.

"I got you something," he told her when they were at the door of Sam's room.

Her eyes sparkled like a child's. "You got me something? What? What is it?"

He took a pendant from his pocket. She had admired it earlier in the day, when they had walked by the Native American artisans in front of the Palace of Governors. On his way from the car to the museum, Eric had given in to temptation and bought it. Now he took pleasure in Sam's expression as he dangled it in front of her face

"Eric!"

"I saw you looking at this with lust in your eyes."

"Eric! Oh, shoot! You really, really shouldn't have!"

"I know. But I did. I wanted to think of you wearing this when you're a great artist in California."

"I can't accept it."

"Yes, you can. It's a memento between friends. We are friends, aren't we?"

"Yes," she barely breathed. "We're friends."

He fastened it around her neck. Her nape was silky smooth and warm. As the rest of her would be. Eric's hands began to tremble.

"I'm a klutz," he admitted.

She reached back and covered his hands with her own, helping him. But her hands shook also. She looked up at him, her eyes uncertain. They were much too close, Eric realized suddenly. Much, much too close. The very sensible reasons for not kissing her burned away in a flame of rising need.

Inevitably, irresistibly, their mouths came together. The kiss began as a hesitant experiment, then escalated into a frantic mating of mouths and tongues. In the middle of it all, Eric took the key card from Sam's hand and managed to shove it in the slot on the door. They tumbled into the room together, still clinging to each other as the door slammed behind them.

"We can't," Sam mumbled.

"We can."

"You love Mary Elizabeth."

"I love you. You know it. You have to know it. And you love me. I saw it in that sketch in the car."

She didn't have to ask him which sketch. "I didn't mean for you to see that."

"I snooped. Since I first saw you, I've tried not to think, not to feel. But it's no good. In just a few days you've become a part of me."

"This is crazy."

"It's insane," he admitted. "You're going to rip my life apart, and draw me a whole new one."

"Am I?" she asked weakly.

"You already have."

She made no attempt to escape as he unbuttoned her shirt and tugged her undershirt from the waistband of her shorts.

"Are we doing what I think we're doing?" she whispered against his neck.

"Yeah. We are."

They fell together to the bed as she struggled with the button on his jeans. Sassy hissed and glared, narrowly escaping with a leap to one side. They didn't notice.

For the rest of the night, they didn't notice much of anything except each other.

Mary Elizabeth's house was tucked into a cul-de-sac against the foothills of Camelback Mountain. Adobe walls and a red tile roof let it blend seamlessly into the desert landscape.

The key was just where Mary Elizabeth had said it would be. When Eric opened the front door, a gust of cool air made him breathe a sigh of relief. Outside, the temperature was 120 degrees. Inside, air-conditioning created an oasis of cool.

A note in Mary Elizabeth's handwriting awaited him on a table in the entrance hall. She couldn't be home at noon, as she'd planned. A viral epidemic was sweeping the local schools, and she was swamped with runny noses and sore throats. Make himself at home, she invited.

Eric had seen the house before, but Mary Elizabeth had redecorated since last Christmas, when he'd been here for a visit. Native American pottery accented the Southwestern decor. Every painting on the walls was dead straight. Not a speck of dust marred the furniture. Outside, palm trees shaded a turquoise swimming pool, and patio furniture was arranged just so. The tautly stretched plastic strips of the chairs gave no hint that they'd ever been dented by anyone's backside.

Eric wandered into the kitchen, where every dish was clean and stacked neatly in the cabinets, organized precisely into shelves of cups, glasses, plates (graded by size, of course), cans (also graded by size), and boxed goods. He poured himself a glass of ice water and carefully mopped the small splash on the countertop.

How much time did Mary Elizabeth spend here? Eric wondered. He would guess not much. The place was lovely, but it certainly didn't look lived in. Her office, on the other hand, was crowded with books and files, along with a gewgaw or two that her clients had given her and a big stuffed bear that she sometimes used to placate her more anxious patients. At least, that was how it had looked the last time Eric had seen it, and he doubted it had changed much. Mary Elizabeth's life was there. She lived where her heart was, and her heart belonged to the children who trooped in and out of her examining rooms.

How had Eric ever believed otherwise?

He loved Mary Elizabeth. He had loved her for years and would always love her, but he loved her as a friend. Not until a different kind of love had dropped out of the blue—or, rather, hitched a ride alongside the freeway—had he recognized the difference. He hoped Mary Elizabeth would still be a friend when this was over. The thought gave birth to a wave of guilt.

Mary Elizabeth gusted out a sigh as she pulled into her driveway and parked beside the little red sports car that nosed up to the garage. Eric was here. Of course Eric was here. Their wedding was only two days away.

"I'm in here," Eric called as she closed the front door behind her.

Mary Elizabeth put a smile on her face and marched toward the kitchen. "There you are," she said. Her heart gave her a jolt. That always happened when she saw Eric. He was much too good-looking for any female not to react to. The familiar charm in his smile inspired a warm rush of affection. "It took you long enough to get here!" she chided, hugging him. "I guess you had a rough trip, huh?"

"In some ways."

Judging by the way he looked, the drive couldn't have been too rough. Mary Elizabeth stood back and surveyed him. "Oh, Eric, you do look good."

"So do you, Mary Liz."

As a matter of fact, Mary Elizabeth mused, Eric looked too good. Even just leaning casually against her kitchen counter, he had a vitality she'd never before noticed. His smile was different. His eyes had a light that made him look as though he'd captured the sun and reduced it to his own special glow. Did the prospect of their wedding do this? She experienced a sickening flood of guilt.

"Uh . . ." Mary Elizabeth had never felt awkward with Eric, until now. "Well, come into the living room and sit down. We have a lot of catching up to do." She put a hand on his shoulder and pressed a light kiss on his lips. His response was warm, but not passionate.

"You must be tired."

"Some." He grinned. "Did you see my hot new car?"

"You call that thing a car?"

Some of the tension dissolved as they sat together on the living room couch and drifted into familiar friendly banter.

Everything was as it always had been, and yet not. Mary Elizabeth told herself to stop putting off the inevitable, but guilt made her hesitate. What she'd done was inexcusably selfish, and what she meant to do was cruel. But to carry on would be crueler.

"Eric . . . uh . . . about the wedding."

A flash of worry darkened his eyes. He must suspect, she thought miserably.

"Yes. We need to talk about the wedding, Mary Liz." He held up a hand to silence her reply. "There's something I have to tell you."

His tone made her hold her breath.

"Mary Liz, this is really a rotten thing to do, but . . . but . . . shit! There's no good way to say this. I can't marry you."

Her mouth fell open.

"Oh, cripes! Don't look like that. It wouldn't work, Mary Liz. This is all my fault, and you should take that piece of pottery over there and break it over my head, but—"

"Eric!"

"I know! I'm a jerk. I'm probably the biggest jerk who ever lived, but—"

"Eric. I canceled arrangements for the wedding yesterday." Mary Elizabeth felt as though a lead weight had been lifted from her heart.

"You what?"

"You heard me." She leaned forward and kissed him again, a true kiss of friendship this time, then hugged him hard. "You'll never believe, Eric. I was convinced I was such a heel! I'll bet we've both been turned inside-out feeling guilty. Who is she?"

"She?"

Mary Elizabeth raised a brow. "Someone's giving you that glow."

Looking like a kid with his hand in the cookie jar, Eric grinned guiltily. "She's someone you're going to like a lot, I hope."

She nodded and pressed a finger to his lips before he could

say more. "Just as you're going to like a certain guy who's waiting back at my office."

"You don't say!"

"I do say!" She smirked. "I think some introductions are in order. And a celebration. Can we take that cute car of yours? I've always liked red."

Eric gave her an enigmatic smile. "Sure thing, Doc. Just watch out for darts behind the seat."

EPILOGUE

*F*lowers heaved a sigh that was appropriately romantic for one in her line of work. "A double wedding! How wonderful! And they're all such good friends. All romances should turn out so well."

"Don't wish us more work than we already have," Hearts warned. "We're already stretched too thin." He smiled in satisfaction, however, as he perused the announcement in the *Phoenix Gazette*. "It says here that Drs. Reirdon and Chambers"—he gave a self-satisfied chuckle—"now Drs. Reirdon and Reirdon, along with the other partners in their practice, are expanding their practice to a second clinic on the other side of Phoenix. Near Chandler. That should keep them busy and out of trouble."

"And Mr. Neal and his bride are settling in Cottonwood, where Eric and a retired Sunbelt pilot by the name of Shepherd are opening a private flight school. Where the heck is Cottonwood?"

Hearts smirked. "Right in the middle of country that would inspire any artist to great work: sweeping vistas, colorful denizens absolutely ripe for character studies, and an extension campus that offers coursework in the arts. I outdid myself on that one."

"Well, don't hide your light under a basket."

"I won't, thank you very much." Hearts leaned back in his white leather chair, folding his arms behind his head. "I hope you observed how creative solutions are sometimes necessary to crack a tough nut like Eric Neal.''

Flowers shrugged. ''I thought the case quite easy.''

''Not easy,'' Hearts corrected. ''Masterfully executed. When an agent picks the right players and stages the right moves, events end up shaping themselves. That is the way it should be. If you have your ducks in a row, only limited intervention should be necessary.''

''Really? Then what was that last-ditch effort of throwing that sketch up in Mr. Neal's face, Mr. Temperamental Sports Car?''

''Eric Neal was an exceptionally stubborn subject. And the Austin-Healey was not an easy medium to work through.'' His expression softened. ''I will miss that car, though. That jet jockey had better take good care of it, now that I'm not there to oversee things.''

''I have to admit that it wasn't all that bad being a computer. Do you believe I had to leave just as they were going to give me a faster modem and sixteen more megs of memory? And you should have seen what was going on in one of the singles chat rooms I found.''

Hearts held up his hand to cut short her reminiscing. ''Let it go, Flowers. We can't afford to look behind when there is still so much work to be done. You have months to go before you've earned vacation.'' He flipped a new set of orders her way. ''This time we're sending you out on your own. A promotion of sorts.''

She scanned the document, and a dark incredulity gathered on her face. ''A cat? You've got to be kidding! I really don't like cats.''

''You don't have to like them to be one. I have the perfect subject to model you after. Her name is Sassy.''

''Oh! That is so stereotypical, Hearts! Not all females are catty, you know. . . .''

Hearts tuned her out, knowing she would give in at the end. He glanced down at the newspaper once more before consigning it to the files. There was a photo of the new Mr. and

Mrs. Neal departing on their honeymoon in a bright red Austin-Healey. Hearts could almost smell the rich leather of the interior and feel the hot asphalt beneath the tires. Next time, perhaps, he might rate an assignment as a Jaguar.

Cupid's Arrow

VICTORIA BARRETT

CHAPTER ONE

Amanda Jensen slammed down the phone.

No grown woman should have to contend with this nonsense. It was enough to drive a stable person insane. Why couldn't her mother just accept her for who she was and encourage her to be the woman she wanted to be?

She supposed that being the only daughter of the Biloxi, Mississippi, social icons, Edward and Veronica Jensen, and not being attuned to them or to their lifestyle, had made her hurting and disappointing them inevitable. Probably inescapable. Oil and water just don't mix. But each does have its value. So why couldn't her mother recognize Amanda's value and spare them both these miserable conflicts?

The motion detector installed to warn her of shoppers' arrival in her mall store, the Card Shoppe, chimed. Hating buzzers that grated on the ear, Amanda had installed a little bell that tinkled softly; a pleasant, soothing sound. Appreciating it even now, she gave the phone a resigned sigh, then did her best to calm down and rid herself of a grimace before greeting her sorely needed customer. Her time for proving the lifelong dream her mother called "Amanda's ridiculous little commercial venture" was nearly up. And failure, God help her, appeared imminent.

She smoothed a wrinkle from the skirt of her red silk sheath, pasted on a smile that probably looked more like a snarl, and then, standing behind the cash register, turned toward the entrance.

Her favorite customer, Chatty, shuffled in. Amanda felt certain Chatty was homeless—all of the signs were there—though the woman denied it. She never had been able to pinpoint Chatty's age. Under the garb it was hard to tell, but she was probably between fifty and sixty. Her pink floppy hat was soaked with raindrops, the sleeves of her three-sizes-too-big army jacket rolled-up, her jeans faded, and her mismatched sneakers dragging shoestrings that left a muddy, wet trail in her wake. Though rain-splotched from head to toe, Chatty looked warm enough, and she was carrying her brown grocery bag, which she'd protected and kept dry, so all must be okay in her world.

Mumbling to herself, Chatty meandered over to the two cushy chairs before the display of the Tender Touch cards Amanda carried exclusively. Amanda wrote the verses herself—another ridiculous venture, according to her mother—and the mysterious Jonathan Maxwell illustrated them. Amanda knew Jonathan only by name and from his notes, though they had worked together via mail for two years, and she'd fantasized about the man every day of them—a fact she admitted, of course, only to her closest confidante, Chatty.

"It's cold out there today, Mandy." Chatty lowered her grocery bag to the teal carpet, near the fern positioned between the two chairs, then sank onto the chair's cushion with a relieved sigh. "Ah, I'm ready for my tea."

Amanda couldn't help but smile. With Chatty's flyaway gray hair peeking out from under the brim of her hat, her vacant glances, and her shade-shy-of-aware ways, she often reminded Amanda of *Bewitched*'s Aunt Clara—or she would have, if Aunt Clara'd had an attitude. "It's already steeping."

"Mmm. It appears the tea isn't all that's steeping around here." Chatty sent Amanda a wary, sidelong look. "What's the matter, pet? You're looking a tad miffed."

"Mother just phoned. Bradley's on his way over."

Amanda didn't linger to hear Chatty's reaction to that disclosure. She knew her retort would be short, snappy, and snippy. Though they hadn't met, Chatty found Amanda's parents' choice of a prospective husband for her about as appealing as their daughter found the man: not at all.

Amanda returned from the little kitchenette in the back of the shop with a tea tray, bearing a steaming teapot, her best china cups, fresh lemon wedges, and snowy linen napkins. She set the tray onto the little table in front of the two chairs, then sat beside her friend and waited. Chatty always poured.

"Why don't you give that man his walking papers?" With a little grunt, she reached for the pot. "He isn't fit to carry your sack."

Glancing up from Chatty's grocery bag, tucked near the leg of her chair, Amanda reached over the fern and accepted the cup. "He isn't that bad."

"He's worse, and you know it. The man drives you up the wall." Chatty filled her own cup. "Ditch him, I say, and get on with finding yourself a real man. Maybe meet your Jonathan. Now, he has potential. You're half in love with him, and you haven't even met him. Imagine what could happen if—"

"I can't." Boy, didn't Amanda wish she could meet Jonathan, or ditch Bradley. She sipped the steamy brew. Japanese green tea felt so good going down the throat. Soothing. "We've been over this a thousand times, Chatty. Jonathan insists on keeping his anonymity, and ditching Bradley would break my mother's heart."

"And I say, maybe her heart needs breaking." Chatty opened her mouth again, likely to express her doubt Veronica Jensen had a heart, but then she thought better of it and held her silence.

Grateful for the reprieve, Amanda watched the fragrant steam lift. "I admit it. She's a snob, an art patroness with a long nose she loves to look down on at other people. But the bottom line is what it's always been: She's my mother."

"And that gives her the right to make you miserable?"

"She doesn't mean to make me miserable. It just kind of happens." Innately compelled to defend her, Amanda frowned. "You don't understand, Chatty. Mother and I live in different worlds. It's . . . complicated."

"I don't see what's so complicated." Chatty harrumped, then muttered, a knowing gleam in her eye, "Your mother—a twit, if you'll pardon my saying so, pet—wants you to marry a man you can't stand because he's a social snob like her. And you think you have to date him just because you've hurt her enough already by bucking her and opening this shop, when she's wanting you to marry a man you can't stand and take your rightful place in society." Chatty blew out a sigh that ruffled the gray silk hangings surrounding the Tender Touch card display. "Pardon my saying so, pet, but you're being a twit, too. About this, anyway."

Amanda didn't take offense. She and Chatty had met during the Card Shoppe's grand opening—months ago—and in the time since then, they had become good friends. The adorable woman was both blunt and honest; she genuinely cared about Amanda. And Amanda loved never having to wonder what Chatty was thinking because she rarely hesitated about speaking her mind. "Twit or not, she's my mother and I love her. I don't like hurting her." Amanda shifted on her seat. "Opening the shop was a real blow. Any more shocks and I'll put her under."

"Bah, she's as healthy as a horse." Knitting her brows, Chatty stuffed a lemon wedge into her pocket. "You, on the other hand . . ."

"She'd be devastated," Amanda countered, rubbing her cup's rim with the pad of her thumb.

"She'd be embarrassed."

She would. Horribly. "That, too."

"I know how you feel, pet, and your not wanting to hurt her is admirable." Chatty patted Amanda's forearm reassuringly. "But the truth of the matter is as simple as sunshine. You stuck out your neck to open this shop because it was what you wanted professionally. Don't you think your personal life deserves at least that same consideration?"

Amanda pushed her spiky black hair back from her eyes and cast her friend a pleading look. "She wants me to marry him."

"No news there. She's wanted that for months."

"Yes, but now she's becoming more insistent, and so is he." They'd joined forces to push her up against the wall, and Amanda hated it.

Chatty stilled. A long moment later, she tilted back her head to look at Amanda from under the brim of her floppy hat. Her soft green eyes glittered resentment and curiosity. "So what are you going to do about it?"

"I don't know. I don't want to marry the man. He irks me, Chatty." Amanda sighed and slumped back in her chair. "But we both know Mother holds the loan on my shop. I have three months. Just three months." Panic laced Amanda's voice. "If I don't prove this shop a success by then, she can call the loan—and she *will* do it. I know she will."

"And then you're up the river without a rowboat." Chatty let her gaze drift toward the front of the store, at the rack of sunglasses and the little table loaded with Valentine's Day goodies: lacy red sachets, velvet-covered journals, sweet-smelling potpourri. "I hate to have to agree with you, pet, but I do. If Veronica can call your loan, she'll do it, to force you to toe the line. But you can't marry the man just to avoid a family feud."

"I know." Amanda groaned, more resentment burning in her stomach. It was a lose-lose situation.

"So what's your battle plan?" Chatty spied the quill pens near the register, and that familiar, appreciative gleam lit in her eyes. "Valentine's Day is right around the corner. It'd be the perfect time, I'd say, to launch a war."

Chatty was right. This was a war. And failure wasn't an option. Amanda would succeed or bust trying. She turned her thoughts to her Valentine's Day plans, and feeling her enthusiasm bubble, she disclosed them to Chatty. "It's going to be a winner. It really is. I know some of my promotional schemes have fallen flat, but this one is going to be a stellar success."

"What is it?" Excitement flickered through Chatty's eyes. She refreshed her tea, then added lemon.

"A 'Meet Your Secret Admirer' party." Amanda's pulse quickened. "I wrote the invitations and hired Jonathan to il-lustrate them. People have been signing up all week." She waved toward the end of the register counter to the mailbox she'd covered in red satin and white hearts. "They fill out their card to their 'admiree,' and then I seal and mail them. The seal proves they're authentic, from the shop," she digressed to explain the safeguard against crazies using them to lure innocents for nefarious purposes. "Then Valentine's night, all of the couples meet here for a formal affair—very romantic. We'll have roses, champagne, the whole nine yards."

"It sounds wonderful!" Chatty set down her cup and walked to the front of the store, her shoestrings still leaving a slinky, wet trail on the carpet. She pointed out into the mall, center court, to the huge bronze sculpture roped off by velvet brass-pole swags. "You can have tables for two out there, candlelight. A band right under the tip of Cupid's arrow, near the little bench, and dancing. . . . Oh, Mandy, people will love it!"

Reassured by Chatty's excitement, Amanda smiled. "I think so, too."

Chatty looked back over her shoulder at Amanda and sobered. "Have you ever really noticed that statue of Cupid?"

"*Cupid's Arrow*?" Amanda asked, reciting the name the renowned and reclusive artist Millicent Fairgate had tagged the sculpture.

Chatty slid her a worried look. "It's the only statue around, pet."

Amanda resisted the urge to squirm. "It isn't easy to miss." The bronze stood a solid ten feet tall. She'd avoided close scrutiny of the piece because her mother had purchased and then donated it to the mall for the holiday. Yet curious now, Amanda walked over to Chatty. "What about it?"

"The arrow nocked in his bow points directly into the entrance of your shop."

Surprised, Amanda studied the giant bronze. "It does." She grunted. "Maybe that'll bring us good luck."

"It hasn't so far, and I'd say it isn't likely to this morning." Chatty grimaced, obviously vexed. "Here comes Mr. Perfect."

Chatty swiped past the fern, rustling its leaves, put her cup down on the little table, and then grabbed her grocery sack. "I don't care if Bradley Wade is the youngest partner in the history of your father's law firm, pet, the man's still a twit. Handsome as sin, but a twit."

Through the store's front windows, Amanda saw women in the mall crook their necks to watch Bradley. He was handsome, in a perfectionist kind of way, and she'd have liked to disagree on the twit remark, but she couldn't honestly do it. "He has good qualities." Weak, but the best she could manage.

Chatty snorted.

Bradley sauntered into the shop, glancing around as if he were appraising it. He did have appeal: dark hair, bedroom eyes. Perfectly dressed in only the best, he carried himself like a winner. A very successful winner. And maybe he would be a winner, if he'd broaden his horizons a little, develop some compassion, and look outside himself to the needs of others just a tenth as often as he looked within to his own.

That was Amanda's biggest gripe about him, and one she just couldn't seem to work past—though she didn't much care for the inspector-general way he looked at her shop or at her, either. The shop was lovely, teal and gray and softly scented with vanilla; warm and welcoming. And her red sheath flattered her coloring, her nape-length, spiky black hair, blue eyes, and pale skin. She was lean and attractive, if not classically beautiful. Certainly she deserved better than him glaring at her throat, her hands, and her earlobes and then giving her a resigned sigh.

Ah. The reason hit her. *No jewelry.* She resisted sighing herself. He knew she hated jewelry, of course, yet he still resented her for not wearing it. As if she hated it to deliberately deny him the opportunity to flash his generosity to observers he wanted to impress. A vintage Bradley reaction, unfortunately. About as deep as a pane of glass.

He cast a disdainful look Chatty's way, as if wondering what in the world a woman wearing rags could be doing in Amanda's shop. "Amanda."

"Good morning, Bradley. I'd like you to meet my friend, Chatty. Chatty, this is Bradley Wade."

Chatty held out a hand and offered him a smile.

Bradley looked at her as if she carried plague. "Charmed." He nodded, then turned his back on her.

Clearly in a snit, Chatty grumbled her way to the cash register counter, picked up the quill pens she'd been eyeing earlier, dropped two of them into her sack, and walked out of the shop.

She headed straight across the mall to the statue of Cupid, sat on the bench, and within seconds engaged in a serious discussion with the bronze.

Amanda saw red. She glared at Bradley. "Why were you rude to her?"

"Me, rude?" He lifted a brow. "Darling, has it escaped your notice that your 'friend' is a bag lady and a thief? She just stole two pens from you. I would think you would ban that kind of riffraff from your shop, not refer to her as a friend."

"Riffraff?" Amanda had to work at it to swallow an outraged bellow. "Don't call Chatty names, Bradley. I mean it." Knowing her voice was elevating anyway, she couldn't seem to stop herself. "She's my friend, and I don't give a damn if she walks out with the whole store."

He crossed his arms akimbo. "Spoken like a true businesswoman."

His sarcasm, and the inference that he shared her mother's certainty that Amanda was doomed to fail, infuriated her. "Look, I realize Chatty's a little eccentric, and she's not apt to find herself welcome at garden club luncheons or country club balls, but she's welcome in my shop any time, and that's that. As for her stealing, well, she knows things aren't important. People are. She cares about me, and I care about her. Now if you can't accept that and be nice to her, then you'd better leave."

Red crawled up his neck, staining his skin, then crept to his face. He was angry all right, nearly choking on it. He glared at her, then left the store without uttering another word.

The bell tinkled, signaling he'd gone. Still trembling from the confrontation and intending to apologize to Chatty, Amanda turned for the entrance.

A gorgeous man stood near the cash register. About six two and dressed in a navy blue suit with an exquisite glove fit, he held his gaze averted so Amanda couldn't see his eyes, but his hair was black, a little shorter on his nape than hers, and he had a strong jaw and the kind of broad shoulders a woman in need could lean on. Appealing package. But why hadn't she heard him come in?

Well, she had been a little preoccupied, screaming like an idiot banshee. She probably wouldn't have heard a bomb explode. *Oh, no. Had he heard her?* Talk about raunchy first impressions.

He glanced her way, and she looked into the most fascinating gray eyes she'd ever seen. Empathy shone in their depths. Her stomach knotted and her face went hot. The man had stood there long enough to witness her confrontation with Bradley, and God help her, he'd heard every humiliating word.

Was there a first impression worse than raunchy?

Doubting it, and wishing for a hurricane, a tornado, or any other disaster that would let her avoid this embarrassment, she paused, but nothing happened. *Figures.* She slid *Cupid's Arrow* a glare for refusing to bring her even a smidgen of good luck, then brazened out meeting the man on her own.

Walking over so the counter would be between them—truthfully, she needed the support of leaning on it—she stepped up to the register and then addressed the man, doing her darnedest to dredge up a smile. "Good morning. May I help you?"

"Good morning, Miss Jensen." His voice sounded soft and rich, as soothing as her Japanese tea. "I understand the woman who was just in your store has been shoplifting."

He knew her name; had to be with mall security. *Oh, God, he couldn't mean to arrest Chatty!*

Amanda's chest went tight. *Think. Think!*

She had to lie. What other choice did she have? "Are you talking about Chatty?"

He nodded, and Amanda let out an absurd laugh, hoping it passed muster and she didn't land herself in jail *with* her friend. "Of course not. That dear woman wouldn't steal from anyone." She pointed to the tray. "We had tea, Mr. . . . ?"

"Jones," he said. "Max Jones." His brows knitted together and his jaw tensed until his discomfort became more overwhelming than evident. "I'm not sure exactly how to put this."

Amanda offered him a tentative smile. No one so gorgeous and gentle-voiced should ever be so uncomfortable. "Just say it, Mr. Jones."

"Call me Max, please. Everyone does."

"Max." He was letting her get away with the lie and, more than a little grateful, she widened her smile. Now here was a man with compassion.

He rubbed his neck and stiffened visibly, as if forcing himself by sheer will to meet her gaze. "Chatty is my aunt."

Amanda blinked, then blinked again. Chatty never had mentioned having family. Especially wealthy family, and from the looks of his suit—definitely custom-made—and the Rolex winking out from under his starched shirt cuff, Max Jones was far more than just financially comfortable.

He dragged a fingertip over his temple. "I'm sure you've noticed that my aunt is a little . . . eccentric, Mandy."

He must be Chatty's nephew. Only she had ever called Amanda "Mandy." "We all have our eccentricities. Chatty's are just a little more visual."

"They are that." He smiled.

Amanda's knees went weak. Gorgeous, compassionate, smells like a slice of heaven, *and* a killer smile. She almost sighed. Forgivable, though. Men like him didn't just walk into her shop, much less walk in claiming to be the nephew of a friend Amanda had thought homeless—despite Chatty's claims to the contrary.

"I've been away on business and just returned to the coast," he said. "I was told you knew about this . . . situation. Now, I learn you had no idea."

He paused, letting his gaze wander over the collection of

wind chimes, then the hourglasses and atomizers, as if weighing his options. Finally he looked back at her. "I'm sorry, but I guess there's no easy way to tell you this."

Amanda braced instinctively. From the tense look of him, whatever was coming had to be god-awful.

He stretched an arm across the counter and placed his hand atop hers, as if by touching her he would absorb the shock. "Earlier this morning, Chatty confessed that she's been 'borrowing baubles' from you since the day you opened your shop."

Amanda stared at him, not sure what to say.

"I'm so sorry, Mandy, and I'd like to make restitution—without involving the police, for obvious reasons—if you'd be agreeable to it." Sincerity radiated from him. "Chatty doesn't mean any harm, she's just . . . well, eccentric."

Relieved that this was all there was to it, Amanda thought she should move her hand. She should, but she wasn't going to. His was large, his fingers long and fluid, his nails short and blunt and well manicured. And his palm was warm on the back of her hand. So very warm. Compassionate, soothing . . . and comforting. She liked all of that about him. A lot. And she felt a deep need to ease his mind. This situation clearly worried him. "I know, Max," she said softly. "Chatty's been rather obvious, at times actually deliberate, in letting me know about her 'bauble borrowing.' "

Surprise flickered through his eyes, and maybe a sliver of admiration, though Amanda couldn't fathom what there was to admire in a businesswoman admitting she'd allowed herself to be duped out of merchandise since the day she'd gone into business. "If it's any consolation, she never takes any of my expensive items. Her cutoff seems to be around the three-dollar mark."

"It isn't consoling. Stealing is stealing. But I appreciate your trying to make me feel better about this." He pulled out his checkbook. "Oddly enough, she's kept an accounting of all her, er . . ."

"Baubles?" Amanda suggested, hating that he felt he sat on the hotseat. Having spent most of her life there, she knew too well what an uncomfortable place it could be.

"Yes." He scratched the tip of his gold pen across the check, filling it out, then tore it from the pad and passed it to her. "I've added sales tax. If you find that's insufficient, please let me know." He let his gaze drift away. "I do feel terrible about this, Mandy."

Terrible *and* embarrassed to the bone. "Please don't." This time her smile was genuine. "I've always had the distinct feeling that if I'd called Chatty down for her borrowing just once, she'd have stopped." Amanda gave his hand a gentle squeeze, then glanced at the check.

Something about his handwriting tugged at a familiar cord in her, but unable to peg exactly what, she put the check into the register, then snapped the cash drawer shut.

"Why didn't you call her down on it?" Curiosity lit the irises of his eyes with mesmerizing silver flecks. "And when I asked, why did you deny knowing about the thefts?"

Even mesmerized, Mandy couldn't hold his gaze. He'd think she was a lousy businesswoman, just like Bradley. And while she didn't give two figs what Bradley thought, for some goofy reason, Max's opinion of her mattered. It had to be her reacting to the compassion in him. Still, truth was truth, and in coming here, he'd earned it. This hadn't been easy for him. That was obvious. "She's my friend. I didn't want her to get into trouble." Amanda shrugged. Sure his censure would follow and not wanting to see it, she dropped her gaze lower, to his gray silk tie, and confessed, "I thought you were with mall security."

A little chuckle escaped him, and from the tender smile that curved his lips, she saw that he didn't think at all like Bradley. "On the q.t., I'm a businessman, not at all secure, and I find your protectiveness . . . touching."

Unaccustomed to praise and to men admitting their flaws, Amanda liked both far more than she should. "What are friends for?"

"Support, caring, sharing—all the things you've given to Chatty. Thank you for that, Mandy." As if he regretted letting her see inside him, Max turned his voice from tender to crisp.

"Tell me, how did you and Chatty become friends?"

Relieved that he hadn't wondered why the daughter of Edward and Veronica Jensen would stoop to "unacceptable commercialism," Amanda felt the knots in her stomach melt. "Chatty's a warm, wonderful woman."

"She is," he agreed. "Though people seldom see that side of her."

Amanda's focus sank deeper into his eyes. They were so beautiful. Magnetic. And she wondered fleetingly how many women had found themselves lost in them.

"Did you meet here?"

"Yes, we did. Grand opening day." Amanda smiled. "Chatty came in cold and wet, bless her heart, carrying her grocery bag, like always. She introduced herself, wished me every success, and then snitched two Christmas ornaments on her way out of the store." Amanda let out a little laugh. "I was so stunned, I couldn't move."

Max looked torn between laughing with her and groaning. "Is that why you didn't have her arrested?"

"No." Amanda shrugged. "I know I should have, but I just couldn't do it."

"Why not?"

She focused on a point beyond his shoulder. "I guess because anyone can get down on their luck." Less than comfortable with being so frank, she shifted on her feet. "It sounds like a silly reason, but it's not. I've become very fond of her. In her own unorthodox way, Chatty is kind and gentle. She really cares about people and their hopes and dreams, and she has a quirky way of looking at things that makes me laugh." Amanda looked back at him, knowing she'd gone solemn and he was far too astute and observant to miss it, knowing she should hush now, before she made a damn fool of herself. But something in his eyes urged her on. "I've heard too little laughter in my life to squander it over the *borrowing* of a few *baubles*."

The look in his eyes told her he understood, and as if sensing her discomfort, he withdrew emotionally. "I trust we're considering this matter settled, then, without the police?"

"Of course."

"Thank you." He smiled, and his eyes lit up from their bottoms. "Chatty's lucky to have you for a friend."

Amanda crossed her chest and rubbed at her arms. "I'm the lucky one."

Looking thoughtful, he turned to walk out of the shop, then stopped and glanced back at her. "Mandy, would you have dinner with me tomorrow night?"

Her heart skidded to a near-halt, then thudded hard, threatening to cave through her chest wall. Liking him, and incredibly intrigued—Why did the eccentric aunt of a wealthy man dress in rags and run around carrying a grocery bag?— Amanda smiled. "Yes, I will. Where should we meet?"

"Antonio's?" he suggested. "Eight o'clock?"

Antonio's? Now what would he know of a place like Antonio's? It was a hole-in-the-wall off Highway 90 near Rue Magnolia, far from the glitz and glamour the casinos had sprinkled along the Gulf Coast, and a choice that would send her mother into a dead faint. Definitely not a socially acceptable restaurant, but Amanda had been there many times, and she loved the food. "Can't wait," she said, chiding herself because that statement held a little too much truth, and Antonio's delectable linguine and white clam sauce had nothing to do with it.

CHAPTER TWO

Antonio's was crowded.

The wonderful smells of tomato sauce, garlic bread, and bubbling hot cheese greeted Amanda. She closed her umbrella and put it in the brass stand near the front door, then slung her raincoat onto the rack with the dozens of others hanging there.

Lightning crackled outside, but only she seemed to hear it over the hum of laughing voices. Waitresses scooted around, winding between the red-and-white-check clothed tables and the thriving green plants that separated the booths. Lining the walls, the foliage gave diners the illusion of privacy. Not seeing Max, she glanced down to check her watch. He had said eight, hadn't he?

"Hi, Mandy." Standing near her shoulder, he smiled down at her. "We're over here."

"Sorry. I didn't see you." She followed him to Antonio's most prized booth. Set slightly apart from the others, it was the only quiet place in the restaurant.

She sat down, a strange fluttering in her stomach. "You know, Max, I have the feeling I've seen you here before."

"You might have." His chair slid across the carpet. "I like the food here, so I drop in a lot."

"Ah." That, and his being Chatty's nephew, had to be why Amanda felt a strong sense of familiarity when there should have been none and why there was none of the discomfort associated with trying to get to know someone you've just met. Though surprised by its absence, she was grateful for it. She hated immensely that part of new relationships.

The waitress came over. Max gave her a heart-melting smile and then asked Amanda, "Would you like a drink?"

"Just a glass of wine with dinner." Thanks to Bradley and her mother, she'd had a wicked day. The last thing she needed was alcohol to heighten the depressing effect.

"Sounds good to me."

They ordered, and then Mandy smoothed down her napkin over the skirt of her royal blue dress. "So tell me about you, Max."

"I'm a businessman." He dropped his napkin into his lap, then grunted. "I've mentioned that, though, haven't I?"

He had, at the shop. "What type of business?"

Max didn't quite meet her eyes. "Actually, a variety of them. Some I like more than others." He waved, greeting a man several tables away.

The waitress returned with their salads. When she'd gone, he lifted his fork. "I have to admit that you fascinate me, Mandy."

"Oh?" Her warning antenna went up.

"Mmm, yes." He sipped from his water glass. Ice clinked against its side. "I've been asking myself all afternoon why such a tender woman would hear too little laughter in her life."

"Nothing fascinating or even mildly interesting about it, I'm afraid," she said, wishing she'd never mentioned it. Why had she? Normally she avoided the topic of her family. "My parents and I have different opinions on what is important in life. It makes for lively exchanges, though few of them involve laughter." Amanda smiled, though it was a little shaky, and changed the subject. "You mentioned just returning home to the coast. Do you enjoy traveling?"

He gave her lengthy, animated accounts of some of his more enjoyable trips and some of his most memorable, humorous adventures.

Amanda laughed until she had a stitch in her side. "Please, stop. Give me time to catch my breath."

The waitress removed their salads and put their plates on the table. The rich scent of clam sauce had Amanda's stomach threatening to growl, and she lowered her gaze to Max's bare throat. In a suit, he looked like her fantasy of Jonathan. In khakis and a soft shirt, Max looked even better. It wasn't fair, his making her laugh and assaulting her senses and then asking her questions she'd rather not think about, much less answer. But in doing so, he had opened the door for her to satisfy a little of her own curiosity. "Do you always laugh so much, Max?"

He hesitated, then reached over and clasped her hand, lacing their fingers until their warm palms touched. "Not really."

Amanda found that hard to believe. He had such a warm and wonderful sense of humor. But his hand felt so solid, so sure, and he seemed too sincere for his comment to be anything except true.

"You're doubting me," he said without censure, sinking his fork into piping-hot lasagna. "I wish I were saying this just to make you comfortable, but I'm not."

He'd done it for her. Deliberately worked at making her laugh. That he would bother touched her heart, and a tear slipped out of her eye. She quickly brushed at it.

Max noticed. "You okay?"

She curved her lips into a smile and nodded.

An awareness that she was not upset but feeling tender lit in his eyes. "May I ask you something . . . personal?"

Here it came: his politely stated demand for an explanation about her parents. Knowing it was inevitable, and she might as well address it and have it done, she braced for it. "Of course."

"Why did you refuse Bradley Wade's proposal?" Max studied the food on his plate. "Chatty mentioned it."

That question, Amanda hadn't expected. It took a second for her to mentally shift gears. "I could be diplomatic—"

"Don't," Max warned her. "Just be honest."

Honest? She could do that. "Bradley's a pompous jerk with

an ego the size of Montana and the arrogance to match. And he was rude to Chatty.'' Amanda felt her face flush. She hadn't meant to be quite that honest.

"So you don't love him?"

"No, I don't love him," she said.

"Egotistical. Arrogant. Rude." Max's lip twitched, as if he wanted to smile but felt it wiser not to. "Refusing him sounds like a good judgment call to me."

Amanda rewarded Max's support with a smile, and it hit her that she'd seldom smiled when with Bradley. Actually, she'd been miserable on their dates. He lived in her mother's world, not in Amanda's.

Yet she felt happy with Max. Sad, too, when he'd been uncomfortable at the shop. Why did it seem she'd known him forever? That sensation made her feel more than happy. It made her feel content. She wasn't used to contentment, but she liked the feel of it.

"I thought that was the reason you refused him, but I didn't want to jump to conclusions . . . again."

When had he jumped before? Ah, about Chatty and her "bauble borrowing," and Amanda not knowing it.

He gazed out of the rain-spattered window. Under the amber street lamp, the wet pavement sheened like a tawny mirror, reflecting but not absorbing shadows. Swinging his gaze back to her, he sobered and looked deeply into her eyes. "Have you ever been loved, Mandy? Not for your money or your work, but for yourself?"

"Not exactly," she hedged. How could she admit she'd never been loved by a man? Her parents' wealth attracted many men, but Amanda honestly couldn't say she'd been loved for herself by any of them.

"I haven't, either," Max admitted. "I guess being judged by others is normal. Everyone types and casts everyone else. But it would be great to be judged just on your worth as a human being."

"Yes, it would," she agreed. However, her recent experiences had left her opinion jaded about the odds of that ever happening.

He held her gaze, seemingly seeing straight through to her most secret self, and sipped at his wine. "Acceptance by someone you care about is a rare gift, but when it happens, it's wonderful, isn't it?"

Shifting on her chair, she debated answering him, then spoke from her heart. "I'll have to let you know, Max."

Surprise had those gray flecks in his eyes turning silver again. But he buried it and smiled. Not a wide smile, but a little curving of lips that came straight from his heart.

The sincerity in it left her breathless, tugged at strong desires for acceptance and approval and caring buried deep inside her. Feelings she wasn't at all sure she wanted aroused. This was too new, happening too fast.

Her instincts urged her to self-protect. She followed them and again changed the subject.

Max must have felt the same way, because he accepted the shift. They talked about little things, about everything and nothing—Max's travels, her struggles to get the store up and running, some of her promotion successes and flops. They laughed, talked about serious things, then laughed some more.

And Amanda watched him. His expressions and mannerisms. And she liked what she saw so much, it should have scared her. Oddly, it didn't, and that set her to worrying. When he found out who her parents were, would he be the same? Treat her the same?

In her experience, too often men became radically different, despite their statements on personal philosophies, such as those Max had made about being judged. And finding Max Jones charming, interesting, and intensely appealing just as he was, she didn't want to risk his changing. Maybe she shouldn't tell him any more about her parents. Maybe—

"Mandy?"

She jerked, dropped her napkin. "Sorry, I drifted."

He passed a fresh napkin to her, frowning more at himself than at her. "I've bored you that much?"

"No, of course not. I've enjoyed your company." She set her wineglass back onto the table. "In fact, I'm glad I came."

His eyes twinkled. "So am I."

Her heart fluttered. Had any man ever before looked at her with such warmth? Not that she could recall. She had dated a lot, but never anyone who attracted her on as many levels as Max, or as quickly. But mutual or not, this attraction was deepening too fast. Way too fast.

Again, she changed the topic to one more generic and less threatening. "I'm sure Chatty's glad to have you home. She really does need you to take care of her, Max. I worry about her being out there on the streets."

He choked on a sip of water, clearly astonished by that remark. "On the streets?"

"She swears she isn't homeless, but I've never known for sure if it was pride talking or the truth. You know how Chatty is. I've tried to get her to come to my apartment, but—"

"She's very independent, Mandy." He dabbed at his mouth with his napkin, then placed it on the table. "But let me put your mind at ease. She is not homeless."

"Thank goodness." Amanda lifted a hand to her chest. "I've really worried about that. I know we don't have blizzards in Biloxi, but we do have cold weather, and the high humidity makes it feel a lot colder."

"She isn't homeless," he repeated, looking more than a little defensive.

"I wasn't trying to make you feel guilty, Max."

His look turned hard, as if he believed that's exactly what she intended.

"Really, I wasn't," Amanda insisted, seeing that she had offended him. "But I am glad you're here now to take care of her."

He stared down at the table. Regret shrouded him and put a defeated edge on his tone. "I can't take care of her."

Amanda stilled, stared at him, stunned. "Why not?"

He clenched his napkin in his fist. "I just can't."

She flinched. He'd seemed so gentle and tender and caring. Now anger pounded out of him in waves. Had she radically misjudged him? "I—I don't understand."

"What's to understand?" His mouth flattened to a slash. "I just . . . can't."

Disappointment, resentment, and a fair share of anger arced through her, crushing all the good and tender feelings he'd aroused. She cocked her head. "What kind of man can be wealthy and yet refuse to help an elderly aunt who's down on her luck?"

Max stiffened. His voice turned as razor sharp as the look in his eyes. "One who respects his aunt's wishes."

Amanda challenged him. "Even when that aunt is eccentric and he knows she needs his assistance?"

He returned her glare with one of his own. "Even then."

Amanda couldn't believe it. Just couldn't believe it. How could she have thought him compassionate when the man clearly was as cold as a stone?

Gathering her wits, she nodded. "I see." That was that, then. Regardless of what he said and how charming he appeared, the real Max had come to light. It was hard to believe he could be so different from the man she'd perceived him to be, but obviously he was, and those differences injected a gulf between them too broad to bridge. It seemed Max Jones was about as selfish as her mother and Bradley.

Disappointment and regret had her food churning in her stomach, and she prayed she could get through the rest of the meal and get away from him before she got sick.

"Have I upset you?"

Yes! I wanted you to convince me I shouldn't feel jaded toward men. I wanted to be right about you, damn it. "No, not at all."

She gave him an icy smile, assuring him everything was fine, and then trudged her way through a sorbet dessert, counting the minutes until she could escape. It was agony sitting across from him, comparing how she felt about him now with how she'd felt earlier. She hated it. And she resented him. Why couldn't he have been as caring as he'd seemed initially, as compassionate as he'd professed himself to be?

Finally, the longest meal of her life ended. The tension at the table was frosty cold and thick enough to slice. A dull ache thudded at her temples, and with the deep freeze seemingly settled between them, she wouldn't have been surprised to see icicles hanging off the tip of her nose.

Seeing an opening to make a gracious exit, she tabled her napkin, then lifted her purse, admittedly angry at him for denying any responsibility toward Chatty and for disappointing her. And angry with herself, because as outrageous as it seemed, she was a scant step from tears and her heart hurt like hell.

"Thank you for dinner." She pushed back her chair and then stood up, close to losing her composure. "I need to get going. I have to be at the shop early tomorrow." She swallowed hard, hating the words about to come, knowing they would leave her mouth and her heart bitter. "Good-bye, Max."

He frowned up at her. "Amanda, wait."

She kept walking.

The last thing she needed in her life was another man she couldn't respect or trust.

CHAPTER THREE

*A*manda dragged herself into her apartment, rattled to the core and hurting more than she thought she could hurt.

Ordinarily the cozy Victorian decor of burgundy and forest green comforted her. But tonight even the subtle sweetness of the vanilla-scented potpourri didn't help her, and she seriously doubted much of anything could.

She toed off her pumps and left them at the entry hall coat tree, dumping her purse on its seat. Being soaked to the skin and chilled from the bone out didn't do her disposition a bit of good, either. She'd all but run out of Antonio's, afraid she'd scream at Max or cry—either of which would have been the last bit of humiliation she could stand today—forgetting her raincoat and umbrella. And nothing in the world could have enticed her to go back in and get them. Three altercations with men in one day was more than any woman could be expected to endure and stay upright. Especially considering two of them had been with Max. She'd really believed he would be different. . . .

Gooseflesh prickled her skin, and she rubbed her arms. She needed to call Antonio's, but first she needed a shower to warm up.

Passing through the galley kitchen, she paused to put the teakettle on the stove, then went to her bedroom, showered, and put on a fluffy, emerald green robe and her fuzzy slippers.

Feeling better now that her teeth had stopped chattering, she made herself a cup of chamomile tea to calm her nerves. Only a master at rationalization would deny they were teetering on the brink of fraying. On her way to the living room, she reached to snag the portable phone, then stopped. The answering machine's red light was flashing.

Her heart skipped a little beat.

Swearing at herself, she firmly insisted Max wouldn't have called her—and if he had, she would *not* call him back.

Resolved, she tapped the button and listened to three messages from her mother. To get through each successive one without pitching a fit, Amanda clenched her teeth a little harder. Her mother's tone went from firm to frigid; plainly irritated, and in each message she demanded Amanda call her immediately.

Already in a sour mood, Amanda figured she might as well get it over with now. If she let her mother stew until morning, it would take that much longer to calm her down. But first she had to phone Antonio's.

Minutes later, her feet tucked under her on the sofa, Amanda was frowning. She braced her head on the heel of her hand, atop the sofa arm. "I'm sorry," said Antonio's hostess. "No one left a London Fog raincoat or an umbrella here tonight."

Amanda hung up the phone, swearing under her breath. She had no one to blame but herself. Still, it'd be at least two months before she could afford to replace the coat. Frustrated to the max, she jerked a warm throw over her feet, shoved aside a stack of novels on the end table at her elbow, and then looked for the coaster. It was missing.

Now why didn't that surprise her? *Couldn't anything go right today?*

She set down her cup atop one of the books, then dialed her mother's private line.

"Hello."

Veronica Jensen answering on the first ring? She was irritated all right. "Hello, Mother."

"Amanda, where have you been? I've been phoning for hours."

"Is something wrong?" She sounded peeved, not upset. Yet to Veronica Jensen, when the two emotions involved her waiting, they were synonymous.

"*Wrong?* This potentially tragic situation is far more than *wrong*, Amanda. I'm doing my damnedest to avoid a disaster—and you failed to answer my question. Where have you been?"

Amanda stared across the room at the lace doily lying across the back of a stuffed chair. "I went to dinner, Mother." Everyone has to eat, right? "Exactly what disaster is threatening?" Could be a broken nail or two equally important social engagements scheduled for the same night. Her father never allowed anything of greater substance to trouble his wife. Was that a blessing or a curse?

Tonight, Amanda admitted, she bent low toward favoring the blessing side.

"What disaster? Bradley, of course. Good God, Amanda. A public scene at your shop? What were you thinking?"

Amanda grimaced. At present she wasn't thinking. She was wishing to hell she hadn't returned her mother's call and that she had installed a zipper in Bradley Wade's mouth only she could unzip. Wasn't it just like him to report the embarrassing incident to her mother?

Chatty was right. He was a twit. "I'm thinking that this isn't anything you should be concerned about. It's between Bradley and me."

"My daughter befriends a bag lady thief, orders the most eligible and sought-after bachelor in the state of Mississippi out of her silly little shop, and I'm not supposed to be concerned? What mother in her right mind wouldn't be concerned?"

"One who respects her daughter's wishes," Amanda said before thinking. She squeezed her eyes shut. Now why had she used the very same words Max had used earlier about Chatty?

"How dare you say that to me? My utmost concern has always been in doing what I think is best for you."

It had. Yet that concern never had warranted a pinch of

consideration—or compassion—for what Amanda felt was in her own best interests. "Bradley was very rude to Chatty, Mother."

"And you weren't rude to him? Elevating your voice in a public place, Amanda. What in the world is happening to you?"

Amanda squeezed her eyes shut again and let her head loll back against the soft sofa, wishing she could crawl in a hole and just hide for a while.

Veronica Jensen had no intention of letting that happen. She droned on and on.

Conjuring her reserves of patience, which were pitifully minute at the moment, Amanda stared at the ivory lace drapes covering the window. Rain tapped softly against the panes, and her mind wandered back to Max, back to her disappointment that he'd taken the attitude he had about Chatty. Why couldn't he have been the man she'd glimpsed as caring, sensitive, and tender? Until Chatty had come up in the conversation, Amanda had thoroughly enjoyed being with him, had found him attractive, charming, and sexy. Fun.

"I wish you'd just stop this, darling." Her mother's voice penetrated her thoughts. "Please. *Please,* give up this ridiculous commercial venture and marry Bradley—before you do your reputation irreparable damage. The only reason . . ."

Amanda tuned her mother out. Let her rant and rave. It was the only way to get past this and back to any semblance of peace between them.

For a while with Max, Amanda actually had stopped fantasizing about Jonathan. Chatty had been right about him, too. Through his notes and his work, Amanda had half fallen in love with him. Any man capable of such sensitivity in his illustrations had to be special. Yet she'd felt content with Max, until—

Something her mother said yanked at her focus, and Amanda twitched. "What was that?" she asked. "The only reason you funded my shop loan was because you had to in order to do—*what?*"

"It's not important," her mother said, sounding decidedly uncomfortable.

Amanda frowned at the phone, grabbed her teacup, and strode back to the kitchen. This was definitely a two-cup-of-chamomile-tea-to-soothe-down night. "I asked you for a straight answer, Mother."

"Oh, all right," she snapped. "I promised the art council I'd purchase *Cupid's Arrow* for the new gallery, but I couldn't acquire it without giving you the loan."

So even that hadn't been a show of support or belief. Amanda started to shake. She set the teapot down for fear of dropping it. "What do you mean?"

Her mother's sigh rippled static through the line. "The bronze had to be placed in the mall so that its arrow tip pointed directly into your shop. In order to do that, you had to have a shop. And in order for you to get the shop, I had to fund the loan."

A shiver streaked up Amanda's spine and set the roof of her mouth to tingling. Chatty had noted that about the arrow this very morning. "Why?"

"Millicent Fairgate insisted on it as a condition of the sale. I had to leave the bronze in the mall outside your shop until after Valentine's Day. Then I can move it to the gallery."

"Whatever for?" Amanda stared into her empty cup, hoping this didn't prove to be a three-cup kind of night. "Why my shop? I don't even know her."

"We've never met, either, but you know how eccentric artists are, dear. During negotiations, we spoke by phone a great deal, so of course Millicent knows a lot about you and Bradley—how you refuse to marry him, and how you entertained the ridiculous notion of opening up your own card shop."

The woman had discussed her personal life with a stranger? *A stranger?* Anger burned in Amanda. She buried it to find out the truth. "Mother, you're digressing. Why did Millicent Fairgate insist the bronze's arrow point into my shop?"

"Well, I told her I was hoping *Cupid's Arrow* would bring me some luck and help you to accept your heart's desire. So, you see, she too is hoping you'll come to your senses and marry Bradley.''

Out of patience, Amanda rolled her gaze heavenward and bit her tongue to keep from groaning or bellowing. Maybe both. Her mother's self-absorption never ceased to amaze her. "I've got to go, Mother. Bye."

Before her mother could object, Amanda depressed the button and then slumped against the kitchen counter, bracing her forehead on her arm. This didn't make a bit of sense. Why would an artist she didn't know from Adam give a flying flip who she married, or if she ever married anyone?

Having no idea, Amanda decided that if she ever intended to calm down enough to sleep, she had to push this whole mess right out of her mind. After grabbing her tea, she lifted the stack of unread mail from the end of the bar.

Two gold-sealed invitations appeared between the light bill and junk mail, and she stopped dead in her tracks.

They were from her store.

Addressed to her.

But she hadn't applied the seals or mailed them.

So who had?

Her hand not quite steady, she opened the first one.

"Bradley." She grimaced. Only he would be arrogant enough to sign his name to an anonymous "Secret Admirer" invitation.

"Twit." She tossed it aside, then opened the second one, chiding herself for the fluttering in her heart, for hoping it was from Max.

> *I've admired you for a long time,*
> *but never more so than now.*
> *Your Secret Admirer*

Her heart started a low, hard beat. The familiar scrawl struck a knowing cord in her, one she'd recognize anywhere. That distinctive ''M'' she'd been seeing in his notes for two years was a dead giveaway. Her spirit soared and sent her sailing straight into fantasyland. "Jonathan!"

Finally, after all the times he'd rebuffed her requests that they meet, of his insisting on retaining his anonymity, she was going to meet Jonathan Maxwell!

CHAPTER FOUR

Chatty came into the shop about ten, grumbling and grinning.

When she poured the first cup of tea, Amanda said, "You're in a great mood today."

"I am. I'm very pleased about you and Max having dinner last night." Chatty filled her own teacup. "So tell me, pet. What do think of my nephew?"

Tired from a lack of sleep due to that nephew, and due to the invitation from Jonathan, Amanda held back, hating the pleading she heard in her voice. "Please, Chatty, don't you start matchmaking on me, too. Mother's doing plenty enough of it already."

"Uh-oh." Chatty grimaced over the edge of her cup. "I figured he'd goof things up. The man has a heart of gold, but I swear, his mouth is pure tin."

Heart of gold? When he could ignore the fact that his aunt was in dire straits? *Ha!*

But not wanting to hurt Chatty's feelings with her true opinion of Max Jones, Amanda pulled out the two invitations from her jacket pocket. "I received these in the mail yesterday. I don't suppose you know anything about them." She had deduced that only Chatty could be responsible. No one else had access to the seals.

Chatty took the invitations, glanced at the first of them, and groaned. "Mr. Perfect. God, spare us. Doesn't the man know 'secret' means you don't sign your name?"

"Evidently not."

"Bah, he knows. The arrogant twit." Muttering, she shuffled the cards to look at the second one. A twinkle lit in her eye. "Well, now, isn't this interesting?"

Amanda suffered a little quiver of excitement. "Did you seal it?"

"No, I didn't." Chatty smiled. "Who do you think sent it?"

Though they were alone in the shop, Amanda leaned closer and dropped her voice to a whisper. "It's Jonathan's writing, Chatty."

She gave Amanda a vacant look.

"See the 'M'?" she said. "It's very distinctive."

"Uh-oh." Chatty glared out into the mall at *Cupid's Arrow*.

Amanda didn't understand that reaction at all, but unfortunately Chatty now had that not-quite-together look. Even if asked, she wouldn't, or couldn't, explain. "Can you believe it? I'm finally going to meet Jonathan."

"I'd say it appears you are." Chatty smacked her lips and added another wedge of lemon to her tea. "I've never seen you this excited about a man, pet."

"You know how I am about Jonathan." She stared down into her cup to avoid Chatty's too-seeing eyes. "He intrigues me. I think about him a lot."

"You fantasize about him a lot."

Amanda chuckled. "That, too."

"Fantasizing isn't a bad thing, but reality has a hard time measuring up."

"I know." Amanda dusted a fern leaf with her fingertip. "But the truth is, between his notes and his work, I've come to know a lot about him. I care for him, Chatty. He's so sensitive. So attuned to my visions. It's like he reads my verses and taps into my soul, and then he does his illustrations." She let her gaze drift to his designs in the Tender Touch display, then, wistful, looked back at her friend. "I suppose that sounds foolish."

Chatty's gaze went tender. She stood up, then lifted her sack and cupped Amanda's upturned chin in her hand. "No, pet," she said softly. "Following your heart is never foolish."

With a little smile, she walked toward the front of the shop, snitched a pair of heart-shaped red sunglasses from the rack near the entrance, then went out to have her customary conversation with Cupid.

Wondering what she talked about when she did that, Amanda eased over to the entrance and eavesdropped shamelessly.

Letting out a sigh that would stop a clock, Chatty frowned at the sculpture. "I hope you know what the spit you're doing, mister, because it sure doesn't look like you know squat from here."

What in the world did she mean by that?

"Hi, Mandy."

Max. Amanda blinked, then looked over, ashamed at being caught red-handed eavesdropping. So much for third impressions. She was really on a streak here. Screaming like a banshee, freezing him out in the restaurant, and now eavesdropping. Would her humiliation never end? "Um, hello, Max."

He ruffled an uncomfortable hand through his hair. "I need to pay for the sunglasses." He hooked a thumb toward Chatty. "And to return these." He passed over her raincoat and umbrella. "You, um, forgot them last night."

"Thank you." She nodded stiffly, stowed the articles behind the counter, then walked to the cash register. What was wrong with her? Her heart was pounding so hard, she expected any second it'd thud right out of her chest, and she couldn't for the life of her seem to hold on to a logical thought. Why did he still attract her? Had she lost her sense, getting lost in his eyes?

She told him the amount, and he wrote out the check. Again as she looked at it, something struck her as familiar. Considering herself overreacting and a little off-balance from all the upset, she tucked it into the cash drawer and warned herself to get a grip on her emotions. That would be a little easier, she reasoned, if Max just weren't so damn appealing. He looked great in a suit and in khakis, and just as good in jeans and a sweatshirt.

"I'm sorry about last night." He looked down at the counter. "I'm not very good at, um, verbalizing, and I think I gave you the wrong impression. Could we try again?" He lifted his gaze to hers. "Would you have dinner with me?"

Still smarting, and too attracted to him to risk it, she stiffened. Her heart screamed yes. But if never again, this time she had to listen to her head. "I don't think that's a good idea."

"Why not?"

"We look at things differently." She hiked a shoulder. "I'm not judging you, it's just that I know me, and I know it wouldn't work out."

"Amanda, I'm not an uncaring bastard. I love my aunt."

Wanting to believe him, she let him see her doubt.

He covered her hand with his, atop the counter. "I do everything for Chatty that she'll let me do. But she's very independent, and she's got a lot of pride. I can't just trample over it and ignore what she wants." He rubbed Amanda's knuckles with his thumb, and a frown knitted his brow. "Like I said, I have trouble verbalizing. I know you thought I didn't want to help my aunt, but I promise, that isn't true. If you don't believe me, ask her yourself."

Amanda's mouth went dry, and she looked up at him, became captured again by those entrancing silver flecks. "I guess I owe you an apology, then, for jumping to conclusions."

"Keep it." A slow smile spread over his face. "And have dinner with me instead."

"No, I owe you the apology." She wrote her address on the back of a business card and passed it to him. "You have dinner with me."

"Beauty, brains, and she cooks, too?"

Amanda laughed, deep and throaty. Outrageous, especially in light of her impressions, but oh so nice. "On occasion. But don't let it get around. You'll blow my image."

"Your secret's safe with me." He dipped across the counter

and pressed a kiss to her temple. "That's a promise."

Amanda gazed up at him. *My secrets, yes. But what about my heart? Is it safe with you?*

That question she couldn't answer.

CHAPTER FIVE

Max was shocked.

He tried valiantly to hide it, and it wasn't a haughty shock like Bradley's—more of an "I didn't expect this" expression he quickly masked. But Amanda would have had to be comatose or dead to miss it. Her tiny apartment was located in a nice neighborhood, but it was modest and evidently far from the elite address he had expected.

And she felt like a fool. Here she'd been agonizing over whether or not to tell him who her parents were, and one look at him made it glaringly apparent she didn't have to tell him a thing. He already knew. Of course, Chatty would have told him. And why that hadn't occurred to her before now had her calling herself forty kinds of fool.

It was him. When Amanda looked at him, she couldn't think straight. Forgivable, she supposed. Dressed in black slacks that hugged his lean hips and a black shirt that left his throat open and bare, he looked devastatingly handsome, and suffering from chaotic senses, who could think at all? Should she say anything about the apartment or just let the matter slide?

He walked into the living room and held out a bouquet of yellow roses laced with ferns and baby's breath. "They got a little wet."

The paper around them dripped. She smiled and took the flowers. "Very pretty." Their fingers brushed, and her breath quickened. She looked up at him, into those fascinating eyes. "Thanks, Max."

She put the flowers into a vase, filled it with water, then returned to Max.

His gaze drifted from her eyes to her mouth, then lingered. "I like your home. There's a lot of you in the feel of it." He grunted. "I mean, it's comfortable."

He wanted to kiss her; she sensed it down to her toes, and heaven help her, if he didn't do it soon, she was going to kiss him. He had trouble verbalizing. She had trouble opening herself up to preconceived notions about being the offspring of wealthy parents. If they both showed themselves willing to communicate, maybe they wouldn't have any trouble at all together. "I'm on my own," she said, deciding to be straight and up front. "It's an unpopular decision with my parents."

He let his thumb slide along her jaw. "I'd think they'd be proud of you for taking the harder road in being independent."

Amanda affected her mother's haughtiest tone. "Damn independence, darling. Appearances must be maintained."

"Ah." He brushed a fingertip over her lower lip, let the pad of his thumb sweep her mouth, corner to corner. "I see."

God, she couldn't think, but she certainly could feel. How could such a simple touch awaken every nerve in her body? "I'm comfortable with it." Did that make sense to him? That she'd choose to live modestly? Most didn't understand.

"You don't have to explain the trials of family to me." He cupped her chin in his hand. "I'm under explicit orders not to so much as mention, er, a certain eccentric aunt's name tonight."

Evidently Chatty had laid down the law. "Why not?"

His eyes twinkled, but he affected an adorable, sheepish look that made smiling nearly irresistible. "She's certain I'll say something stupid and upset you again."

Amanda laughed.

So did he.

It felt good to laugh with a man. Especially with Max. Oh, but the way he made her feel. Desirable, accepted, content. *Content.*

Her throat went thick. Taking a bold leap of faith, one totally out of character for her, she lifted a hand to his chest. His heart beat hard against her fingertips. "Let's make a deal."

"What kind of deal?"

"One where we can say or do anything with each other, and if it should hit the other of us wrong, then we'll stay calm and talk it out."

He palmed her hand on his chest. "I like the sound of that."

"Then we'll consider it done."

He gave her a slow negative nod that was at odds with the warm acceptance in his eyes.

"No?" she said, confused.

"We have to seal the contract."

Max dipped his chin, touched his lips to hers for the merest twinkling, then pulled her closer and claimed her mouth completely.

Amanda settled against him, enticed and eager to be thoroughly kissed; and Max didn't disappoint her with a tender touching of mouths or a tentative exploration of the new and untested. His kiss was firm, possessive, hungry. It burned with longing and desire and ignited a passion that flared, flamed, and threatened to consume, unleashing a surge of emotions that had her light-headed and swaying on her feet. A thought ran through her mind that thrilled and chilled her. *I've kissed him before. At some time, I've kissed him before.* But that was impossible, wasn't it? They'd just met.

You know him, Amanda. Heart to heart. Soul to soul. Don't deny this gift.

Acknowledging her conscience, she admitted the truth. She *did* know him. On some level, she knew all of him. Acceptance had a burst of heat swirling low in her abdomen, and she nestled closer, drank greedily from his lips, hoping this bond she sensed between them lasted forever.

Long before she was ready to let him go, Max parted their mouths and let his lips trail to her cheek. "Mandy?" he whispered, his voice a husky rasp.

His breathing was as erratic as her own, warm against her

skin, and his fingertips spanning her ribs trembled. Drifting in the sensual, feeling kind of dreamy, she felt her throat vibrate against his chest. "Mmm?"

He gave her a lazy smile. "I think that's the timer."

As he said the words, the stove timer's incessant buzz caught her ear. How long it had been droning on, she had no idea. Just as she had no idea if Max had backed away because of it or because of the impact of their kiss. She wanted to know, but no longer wrapped in the warmth of his arms, she didn't feel brave enough to ask.

"Dinner's ready," she said. "I hope you like New Orleans–style red beans and rice and Mexican cornbread." Getting a whiff of the mouthwatering Creole spices, she moved to the stove and gave him an impish grin. "I fixed you my favorites."

"You're in luck." He winked at her. "I'm starved."

Not at all sure he meant starved for food or that she wanted him to mean that, she directed him toward plates and napkins, then lectured herself on getting a grip on her emotions and her hormones. The problem was, she didn't want to get a grip on anything but Max. And unless her instincts were out of whack, he wanted her just as much as she wanted him, which only excited her more.

He set the table, and she arranged the food on the server. She removed her apron, and he poured the wine. All the while, they talked. And over and again she kept thinking that it would be so easy to get used to this kind of sharing with him. The little things. The inconsequential details that wove the tapestries of their lives, the unguarded remarks and the sultry looks, and the secret smiles. God, how she loved those secret smiles.

They sat down with their plates, and Amanda sighed. "I forgot to light the candles."

"Let me." He took the matches from her, pressed a tender kiss to the back of her wrist, then held her hand against his warm face. "Amanda, I take it back."

Breathless. Only that, and she felt breathless. "Take what back?"

He let his gaze roam over her, wandering at will. "My

thought that you couldn't be sexier without the apron.''

Stated so matter-of-factly, yet he had her heart threatening to careen right out of her chest. She cast him a warning look. "If you keep this up, Max, there's no way I'm going to be able to swallow a thing."

He looked pleased with himself about that admission. "I'll behave, then—can't have you hungry—but, um, you'll have to tell me exactly what I'm doing that's getting to you."

A lopsided grin. A mischievous glint in his eye. The man knew exactly what he was doing. And even though she knew it, too, it was still working. She gave him a frown to let him know how she felt about that bit of business. "Just eat, Max."

"I will." He cocked his head. "And I'll behave, if . . ." He let his voice trail away.

"If *what?*" She loved his teasing as much as everything else about him.

"If you'll show me some of your work after dinner."

Mildly surprised he'd be the least bit interested—God knew no one aside from Chatty ever had been—Amanda asked, "My work? Whatever for?"

He shrugged as if it were a minor matter. "I like your way with words."

Her surprise deepened, and a flood of sheer pleasure washed through her. She smoothed her napkin over her lap with an unsteady hand. "You've read my verses?"

He nodded. "There's a lot of beautiful emotions in you."

Never in her life would she forget those words. Never. Because they mattered so much, she wrinkled her nose and waved a warning fork at him. "There's some nasty ones in me, too."

"Good." He let out a totally faked sigh. "I thought for a while there you were perfect. It's intimidating."

Max Jones intimated? Impossible. She laughed in his face. "You're outrageous."

"At times." He dabbed his lips with his napkin, making it impossible to determine if this was one of those times. "So do we have a deal?"

She swallowed a bite of hot cornbread, then pursed her lips. "Pass the butter while I think about it."

She took it from him, then slathered some on the steaming cornbread. "After dinner I'll show you my work, if you'll dance with me."

His gaze warmed. "A deal inside a deal, eh?"

"I need the practice." She shrugged a delicate shoulder. "For the Secret Admirer party."

"Ah, that woman I'm sworn not to mention told me all about it. Sounds like a great promotional plan."

"I hope so." Amanda's stomach furled. If it failed, she was in deep kimchi.

"Okay. You show me your work, and I'll dance with you."

She smiled. "Fair enough."

"Now, tell me why the success of this promotional plan has you worried."

She should keep her business to herself, but the temptation to share proved too great. She explained, thinking it felt good—alien, but good—to have a man to talk to about her challenges.

By the time they finished dinner and, at Max's insistence, cleaned the kitchen, she felt better about her work, her challenges, and life in general. Amazing how much clearer things became just by talking about them out loud. Max didn't act as if she expected him to solve her problems; he just let her vent, talk, and discuss them. She liked that about him, too.

While she was up to her elbows in soapy water, and he was drying her bean pot and explaining the intricacies of organization in freelance business operations, Amanda underwent a major awakening. A realization she both feared and longed for seeped into her mind. She could fall in love with this man. So easily. Totally and irrevocably, and so darned easily. . . .

"What is it?" The pot clinked against its lid, and he straightened up from stretching to reach deep into the cabinet.

Slumped against the counter, feeling water soak the front of her apron, she looked down at him, squatting before the open cabinet door. "Excuse me?"

"Something's on your mind. What is it?"

Nothing she felt ready to share. Not yet. "I was just thinking that you're a really nice man, Max."

"Uh-oh." He stood up and his knees cracked.

"That was a compliment."

"I don't think so. Nice guys always finish last." He set down the dishcloth, reached into the sink, and pulled out the drain plug.

"Not from where I stand." Beneath the soapy water, her fingers sought his and she stroked the backs of his knuckles.

He turned his hand over, laced their fingers, and then squeezed gently, dropping his voice to a raspy whisper. "You have bubbles on your nose."

The warm water surrounding them felt good, sensual, intimate, and her breathing shifted to shallow puffs. "I sneezed." She reached up to wipe away the bubbles.

He caught her free hand midair and laced it with his. "I'll get them." He leaned close, then rubbed their noses.

Amanda closed her eyes, reveled in the feeling of their holding hands, in and out of the warm water; of their noses lightly brushing; his breath warming her face; of the sweet pressure of their bodies touching. He didn't speak, but he didn't have to use words; his fingertips told her all the things her woman's heart wanted to hear: *You're beautiful, Amanda. I love touching you. I love feeling you touch me. I want you . . .*

The water drained away. Locking his gaze with hers, he turned on the tap, rinsed the bubbles from her hand, and then lifted it to his lips and swept at the droplets of water with his tongue.

Her knees went weak, and she gasped softly. Water ran in a rivulet down his chin. Too tempted to resist, she touched her tongue to it, and when he let out a groan from deep in his throat, she shifted and captured his lips, opening her mouth, inviting him to explore. And he did. Sweetly, tentatively, and then aggressively, lifting her to him, tightening the circle of his arms. Her wet hand soaked his back, and the water ran on in the sink, heard but ignored. She curled her arms around his neck, tousled the hair at his nape, splaying her fingers against his skull and taking the kiss even deeper.

He parted their mouths. His eyes glazed with desire; he sighed his contentment and reached for the faucet.

Instead he hit the sprayer—and doused them both.

Getting hit in the face with a stream of water, she sputtered, "Hey!"

"Sorry." Laughing, he shut down the tap. "It got me, too."

She blew her dripping bangs out of her eyes, slinging speckles of water onto his face. The absurdity of the situation struck her as funny. There they stood at her kitchen sink, water dripping down their faces, their clothes soaked, looking wilted and goofy, and they were laughing. Deep from the stomach, laughing. Deep from the heart.

He grabbed the dishtowel and dried her face, his touch so gentle that she had a hard time reconciling it with the man who'd held her so greedily just moments before. She grabbed the free end of the cloth and patted his cheeks, his eyelids, his mouth, and his chin, then lowered the cloth to his neck and felt him touch hers, mirroring her move. The heat of his fingers seeped through the cloth, and she spread her fingers over his chest.

He stilled, his heart rocketing against her breasts. "Mandy?"

"Mmm?" She couldn't talk. She just couldn't. She'd never been this intimate with a man. She'd had a select few lovers, but never before had she been intimate. Not like this.

Those silver flecks in his eyes turned molten. "You're a beautiful woman, inside and out. Would it upset you if I told you that I want to kiss you again, and to keep on holding you?"

She nearly melted. "No, it wouldn't."

He feathered a thumb over the blade of her cheekbone. "I can't believe I'm admitting this to myself, much less to you. I want to know more about you, everything about you." He dropped his voice, low and throaty. "I know this probably seems soon to you, Mandy, but I want to be with you. Today, tomorrow, at the Valentine's party—as much as we can manage."

He couldn't believe he was saying these things, and she

couldn't believe she was hearing them being spoken, not to her. Max, whose kisses excited her, scorched and soothed and touched her heart, offered her everything she had ached for and wanted for so long.

The Valentine's party? The unwelcome thought intruded. *Jonathan.*

Misery infringed on her elation and streamed through her in a rush. How was she going to explain Jonathan to Max? Of course she had to explain him. "I want to be with you, too," she said softly, her wariness rippling her voice.

"But you can't."

So perceptive. So attuned. "I can, just not at the Valentine's party."

"Why not?" No anger or resentment tinged Max's tone or his expression, only curiosity.

She admired his control and braced for it to snap. "Jonathan sent me a Secret Admirer invitation, Max."

Surprise burned in his eyes. He blinked, then blinked again. "But they're anonymous. How do you know—"

"I might not know the man's face, but I do know his handwriting. After two years of dealing with him by mail, I recognized it in under two seconds."

Max paled and his jaw gaped open. Why did he seem so shocked? "Max?"

"So you're going to meet him at the party, then?"

He didn't sound angry or sad; he sounded stunned. "Yes, I am," she said. "I know you probably won't understand this, but—"

"No, I do," he interrupted, clearly irritated with himself. "You have to know."

He understood perfectly. Tears welled in her eyes, and she blinked hard to keep them from falling. "If I don't find out, I'll always wonder."

"So will I." A stream of heat from the air vent whipped at Max's hair.

He would wonder. He too recognized their bond, and he recognized that if she didn't meet Jonathan, he could always be there, like a ghost between them. She smoothed down a strand of Max's hair, feeling physical cravings for him that dulled her logical thoughts. If he understood and he too would wonder, then why did he look as if she'd just dropped a bomb on his head?

She let her hands glide down his lean sides and paused at his waist. "I really do want to be with you, Max."

He looked doubtful, crinkling the tender skin at the outer corners of his eyes. "Does that mean you're having the same kinds of feelings I am about us?"

Another leap of faith. Her heart stuck somewhere in her throat, she swallowed hard. "If they're good feelings—"

"They are," he assured her. "Very good feelings. Strong ones."

Her heart warmed. "Yes, then. I am."

He let their foreheads touch, then whispered, "I'm glad."

"I think I am, too, but I'm not sure." She ran a fingertip down his shirt placket, then over his broad chest, loving the feel of his muscles quivering under her hand, and she said aloud what she'd felt since the first time she'd seen him. "I'm afraid you could steal my heart, Max." Her mouth incredibly dry, she moistened her lips with her tongue. "I wouldn't mind that, but I'm not eager to be hurt."

"Neither am I," he confessed. "Would it help if I told you I'm having those same fears?"

Her heart nearly burst in her chest. Could he be? Did she dare to believe it? "If it's true, it would help. Yes."

"It's true, and I am." His expression shifted from tender to hard, almost as if he'd been confronted by a demon he couldn't quite believe had exposed itself. "It's happening too fast."

"Yes, it is."

"It's your fault," he said without heat, and pulled her closer, until they met chest to breasts. "A gracious, beautiful woman wearing a slinky black dress and a sexy apron does things to a man."

The apron had nothing to do with it. It was what they did to each other inside. She wrinkled her nose at him. "I'll have to remember that."

"I like it. He let his hand skim over her side, down to the apron, then inched beneath it and glided over her abdomen. "So do you want to slow things down?"

"Frankly, no, I don't," she said, surprising even herself with her lack of discretion. She'd never felt swept away before. It was kind of magical.

A lazy smile curved his lips and touched his eyes. "Kiss me again, then."

Oh, it'd be so easy. But several kisses hadn't been enough, and with another, neither would just kissing him. Max called to her at core level, and she did to him; she knew it as well as she knew she stood in his arms. As well as she knew if she dared to kiss him again, she wouldn't be satisfied until they'd made love.

She'd just told him she had to meet Jonathan to know for a fact the deepest desires in her heart. Yet she wanted Max in every way a woman could want a man. What was wrong with her? How could she feel this way about Max with Jonathan between them? "It's too soon, Max. We'd kiss again, and make love, and then we'd regret it. I don't want us to take something I know will be beautiful and taint it with regret."

Disappointment shadowed his eyes. Acceptance followed on its heels. "Neither do I." He loosened his hold. "Let's look at your work."

She loved and hated his disappointment and quick acceptance. It didn't make sense to feel both, but she did, and she wasn't going to lie to herself about it.

Ten minutes later they were in the second bedroom she'd converted into a home office, surrounded by designs spread out on her desk, on the top of the file cabinet, and on her pride-and-joy drafting table.

He pointed to a card on it. "This is my favorite."

"Really?" She looked from her newest "I'm sorry" card to him. Secretly she too felt it was one of her best.

"It's great for people who have trouble with words." He glanced from the card to her. "Saying 'I'm sorry' is never easy, but when you're lousy with words, it's sheer hell."

"And sometimes, no matter how many words you have, they aren't enough."

"You're very talented, Mandy. Not everyone can put on paper what's in a person's heart."

Warmth flooded her inside, spread through her chest and limbs, and her eyes grew suspiciously moist. "Thank you."

He frowned. "Why do I have the feeling no one's told you how good you are before?"

Should she answer him? Debating, she lifted a crystal paperweight from her desk, then set it back down. "Maybe because they haven't." She wanted to look at him, to see his reaction, but she couldn't make herself do it. More censure she didn't need. "Chatty's been supportive," she said, more to break the silence than because she wanted to let him see this deeply inside her. "But . . . well, that's just not the kind of thing she'd say."

Worrying her lower lip with her teeth, Amanda glanced at the card. From now on, it would hold a special place in her heart.

He sat in her desk chair, swiveled toward her, then urged her to turn to him with a hand at her waist. "I didn't mean to embarrass you."

"You didn't." She looked down at him. "Well, you did, but it was worth it."

He tugged her closer, between his knees, then applied pressure at her waist, inviting her to sit on his lap.

She let her knees fold and settled against his hard thighs. Wrapping her arms around his shoulders, she whispered against his neck, inhaling his musky cologne. "I'm sorry. I didn't mean to get so emotional. It's just that . . ." She couldn't go on. A knot of tears had lodged in her throat.

"Approval is an elusive thing," he said softly, breathing against her hair. "I understand."

He did. Perfectly. "It's powerful, too."

"Yes," he agreed, smoothing a hand against her back. "Yes, it is."

They sat there for a long moment, then he asked, "Did Jonathan Maxwell illustrate all of these?"

The strength returned to her voice, and she pulled herself to her feet. "Yes. I admire his work immensely."

"I can see that."

"He's very gifted, Max." She fingered the smooth ledge of her drafting table. "And, in a way, he's frightening."

"Frightening?" Max frowned and curled his fingers around the chair arms, whitening his knuckles.

"Not negatively," she explained quickly. "He's just . . . disconcerting."

"How?"

She turned to the cards, letting her fingertips glide over one of Jonathan's illustrations, and felt its power, as she always did on touching them. "Sometimes I look at his work and I feel as if he's looked straight into my soul."

Max paused a beat. "Mandy, are you in love with him?"

Her face went hot, and she looked back at Max. "I love the way his work makes me feel." She shrugged. "I know it sounds bizarre, but he really must see inside my soul. His illustrations are just so . . . perfect. Somehow, he attunes to my visions. That's what's frightening. He couldn't attune to my visions unless he could see inside me."

"Maybe. But it could be that, with what you write, you see inside him." Max's voice softened even more. "You didn't answer me. Are you in love with him, Amanda?"

"Amanda," not "Mandy." She studied Max's face and saw all the signs of jealousy. She loved and hated them. "I've never even met him."

Max stared at her, as if by holding his silence he would force her to accept that she still hadn't given him a straight answer. He wanted one, deserved one, but that she couldn't give him. It wasn't that she didn't want to, she couldn't. Because the truth was, she herself didn't know.

Instead she smiled. "Ready to dance?"

Max hesitated a long moment, clearly fighting the dilemma of whether or not he wanted to push the issue. She waited, her nerves stretching taut, and finally he stood up.

"The stereo's in my bedroom." Her stomach fluttered.

"We'll have to dance in there, or else disturb the neighbors. Is that, um, comfortable for you?"

He answered with a nod.

She walked out into the hall, then took a right into her room and turned on the overhead light. Her face felt as hot as if she'd been blasted by a heat wave.

Max paused at the doorway and looked around. She did, too, seeing her room through his eyes. A cherrywood four-poster bed, draped with white diaphanous hangings; an antique dresser with a huge oval mirror; a reading nook, with yet more novels spread on the little marble-topped table beside it; and a throw with pictures of quill pens scrunched up on a wing-back chair. Surrounded by the room's soft blues and warm creams, she had always felt comfortable here. But her domain would feel too prissy and frilly for a man as virile looking and masculine as Max. He'd like leather, she thought. Dark and bold and lots of it. And yawning chairs to accommodate his size that she'd feel lost in. He was a big man. Lean and fit, but both tall and broad. He'd definitely appreciate less fuss and more mass.

She selected a Genesis CD and inserted it in the player. A soft ballad filled the quiet, and she adjusted the volume. The beat of the music was slow and sensuous. Oh, this wasn't a good idea. Not at all. Not in here.

He opened his arms.

She stepped into them, felt his arms close around her, curved hers against him and her face against his chest. "Your shirt's wet."

He released her, stripped off the shirt, and then hung it on the doorknob.

God help her, he was gorgeous. Rippling muscle, smooth skin covered with soft black down. When he again opened his arms, her senses went into full riot. She swallowed hard, then fitted herself against him, her face hot against his bare chest. He began to move, swaying to the music, and she drifted into that world of the senses where reason and logic cease to exist, knowing that drifting was dangerous—*it was soooo soon*—and yet the truth seemed amazingly simple and clear.

What had begun as attraction was strengthening, deepening, regardless of time, as if time had no more place here than reason or logic, and for the life of her, she couldn't think of a single reason why it should matter. Did anything but feelings matter? Was anything equally important? More honest? She'd tried being logical and wise, and it had gotten her Bradley. Max felt so much better. He felt . . . right.

He pulled her closer, rubbed delicious circles on her spine that had her snuggling, inhaling his musky scent, and wanting to purr. "Max," she whispered against his shoulder, "I'm tired of being wise. I want to just be."

He hooked her chin with the back of their clasped hands. She tilted back her head and glanced up at him, looking down at her. Hunger and heat raged in his eyes, so stark that it startled and stunned and elated her.

"Finally." A gravelly groan vibrating deep in his throat, he bore his lips down on hers.

No simple kiss, this. Pure passion and heat. Commanding and luring. Chest to breasts, thighs to thighs, they clung, tongues swirling, hands eagerly claiming yearning flesh. He wrenched his mouth from hers to whisper, "I knew, Mandy. I knew it'd be like this," and then he kissed her again, even more ardently. And he went on kissing her, until she couldn't think at all, could only feel the intense longing in him and in herself. She'd kissed and been kissed. But never like this. Never by all of a man . . . except in her fantasies of Jonathan.

And in her mind, fantasy and reality melded; the men became one, and she treaded in life to the place where, before this moment, she'd visited only in dreams.

He lifted his mouth from hers and just held her close. Woozy and weak, she kept her eyes closed, hanging on to the potent, magical feelings, lingering as long as she possibly could in the netherworld where she'd first experienced this kiss. "Oh, Jonathan," she breathed against the curve at his shoulder. "I knew, too."

He stiffened, stilled, and what she'd said hit her. Too mortified to speak, she sucked in a breath so deep that her stomach went concave, and she squeezed her eyes shut to block out the pain shining in his eyes.

Grimacing, he clenched his jaw, anger seeping from his every pore, and grasped her face in his hands. "Look at me."

She didn't want to. *Oh, God, but she didn't want to!* Regret and remorse blanketed her. Guilt and shame arrowed through her, sharp and swift and merciless. How she must have hurt him!

"Look at me, Amanda." His grip on her face tightened, just short of painful, and his voice shook with bitter rage.

More embarrassed than ever in her life, she opened her eyes, praying he'd see past his anger and her disgrace and understand all she was feeling.

"Max, Amanda," he informed her, his voice raw, his expression ravaged. "My name is Max, and I'm the man holding you."

Her chin trembled, and her blood felt as if it had drained to her feet. "Oh, God, Max. I know that. I—I don't know why I said it. I don't know why . . ." Anguish flooded her voice. "I'm so sorry. I—"

"Just stop, okay? Just . . . stop." He backed away from her, snatched his shirt from the doorknob, and then slung it on, shoving his arms into the sleeves. His face had paled to the pasty white of her bed hangings. "I guess I asked for it. When you showed me his illustrations . . . your voice . . . I suspected you were in love with him." Max worked at the buttons of his shirt, his hands jerking and rough.

"You didn't ask for this. I—I, oh, hell, Max, I don't know what to say. I wish I did, but I . . . don't."

His expression only got harder. "I'm hurt. I'd be lying if I didn't admit it. But I'm not stupid, Amanda, and I won't play substitute for someone else. I made a mistake. I thought . . ." He paused, dragged a hand through his hair—hair she'd ruffled only minutes ago, lost in passion. "Well, it doesn't matter what I thought."

Abject misery twisted his face. "Yes, damn it, it does matter. It matters a lot because you mattered a lot. I thought you'd be different. How can you react to me the way you do and love him? How can you do that, Amanda?''

''Max, please.'' She stepped toward him. ''You don't understand.''

''You're right. I don't.'' He finished with his buttons and shook his head. ''I thought having come from where you have, and living with what you've lived with, you might just come to care about me for myself.'' His voice went stone cold. ''Obviously, I was wrong.''

He walked out of her bedroom.

Understanding his anger but not his comment, she followed him into the hall. ''Max, please listen to me.'' How could she explain? How could she tell him now that she *had* come to care for him for himself? That only with him had she slipped into a two-year-long fantasy she'd never once before glimpsed while awake, or so vividly in sleep? He'd never understand or believe her. How could he? How could she expect him to, when she didn't believe it herself?

What was happening between them was too fragile and new. It was just too soon. It didn't make sense, it was just . . . real. Real, and there.

He kept walking.

She screamed silently, *You're part of me now, damn it, and I don't know how to make you stay!*

Her conscience prodded her. So what if this didn't make sense? When did sense ever rule in matters of the heart? Feelings and emotions were notoriously crazy, making the absurd reasonable *and* inconsequential. Because when the heart decides, it decides. The head just doesn't stand a chance, not when it goes toe to toe with the heart.

Unfortunately for her, her heart had decided too late. She'd let him inside her, something she'd avoiding risking until now. Yet taking those risks hadn't changed a thing.

Have you ever been loved? Not for your money or your work, but for yourself?

The weight of the question he'd asked her hit her full force. He hadn't been loved for himself, either. And, God forgive her, she'd called him by another man's name.

She'd hurt Max deeply. Too deeply. They'd never get past the pain. Her heart turned wooden in her chest, and her face stung like fire. Never in her life had she felt so guilty and full of remorse, so ashamed. And she'd done it to herself.

His eyes anguish-ridden, he strode to the front door. "Good-bye, Amanda."

"Oh, Max. Please, forgive me. I didn't mean—"

His glare had her stopping midsentence, then trying again, tears welling in her eyes. "Can we talk about this? Please, Max?"

The door open, he gripped its edge and stared at her. "Discussing it won't change anything."

Word upon word tumbled through her mind and ripped through her heart. So many words, yet none of them would make him understand or forgive her. There was nothing she could do. Nothing, except to accept the inevitable. "No, I guess not." Flustered, she forced herself to meet his gaze, knowing her chagrin and regret at having hurt him shone in her eyes. How could she have let this happen? "I am so . . . sorry, Max."

He walked out without acknowledging her.

She watched him go, her eyes burning, the back of her nose stinging, her heart aching so much, she thought she'd die from it.

The door slammed shut.

"Good-bye, Max," she whispered, the first tear trickling down her cheek.

CHAPTER SIX

*A*manda hadn't slept.

She untangled herself from the covers, showered, dressed in a deep green skirt and soft sweater, drank two cups of coffee, and then went to work, convinced that concealers did not hide dark circles under the eyes and teabags pressed to the eyelids did not reduce swelling caused by crying.

In her calmer moments, she told herself she was acting crazy and not at all like herself. She didn't know Max well enough to feel this strongly about him. But even as she uttered those words, she knew they were lies. On some level she'd always known him. Not in a physical sense, but in her heart and soul. Everything that really mattered in a relationship—caring, tenderness, concern—they were all there. The details would have come with time.

Would have come. But she had messed things up. Now they'd never have the chance.

She opened the shop feeling so low, she'd have to look up to see down. By lunchtime things weren't any better, and she was constantly telling herself to just concentrate on getting through the day.

In the kitchenette, she put water on for tea, then squeezed her eyes shut, waiting for it to heat. "Please," she whispered. "Just let the rest of the day be calm and peaceful. I've had all the upheaval I can stand. . . ."

"Amanda?"

She went as stiff as a board, and her eyes flew open. Her mother? *Oh, no. Not now. Please, not now!*

"Amanda? Darling, are you here?"

She straightened her shoulders and pulled in a calming breath. "You can deal with this," she told herself. "Seriously, you can. If you couldn't, then it wouldn't be happening."

Whatever doesn't kill you makes you stronger, right?

Wrong, she told her conscience. *Whatever doesn't kill you drives you insane.* Pitiful, but right now, insane didn't sound half-bad.

She walked out into the shop. Bradley was with her mother. Stifling a grimace, Amanda stared at them. "Well, I didn't expect to see you two here today."

Her mother, perfectly coiffed and wearing a sapphire raw silk suit, slid Amanda a silent reprimand. "Darling, we're concerned." She sat on the edge of Chatty's chair.

That grated at Amanda, but she saw humor in it, too. Maybe she had slipped over the edge into insanity. "Concerned about what, Mother?"

Bradley interceded. "We're trying to save you from yourself, darling."

She rolled her gaze heavenward, praying for patience. This, she never needed, much less today. "Thank you for your concern, but I don't need saving." Hell, maybe she did. Falling in love with one man and hurting him; half in love with another man, one she'd never met. Maybe she needed saving in the worst kind of way.

"Amanda." Her mother leaned forward, perching on the edge of the seat. "You look dreadful, dear. Are you ill?"

Did being brokenhearted because you'd hurt a man who'd been courageous and comfortable enough with himself to admit that he feared you'd hurt him count? Not in Veronica Jensen's book. Not unless that man's name was Bradley Wade. "I'm fine, Mother."

"Good," Bradley said, dismissing the issue and proving himself as dense as a doornail. "Then perhaps you're ready to see reason."

From the looks of Mr. Perfect, he had run out of patience.

Though mildly tempted to give him that little shove so he would lose his composure and she would finally get a glimpse of the real man behind the snobby facade, she just couldn't muster the energy or harness enough interest to bother. "What reason, Bradley?"

"Our engagement, darling."

"Our *what*?" Good grief. Not this, too, and not now. She folded her arms over her chest and dug in her heels. She might fall, damn it, but she wasn't going to fold. "There is *no* engagement between us."

"Amanda," her mother said, sounding a tad sharp. "Be reasonable, darling. Bradley has been extremely patient while you've indulged in your little whims. But it's time now to stop this nonsense."

Nonsense?

You're very talented. Why do I have the feeling no one's ever told you that before?

Maybe because they haven't.

"Indulged?" Her incredulity slipped into her voice. So did her anger. "Patient?" Her voice raised yet another notch. "My little whims?"

"Yes, Amanda, your whims." Bradley clenched his jaw. "Why can't you think of anyone other than yourself? I just don't understand you." He looked at her as if he had no idea who she was inside.

She supposed he truly didn't have a clue.

His face reddened and a vein in his neck bulged, but he didn't shout. Not Mr. Perfect. He'd never lose his composure as Max had. "Do you even understand yourself?"

She didn't answer. She couldn't answer. Even privately she shunned looking inward deeply enough to find out.

"I didn't think so," Bradley said on a frustrated sigh. "For once, why don't you consider what you're doing to your mother? You're breaking her heart."

What about my heart? Doesn't it matter? Doesn't what I want and what I need matter? Hanging on to her sanity by a thread, Amanda looked up and saw the anger in his eyes. It was the last straw. Shaking inside, she opened her mouth to tell them both she'd had it—and heard the motion detector's chimes.

Swinging her gaze to the entrance, she saw Chatty come into the shop.

At least, Amanda thought the woman was Chatty. She looked like her, only her clothes were all wrong and her grocery sack was missing. This pint-size woman wore a deep blue-red suit—Amanda didn't recognize the designer, but it definitely had not come off any rack—and pumps with a black cape that swung softly at her hips with her every step. She looked radiant. Elegant. And, though older, she could hold her own against Veronica Jensen on the taste-and-sophistication, wealth-and-class fronts.

Amanda's heart swelled. "Chatty?" She walked over and clasped her friend's hands. "Oh, Chatty. You look . . . beautiful."

A faint blush tinted her cheeks. "Don't get carried away, pet. I'm doing this clotheshorse stint today for you. Tomorrow, I'm back to the old me again."

For her? What did that mean? Oh, who cared? "I love you both ways," Amanda said, giving Chatty's fingertips a pleased squeeze.

"Of course, pet." Chatty smiled.

"Darling," Veronica called out, "I hate to intrude, but we need to resolve this matter."

Amanda whispered to Chatty, "It's round four, and I'm fading fast."

"Dignity, pet. You hang on to that, and you'll do just fine."

"Confidentially, at the moment I'd settle for stuffing socks in their mouths."

Chatty cleared her throat to muffle a chuckle and smoothed her cape. "The cavalry has arrived. Let's battle."

"Amanda," Veronica called again. "Please, darling. Bradley and I have an appointment with the caterer—to discuss the menu for the engagement party."

Amanda swung around, horror in her eyes. "Oh, no. No. Absolutely not." She stared at her mother, who seemed stunned. Amanda had her same black hair and light eyes, but

Veronica's features were more finely chiseled. In a way she looked vulnerable, almost naive, though Amanda knew better than to accept that as more than a well-practiced facade Veronica employed to get what she wanted. "I did not agree to any engagement, nor do I intend to agree to any engagement. And I certainly won't attend a party to announce an engagement that doesn't exist."

"Oh, Amanda, you must. Bradley and I have arranged everything, darling—because you're so busy here."

With a clean conscience and a good heart, she could smack them both. Yet this woman was her mother, and even beneath all the anger, Amanda didn't want to hurt her. "I'm sorry you've wasted your time." She turned to Bradley. "My answer is no."

"Answer . . ." he started to protest.

"I hate to interrupt," Chatty interceded, pointedly checking her gold watch. "But if you don't leave now, Amanda, you'll be late for your luncheon. The reservations are for noon."

Luncheon? Reservations? Chatty's intent slammed into Amanda. She could have hugged her friend. Instead she blessed her silently. "Thanks for reminding me." She turned to her mother and Bradley. "I'm sorry. It's a business luncheon, and I can't be late."

"Amanda . . ."

She glared at her mother. "We'll talk later, but I will not do this, Mother," she said, then turned and walked toward the front of the shop.

When she and Chatty stepped out of hearing range, she whispered, "I owe you one."

"You owe me two," she corrected Amanda, giving her arm a gentle squeeze.

"Two," she agreed, assuming the first was for Chatty having to dress up. "But I can't leave for lunch."

"Why not?"

"The shop."

"I'm going to watch over things here."

Surprise streaked up Amanda's back. Her adored, light-fingered friend? What kind of businesswoman left her favorite thief to mind the store?

I'm doing this clotheshorse stint for you.

She'd planned this. Lunch—actually, time alone. For Amanda. Her heart full, she knew exactly what kind of businesswoman left Chatty in charge of her store. Amanda's kind. She pushed aside her misgivings and smiled at Chatty. "Why?"

"To give you time to think." Chatty stepped behind the register and perched a pair of Dior frame glasses on the tip of her nose. "May I speak frankly, pet?"

Hadn't she always? "Of course. But not too loudly. I'd prefer Mother and Bradley didn't hear."

Chatty nodded and dropped her voice to just above a whisper, and her gaze turned tenderly solemn. "Everyone craves approval, dear heart. Grown men and women are no more immune than children, especially if approval has been nonexistent or rarely glimpsed."

Amanda's face heated. "I've accepted that Mother will never approve of me, Chatty."

"Have you?" She looked deeply into Amanda's eyes. "I've told you before that I admire you for not wanting to hurt her, and I do. But there's something you need to think about. In any relationship, no matter how intense the craving for approval, or how strong the desire not to hurt or disappoint, there comes a time when you're forced to choose. You must hurt someone else, or hurt yourself. For you, that time is now." Chatty gave Amanda a bittersweet, sympathetic smile. "Either way, the pain is challenging, pet. But there is solace in suffering its sting when you're following the decisions of your own heart."

"Is that what you want me to think about?"

"I want you to look deep inside, beneath all the feelings of what you think you should want and what others want for you, and decide what *you* want. You're going to live with those decisions a long time, so it's important you make the right ones, mmm?" Chatty gave her hand a motherly pat. "Now, you go on. And don't hurry back. I'll be here until closing."

Veronica and Bradley stood near the chairs, seething. Taking in a deep breath, Amanda walked out of the shop.

She left the mall and strolled to the park. The weather had cleared, and the sun felt warm on her face. She grabbed a hot dog from a stand near the street and squirted a healthy dose of mustard on the bun. Chatty had made a lot of sense, not only about her relationship with her mother, but about her feelings for Max.

By the time Amanda wandered through the path of winter-barren oaks and finished the hot dog, and then fed the saved bits of the bun to the mallards swimming in the little pond, the truth hit her right between the eyes. She hadn't once thought of Jonathan, only of Max. She wanted Max. He was in her heart, and she wanted him in her life—and at her party.

She rushed back to the shop, hugged a surprised Chatty, and rushed straight to the little Valentine mailbox and filled out an invitation.

"Mind if I ask who you're inviting?"

From the twinkle in Chatty's eyes, she knew exactly. And the truth that she'd probably known *before* she'd come into the shop today settled over Amanda like a warm cloak. "Max." A fissure of fear opened in her stomach like a bottomless chasm. "I just hope it's not too late."

Chatty stared out of the Card Shoppe's front window, across the brick flooring into the center of the mall. Amanda stood between the brass poles, near the burgundy velvet ropes that kept spectators a safe distance from *Cupid's Arrow*. She just stood there, gazing up wistfully at Cupid's face, looking so unhappy that Chatty could feel the force of it weighing her down.

"Good grief." The last thing Mandy needed was more pressure, what with the Meet Your Secret Admirer party tonight. Worry rippled through Chatty—and a fair share of irritation. What had that distrustful, misguided misfit of a beloved nephew of hers done this time to hurt the woman?

Grimacing, Chatty shifted her gaze to glare at Cupid. "Some aim you've got, you overgrown lump of worthless metal. I ought to melt you down and sell you for scrap. Three men in my pet's life, and she hasn't got a single Valentine."

*T*he Meet Your Secret Admirer party was in full swing, and according to everyone—including the WLOX news crew taping the event, the reporter from the *Sun Herald,* and Amanda's mother—it was a huge success. Everyone, that is, except Amanda.

She felt relieved by the positive feedback, but not euphoric, as she'd expected she would feel. Of course, there were extenuating circumstances coloring her perception, and she knew it.

Standing near the shop entrance, she looked out at the crowd of several hundred who had gathered for the celebration. She smiled at the right people, at the right times, and admitted that most of the couples did seem to be having a wonderful time. Some were dancing to the band's gentle, romantic ballads beneath tiny twinkling lights that had been strung on tall potted plants to define the dance floor for the occasion. Some were laughing and talking, and others were sitting at the tables, sipping champagne and gazing through soft candlelight into each other's eyes.

Romance and magic were definitely in the air.

Everyone looked beautiful, too. The men in the tuxes they hated and women loved; the women in their formal gowns and the sparkles that made them feel as beautiful as they looked. Chatty looked positively stunning in her sophisticated black Dior, and even Amanda had been told at least a dozen times that she looked lovely tonight. She had taken painstaking care to look her best, dressing in a deep purple gown that hugged her curves like a second and third skin. The gown wasn't tight or low cut so much as suggestive. Its beaded collar circled her throat, and its steep-cut bodice bared her shoulders. She'd opted for more dramatic makeup, too, to emphasize her eyes, gratis Veronica Jensen's Fashion Tips 101.

She needn't have bothered.

At least she appeared to be the only person around who felt miserable. While she was grateful for that, her heart sank, and the wave of depression she'd been struggling against for hours threatened to overwhelm her. She wanted to keep fighting it, but, damn it, she hurt: Max hadn't forgiven her. Chatty had said he had gotten the invitation, but he hadn't come. And, not that it much mattered, Jonathan had stood her up, too. Getting jilted, so to speak, twice on one Valentine's Day seemed like overkill. And it felt worse.

Amanda leaned a shoulder against the shop entrance's glass wall and looked up at *Cupid's Arrow*. Jonathan wasn't the man she'd fantasized. That man never would have humiliated her by just not showing up. That man was good and kind and understanding. He cared about her feelings, her thoughts and dreams and desires. He . . . was Max.

Caring and concerned, supportive and compassionate, Max personified everything Jonathan's work had made her feel, everything she had fantasized. And she'd hurt him. He could have been here with her—he'd *wanted* to be here with her— but she'd had to chase a damn fantasy, and now it was too late.

Max hadn't come. He hadn't forgiven her.

When it came to making mistakes, she was certainly no slouch. "Major league all the way," she mumbled to herself, wondering just how long she'd regret this one. Years? The rest of her life?

Forever. She would regret losing Max forever.

Plunging into despair, she walked into the shop, needing a few minutes alone. At the Tender Touch display, she let her hand skim down the silk hangings draping the sides of the card rack, then drifted her fingertips over the cards. Maybe Max had been right. Maybe her words had touched Jonathan's feelings, but that's all that had touched him. Not her, just her words.

Was that really possible? Could it be? And if it was, then why did it feel so . . . wrong? Her words were a part of her. The sentiments expressed, ones she held in her heart. How could he and his illustrations be separate?

Yet he hadn't come.

Nor had Max.

And that's where her true regret lay. She wanted Max more than anything. She always would.

"Pet?" Chatty said from behind her. "What's wrong? I thought you'd be on top of the world."

Amanda blinked hard to keep the tears blurring her vision from falling. "Oh, Chatty . . ." The words tumbled out of her mouth in a rush. "I've made the worst mistake of my life."

"But the party is—"

"A success." Amanda sucked in a breath to keep from expelling a sob. "I know." She wrung her hands, let Chatty see her misery. "But he didn't come. God help me, Chatty, I've fallen in love with the man, and I've lost him."

Chatty gave her a vacant look. "Did you tell him you loved him?"

"You don't just put that in a card." Amanda lifted an arm, then let it fall back to her side. "Well, you do," she amended, realizing people did exactly that all of the time. "But I wanted to tell him in person. I wanted to see his face when I told him."

Chatty gave Amanda a bewildered look. "Just so I'm perfectly clear, pet, are we talking about Jonathan here?"

"Of course not. It's Max I love."

"Ah, good." She smiled, overjoyed by that news.

Amanda cast her a solid frown, wishing this weren't one of Chatty's shade-less-than-aware times. "There's nothing to be happy about. He *didn't* come." She pulled the rose corsage off the bodice of her dress and slung it onto the counter by the register. "I blew it, Chatty. I told Max I'd gotten the invitation from Jonathan. I had to tell him, of course—''

"Of course."

"But he was so hurt."

"Yes, I expect he was," she agreed. "Probably far more than you realize."

"Oh, I realize it," Amanda assured her, then turned to lean back against the counter. "The worst part is, even hurt, Max really understood why I needed to meet Jonathan. Or why I thought I needed to meet him."

"You mean you don't?"

"No. When he stood me up tonight, I was relieved."

"Relieved?"

"Well, okay. My pride was bent a little, but it's true. I was relieved."

"Pet, you're not making a spit of sense. I thought you wanted to meet Jonathan."

"I did until I realized I love Max." A frown wrinkled Amanda's brow, and a sob thickened in her throat. "But I guess he just couldn't forgive me." She looked over at her friend, misery in her eyes. "I love the man, and I've lost him. What am I going to do, Chatty?"

"Oh, my. This is a dilemma." Chatty walked to the chairs and then paced in front of the little table, rubbing her temple, mulling over the matter.

"It's my own fault," Amanda went on. "Max couldn't risk letting me stomp on his heart again."

A pensive gleam in her eye, Chatty opened her mouth to say something, but before she could get it out, Amanda's mother swept in on a cloud of perfume. And, God help Amanda's pounding head, she was towing Bradley.

She withheld a grimace by the skin of her teeth. The last time she'd seen them, they'd been on the dance floor, conspiring. She had hoped they would stay there a good long while, but no such luck.

"Amanda." Bradley offered her a tentative smile. "I know we said some things in anger earlier."

"Yes, we did." Amanda hoped this conversation wouldn't lead to more being said in anger. It required an enormous amount of energy, and her emotional reserves were depleted.

"I'd like to forget them."

Thank heaven. "So would I." She was too down to fight anymore. With anyone. Over anything.

"Wonderful." Bradley's confidence returned with a vengeance. "Then I'll ask you one last time to become my wife." He held up a hand to keep her from answering. "You should know that I won't ask again. Ever."

That was the best news she'd heard all day. She looked at her mother's hopeful expression, regretted that she had to be the one to crush it, and then back at Bradley's haughty one. As ungracious as it was, she wasn't sorry she'd be crushing his.

Their hands were linked.

Linked.

Finally, she knew exactly what she wanted to say. "You know, I'm weary of this. If you two want a Jensen/Wade marriage so desperately—even with you both knowing I don't love you, Bradley—then all I can suggest is that you, Mother, divorce Father, and then marry Bradley yourself. Because I'm certainly not going to marry the man you want. I love you, Mother, but who I marry is my decision."

Amanda looked at Bradley. "I don't want to hurt you. Either of you." She added in her mother with a glance, then focused again on him. "But if the truth is known, I doubt I *could* hurt you. I'm not my mother, Bradley, and I'll never be like her. Her role in society is comfortable for her, but it would never be comfortable for me. I'll never be the perfect hostess, or the perfect wife. The man I marry is going to have to love me anyway, for what I am, not for what he'd like me to be. And certainly not for what my mother is."

Her mother's face bleached white. Rarely had Amanda seen Veronica Jensen livid, but she was livid now.

"Amanda, I refuse to believe—"

"Believe it, Mother," Amanda cut in, her voice serious. She lifted a hand, motioned around the shop. "This is who I am, and I like me. If I embarrass you, I'm sorry. Either accept me, or I'll just stay out of your way. What I cannot do, *will not do,* is let you define my life. I have the right to pursue my own dreams and to live my own life my own way. I have to answer for it, Mother. And I'm the one who has to live with the decisions I make. I hope you understand that I mean this, because I'm through tolerating schemes such as this one with Bradley."

Chatty beamed, mentally flooding Amanda with her support.

Veronica looked torn. A long minute passed. Then another. Finally she collected herself and made her decision. "I'll try. It won't be easy. This is a radical change from all I've envisioned for you. But I will try." Her expression turned pleading. "Just please stop keeping friends with that bag lady, darling. For your own safety."

One last grapple for control. And clearly her mother didn't recognize Chatty. Silently amused by that, Amanda forced herself to respond seriously. "No."

"No?" Her mother's brows shot up. "But it's a disgrace, Amanda. The woman is a thief!"

"She's my friend."

Max stepped out from behind the rack of sunglasses, looking stunningly handsome in a tux and laughing deeply.

He came! Amanda's heart turned over in her chest. But rather than seeming pleased to see him, she glared at him as if he'd lost his mind. "What in the name of heaven is so funny, Max?"

"Your mother," he said between waves of laughter.

Bradley tensed. Her mother grimaced. And Chatty just kept beaming.

"I beg your pardon." Veronica leveled a haughty glare on Max that should have had his knees trembling.

He laughed harder, deeper. When he gained semicontrol, he swiped at his damp eyes. "Oh, no, Mrs. Jensen. There's no need to beg my pardon."

Her mother fumed.

Amanda studied him suspiciously. "Are you drunk, Max?"

"No, darling, I'm not." He stepped to her side. "I'm amused."

"Amused?" Veronica interrupted. "There's nothing amusing about my daughter consorting with a thief."

"I agree," he said, which had Veronica looking at him as if he'd lost his mind. "What is amusing is that you paid seventy thousand dollars for that 'disgraceful, bag lady thief's' latest work of art."

Veronica gasped.

Amanda did, too, and swung her gaze to Chatty. "*You're* Millicent Fairgate?"

Her eyes twinkled. "Guilty, pet."

Laughter bubbled deep inside Amanda. "But why did you pretend—Ah, I see." The negotiations for *Cupid's Arrow*. Her mother had told Chatty all about Amanda, and Chatty had decided to intercede. Not in the hope Amanda would marry Bradley, though, as her mother had claimed. But because Chatty loved unconditionally, and she wanted to help Amanda realize her dreams.

Veronica shouted at Max, "Just who are you to insinuate yourself into my family's affairs?"

"My friends call me Max Jones." The laughter left his voice.

Totally vexed, Veronica pinched her lips into a tight line. "Do nonfriends call you something else, then?"

A shiver of knowing streaked up Amanda's back. She swiveled her gaze from her mother to Max, afraid of what she was about to hear, but even more afraid not to hear it.

Avoiding Amanda's eyes, he circled her waist with his arm. "Most people call me Jonathan Maxwell."

Her knees turned to water. She slumped against him. The checks. The distinctive "M." *That's* what had been familiar about them. Max *was* Jonathan.

"And very soon"—he turned his gaze to Amanda—"I hope I'll also be called your daughter's future husband."

"Future *husband?*" Amanda gasped. "You've forgiven me, Max?"

He nodded.

Her jaw dropped loose. No wonder she'd recognized him heart to heart. Known him so well, so quickly. They were the same man, and now he wanted to marry her. "Why didn't you tell me?"

Leaving a gape-jawed Veronica and Bradley standing there with the beaming Chatty, Max led Amanda out into the mall, then over to the bench beneath the tip of Cupid's arrow. He clasped both her hands in his, looking as nervous as she'd ever seen any man. "You should have told me, Max."

"I know. I wanted to tell you. Yet twice I've loved and believed I was loved back. But they loved my money and my work, not me. I promised myself I'd find a woman who'd love me, Mandy. Just me. Just the man."

He grunted. "Things weren't supposed to go this far, not without you knowing the truth. And they wouldn't have, except that you recognized the handwriting on the Secret Admirer invitation as Jonathan's. Everything got so . . . complicated."

"But you knew I was torn up about loving you both."

"I strongly suspected it, but I also suspected that if I admitted to deceiving you, then you'd hate us both."

Amanda stared at him. He didn't quite meet her eyes. "Uh-uh, Max. Tell me the truth."

"That is the truth." Resignation slid over his face. "But, you're right. It's not the whole truth." He swallowed hard, bobbing his Adam's apple. "I intended telling you after dinner, at your apartment. But then you called me Jonathan, and I was afraid what had happened before was happening again. That you'd somehow found out who I was and you were falling in love with the Jonathan persona, and not with me."

"I believe you're being honest, Max. But I know in my heart that there's more. I won't marry a man I can't trust. I don't care what his name is, or how much I love him."

He locked his gaze with hers. "Do you love me, Mandy?"

"Answer me," she insisted, ignoring his question.

Nodding, he went on, "At the apartment, I also realized I'd committed the ultimate foolish act."

What did he mean by that?

"After what happened to me, I never would have believed it possible that I'd do something so asinine, but I did. I fell in love with you through your work." He shook his head, as if that fact still sent him reeling. "Chatty had sworn to me that prince or pauper, it wouldn't matter to you, and yet . . ."

Understanding welled in Amanda and softened her voice. "You didn't believe her."

"I didn't dare to believe her. Not after being wrong twice before." He took in a deep breath and then blew it out slowly, calming himself. "Then she forced my hand, confessing her 'bauble borrowing' as proof of what kind of woman you are. I couldn't believe you were real. I had to see for myself." He lifted an unsteady hand to her face. "It got messy. I was neck-deep into this, and I didn't know how to get out of it without losing you."

A flash of insight had her heart feeling squeezed. "You were jealous of Jonathan."

"Hell, yes. And I don't mind saying it's unadulterated agony being jealous of yourself. I felt like an idiot, Mandy. I loved you, and until he came up, I was just crazy enough to believe you loved me, too. Or that, with time, you could love me."

"I do love you."

Max stilled. His expression turned tender, and the anguish left his eyes. "Really?"

She nodded and pressed her hands flat against his chest. "And I believe I owe you another apology. Will two kisses do?"

He anchored his hands at her waist and gave her that adorable, lazy grin that melted her heart and turned her mind to mush. "After all this hell? I need at least ten kisses just to feel human again."

"Mmm." She looped her arms around his neck and let her fingertips dangle off his shoulders. "A woman certainly appreciates a greedy lover, but ten kisses is a steep price for a future bride to pay."

"You'll marry me, then?" He sounded positively stunned.

The hint of a smile curving her lips, she shrugged. "Of course."

A slow smile spread over his face, and the look in his eyes heated and turned possessive. "Of course."

She kissed him lovingly, longingly, her heart full and content. And when their lips parted, she whispered, "I think I like being in debt to you, Max."

He pulled back to look at her face, his expression wary. "Then why does that little tremor in your voice make me uncomfortable?"

"Trust me, darling. You're going to come to love that tremor." He would. Just as soon as he figured out what it meant.

"What do you want, Amanda?"

"I want you. Only you." She let the truth shine in her eyes. "All of you."

His fingertips tightened at her waist. "You were right. I do love that tremor." He curled an arm around her waist. "Let's go home."

"Now? But it's my party."

"Chatty will close the store." He nuzzled the shell of her ear, longing shaking his voice. "I want all of you, too."

Thinking those the most heavenly words she'd ever heard, Amanda smiled up at Cupid and hugged Max tighter. Their lives would be full of ups and downs, and of all the magic and romance possible in any marriage founded in love. Chatty had been right about many things, but about one thing, she'd been wrong. When it came to Amanda's fantasies of Jonathan, the reality of Max had no trouble whatsoever measuring up.

And Chatty had known he wouldn't. Amanda would bet her baubles on it . . . later.

Arm in arm with Max, Amanda left for home, eager to begin their life together.

Chatty watched them go and sniffed, her heart finally at peace. Sighing her content, she let her gaze drift up the giant bronze she'd crafted while praying for exactly this. Her pet and her nephew—the two people she loved most—loving each other. Life just didn't get any better than this.

Her eyes moist, Chatty smiled straight into the heart of *Cupid's Arrow*. "Well, mister, I guess I won't melt you down and sell you for scrap. Your aim was perfect, after all."

Top Cat and Tales

Elizabeth Bevarly

PROLOGUE

"*O*h, I'll bet you Trojans say that to *all* the girls."

Aphrodite, goddess of love, fluttered her golden eyelashes coyly, then drew her finger along the chiseled jaw of the closest of the three men she'd brought home for cocktails. No wonder those twentieth-century folks named a contraceptive after the men of Troy. They were indeed a randy bunch. Just the way she liked them.

"Do come in," she instructed her guests as she pushed open the door to her temple. "Artemis just turned me on to this new label of ouzo that's absolutely—" She halted midsentence as she stepped inside, the acrid stench of cat refuse filling her nose and burning her eyes.

Not again. Honestly. You ask your son to perform one lousy chore before he goes out charioting with his friends, and what happens? He completely ignores you. Then again, what did she expect from a surly adolescent like Cupid? Changing the litter box was obviously beneath a god, even one who was still too young and impulsive to have achieved full deity status.

Aphrodite spun around to offer her apologies for the stench, but her gorgeous, ebony-haired Trojans were already backing away. "I am *so* sorry," she said, trying anyway. She chuckled a little anxiously. "We can take our party out to the pool. How would that be?"

But the men evidently had other ideas, as each suddenly began to mutter an excuse for having to be elsewhere immediately. Aphrodite frowned as she watched the Trojans make their escape, then sighed with much gusto. Unfortunately the gesture only filled her nostrils with *eau de* wet litter. There was nothing like the smell of cat pee to ruin an otherwise promising romantic interlude. She was going to strangle Cupid when she got her hands on him.

As if conjured by her murderous thoughts, a door slammed somewhere at the back of her temple, and an uneven voice, sometimes tenor, sometimes baritone, called out, "Yo, Mom! I'm home! What's for dinner?"

Aphrodite spun around and made her way toward her son's voice, her gauzy white robes swishing around her silver sandals, her golden hair dancing about her shoulders. She found him in the kitchen, standing in front of the open refrigerator door. As always, she softened some when she saw him. Even at thirteen he was nearly as beautiful as she, with blond curls that hung to his shoulders and eyes bluer than the Aegean. Her son would be a gorgeous hunk of manhood someday, she conceded. If he lived that long.

"Cupid, I told you this morning to clean out the catbox," she stated without preamble.

He shrugged without concern and snatched a golden apple from the crisper. "I had other things to do."

And that was it—no explanation, no apology. For that as much as anything, Aphrodite decided, her son was going to pay. He might be a god, but *she* held an infinitely more powerful position than mere deity—she was a mother.

"This is the last time you're going to find other things to do when I assign you a chore," she told him. "So far this week, you've refused to walk Cerberus for your Uncle Hades, you didn't take out the trash, and you ignored me when I reminded you that it was your turn to mow the Elysian Fields." She crossed her arms menacingly over her midriff. "Medea and Ione are *your* cats, buster, and you promised to take care of them."

"Yeah, but—"

"Don't you 'yeah, but' me, young man. That catbox smells bad enough to make a minotaur heave."

"But, Mo-o-om, my homeys and me were going down to the arcade to—"

"I don't care what you and your homeys were going to do. You and those boys spend far too much time playing those bloody gladiator computer games as it is. You've left me no choice but to do something that will ensure you don't conveniently forget to do your chores in the future."

Cupid eyed her warily. "Whaddaya mean?"

Aphrodite smiled and pushed back the sleeves of her translucent white gown to her elbows. She gave her fingers an experimental wiggle—it had been a while since she'd cast anyone down from Mt. Olympus—then cracked her knuckles one by one.

"Yo, Mom?" Cupid asked, his eyes widening when he noted her gesture. "What are you doing?"

Aphrodite arched one perfect blond eyebrow. "I'm going to send you on a little quest," she told him. "And you're not coming back until you've proved yourself worthy."

"Worthy?" he echoed with obvious trepidation.

"Yes, worthy. You haven't behaved in a godly fashion at all lately," she said simply. "And now you're going to have to perform a deed for me."

He panicked visibly at her announcement. "Oh, no. Please. Not that. Not a deed."

She ignored his plea and told him, "If you're successful, you can come back to Mount Olympus with my blessing, provided you do as I say in the future. But if you fail . . ." She deliberately left the threat unfinished. Let the little blighter chew on that for a while.

"If I fail?" Cupid asked, his expression growing even more concerned.

"Then you'll remain an outcast until you succeed. Now then," she hurried on before he could object again, "what would be a suitable deed for you to perform? Hmmm . . ."

"How about I just, like . . . run down to the Agora and pick up some groceries for dinner?" Cupid suggested quickly. "I'll cook tonight to make it up to you. Tacos," he added, knowing they were her favorite.

"No, I don't think so." Then an idea came to her in a flash, and she smiled. "You're a god of love, too. It's about time you proved yourself in that respect."

"*Love?*" Cupid fairly spat the word at her. "Oh, gross. Don't make me hurl."

She chuckled merrily. "Ah. Well, then. That's it. Your deed is to go down to earth and bring two mortals together in a love to transcend all time. And not to the classical Greece we've all come to know and love here on Mount Olympus, either," she added quickly when she saw her son begin to grin smugly. "They're far too romantic. It would be too easy for you."

"But, Mom—"

"So I'm sending you to . . . hmmm . . . let's see now . . ."

Aphrodite thought for a moment, then smiled as she recalled her earlier reflection about those twentieth-century folks and their classically inspired contraception. "You're going to the New World, Cupid, darling. At the end of the second millennium, where rabid fear of commitment makes it nearly impossible for two people to get together for any length of time." She nodded at her brilliant idea. "Yeah, that's the ticket."

"Mom! That's like . . . *so* harsh!"

"So is coming home with some truly lovely people with whom you've looked forward to having hours and hours of, um . . . stimulating conversation, and having the house smell like a catbox." Aphrodite raised her arms above her head and flexed her fingers lightly. "Off you go, then," she said. "Happy trails."

And . . . poof! Cupid was gone.

He landed with a thud in a cold, wretched downpour, in the middle of the night, without a friend to be had. Icy water slammed down around him, clinging to his face and back and tail, and he—

Wait a minute . . . tail?

Cupid glanced down at himself, then howled a loud curse toward the dark night sky above him. Only instead of a shout, the sound that emerged was a strangled, feral growl. His mom had not only cast him down among those lame mortals, but she'd turned him into a cat. Oh, man. And with that babe Andromeda waiting for him at the arcade, too. Perseus was sure to move in on her now.

Standing, Cupid shook all four paws fruitlessly and glanced around at his surroundings. A tall brick building silhouetted against the night sky caught his attention first. All the windows there were dark, except for one near a metal staircase that wound up one side. "Archer Arms Apartments," read a sign over the front door. At least, he was pretty sure that was what it said. His grades at school in modern languages hadn't been so good lately.

Might as well get this over with as quickly as possible, he thought. Surely there were two people around here somewhere who could stand each other for an eternity. Cupid squinted through the cold rain, then stumbled haphazardly toward the building as he maneuvered four feet instead of his usual two. And he wondered who could be up so much later than everyone else.

CHAPTER ONE

*A*bby Walden watched the cursor on her computer screen go *blink blink blink* and listened to the rain pelt the dark window beside her with an identical staccato beat of *plink plink plink*. Halfheartedly she gazed down at the keyboard and pushed the shift key, followed by the letter *D*. Then a small-case *e*. Then an *a*. And finally an *r*. Sighing, she brought her other hand into the action, thumbed the space bar, and added *F-r-u-s-t-r-a-t-e-d i-n F-r-e-s-n-o*. Then she sat back to admire her handiwork. There. She had the first full line for her latest column. She was going like gangbusters.

Exactly *where* she was going, however . . . now that was a mystery. Just what exactly did one say to a man who was worried about the size of his penis? Not that she hadn't pondered such a dilemma before. An inordinate number of her readers seemed to be concerned about that very thing. But she was no closer to providing a convincingly reassuring answer now than she'd been when she started writing her column for *Cavalier* magazine two years ago.

Maybe she could just ignore Frustrated in Fresno this month, she thought, and include his letter in next month's column instead. There was a pile of other questions addressed to Abby's alter ego, the celebrated Candida. And they were questions that were infinitely more interesting than Frustrated's. That one about zucchini, for example, was just begging to be answered. Or the one about feather dusters. And she couldn't possibly ignore the Cheez Whiz guy any longer, could she?

Abby highlighted the greeting she had just typed and reached for the delete key. Then she paused before completing the action. "Candida's Room," the erotic advice column she authored for *Cavalier*, was the most frequently and faithfully read part of the men's lifestyle magazine, a regular feature that had driven subscriptions way, way up since its introduction. She owed her readers the frank, in-your-face answers for which she had become famous, meeting, without flinching, their queries as to what it took to please women sexually, romantically, and emotionally.

Even if half the time she had absolutely no idea what she was talking about. Not from personal experience, anyway. She'd proposed "Candida's Room," a playful sexual advice column for men written by a woman, to *Cavalier*'s publisher on a lark, only half-serious about it. But the publisher, who also happened to be Abby's Aunt Victoria, had thought the proposed column was a fabulous idea, and who better to write it than Abby?

Who better? she wondered as she invariably did whenever she sat down at the computer wearing her Candida hat. Who better to write a hip, happening, how-to column for young, upscale men who were hungry for sexual and romantic expertise? Oh, gee, Abby didn't know. . . . Maybe someone who *hadn't* majored in medieval studies? Maybe someone who *didn't* teach Chaucer to dozing college students in her real life? Maybe someone who actually *had* sex on a regular basis and could claim *some* working knowledge of such a thing?

No, no, Aunt Victoria had assured her. Abby was perfect. Literary background. Extensive vocabulary. Irreverent outlook on life. Used to working on a deadline, thanks to that obscure underground fiction magazine she'd edited in college. And unafraid of strong language. Best of all, she was female. Abby could make such a column tasteful and fun, Aunt Victoria had insisted. Even if she wasn't exactly an expert.

And she could make it fictional, too, Abby thought wryly as she shoved her big glasses up higher on her nose and ran a quick hand through her long dark bangs. Which may have been why the column was so wildly successful with her predominantly male readers. Candida was the ultimate fantasy female for them. Now whether or not her advice was at least *grounded* in reality, well . . . Maybe Abby would find out for herself someday what these things called love and sex and romance were really all about.

In the meantime, she had a column to make up . . . er, write. She snuggled more deeply into the wool afghan she'd wrapped around her flannel pajamas, reached for her chamomile tea, and thought about penis size. Hmmm . . . this was going to be a hard one. . . .

A movement outside the window by her desk brought her attention around with a start, and she cried out when she saw a face peering in at her from the other side. Then she realized that the face was kind of . . . fuzzy. With a little pink triangle nose. And pointy ears and huge blue eyes and droopy little white whiskers. As Abby watched, the wet, shivering cat opened its mouth and cried out at the storm attacking it.

As quickly as she could, she set down her tea, leaped from her chair, and shoved the window up high. The icy February rain assaulted her as she stuck her upper body outside and scooped the soggy buff tabby off the fire escape. The scrawny creature was shivering wildly, so Abby shrugged out of the afghan and wrapped the warm wool around it, rubbing gently to jump-start the cat's circulation.

"Poor little thing," she cooed softly. "What are you doing outside on a night like this?"

With no small effort, and ignoring the puddle of water on the hardwood floor, she tried to shut the window with one hand. Unfortunately it got stuck with a good four inches or so left to clear, and no amount of shoving on her part would close it completely. Ignoring it for now, Abby made a mental note to call Billy-the-Super about it in the morning. Right now she had a frozen catsicle to thaw out.

The radiator hissed as she padded to the kitchen, her heavy socks muffling her footsteps as she went. She continued to cuddle and dry the stray as she fumbled to warm milk in a pan. Then, when she'd done all she could to dry it, she set the animal on the floor. Immediately it sneezed hard enough to knock itself down, and Abby bit back her laughter.

"Where on earth did you come from?" she asked aloud. "You can't be from here, because pets aren't allowed at the Archer Arms."

In response, the damp cat took a few steps forward, shaking each of its paws in turn, as if it were doing a drunken samba. When Abby laughed again, it halted and glared up at her. Actually *glared,* as if her chuckles had insulted it. She laughed harder.

"Boy, you are one pathetic-looking little refugee." She shook her head at the limp animal. "Are you a boy cat or a girl cat?"

Without awaiting a reply, she lifted the cat from the floor again, snatched up its tail, and inspected it from behind. "Boy cat," she said as she set him down again.

The moment she did so, he spun on her, bucked up his back, fuzzed out his tail—well, as fuzzy as it could go, all water-logged as it was—and hissed at her long and low.

She arched her brows in surprise. "Don't tell me I insulted you," she said. When his expression suggested she had done just that, she added graciously, "I do beg your pardon."

The cat eased off some at that but still eyed her warily. Abby poured the warm milk into a bowl and placed it on the floor before him. He dipped his head and lapped experimentally, gagged a bit, then lapped a little more. He wasn't quite a kitten, but he didn't seem full grown yet, either. Funny how he'd come out of nowhere like that.

Satisfied that he was okay for the time being, she fished a roll of paper towels from above the sink, then returned to the dining room that doubled as her office, to wipe the rain off the floor. That done, she put both hands and arms to work closing the window, but the fool thing refused to budge. Instead it only seemed to get jammed even tighter.

Then a quiet sound outside suddenly cut through the darkness and the downpour, a steady hum that halted her efforts completely and nearly stopped her heart. As quickly as her pulse rate ceased, however, it jumped to life again, now pumping double time. Abby switched off the single lamp burning on her desk, then gazed through the window, beyond the black zigzag of the fire escape, down to the alley behind the apartment building where the Archer Arms residents parked. A single white light cut through the darkness at the very end of the alley to announce his arrival, followed by the shadow of a motorcycle.

And then she saw *him*. The man in black. Her upstairs neighbor, who'd fascinated her from the day he'd moved in nearly three months ago. His last name was Tandem—at least, that was what the label beside his door buzzer said. And his first name was Joel, if the oversize mail the postman left on the floor from time to time—mail she might have accidentally glanced at once or twice—was correct.

Automatically her gaze flew to the green numbers illuminated by the clock on her desk. Four-fifteen A.M. on the nose. He was right on time.

Just where did a man who dressed in black leather and drove a Harley go every single night except Sundays, at exactly ten forty-five in the evening, only to return five and a half hours later on the dot, when most normal people would be fast asleep? The question erupted in her brain, as it always did this time of the morning, when he was returning home from whatever strange place he visited night after night after night.

Occasionally the sound of his motorcycle woke Abby from sleep. But more often she was still wide awake whenever he returned home, writing Candida's column or working on her class notes for the following day.

A night owl since childhood, she taught classes only in the afternoons and evenings, and she always wrote Candida's column during the darkest hours of the morning. It just seemed appropriate somehow to be Candida only after midnight. Something about the wee hours made her feel less inhibited, more inspired. Well, that and the generous two fingers of vodka she normally poured into her chamomile tea.

But at least she was at home during the darkest hours of the night, she reminded herself. Joel Tandem was out running around on his motorcycle, performing heaven only knew what kind of black deeds. Not that there were necessarily all that many black deeds to be performed in a little town like Kenwood, Massachusetts, where the only thing of note was tiny Kenwood College, where Abby taught. But still . . .

You never could tell about some people. Especially people who wore black leather all the time and drove big ol' Harley hogs.

She moved closer to the window and watched with interest as her neighbor pulled his motorcycle into its usual place. Because it was still raining, he didn't remove his helmet, as he normally did the minute the kickstand went down. So tonight she wasn't rewarded with the sight of his glossy, shoulder-length black hair reflecting the blue light of the street lamp. And even if he had taken off his helmet, she was still too far away to see his mesmerizing midnight blue eyes.

But she knew for a fact that he did have mesmerizing midnight blue eyes. She knew because he'd mesmerized her with them on more than one occasion. He lived in the apartment right above hers, after all, and from time to time she ran into him on the stairs or in the elevator. Naturally she'd never actually *spoken* to him—who on earth could actually *speak* to a man who looked like . . . like . . . like *that?* But she had admired him from a distance once or twice. Or more.

Okay, so she'd admired him from a distance lots of times. Almost every night, in fact. She had to admire him from a distance, because she was way too scared to admire him from up close. Getting up close and personal with a guy like him would probably make her spontaneously combust. The two of them would doubtless mix about as well as baking soda and vinegar. Or gasoline and matches. Or matter and antimatter. That kind of thing.

As if he knew he was being watched, however, her neighbor in black leather suddenly halted in the courtyard below and glanced up at the window from which Abby was observing him. Then, despite the rain, he stopped dead in his tracks and slowly unsnapped the chin strap of his helmet. Then, even more slowly, his attention still fixed on her window, he eased the helmet from his head.

· And returned her inspection quite openly.

Abby assured herself he couldn't possibly see her standing in the darkened window, even with the screen saver scrolling across the computer behind her. But somehow she was certain that he knew she was there. And although she told herself to move, to dart away before she embarrassed herself any more than she already had, something in his posture froze her in place.

She watched from two stories up as he stood there watching her back, as he lifted a hand to rake his fingers leisurely through his long, wet hair, as he settled both hands casually on his hips, his helmet tucked under one arm. For long moments he only rested his weight on one foot and stood there in the rain, staring up at her window. And with each passing second, Abby's heartbeat quickened and her temperature soared.

Why was he staring at her? she wondered. Even if he knew she was there watching him, surely he was used to having women ogle him all the time. Why would he find her interest in him so, well . . . interesting?

She swallowed hard and somehow forced her feet to propel her backward, until the corner of her desk poked her in the fanny. Only then did she remember to breathe, and she gulped in one great lungful of air after another, until her pulse began to slow and her brain waves began to steady. Unfortunately the action also left her feeling dizzy and unbalanced, and not a little excited.

And as always, she realized that whoever Joel Tandem was, it was going to be vital that she continue to avoid him at all costs. If he could make her hyperventilate simply by staring up at her window through the rain, silently and without moving, then what kind of reaction would actual physical contact with him wreak?

Something made Abby turn toward the kitchen, and she saw the silhouette of her fuzzy little refugee seated like an isosceles triangle in the doorway, watching her with as much interest as her black-clad neighbor had only a moment ago. Then the cat stood and sauntered over to the window, leaped onto the sill, and looked outside. For a long time he stared into the darkness, his tail swinging from side to side like a pendulum. Then he turned toward Abby again.

How odd. In the scant light of the screen saver, he seemed almost to be smiling at her.

She shook her head to clear it of its whimsy and switched on the desk lamp again. In full light, her feline guest's expression returned to the mild sort of indulgence that cats normally reserved for lesser humans. But when he leapt down from the windowsill and sauntered toward the kitchen, she wondered if he'd hurt himself. He didn't seem quite steady on his feet, stumbling half the time as he was. Shrugging, she moved to the open window and devoted the next ten minutes of her life to closing it. But it had jammed itself completely.

Surrendering, knowing it would be fruitless to try to reach Billy-the-Super in the middle of the night, because he was anything *but* super when it came to fixing things, Abby resigned herself to a chilly night's sleep. Then she wrapped herself once more in the afghan and returned to her seat, skittered the mouse across its pad to dispel the screen saver, and returned to Candida's column. But as quickly as it appeared on the screen, she closed the file and pulled up computer solitaire instead.

There was no way she could think about things like zucchini and Cheez Whiz and penis size right now. Unfortunately, when she heard the slow scuff of boots sauntering across the hardwood floor in the apartment above hers, Abby realized she could think about little else. And even the cold wind blowing through the open window could do nothing to cool her off.

Oh, man, this was going to be sooooo easy, Cupid thought as he studied the woman who had rescued him from the rain. She was already gone on somebody—though what she saw in some dude that didn't even have sense enough to come in out of the rain was a little weird. But seeing as how the dude had just stood there looking lame, maybe he had ideas about the babe, too.

Babe, he thought again as he glanced back at the woman playing solitaire. Okay, so maybe the word wasn't the best one for her. Still, she probably wouldn't be too bad cleaned up a little. In dim light. After a couple of bottles of brew. It was something he could work on.

As the sound of footsteps overhead alerted him to the fact that the dude in question lived right upstairs, the rumble of a contented purr tickled the back of Cupid's throat. Oh, wow. That felt *so* cool. Yeah, he thought further as the vibration intensified, his mom wasn't so smart. Sending him right down into the middle of two people already half-sprung. All he had to do was hurry them up a little, then he could get back to the arcade—and Andromeda—and beat the Nikes off of Perseus once and for all.

Wrinkling his nose at the empty bowl on the kitchen floor, Cupid headed for the woman. If she thought he was going to be satisfied by one lousy bowl of warm milk, she was out of her mind. Hey, man, he was a growing boy. . . .

Chapter Two

Joel Tandem tore open the snaps and unzipped his wet leather jacket, tossed it and his helmet onto the chair by the radiator, and headed for the kitchen to grab a beer. For some reason, he was really, really thirsty, for something really, really cold, in spite of the icy rain that had soaked his clothes and chilled his skin. After filling his mouth with the cool, bittersweet flavor of ale, he fell back onto his sofa, unmindful of his wet leather pants, and concentrated on slowing his heart rate.

His downstairs neighbor was going to give him a heart attack one of these days. And he'd barely exchanged a dozen words with her.

She sure was cute, though, he thought further as he closed his eyes and lifted the cold bottle to his forehead. Those huge, espresso-colored eyes, made even larger by her big glasses, that fall of dark auburn hair that would look like fire in a storm all love-rumpled and laid out across a man's pillow. Joel lowered the bottle to his lips and drank thirstily again. Yep, that Abby Walden was some kinda woman, all right.

He just wished he could figure out exactly what kinda.

Hiding her incredible eyes behind those big, tortoiseshell glasses, with her fiery hair almost always wound down her back in a tight braid, she gave the impression of being the stereotypical schoolteacher, librarian, or IRS employee. And although he'd heard through the apartment grapevine—all right, he conceded to himself, he'd discovered through a flat-out Spanish Inquisition of his neighbors—that she did teach at the local college and volunteer at the library and was, in fact, perfectly capable of preparing her own tax returns (not to mention those of many of their elderly neighbors), Joel suspected there was a lot more to Abby than a simple stereotype.

Something in her eyes hinted at a limitless and not quite satisfied passion. At dreams unspoken and wishes unfulfilled. At a need and desire that was so profound, she felt compelled to bury it far inside herself lest it overrun her completely. And every time he ran into her, he found himself wanting to unleash whatever it was that Abby Walden guarded so carefully inside.

And after three months of accidental run-ins with her, he got the distinct impression that she was attracted to him, too. Why else would she do something like turn out her light just so she could spy on him through the darkness? On those few occasions when he'd encountered her in the building, her gaze inevitably flew to his person with absolutely no coaching on his part. Oh, yeah. She was interested.

So why did she run like a scared gazelle every time he came within ten feet of her? Why did she deny that need inside her that he was perfectly willing to fill?

He glanced at his coffee table, where he'd deposited his mail that afternoon without looking at it. Beneath the jumble of bills and advertisements lay the latest issue of *Cavalier*. Joel smiled as he reached for the magazine. Candida. His favorite woman in the whole wide world. Maybe he should write and ask *her* why a seemingly interested woman would bolt in terror whenever the object of her affections was within grabbing distance, fully willing to be grabbed.

Joel flipped immediately to "Candida's Room" and leaned back on the sofa again. As he read, his thirst grew, his temperature rose, and his body tensed. My, my, my, but that Candida had a mouth on her. He wondered what it would feel like on him. Oh, baby.

He snapped the magazine closed before finishing the column. He was already worked up enough as it was after that little interlude with Abby, however distant she'd been at the time. Then he stood and stretched, a long, lusty stretch, forcing the kinks out of his body. He hated working nights, but that seemed to be the best time for what he had to do. He'd tried mornings and afternoons both, but he'd discovered, much to his annoyance, that nighttime hours were by far his most productive. Ah, well. It wasn't as if he had a lot of places to be during the day, anyway. Might as well sleep then as any other time.

He ended the stretch by reaching behind himself to bunch the fabric of his black T-shirt in one fist. Then he drew it easily over his head and wadded it up on his way to the bathroom. A quick shower and a little sleep would work wonders to ease his tension.

Of course, there were other, infinitely more enjoyable ways to fend off the stress and fatigue that came with his line of work. But Abby Walden was probably on her way to bed by now. It was nice of her to wait up for him night after night the way she did, he thought with a fond smile. But he supposed she had to sleep sometimes, too.

Thoughts of Abby in bed were a bit more than Joel could handle at the moment, so as he stepped naked into the hot jet of the shower, he pushed them way far to the back of his brain. Unfortunately that still wasn't quite far enough. Because as he closed his eyes and soaped himself up, the visions that danced in his head were a combination of the big-eyed, auburn-haired woman who lived downstairs and the heated suggestions he'd just read in ''Candida's Room.''

He awoke with a start later that morning and right away wondered what had roused him to consciousness so quickly and completely. Immediately he had his answer. A buff-colored cat with stripes the same shade as coffee ice cream sat on the pillow opposite him, its blue eyes depthless and moderately curious. Pushing himself onto his elbows, he eyed the creature back with what he hoped was an equally bland expression.

''Where did you come from?'' he asked.

The cat glanced toward the bedroom window, and Joel's

gaze followed. He'd opened it about five inches before turning in that morning, not enough to let in the rain, but enough to allow the fresh air—however cold—that he demanded while he slept. And, evidently, enough to provide entrance for a stray cat with curious eyes.

He shook his head and chuckled. "Came up the fire escape, huh? Guess that makes sense."

Slowly he extended a hand toward the cat, but the little guy stood and backed away before Joel could make contact. "Skittish, hmm?" He yawned with much enthusiasm. "You're just like a certain downstairs neighbor I know."

Joel rolled over and slung his feet to the floor, scrubbed a hand through the pelt of dark hair covering his chest, then raked his fingers through his long black hair. "You know, pets aren't allowed here at the Archer Arms," he told the cat as he reached for a pair of sweatpants at the foot of the bed. "So what am I supposed to do with you?"

The cat blinked at him but offered no suggestions.

"How about breakfast, then?" Joel suggested. "Bacon and eggs all right?"

The animal twitched his ears at that, then jumped from the bed and headed straight for the kitchen. Joel laughed as he followed, loosely tying the drawstrings of his sweatpants and thinking his feline visitor must be even hungrier than he was himself. His chuckles halted abruptly, however—just as Joel did himself—when he entered his dining room. Everywhere he looked, the floor was cluttered with . . . stuff. All kinds of . . . stuff. Unfortunately, none of it appeared to be *his* stuff.

The card table and folding chairs that passed for his dining room suite, the rag rug his Aunt Margie had given him as a housewarming gift, even the slouching potted palm his sister Cathy tried to maintain for him when she came to visit weekly, were all obscured by dozens of . . . things. Joel stepped carefully into the room, bypassed a string of pearls—*Please don't let them be real,* he prayed—edged past a jumble of clothing he *really* hoped wasn't women's underwear, and reached simultaneously for a ring of keys and a leather wallet.

"What the . . . ?"

His question trailed off before he could finish it, because the cat who'd come in from the cold began to wind affectionately around his ankles, obviously quite pleased with the results of his hunting-and-gathering expedition.

"This is your doing, isn't it?" Joel asked unnecessarily. When the cat only dropped back on his haunches and refused to answer, he frowned. "I thought beagles and mynah birds were the only animals that did this kind of thing."

The cat blinked but refrained from comment, only lifting his nose distastefully into the air. For some reason, Joel got the impression that he'd insulted the animal by comparing him to first a dog and then a bird.

He glanced down at the keys and wallet he gripped in each hand. Someone was sure to need these things right away, if they hadn't missed them already. Yeah, today was Saturday, but people still had places to go and things to do on the weekends, right? Well, most people, he amended. Other people. People who *weren't* on a tight deadline.

More concerned about returning what didn't belong to him than he was about invading anyone's privacy, he unsnapped the undoubtedly feminine wallet and peeked inside. He was relieved to find the cellophane driver's license window right there in front—until he saw the photograph and name behind it.

Abigail Walden. Archer Arms Apartments.

Oh, swell.

He wondered if the keys and pearls were also hers. Then, unable to stop himself, he wondered if that really had been women's underwear he'd walked by a second ago and whether or not *that* belonged to her, too. Helplessly he glanced over his shoulder at the froth of lavender lace that lay pooled on the floor scarcely two feet away. Then he tossed the wallet and keys onto the card table and bent to scoop up the mysterious garments instead.

Yep. It was women's underwear all right. Skimpy little bikini panties and an even skimpier little bra that couldn't possibly be effective in doing whatever it was bras were supposed to do. Before he realized his intentions, Joel lifted the lingerie to his nose and inhaled deeply. Oh, baby. Sachet. A combination of cedar and cinnamon and a half dozen other spicy aromas.

No way could these belong to Abby Walden. All buttoned up, smoothed down, and ironed out as she was all the time, she was undoubtedly the cotton, Jockeys for Her, no-nonsense underwear kind of woman. Obviously this particular cat burglar had hit more than one apartment last night.

"Okay, I give up," he said as he turned to face the cat again. He held up the lavender confection of lace for the animal's inspection, trying not to notice how flimsy and filmy the material was. "Who do these belong to? Show me that woman, and I'll reward you with a T-bone steak. Rare."

The cat licked his lips and set to a loud purring, then scampered toward the bedroom again. By the time Joel followed, all he saw was a ringed tail disappearing through the open window. He shook his head and sighed, then padded over barefoot to close it. No sense abetting the animal in any more larcenous endeavors, he thought. He was already going to have some serious explaining to do about having received all that stolen property in his dining room.

As he returned to inspect the pilfered loot again, Joel decided to post a note on the community bulletin board in the laundry room, explaining how he'd come into possession of his neighbors' belongings. At least he knew the identity of one victim, he thought as he reached for Abby's wallet. Then again, it would probably be best to invite her up to his apartment, just to see if anything else the cat had stolen was hers.

After a quick look in the White Pages, Joel was punching numbers on his phone. He ignored the strange, heated sensation that erupted in his belly as he waited, swallowed against the dryness that suddenly overcame his mouth and throat as the line rang once . . . twice . . . three times . . . four . . . But he couldn't quite dispel the explosion of utter terror that shook him when a muffled, sleepy, utterly erotic, feminine voice answered, "Hello?"

"Uh, Abby?"

"Mmm?"

He cleared his throat indelicately, licked his lips to no avail, and began, "This is, uh . . ." Well, hell, he thought irritably. He didn't even know if she knew his name. "This is your upstairs neighbor, Joel Tandem?" He squeezed his eyes shut at the shaky, adolescent quality his voice seemed to have suddenly adopted.

A long silence ensued, followed by, "Uh . . . who?"

"Joel?" he repeated. "Joel Tandem? I live right upstairs?" He cursed himself for suddenly being able to speak only in the inquisitive tense.

Another long silence, then, "Yes?"

Okay, so obviously he wasn't the only one speaking in the inquisitive today. Strangely, the realization heartened him some. "I, uh, I seem to have something that belongs to you?"

"Oh?"

"Your, uh, your wallet?"

"My wallet?"

"And maybe some other things, too?" he added.

"What, um . . . what kind of other things?"

"Some keys, maybe? And some jewelry? Possibly even some under—" He halted, reminding himself that the bra and panties undoubtedly belonged to someone else. "Ah . . . some other stuff," he concluded quickly to cover his gaffe, pleased that he finally seemed to have found some form of punctuation other than a question mark to end his sentences.

"I'm sorry," Abby's voice came from the other end of the line. She was still obviously not quite awake. "I don't understand. What are you doing with my wallet?"

Joel opened his mouth to explain, then decided it would be better if he had visual aids to assist in his presentation. "It's kind of a long story," he told her. "Maybe you should come up here and let me explain. If you haven't had breakfast already, you're more than welcome to join me for coffee. And I think I have some bagels or something."

Another lengthy silence, then Abby said, "I still don't understand."

"Just come up here as soon as you can," Joel told her. "I'll explain everything then." And without waiting to hear if she agreed or declined, he dropped the receiver back into its cradle.

Cupid flattened his feline body and squeezed back into the woman's apartment, just in time to hear her mumble a half-conscious greeting into the phone. Yeah, this was going to be like . . . *so* not hard, he thought again as he trotted into her bedroom and leapt onto her bed. He watched as she shoved her hair out of her eyes and braced herself on her elbows, then would have laughed out loud—if cats could manage such a thing—when she pulled the phone away from her ear and gaped at it.

Okay, so he'd stolen a few of her things. So what? It wasn't like he'd lifted CDs and game cartridges from Aristotle's House of Entertainment, was it? No way. She'd be getting her stuff back. And then some—stuff she'd never bargained for. Hey, man, bonus, right?

Besides, it wasn't like she didn't already have a major thing for the guy upstairs. And now she had an excuse to meet him face-to-face. No more staring down at him longingly from two stories up. And the dude wouldn't have to stand out in the rain like some half-drenched satyr, pining for her. This was like *so* perfect.

Yeah, Cupid could already taste the T-bone steak he'd been promised as a reward—though it was really uncool, this sudden craving for meat. He'd always been a vegetarian before, because Andromeda was a vegetarian. And he couldn't wait to see the look on his mom's face when he delivered these two sappy mortals in record time.

Being a god of love suddenly didn't seem to be quite as lame as it had before. Andromeda, for example, he thought with another purr, was sure to be impressed.

CHAPTER THREE

Abby lifted her hand to knock, but she couldn't quite convince her fingers to make contact with Joel Tandem's front door. Like her fingers, she was simply too terrified to move. Female professors of medieval studies, regardless of whether or not they wrote risqué advice columns under cover of darkness, simply were not equipped to go up against male sexpots who dressed in black and rode big motorcycles. There was absolutely no literary precedent for Abby to fall back on in this situation. The occasional encounter with Mr. Leather Pants in the elevator or the laundry room in no way prepared her to face him on his own testosterone-filled turf.

Then again, she reminded herself, Candida was lurking somewhere inside her. What would *she* do in a case like this?

The first thing Candida would do, Abby thought, was pour herself a drink. But seeing as how it was barely ten A.M., that probably wasn't a good idea at the moment. The second thing Candida would do was put on some Really Red lipstick. Again, however, Really Red wasn't exactly Abby's color. Her tastes ran more along the lines of Barely Beige. The third thing Candida would do was light a cigarette. Of course, Abby didn't smoke, because it was far too hazardous to her health.

She sighed dispiritedly. She and Candida really had very little in common. How could they both be dwelling inside the same body?

Okay, she could do this, Abby told herself firmly. Hey, writing as Candida only hours ago, hadn't she told the Cheez Whiz guy that it was perfectly all right to squirt a nondairy product onto a woman's toes and call it foreplay, even if he *wasn't* a podiatrist? Provided the woman in question was a consenting adult, naturally. The point was that Joel Tandem wasn't going to overpower Abby unless she let him, right? So all she had to do was make sure she kept the upper hand.

Squaring her shoulders, she clenched her fingers tight and urged her fist toward the door. *Rap. Rap rap. Rap rap rap.* There. That ought to do it. She smoothed a hand down the massive, oatmeal-colored sweater that hung over her jeans to nearly her knees, shoved her glasses up on her nose again, and waited.

She didn't have to wait long.

She was still adjusting her glasses when the door was yanked inward, and she stood libido-to-libido with the man in black. Only he wasn't wearing black this time. In fact, he wasn't wearing much of anything at all. Just heather gray sweatpants and a colossally surprised expression.

"You got here fast," he said by way of a greeting.

"Well, you did indicate that it was important that I hurry," she reminded him.

Unfortunately she uttered the sentiment not to Joel, but to his chest. His naked chest. His naked chest that filled her vision from only inches away. She tried not to faint.

So much for keeping the upper hand.

Inhaling deeply, she forced her gaze upward, told herself not to be mesmerized by his mesmerizing midnight blue eyes, and said, "Mr. Tandem?"

He blinked as he returned her perusal, almost as if he were battling an enchantment of his own. "Uh . . . yeah. That's me."

"I . . . Abby Walden," she said, thrusting her hand forward, hoping it wasn't shaking as badly as she was.

He smiled as he folded his fingers over hers, a decidedly interested smile that made her tremble even harder. "Yeah, I know," he fairly purred.

"Of course," she returned, mentally smacking her forehead. Hard.

She tried not to notice how warm and rough his hand was over hers, how much larger and stronger it was than hers, how much more powerful. And she scrambled to squash the ideas parading around in her brain about having his hands covering other parts of her body as well.

"You, uh . . ." She cleared her throat with some difficulty and tried again. "You said you have my wallet? And maybe some other things, too?"

He nodded as he released her hand, and she tried not to become suicidal about the loss of skin-to-skin contact.

"Come on in," he told her.

Inhaling a deep, fortifying breath, she instructed herself to remain calm and willed her feet to go forward. Oh, yes. Definitely a testosterone kind of place, she decided immediately upon entering. The man's furnishings were Spartan, to say the least, without a woman's touch to be had anywhere. Even the potted palm in the corner looked ready to succumb to Joel Tandem's overwhelming presence.

Then she noted that although the man's apartment was short on furniture, it seemed to be long on clutter. Why, his dining room floor alone was scattered with a variety of items, none of which seemed appropriate for his lifestyle—whatever, precisely, that lifestyle was.

"What went on in here?" she asked as she nodded toward the mess. "Did a gang of salesgirls from The Limited break in and try to accessorize you within an inch of your life? I hate it when that happens."

Then she noticed that some of the accessories in question looked rather familiar. "Hey!" she exclaimed as one item in particular caught her eye. "Those are my mother's pearls!"

She scampered over to the string of pearls and lifted them from the floor, cradling them in her palm when she spun around to face Joel. "My mother gave these to me when I graduated from college. What are they doing here?"

Her upstairs neighbor blew out an exasperated breath and

slowly raked his fingers through his hair. "Those are yours, huh?"

She nodded.

"You positive?"

"The clasp is kind of unusual—a silver maple leaf," she pointed out. Then she asked again, as emphatically as she could, "What are they doing here?"

He lifted one shoulder in a halfhearted shrug, a gesture that made Abby's heart go all pitter-patty, thanks to the way it made the muscles in his abdomen dance. Actually dance. Wow.

"You're not going to believe this," he began by way of an explanation.

"Try me."

He inhaled deeply again, another action that played his torso like a harpsichord. Jeepers. "There's this cat, see? He sorta showed up last night out of nowhere, and—"

"A tabby cat?" she interrupted. "A buff tabby with big blue eyes?"

His expression cleared of its obvious anxiety. "Yeah. Yeah, that's him."

She nodded, amenable to giving him the benefit of the doubt. For now.

"I just woke up this morning," he went on, "and there he was, sitting on my bed. He came in through the window."

"You keep your window open at night in the dead of winter?" she asked.

He made a wry face. "I like fresh air. I grew up on a farm. Sue me."

He grew up on a farm? she thought. Surely he was joking. He seemed more like the kind of man who had been, oh, say . . . molded by the hands of the gods.

"Anyway," he continued, "the cat came in through my bedroom window—several times, evidently, because he brought all this stuff with him." He swept a hand toward the assortment of items on his floor. "Looks like I'm not the only person who sleeps with his window open in the dead of winter, because I can't begin to imagine were he found all that stuff."

Abby inspected the collection again. "He found it all at my place," she said.

"Oh, so you sleep with *your* window open?" he asked in a sarcastic drawl. "In the dead of winter?"

This time Abby was the one to make a wry face. "No. Not by choice, anyway. But the cat you're talking about came to my window—the one by the fire escape—soaking wet and shivering last night. I couldn't let him stay outside in the storm. Then, after I let him in, I couldn't get my window closed. I left a message for Billy-the-Super to come unstick it this morning. Who knows when he'll get around to fixing it, though?" she added morosely.

Her neighbor nodded his understanding. It was common knowledge to the residents of the Archer Arms that Billy-the-Super wasn't a particularly super super. In fact, he was more of a pooper super than anything else.

"Don't wait for Billy-the-Super to do it," Joel told her. "It'll take him forever. I can come down after you've collected your things here and unstick it if you want."

If you want. For some reason, those words made Abby feel dangerously warm and gooey inside. "Uh, that's okay," she said quickly. "It can wait."

"We're supposed to get an ice storm today," he pointed out.

"I—all right."

As she uttered the words, her gaze fell to his naked chest again, and heaven help her, she just couldn't rein it back. Joel seemed to notice her extreme fascination with that particular part of his anatomy, because he hastily opened his palm over his heart and rubbed his chest absently. The singularly male gesture sent another Molotov cocktail whizzing with a fiery crash into Abby's midsection, and she swallowed hard. Oh, boy.

"Maybe I should go put on a shirt," he offered.

She nodded quickly. "Maybe you should."

"In the meantime, you can go through all this and make sure it's yours. I still think some of it must have come from somewhere else."

He left before she could assure him that no, she was fairly certain she'd been the only victim of Buffy the Thieving Wonder Tabby, but she made a thorough inspection of everything as she moved it all to his dining room table, just to be sure. By the time Joel returned, having thrown on an exhausted denim work shirt over his sweatpants, Abby was convinced that the loot was hers exclusively.

"What's the verdict?" he asked as he approached her.

She tried not to notice that he'd bothered to button only the bottom three buttons of his shirt. Tried, and failed miserably. "It's, uh, it's all mine," she said.

He arched his eyebrows in surprise. "All of it?"

She nodded.

"Are you sure?"

She nodded again.

"Oh."

His expression was oddly troubled, so she asked, "What's wrong? I thought you'd be happy to discover you won't have to locate any other victims."

"Uh . . . actually . . . um . . . " he hedged.

"Yes?"

"There, uh, there was . . . something else . . . that the cat dragged in, so to speak. But I figured it must belong to someone else, so I kind of, um . . . kept it. But only until I found the rightful owner," he hastened to add.

This time Abby was the one to arch her brows. "Oh? And what might that have been? I may very well be the rightful owner."

His gaze ricocheted around the room, landing on everything except her. Finally, nervously, he licked his lips and said, "Some, uh . . . some women's underwear."

"Oh."

The single-syllable response was all Abby could manage. Simply put, she *really* didn't want anyone to know anything about her underwear. Especially a man who favored black leather and who seemed to do most of his living during the night. Such a man was sure to misconstrue her reasons for wearing what she chose to wear against her skin. He was probably going to think she was wanton, or something silly like that, when in fact she was merely a lover of beautiful things—like lingerie. She chose her underwear for aesthetic purposes only. There was nothing more to it than that. Truly. There wasn't. Honestly. Really.

Straightening, Abby willed herself not to blush and asked in as matter-of-fact a manner as possible, "May I, um . . . see the underwear in question?"

Joel smiled, a decidedly suggestive smile that put her slightly off-kilter. Jerking a thumb over his shoulder, he said, "I put it in my room. In my, uh, in my underwear drawer. For safe keeping."

"I see."

Abby's battle with the blush wasn't going well at all. At the thought of her underthings mingling with his, heat crept from her chest to her neck to her cheeks. Vainly she tried to pretend she didn't notice and instead tilted her head toward the direction he indicated. "Would you mind . . . ?" she asked softly.

He eyed her with intense concentration for a moment, as if he were thinking very hard about something. Then, suddenly, his expression cleared, and he said quickly, "Oh. Yeah. Yeah, sure."

Then he spun around and beat a hasty retreat. Abby took advantage of his absence to try to steady her breathing, but he returned far too quickly for her to manage it. Which was just as well, because when she saw what he was carrying in his hands, she nearly went apoplectic. There, cradled in his fingers with *much* affection, lay her latest acquisition from the Victoria's Secret catalog. Oh, dear.

"Yes, those are mine, too," she said quickly, lunging for the garments in question.

But before she could seize them, Joel snatched them out of her reach. "Are you sure?" he asked, smiling broadly.

There was a distinct playfulness in his words and expression, Abby noted uncomfortably, though why he would bother playing with a neighbor he'd only just met was beyond her. "Yes," she told him evenly. "I'm sure."

"Maybe you better take a good look," he suggested sagely, "just to be sure."

To make her job easier—or more difficult, depending on her perspective, which at the moment was wavering staunchly toward the latter—he held the brassiere half of the combination at arm's length by each of its wispy straps.

"Wow," he said, gazing at her through it. "I only just now realized how revealing this thing is. That's amazing. Does it really work?"

"Yes," she said, her voice almost inaudible.

He shook his head in obvious admiration, whistling low as he gently fingered the froth of lavender lace. "Boy, you gotta love those guys in research and development, don't you?"

"Do I?"

He nodded. "Modern lingerie technology is clearly making big, *big* strides, isn't it?"

"Is it?" she asked, striving for blandness, again reaching ineffectually toward the garments in question. But Joel simply pulled them back toward himself, just beyond her grasp. Softly she added, "I don't know that I'd use the word 'big' in regard to—"

"And the panties," he interrupted enthusiastically, extending them toward her a bit this time, but still not quite close enough for her to grab them and put an end to her humiliation. "This is what they call a thong bikini, isn't it?"

"Yes," she admitted helplessly.

"I've never seen one this close up before."

"Really?"

"Really."

"I find that rather hard to believe, Mr. Tandem."

"Joel," he corrected her easily, smiling that roguish smile again. "And it's true. I haven't. Why do you find that so hard to believe?"

Instead of pointing out that most leather-wearing, motor-cycle-straddling, drop-dead gorgeous men would doubtless have experienced a rather wide array of women's underthings, she remained silent.

"Abby?" he prodded when she failed to respond. "Why do you doubt me?"

She swallowed hard. "Because." It was a lame reply, but the only one she could put voice to without embarrassing herself more than she was already.

"Because why?"

"Because . . ." She inhaled deeply and released her breath in a ragged rush of air, biting her lip before she could blurt out, *Because you're a gorgeous hunka man who wears leather pants, that's why.* Instead, without thinking, she told him, "Because I find it difficult to believe that an attractive adult male such as yourself would never have encountered at least one thong bikini before."

Oh, nicely done, Abby, she congratulated herself. No way had she compromised herself with that confession.

His smile grew absolutely predatory as he caressed the tiny garment again, rubbing his thumb confidently, even possessively, over the lacy confection. "You think I'm attractive?" he asked in that velvety smooth voice.

How strange that such a big man could be so gentle, she thought as she watched him fondle her underwear. Then she realized that he was coming closer, and suddenly it didn't seem quite so urgent that she rescue her bra from his clutches. No, suddenly it seemed much more imperative that she rescue her*self* from his clutches. So she took a step backward.

And he took a step forward.

So she took another backward.

And he took another forward.

They continued with the impromptu little dance until Abby's back came into direct contact with one of Joel's dining room walls, something that rather impeded her ability to go any farther. Joel, however, still had plenty of opportunity, and he didn't stop moving until nothing more substantial than a breath of air separated them. Still holding on to her underthings, he fisted the hand holding her bra on his hip and settled the one still grasping her panties flat against the wall beside her head.

Abby closed her eyes as the heat of him surrounded her,

but that served only to set her other senses on full alert. When she turned her head to the side, she heard his respiration, its rhythm as rough and rapid as her own. When she inhaled a deep breath to calm herself, she filled her nose and lungs with the scent of him, something earthy and musky and far too masculine for her inexperienced sensibilities. When she licked her lips nervously, she even fancied she could taste him, a mixture of salt and flesh and leather.

"You know," he said softly, his voice rich and intoxicating, "now that I know your underwear so intimately, maybe it's time you and I became better acquainted."

She opened her eyes and turned her head to look at him, his face filling her vision, those mesmerizing midnight blue eyes utterly captivating her. Seemingly without moving, he came even closer, his gaze penetrating hers, his mouth hovering scant millimeters above her own.

"I—I—I," she stammered. She inhaled another gulp of air, but that only filled her nose with the scent of him once more. So she squeezed her eyes shut and tried again. "I—I—I don't think that will be necessary."

"C'mon," he cajoled in that deep, sexy baritone of his. "Have dinner with me. Tonight."

She shook her head. "I, um, I—I—I have other plans." Frantically she scrambled to fabricate an excuse that sounded plausible. But all that came out was, "I have to wash my hair."

Immediately she gave herself a mental slap. *Lame, lame, lame.* Instead of being put off by her idiotic excuse, Joel seemed to be delighted, because he smiled at her again. A toe-curling, hormone-steaming smile that left her completely breathless.

"Maybe I could help you . . . rinse," he said softly.

Oh, *wow,* Abby thought. Her knees went weak as all kinds of hot, liquid things began to gush inside her. She had to get out of there. Joel Tandem was just way too much hombre for her to handle. Candida, she tried to remind herself. What would Candida do in this situation?

Idiot, she berated herself. Candida would have been tangling naked with Joel right there on the dining room floor within two minutes of entering the apartment. How many times did she have to remind herself that Candida, although a lovely and exciting woman, was a complete *figment of her imagination?*

"I gotta go," she said quickly, dipping below Joel's arm and heading straight for the front door.

"But what about your stuff?" he called after her.

So much for a clean escape. "Oh. Yeah. Um . . . do you have a grocery bag or something I can put all this in?"

He smiled that wild-animal smile again, and for a moment she feared—perhaps hoped?—he was going to say something like "I'll wrestle you for it—best two out of three falls." But he remained silent behind that knowing grin and pivoted around to stride easily into his kitchen. When he returned, he was holding open a brown paper sack with her underwear already inside. She was thankful he remained silent as they gathered up the rest of her things.

Then, clutching the bag to her chest, Abby turned to leave. Unfortunately, so did Joel. He followed her, still barefoot, out the front door and into the hallway, all the way to the stairs. When she turned her inquisitive gaze on him, he only shrugged, as if he didn't understand her confusion.

"Good-bye," she said pointedly.

"Your window," he reminded her.

"Oh. I forgot."

"It's the least I can do after having acted as fence for some of your prized possessions."

Not to mention fondling her underwear, she added to herself. But instead of commenting, she only nodded. Joel extended his hand toward the stairs, indicating she should precede him, and she was left with no choice but to comply.

CHAPTER FOUR

Cupid was lounging on the couch in the woman's apartment, watching a Saturday morning trash talk show on cable and thinking he and his mom would make the perfect guests for one of those things—"My Mom Is a Total Love Goddess! Next on *Sally*!"—when he heard the scrape of a doorknob turning. Hastily he fumbled with the remote control—no easy feat when your mother hadn't seen fit to give you opposable thumbs upon casting you down from Mt. Olympus—then knocked it to the ground before he could snap off the TV. He did, however, manage to turn up the volume with the gesture. Way loud, too.

"That's funny," he heard the woman say over the noise. "The TV wasn't on when I left."

She crossed the room quickly and turned it off the old-fashioned way—by pushing the button on the television itself—then moved back toward her companion near the front door. Cupid peeked around the sofa and purred in relief when he saw that she had returned with the man who lived upstairs. Finally. Not only were they in the same room together, but they were even . . . almost . . . touching. And they were definitely looking all gooey-eyed at each other. Yeah, they were on the road to righteous lust all right. Mortals were like . . . *way* predictable.

Any time now, Mom, he thought.

Unfortunately, the minute the man closed the door behind

them, the woman jumped about two feet away from him and fumbled wildly not to drop the paper bag she'd been clutching to her chest. Cupid watched as the man easily recovered the distance, plucked the bag from her grasp, and tossed it casually onto a nearby chair. The woman's eyes widened in panic as the man drew nearer, and she uttered an odd, strangled little cry before dashing to the other side of the room.

Now *this* was getting interesting.

Playing hard to get, was she? Cupid thought. Hmmm ... This might just be a little tougher than he'd planned. Then again, the game wasn't any fun at all if there wasn't *some* kind of challenge to it.

Oh, yeah, he thought as he curled his body around the corner of the sofa and approached the couple, surprised to discover that he was actually kind of enjoying himself. This was definitely getting interesting.

Gleefully Joel closed the front door behind them with a resolute thump, a sound Abby punctuated by jumping nearly a foot in the air. At last he had breached the barricade of her fortress. And, not surprisingly, he'd found it to be everything he'd imagined it would be—warm and inviting and redolent of Laura Ashley.

He couldn't think of a better way to spend a cold, icy, lonely Saturday afternoon than with a warm, enticing, beautiful— albeit puzzling—woman. Even if she was doing everything within her power to maintain a safe distance between them. He wasn't about to be put off by something as insignificant as a little breathing space, especially when where he wanted to be breathing was down the sweater of his hostess.

"Is that the window?" he asked unnecessarily, pointing to the one open a few inches in her dining room.

She nodded quickly and backed away some more.

Joel couldn't help but smile as he took a few steps forward—not toward the dining room, but toward Abby. "Interesting," he murmured. "The fire escape outside *my* apartment is attached to my *bedroom* window."

She cleared her throat a little erratically, took another step away from him, and said, "Why, um, why would you think that I might find that particular fact interesting?"

He shrugged and took another step toward her. This was getting to be kind of fun. "Oh, I don't know," he told her. "Just an observation. FYI and all that. Should you ever find yourself in the mood to, oh, say . . . venture out your dining room window."

"Mr. Tandem—"

"Joel."

"Would you mind having a look at the window?"

He smiled at her nervousness, still wondering about the source of it. "Not at all," he told her.

The ice storm had begun with a whimper, he noted as he approached the window, softly pelting the foggy panes with tiny crystals of ice. Joel braced the heels of his palms against the window sash and pushed up hard, once, twice, three times, before he finally dislodged it. Then he eased it down slowly, settling it back into place and shutting the cold air outside.

For some reason, though, he couldn't quite bring himself to lock it, in spite of the fact that a woman like Abby would doubtless be militant in making sure such things were done before turning in at night. Let *her* be the one to lower that final barrier, he thought. Why should he, when he was the one who was doing everything he could to weaken her battlements? Sheesh.

"There," he said when he was finished. Would that all his life's endeavors turned out as well, with as little effort, he thought. "All better."

"Thank you."

For some reason, Abby's voice seemed softer now, a bit more hollow. When he spun around to look at her, he found her gaze lingering at what would have been his, well . . . his butt . . . when he'd had his back to her. Now that he'd turned around, though, she was staring rather blatantly at his—

"Abby?" he said, swallowing hard.

Her gaze unmoving, she murmured a bit dreamily, "Hmm?"

"I, uh . . ."

For some reason, Joel suddenly forgot what he was going to say. He was far too caught up in studying her face and being thrown by the way it seemed to be all warm and rosy, lit up from the heat of some furnace deep inside her. Wow. He'd never seen a woman's face do something like that before. Certainly not while she was looking at him.

"Abby?" he tried again.

This time her gaze skittered up to his face, and when it did, her eyes widened in panic. "Oh," she murmured. "Oh, dear."

Joel licked his lips, wondering if he should press his luck. "Abby," he tried again, immediately deciding he had absolutely nothing to lose. "I think we need to talk about this thing that's going on between us."

If possible, her eyes grew even larger behind the big frames of her glasses. "Thing? Between . . . us?" she echoed. "But . . . but there is no 'us.' There is no 'thing.' We only just met today."

He shook his head. "Maybe we just met formally today, but you know as well as I do that there's been an 'us'—not to mention a 'thing'—since that first day we ran into each other in the laundry room."

"I don't know what you're talking about."

Her actions belied her words, however, as she hastily dropped her gaze and began to fiddle with the hem of her sweater.

"Oh, I think you do," he countered. "Think about it."

But still she kept her attention fixed to the floor, maintaining her silence in response to his charge.

"If there's nothing between us," he began again, "then how come you're always up waiting for me when I come home from work?"

At last she jerked her head up to look at him, her expression one of abject embarrassment. "I do *not* wait up for you to come home. I work at night, too, sometimes."

"Doing what?" he asked. "I thought you were the Chaucer scholar at Kenwood College."

She narrowed her eyes at him now. "No, I'm the medieval drama scholar at Kenwood. I'm just teaching the Chaucer course while Dr. Morehead is on sabbatical. And how did you know I was teaching Chaucer this semester?''

This time it was Joel's turn to drop his gaze to the floor. ''I, uh . . . I might have glanced at the spring schedule,'' he confessed. ''I was thinking about going for some continuing ed classes in, um . . .''

What? he asked himself. Chaucer? Because in spite of having more than completed his own higher education years ago, he'd given more than half-serious consideration to enrolling in one of Abby's evening classes, just to have an excuse to talk to her. Even if it had to be in iambic pentameter.

''In what?'' she prodded.

''In . . . uh . . . creative writing,'' he threw out impulsively. ''They say everybody has a novel in them, right? And just between you and me, I have one or two stories I could tell.''

''I'll bet.''

Something in her voice eased his tension, mainly because he could see her tensing up herself. Feeling the upper hand slip easily back into his grasp, Joel crossed the dining room.

''You almost sound jealous,'' he said softly.

She shook her head slowly, her gaze fastened on his. ''Not at all. I have no desire to . . . to . . . do whatever it is you do at night all dressed in leather.''

That made him chuckle. ''Why, Abby. I'm flattered you've noticed.''

''I didn't,'' she began, blushing again when she realized how obvious it was that she was lying.

''Did it ever occur to you that the only reason I wear leather is to protect myself from physical harm when I'm on my bike? A motorcycle isn't exactly the safest mode of transportation around, you know.''

''Then why do you ride one?''

He didn't even bother to hide the salacious smile her question stirred. Instead he took another bold step toward her and murmured, ''I *could* say it's because I like to have something hot and shuddering and wild between my legs.'' He laughed, low and leisurely, at her expression when he uttered the remark. Man, but she was skittish. He wondered what—or who—had made her that way. Then he wondered what it would take to tame her. "But the fact of the matter is," he continued easily, "I just don't like being . . . confined."

Oh . . . my . . . God, Abby thought after he'd offered the statement. *He's been in prison.*

Why else would he have made such a comment about being confined? What other confinement was there worth mentioning, other than being convicted to a penitentiary? Oh, dear. *Oh,* dear. Oh, *dear.*

"Mr. Tandem—"

"Joel," he corrected her. Again.

But Abby wasn't going to fall for it. Nuh-uh. No way. Nohow. The only thing more self-destructive than getting involved with a man who wore leather pants would be getting involved with an ex-con who wore leather pants.

"Thank you for fixing my window," she said as politely as she could. "Good-bye."

She started to reach for the doorknob, then realized that it was behind him. Her brain noticed that fact long before her body did, however, because her arm kept reaching forward even as her mind urged her to pull back. In the end, she wound up stopping only because she'd barreled headfirst into Joel. Immediately he jerked up his hands to steady her, curling his fingers gently over her shoulders.

Gee, for an ex-con he certainly had a soft touch. And he smelled good, too, she noted further, fighting to keep herself from burying her nose in the hollow of his neck. Clean and fresh, like Ivory Soap—ninety-nine and forty-four one-hundredths percent pure. Inevitably she found herself wondering what the other fifty-six one-hundredths were. Something impure, obviously, she decided. Because there was nothing at all refined about the way he was making her feel at the moment.

"Mr. Tandem," she tried once more, marveling at the deep, husky quality her voice seemed to have suddenly adopted.

"Joel," he stated emphatically again, brushing his fingertips slowly, rhythmically, hypnotically, over her shoulder blades. "Call me Joel."

"Joel," she repeated in a hoarse whisper. Good heavens, but the man was potent.

He grinned at her capitulation, then lifted one hand to her temple, gently removed her glasses, and placed them carefully on the table beside them. Then, just as she realized his intention, but before she had a chance to object—not that she necessarily wanted to object—he lowered his head to hers. A voice inside told her that what was happening had been coming since the moment he'd sauntered into the Archer Arms laundry room three months ago, looking so incongruous—and endearing—in his black T-shirt and leather pants, with a basket of dirty underwear tucked beneath one arm.

She remembered thinking at that moment that he was every woman's fantasy—a bad boy with a box of Biz.

And then Abby couldn't think at all, because Joel's lips grazed her own, warmly, tenderly, and again she was overcome by the puzzle of the tough exterior that housed such a seemingly gentle disposition. Almost gracefully he dipped the fingers of one hand inside her sweater to waltz them along her collarbone, then skimmed them higher to curve over the warm, naked skin of her neck. And when a wild little cry escaped her, he silenced her by covering her mouth completely with his own.

Oh. Oh, my. Oh, my goodness.

Abby's eyes fluttered closed, and she felt herself go limp at the murmuring brush of his mouth against her own.

His lips on hers began as a mere caress, a leisurely stroke back and forth . . . back and forth . . . back and forth . . . Then, unbidden, she felt him pull back. She was about to open her eyes and cry out an objection when he moved his entire body forward and looped his arm around her waist to pull her body flush with his own. Then he curled the fingers of his other hand around her nape, urging her closer still. And then he was moving against her from shoulder to knee, abrading her from chest to thigh, taking her mouth more completely with his . . .

And then Abby did go limp.

But Joel was there to catch her, holding her more tightly, kissing her more insistently. When she gasped at his forwardness, he thrust his tongue into her mouth, and she went utterly still. Over and over he tasted her, more and more deeply with every turn. The hand at her waist crept higher, opening over her back, pushing her forward, more fully into his embrace. And all Abby could do was stand there, feeling hot and greedy, succumbing to the euphoria that overtook her.

She opened her own hands over his chest, one reveling in the soft, worn fabric of his shirt, the other dallying in the crisp dark hair beneath it. His heartbeat thrummed rapidly under the pad of her thumb, his skin hot and rigid beneath her fingertips. And still he kissed her, again and again, until she could scarcely remember who she was.

But she *could* remember who he was. A big, strong man with a questionable background, one who dressed in black and lived at night. A man she barely knew, in spite of the dizzying way he made her feel, and one a woman like her was totally incapable of handling. With what little sense and reason she had left, Abby reminded herself of all those things, and somehow she found the strength to push herself away from him. Hard.

Surprisingly, he let her go. But his release hadn't come easily, she could tell. His breathing, like hers, was quick and uneven, and she wondered if he, too, felt the electric charge of a live wire like the one that was shuddering through her. His eyes were wild with unfulfilled need, and she suspected that her own face reflected the evidence of her equally unrequited desire.

. Desire. It had been a long time since she'd been so overcome with it. Perhaps she'd never quite felt it in the abundance she did now. Joel Tandem, whoever he was, made her want. Badly. Things she really had no business wanting. She just wished he were the kind of man from whom she could take.

But that, she was sure, would be a mistake. Because he was the kind of man who gave freely for the moment, but whose resources doubtless dried up in no time at all. Abby's experience with men was in no way extensive. But she'd learned a lot from the letters she received as Candida. And for women like her, men like Joel were the most dangerous kind. Seductive. Charming. Tempestuous. But also capricious. Risky. And temporary.

In short, he would be the perfect lover for Candida. But he would wreck Abby's life completely.

"That . . . " she began, her voice raspy and harsh and completely unfamiliar. She cleared her throat, inhaled deeply, and tried again. "That shouldn't have happened," she finally managed to say.

"Why not?" Joel immediately asked her, his own voice none too smooth.

"Because." She squeezed her eyes shut even as she uttered the one-word reason, knowing it was totally inadequate for what had just happened but unable to come up with a better one.

He nodded, then ran his tongue slowly across his lower lip, as if he were savoring the flavor she had left behind. "Because," he repeated blandly. "That's a conveniently vague reason. Tell me, do you ever really come up with an explanation to go along with it? Or do you just hide behind it without ever questioning it?"

Abby hauled herself up with as much dignity as she could muster, then assured him, "I have a perfectly good explanation to go along with it."

His eyes flashed with a dark warning. "Oh? I'd like to hear it."

She turned her chin up a fraction more. "It's personal."

"In that case, I'd *love* to hear it."

"Well, you won't."

"Why not?"

"Like I said. It's personal. And you're a virtual stranger."

His lips twisted into a wry smile. "Yeah, well, in case you hadn't noticed, I was kind of doing my damnedest to change that."

Abby said nothing. Instead she snatched her glasses from the table and settled them back on her nose, then met his gaze as coolly as she could—which was no easy feat, considering her insides were still on fire.

In response to her silence, Joel only shook his head. "Guess there's no reason for me to hang around,'' he said softly.

"No, I suppose there's not," she agreed.

She hadn't realized she still stood within arm's length of him—not until he lifted a hand and skimmed the backs of his knuckles along the line of her jaw. The touch caught her by surprise, not just because it was unexpected, but because it was so gentle. Again she was struck by the way his outward appearance masked what seemed to be a tender interior. But gentleness and tenderness didn't necessarily equal devotion, she reminded herself. And he was moving far too quickly for her to make any rational decisions.

"See ya later, Abby," he said quietly as he dropped his hand back to his side.

She swallowed hard, then, almost silently, she told him, "Good-bye."

For a moment she thought he was going to stay, because he didn't move at all. He just stood with his hands settled on his hips, his gaze fixed on her face, as if he were thinking very hard about something. Then he shook his head almost imperceptibly and pivoted around. Without a further word, without looking back, without even a minor hesitation, he strode to the door and tugged it open, then left without a backward glance.

Oh, man. Bummer.

Cupid twitched his whiskers as he watched the kiss that had promised to be his ticket back to Mt. Olympus fizzle out and die. Without thinking about what he was doing, he scurried to follow Joel out before he closed the door completely. He wasn't sure what he was going to do, but since Abby was clearly the unwilling party here, it was probably pointless to hang around with *her*. So he trotted along behind the male half of the mortal couple, scrambling for plan B, wondering why plan A had backfired in the first place.

Abby was clearly scared of something, but Cupid couldn't figure out what. This Joel dude seemed like a nice enough guy. For a grownup. And his motorcycle was way, *way* cool.

So it must be some hangup with her. But what?

Suddenly he regretted leaving with Joel. He was about to turn tail—literally—and try to meow his way back into Abby's good graces, but Joel suddenly halted and spun around. For a moment Cupid thought his mortal companion was going to go back and fight like a man. In fact, Joel did take a step back toward Abby's place. But just as suddenly he changed his mind again and turned back toward the stairs.

Curious now, Cupid followed. He didn't think Joel had even noticed his presence until the man opened his own front door and waited inside for the cat to join him. When they had both retreated inside, he closed the door behind them, clearly lost in thought. But Joel never said a word as he fell back onto the sofa and stared up at the ceiling.

Maybe, Cupid thought as he watched Joel gaze up at nothing, the secret lay with him, after all.

CHAPTER FIVE

*T*hat night, long past dark, as the sky continued to scatter ice against the windows, Joel sat in his apartment, sulking. No sense trying to get to work, he thought. Not only were the roads completely impassable, but his earlier, dissatisfying little impromptu with Abby had left him feeling anything but productive. No, the last thing on his mind tonight was work. Instead he was pretty much consumed by a preoccupation with his downstairs neighbor.

"Wow, what a woman" didn't even begin to cover his reaction to that kiss. As hard as he'd tried to recall, he couldn't remember ever experiencing an atomic meltdown quite like that with anyone else in his life. And no matter how many times he replayed the scene in his head, he couldn't think of a single reason for Abby's sudden withdrawal. She'd seemed to be having as good a time as he, and she'd certainly joined in the fun readily enough. So just what, exactly, had gone wrong?

He started to rerun the scene in his head—again—but when he felt a certain part of himself jump to life—again—he decided that he might be better off thinking about something else for now. Idly he reached for the copy of *Cavalier* that was sitting on his coffee table, then flipped through the magazine until his attention settled on an article entitled "What Do Women *Really* Want, Anyway?"

Good question, he thought. Unfortunately the article's female author did absolutely nothing to answer it. Uttering an exasperated sound, Joel tossed the magazine back onto the table. And when he did, almost as if by magic, it flipped itself open to "Candida's Room."

Helplessly he picked up the magazine again and glanced over the featured questions for the month. Now that Candida, he thought, *she* knew about men. Why couldn't he find a woman like her? When he came to the end of the column, he noticed the little paragraph in italics that was always there. However, instead of ignoring it as he usually did, he took the time to study it.

"Got a problem with your sex life?" the paragraph began. "Looking for a little romance? Can't figure out what it is women want? Tell Candida all about it. Write me c/o the magazine. Or, if you're in a hurry, e-mail me: Candida@cavalier4men.com. I do so look forward to hearing your wildest dreams."

Joel had never considered himself the Dear Abby type—or the Dear Candida type, for that matter—but something about Candida's come-on inspired him. Hey, she was a woman who could appreciate a man, right? And she did, in every column she wrote. Maybe she'd understand where he was coming from.

Nevertheless, he felt like an idiot as he approached the laptop computer in his bedroom and switched it on. He tried to reassure himself that there was nothing wrong with what he was about to do, that there must be hundreds—perhaps thousands—of men in America who wrote to Candida every month. He sat down, pulled up his Internet access, highlighted the "Compose Mail" selection, and clicked the mouse onto the "To:" box. For one long moment, though, his fingers only hovered over the keyboard, unmoving, as he gazed at the almost blank screen.

Then his new feline companion jumped onto the desk and sat himself contentedly beside the computer, gazing at the flickering cursor on the screen. When he turned to look at Joel, the cat's expression seemed to be saying silently, "Yeah, so? What are you waiting for?"

"Nothing," Joel told the cat, wondering if he was really beginning to lose it, talking to an animal. Then, shoving aside his worries for the moment, and with a chuckle that was more than a little anxious, he forced himself to type out "Candida@cavalier4men.com . . ."

Abby really hated winter. There was nothing worse than the cold and damp and snow that plagued New England for months on end. It was a cold that seemed to settle into her body for the winter, chilling her to the bone with relentless glee. As she steeped her chamomile tea, inhaling deeply of the clean, soothing aroma, she resigned herself to not feeling warm again until well into June.

Oh, you could be warm in no time at all, and you know it, a voice deep inside her piped up unbidden. *Just call that yummy Joel Tandem to come down and kiss you senseless again. That'll warm you up big time.*

She told the voice to shut up and go away but knew she couldn't deny the reminder. Maybe that was why the cold outside that had crept inside was so much more insufferable than usual. Because now she knew there was an alternative. Joel Tandem was one hunka hunka burnin' love, no two ways about it. A man like him would never make a woman feel cold and lonely. Not as long as he was with her, anyway. Not until after he left her.

Not until he got sent up the river for five to life.

She pushed away the thought as she went to retrieve the bottle of Stolichnaya she kept in the cabinet beside the refrigerator and carefully measured out the usual two fingers for her tea. Then, as an afterthought, before recapping the bottle, she sloshed a generous addition to the brew. What the hey, she thought. With all that ice outside, she wouldn't be going anywhere for a while.

Plus, she still had work to do. She needed one more letter for Candida's column, then she could e-mail that puppy off to her editor and not worry about another one for a couple of weeks. But the list of letters and e-mail she'd saved for this month hadn't really been up to Candida's usual challenge, so

Abby decided to check her e-mail from the magazine, in the hope that there was something she could use there.

Within a matter of minutes she'd downloaded more than a dozen new inquiries, and she scrolled through them casually as she sipped her tea, letting the temperature of the beverage and the false heat of the vodka warm her. The window beside her grew foggy with the steam that curled up from her mug, ice pelted the glass softly, and she wondered what had happened to her cat.

Then a letter caught her attention.

The return address was JoJaJe@NECom.com, not one she recognized. Many of Candida's letters came from a small pool of regulars that Abby had dubbed "The Usual Suspects." Even beyond those, she had an uncanny ability to recognize repeat offenders. This was definitely a new one. Her interest piqued, she opened the file and read:

> Dear Candida, There's this woman in my apartment building I'm crazy about, and I'm fairly certain she's crazy about me. So what's my problem? Every time I come anywhere near her, she gets edgy as a skittish cat and bolts. I'm a nice guy with no social, medical, or political embarrassments in my past or present. So what gives?

It was signed "Finishing Last."

Abby narrowed her eyes as a thrill of electricity shot through her, and she couldn't help but wonder if the timely appearance of the missive was a coincidence or something more. Another look at the return address offered her no real clue to the writer's identity, except for the fact that NECom.com was a local Internet server. And "Joel" did begin with "Jo," just as the return address of the letter's author did.

Of course, the "JaJe" part of the address had nothing to do with "Joel" or "Tandem," and NECom.com served a good portion of eastern Massachusetts, including the millions of people in the Boston area. Certainly there was nothing else there to suggest the letter had originated with her upstairs neighbor. Even the reference to a cat didn't necessarily mean anything in particular.

· Too, the content of the letter was anything but unusual. There were *a lot* of men out there who were absolutely convinced that the object of their affections must *of course* return their loving feelings, regardless of how icky the letter writers probably were in real life.

In the scheme of things, the chances that this letter came from Joel Tandem were pretty slim, she told herself. In spite of that, something about the guy's plight touched a tender spot inside Abby. She assured herself it was only because of her own experience with Joel that afternoon. Maybe Finishing Last really was finishing last. It happened to the best of nice guys.

The letter wasn't one she could use for her column—it wasn't nearly demented enough—but it deserved an answer. If nothing else, she could reassure the writer in a way that would bolster his ego without making him further hassle the woman, who obviously *didn't* welcome his overtures. So Abby sipped her tea a few more times and moved the cursor over to the reply button. But instead of clicking the mouse, she let her finger linger on the button for a moment as she considered the options for her reply.

Then she nearly had a heart attack when she saw a face at her window again. Because this time it wasn't a cute, cuddly, furry face with a little pink triangle nose. It was the face of a man, one who was shivering, wet, and obviously very angry.

Immediately Abby leapt up from her chair and shoved open the window, trying to shake off the feeling of déjà vu that washed over her. Two nights in a row rescuing refugees did not a habit make, she told herself. Still, it was with more than a little trepidation that she watched a bedraggled Joel Tandem crawl through her window and land in a heap on her dining room/office floor.

"What on earth are you doing out there?" she asked as he pushed himself up on his hands and knees.

When he rose, he was shuddering like a jackhammer, the clothes he'd worn earlier that day—or rather yesterday, Abby realized as she glanced at the clock—clinging to him like a frigid second skin. She pulled the lapels of her pink chenille robe more snugly around her, feeling her own temperature plummet as she gazed at her iced-over guest.

Before he answered her, Joel reached for the window, hesitating before he closed it. "Well?" he said crossly to someone on the other side. "Are you coming in or not?"

She opened her mouth to inquire as diplomatically as she could into the status of his mental health, when a buff-colored streak of wet cat bulleted through the window in response to his question. Only then did Joel shove the window back down into place and turn to glare at the bedraggled blob of soaked fur that had seated himself in the middle of the dining room.

"Uh, Joel?" Abby tried again.

He grumbled some ripe curses under his breath at the animal, then turned his angry gaze on her. "What?" he barked.

She eyed him warily in return. "What were you doing out on my fire escape?"

He sighed, shivered some more, then raked his long fingers restlessly through his wet hair. "Actually, Abby, that fire escape belongs to all of us who live on this side of the building. So if you want to get technical about it, it's *our* fire escape."

She frowned at him, miffed that he was still trying to join the two of them as a unit, however dubiously. "Okay, what were you doing out on *our* fire escape, in the middle of the night, in the middle of an ice storm?"

He inhaled deeply, fisted one hand on his hip, jerked up his chin defiantly, and thrust a finger at the cat. "Maybe you better ask *him* that question."

Without missing a beat, Abby turned to the cat. "Okay, Buffy, what were you and Joel doing out on the fire escape at this time of night, in weather that's fit for neither man nor beast?"

Oh, yeah. She'd definitely overdone it on the Stolichnaya tonight. A ripple of whimsy wound through Abby, and she bit back a giggle. If she didn't know better, she'd swear the cat was mad at her for calling him "Buffy."

She turned back to Joel. "Buffy's not talking."

Joel rolled his eyes. "Yeah, well, he should be. That damned cat is nearly human."

The cat uttered a low, rowdy sound at that, as if he'd just been handed the ultimate insult. Abby and Joel both turned to glare at him this time, but he glanced haughtily away.

"What is going on?" she demanded again.

Joel continued to look at the cat as he spoke. "Buffy there went to my bedroom window a little while ago and started scratching on it like he wanted to go out. I figured he had to ... you know ... answer the call of nature or something. Since I didn't want cat ... stuff ... on my floor, I opened the window for him. And since it was so cold and icy out, I left the window open so he could get back in when he was done. But he didn't come back."

Now he turned to look at Abby, still wet, still shivering, still obviously freezing to death.

"I'm sorry," she apologized. She waved a hand toward her kitchen. "You must be half-frozen. You want some hot chamomile tea?"

He glanced in the direction she indicated, where the evidence of her usual nightly concoction still sat on the counter. "No thanks," he told her. "But I'll have a shot or two of that Stoli, if you don't mind."

"You need to put on some dry clothes," she told him as she crossed to the kitchen.

"Yeah, well, that's going to be kind of hard to do, seeing as how I'm locked out of my apartment."

Abby halted as she reached into one of her cabinets for a juice glass, her fingers convulsing over a delicate tumbler. "Locked out?" she repeated as she uncapped the bottle of vodka and splashed a generous amount into the glass. "How could you be locked out?"

When she turned, Joel was glaring at the cat again. "I don't know," he said. "Only *he* can answer that question."

Abby strode carefully toward Joel again but maintained an arm's length as she pressed the glass into his hand. Immediately he lifted it to his lips and threw back his head, draining the full amount in a matter of seconds.

He grimaced as he swallowed, then expelled a long, satisfied sigh. "Oh, yeah. That helps."

"More?" Abby asked halfheartedly.

He nodded as he handed the glass back to her. "Yeah. Make it a double."

"That was a double."

"Then make this one a quadruple."

She opened her mouth to object, but the look on his face warned her not to. So she only reiterated her earlier suggestion. "I still say you need to get out of those clothes."

A warm, wonderful, *wicked* smile curled his lips at her statement. "Why, Abby, I didn't think you cared."

"I mean, uh . . ." Her voice trailed off through several time zones as she scrambled to cover her gaffe.

Obviously taking pity on her, Joel didn't press the issue. Instead he asked, "Mind if I use your phone to call Billy-the-Super?"

She shook her head eagerly. "No. Of course not. He's on the speed dial. Number two."

Joel moved over to her desk and lifted the receiver. "Who's number one?" he asked as he waited for a reply from the other end of the line.

"My mother."

He nodded with a knowing grin, as if that news came as no surprise at all. What was likewise no surprise at all was that Billy-the-Super wasn't answering his phone, so Joel had to leave a message. When he hung up, he plucked at the collar of his shirt and said, "You know, this really is uncomfortable. And Billy-the-Super probably won't get around to calling back for another two or three days. Do you mind . . . ?"

Abby stared at him dumbfounded for a moment, completely mired in denial. What, exactly, was he trying to tell her? she wondered. Surely not what she suspected he was trying to tell her. "Do I mind . . . ?" she asked.

He stared back at her in silence, his expression not unlike that of a koala bear high on eucalyptus. "Uh . . . " he began eloquently. "I'd like to take my clothes off," he announced for clarification. "All of them. Do you have anything I could wear?"

"Uh . . . " she replied just as eloquently. "No."

"Uh, no, you don't have anything for me to wear?" he asked. "Or uh, no, don't take my clothes off?"

"Yes."

"What?"

"That."

"What?" he repeated, his exasperation clearly multiplying. "The nothing-for-me-to-wear thing, or the don't-take-off-my-clothes thing?"

"Both."

He chewed the inside of his jaw for a minute, then, obviously unconcerned about her concern, began to unbutton what few buttons on his shirt were fastened. "Abby," he said as he peeled his shirt off his magnificent torso, "I'm freezing my butt off here. No offense, but either get me something to wear, or we're going to be *very* intimately acquainted in less than a minute."

CHAPTER SIX

*A*bby widened her eyes in panic at Joel's assertion, then, when she saw that he was perfectly serious, bolted from the dining room. A quick search of her closet, which she knew would be fruitless, was fruitless. Although a couple of her Carole Littles—which she had deliberately bought big to enhance the flow of the design—were the perfect color for him, she decided some of the prints were just a tad too bold. So, as a last resort, she snatched the heavy Wedgwood blue cotton throw from her rocking chair and raced back out to where she'd left him. Feeling like a trembling debutante—except for the fact that she'd never been to a cotillion in her life—she covered her glasses with her open hand as she held out the throw at arm's length. Which was redundant, really, since she also had her eyes closed. Still, no sense taking chances.

"Are you decent?" she asked.

A moment of silence greeted her, then she heard his deep voice coming from much closer than she'd anticipated. "Um, define 'decent.' "

"Never mind," she said hastily, blindly thrusting the throw in the general direction of his voice.

He took it from her right away, and she heard the soft whuffle of fabric brushing along bare skin. Swallowing hard again, she tried not to panic at the realization that there was, quite simply, a naked man in her apartment.

"Okay," he said after a moment. "I'm covered."

Slowly, reluctantly, she dropped her hand from in front of her glasses and opened her eyes, hoping her gaze would fall on something that wasn't Joel. Unfortunately, like two heat-seeking missiles, her eyes were drawn immediately to him. To his chest. To his naked chest. To his naked, incredibly sexy chest. Oh, dear.

"I—I—I wouldn't exactly say you're covered," she stammered quietly.

He glanced down at himself, wrapped from waist to midcalf in Wedgwood blue, then back up at Abby. And he shrugged with much nonchalance. "I got all the naughty parts, didn't I?"

That, she decided quickly, was a matter of opinion.

"I—I—I," she tried again. That incorrigible, damnably knowing smile he kept throwing at her didn't help matters at all. She inhaled a deep, fortifying breath, then boldly ventured forward. "Why-yi-yi don't I run down to the laundry room and put your clothes in the dry-yi-yier?" she said in a rush of words.

"That's okay," he told her, shrugging off her offer, swirling his vodka absently in his glass. "I just draped them over the radiator. That'll probably dry them as fast as anything would."

Yes, but then she would be stranded in the same room with him, Abby thought. And that just would not do at all. Especially when every little move he made orchestrated a veritable ballet in his torso. Her gaze was riveted to the ripples and bumps of muscle and sinew even the rich spattering of black hair could do nothing to hide. Try as she might to close her eyes and think of something else, all she could do was stand there and stare at Joel. Stare at him and hope that she didn't start drooling and yammering incoherently, like a sexual dynamo churning at peak production with a stark, raving hunger in the factory of love.

Wow, she thought as the image materialized more fully in her brain, that was good. She'd have to remember that for Candida's column. Instinctively she moved toward her desk to retrieve a pen and pad of paper. She always forgot the good stuff unless she wrote it down.

"What are you doing?" Joel asked as she scribbled the thought over a few blue lines of notebook paper.

She held up one index finger to silence him so she wouldn't get distracted. "Peak production . . . raving hunger . . . in the factory . . . of . . . love," she mumbled absently as she finished recording the phrase. She tore the page from the pad of paper, folded it about twenty times, and stuffed it into the pocket of her robe.

Only then did she remember that she had a naked man in her apartment, and her pulse rate, which had begun to slow once she'd become preoccupied, began to race once again.

" 'Factory of love'?" he echoed. "What the hell does that mean?"

She squeezed her eyes shut in mortification that she had actually spoken her thoughts aloud. "Nothing," she said quickly, glancing guiltily around the room as she tossed the pad of paper back on the desk.

"You just wrote that down," Joel said, clearly unwilling to let the subject drop. "What does it mean?"

"Uh . . ." She scrambled for some excuse. "Nothing," she insisted. "It was a, um . . . a reminder. Yeah, that's it. I just remembered that I'm out of milk, and I, um, I started a grocery list."

" 'Factory of love' is a reminder to buy milk?" he asked doubtfully.

She nodded quickly but didn't elaborate. Instead, to emphasize her point, she withdrew the piece of paper from her pocket, unfolded it, and began to write again as she murmured, "Eggs . . . bread . . . bagels . . ."

"Cat food," he added helpfully.

"Right," she said without looking up, punctuating the word by jabbing the air with her pencil.

"Wine, candles, T-bone steaks," he continued. "Bubble bath, pudding, whipped cream . . ."

Abby stopped writing and looked up to find him smiling. And still half-naked. "I beg your pardon?" she asked.

He shrugged, all those muscles quivering again. She closed her eyes. "Just trying to help you out with the menu."

She opened her eyes and focused her attention on a cobweb dangling from the dining room archway behind him. "What menu?" she asked.

"For when you invite me to dinner."

"But I'm not inviting you to dinner."

"Fine. Then I'll invite *you* to dinner."

"No, thank you."

He sighed in what she could only liken to exasperation, and that was when she remembered that, speaking of exasperation, she still didn't know how he'd come to be locked out of his apartment and settled nicely into hers. For some reason, she glanced down at the cat, who had moved closer to the radiator himself and who was lapping contentedly at a paw. As if he noted her perusal, however, the cat snapped his head up and met Abby's gaze levelly. Something in his blue eyes tugged at her soul, and a frisson of strange electricity sizzled down her spine.

Shaking off the odd sensation, she tossed the pad of paper onto her desk and turned back to Joel. "Will you *please* tell me what you were doing out on the fire escape?" she asked.

Joel shook his head slowly, annoyed that Abby fought so desperately what he was beginning to think was completely inevitable. He lifted the juice glass to his lips, sipped a bit less greedily this time, then closed his eyes as he felt the heat wind through him. Not so much to better enable him to enjoy the soothing warmth, but because the sight of Abby Walden in her jammies was just too much for him to bear.

How any woman could make flannel and that fuzzy stuff on her bathrobe look sexy was beyond him. But even when he'd been fairly encrusted with ice, seeing her all dressed for bed had steamed up his insides faster than a sauna would have. Now, as he opened his eyes again, all he could do was wonder if the skin beneath her winter trappings was as pink and warm and soft-looking as her face was at the moment. And he discovered, not much to his surprise, that he really, really, *really* wanted to find out.

"It's the damnedest thing," he said in response to her question, shoving aside his curiosity about what lay under Abby's robe. For now. "Like I was saying, Buffy went out, and when he didn't come back, I went to the window to see where he was." He shrugged a bit sheepishly. "I was worried about him. Then I heard him meowing, this really pitiful meow, way off in the distance somewhere. I was afraid he'd hurt himself. So I climbed out the window to see if I could find him."

"Dressed like that?" Abby asked. "Without even putting on shoes and socks?"

He expelled an incredulous sound. "I was afraid he was hurt," he repeated, wondering why she had trouble grasping the concept. "I didn't waste any time getting dressed."

Her mouth dropped open and she gaped at him, as if she couldn't believe he'd said what he'd just said. Joel brushed off his irritation that she could find his intense concern for an animal so incredible and continued with his explanation.

"I got halfway up the fire escape when I realized the sound was coming from the ground instead of the roof, which was what it had sounded like at first. It took forever for me to climb down—the steps are coated with ice—but when I got back to my apartment, there sat Buffy, wet and cold, but happy as you please otherwise, right outside my window." He paused meaningfully before adding, "My *closed* window. My *locked* window."

Abby eyed him warily at that. "How did that happen?"

"I have no idea. It was as if Buffy closed and locked it himself or something."

"That's impossible," Abby pointed out. "He doesn't have opposable thumbs. Not to mention the strength to manage it."

Joel thrust one of his own opposable thumbs over his shoulder, toward the window through which he had just come. "Look, if you don't believe me, then you can climb back up there and check it out for yourself."

For a moment he thought she was going to take him up on his suggestion, but the soft skitter of ice against the windowpane seemed to make her change her mind. "No. That won't be necessary. I believe you."

Simultaneously they turned their attention to the cat. Under their perusal, he halted his grooming and stared back at them.

He blinked once, a slow, self-satisfied blink, then lifted his other paw and, still watching them, began to lap at it and rub it over his ear.

"He doesn't seem to be any the worse for wear," Abby noted unnecessarily.

Joel shook his head again, still mystified by what had happened. "It just doesn't make any sense. I mean, that window *is* kind of loose, so I can almost convince myself that it would have fallen back down into place. But how could it get locked from the inside?"

Abby shrugged. "Maybe the lock is loose, too? Maybe the jolt of the window falling knocked it into lock mode?"

Joel emitted a single chuckle completely lacking in humor. "Yeah, sure. And maybe I'll be a Supreme Court Justice someday."

"Not with your rec—"

Abby slapped a hand over her mouth before completing whatever odd comment she had been about to make, and Joel narrowed his eyes at her when he noted the panic in her eyes.

"Not with my what?" he asked.

But she only shook her head hard and remained silent.

"No, come on," he cajoled. "You were going to say something. What?"

"Nothing," she said quickly. A little *too* quickly. "That, uh, that just popped out. It wasn't important. Honest."

Joel eyed her suspiciously but didn't push. "Look, I apologize for the intrusion," he told her. "I know it's after midnight, and you were probably on your way to bed."

She blushed furiously at what should have been a completely innocent statement. Joel did his best to ignore it, but he knew that her thoughts were probably running pretty parallel to his own. Which meant that she was most likely feeling nearly as hot and bothered as he was, in spite of the frightful weather outside.

"So," he began again, nearly choking on the word, "don't let me keep you up. I can wait out here for Billy-the-Super to call." He glanced over at her computer. "Nice setup," he said, feeling a ripple of envy at the elaborate, state-of-the-art system. "Hey, you got *Myst* by any chance? Or *Doom?* That'd pass the time while I wait. I'm kind of a night owl anyway."

He started toward the computer, where a screen saver that scrolled the message *Call your mother. . . . Call your mother. . . . Call your mother. . . .* rambled slowly across the screen. He smiled as he reached for the mouse and skidded it along the pad.

"No!" Abby screeched from behind him.

The screen filled with words typed in standard Courier 12 as she blurted out the warning. Startled by her vehemence, he spun around so quickly that he almost lost the big coverlet he had wrapped around his midsection, catching it loosely just before it drooped dangerously low. "What?" he shouted in surprise. "What'd I do?"

Abby bolted toward the computer and placed herself stiffly between it and Joel. "Just . . . don't touch it. Don't touch anything."

Somehow he knew she was talking about a lot more than her computer. "Okay," he conceded. Nevertheless, his gaze was unavoidably drawn to the words she seemed so desperate to hide. When she volleyed her body to block his vision, he frowned. "I'm sorry. I didn't know you and your computer were intimately involved."

She swallowed visibly. "I'm just very particular about my work. Okay?"

"Okay."

He started to retuck the coverlet around his waist, noting from the corner of his eye that Abby seemed to be taking an inordinate amount of interest in his activities. So much interest, in fact, that she relaxed her body some to reveal the screen behind her again. He was halfway tempted to just drop the damned throw to the floor and give her a real show. Another shot of that Stoli, and he just might.

Then he caught sight of a word on the computer screen beyond Abby, a very distinctive word, one whose significance only he and about a million kids in America would recognize: "JoJaJe." For one moment he only stood, staring at that word in total confusion. Then he forced his gaze lower and saw two more words of momentous importance: "Dear Candida." As understanding dawned, a burst of fireworks backfired in his belly, and he cupped a fist loosely over his mouth.

Abby must have noted his monumental shock, because he heard her voice, as if from a very great distance, ask, "Joel? Is something wrong?"

Unable to utter a word in response, he only remained silent as he pondered his current predicament. Trapped during an ice storm, all but naked, with a beautiful, pajama-clad woman whom he'd been lusting after for months, a woman he'd just learned was none other than Candida, the object of every *Cavalier* reader's fantasy life, and he had completely frozen up. What on earth could make the situation any worse?

As if playing a bad joke, the lights flickered, dimmed, and went out.

"Oh, no. No, no, no," he heard Abby say helplessly through the darkness.

And then he felt the clingy wet fur of a damp cat rubbing affectionately around his ankles.

Okay, so they needed a bigger nudge than the average mortal, Cupid thought as he wound first around Joel's legs and then headed for Abby's. The total darkness should do the trick, although he was frankly surprised he'd been able to manage it. He'd been afraid he'd used up every ounce of his power to arrange for that locked window upstairs. Puberty really messed with a god's abilities, man.

Now if he could just come up with some way to get Abby to ditch those lame pajamas and that stupid robe. As soon as the thought materialized, the hiss of the radiator provided him an answer. If he could just corral a little bit more of his power—or, better yet, if the heat control on that thing was loose, thereby disposing of the whole opposable-thumb problem—then maybe, just maybe, he could really heat things up in this apartment. . . .

CHAPTER SEVEN

"You're Candida?"

The question was completely unexpected, came at Abby through total darkness, and hit her like a ton of tacky fan mail. "What?" she asked, her voice barely audible, even to her own ears.

"You're Candida."

This time Joel uttered the two words as a statement, not a question, and she felt something tighten inside her. She struggled frantically to adjust her eyes to the darkness, but not even a sliver of moonlight eased the velvet blackness surrounding them. When she felt a nudge against her calf, she nearly jumped out of her skin. Then, when she understood that it was the cat, and not Joel, who had caressed her, she felt inexplicably disappointed.

"Abby?" His voice sliced through the darkness again.

"What?" she asked.

"You're Candida, the columnist for *Cavalier* magazine, aren't you?"

"Wh-why do you say that?" she said, stalling.

"Because just before the power went out, I saw what was on your computer screen." His voice seemed to draw nearer as he spoke. "It was a letter to Candida."

"You saw that?"

"I saw that."

"You're sure?"

"I'm sure."

"Oh." In a sudden burst of inspiration she asked, "Well, how do you know that wasn't a letter I was *writing* to Candida?"

His reply was a soft, disembodied, "Oh, I know."

"Oh."

Even though she had been the last one to speak, Abby knew Joel was waiting for her to say something more. Unfortunately, for the life of her, she had no idea what to say. Although Candida's true identity was a well-kept secret at *Cavalier*, both to protect Abby from any potential weirdos and to boost sales by promoting a sexual mystique that was every man's fantasy, the fact that one person had learned the truth didn't necessarily spell disaster. Not for the magazine, at any rate. For Abby, well . . .

Frankly, she wasn't sure what this meant. Joel seemed like a nice enough man, in spite of his criminal record. Of course, she thought further, that probably kind of depended on what, exactly, his crime had been.

"Are you going to admit the truth or not?"

His voice was definitely closer than it had been before, she thought. Still, she couldn't answer him. But Joel didn't seem to need her verification of his charge, because he continued speaking as if she had just assured him that yes, she was in fact Candida, and it was just *so* nice to make his acquaintance, especially in the dark this way, when he was, for all intents and purposes, naked.

"I can't believe it," he said softly, his tone of voice belying nothing of what he might be thinking. "All this time, I've been picturing you as a blonde."

His comment reminded Abby that there was another reason she'd wanted to keep Candida's identity a secret. If she ever met a man she found interesting, who was likewise interested in her—a long shot, certainly, but not completely outside the realm of possibility—she'd wanted to be sure that man cared about her as Abby, not as Candida. And even though she told herself that Joel was in no way the kind of man who would interest her, something hard and cold settled in her midsection at his assertion.

"I'm not Candida," she told him outright.

"Abby, don't bother to deny it. I just saw for myself that you—"

"I'm not Candida," she repeated.

"But I saw—"

"Candida doesn't exist," she interrupted him. "She's imaginary. There is no Candida."

There was a moment of silence, then Joel said, "You know what I meant."

"Yes, I know what you meant. And I'm sorry to disappoint you, but there is no Candida."

"Hey, Abby, *some*body's been writing those columns."

She inhaled a deep breath, not sure how to respond to that. So she only stood silent in the dark room, her body temperature starting to rise. Boy, it was getting awfully warm all of a sudden, she thought, even for someone who wasn't currently very embarrassed and trapped with a naked man who really turned her on.

"Did you turn up the heat?" Joel asked her.

"No. I was just about to ask you if you did, because you were so cold."

"Oh, believe me, Abby. I haven't been cold for some time now."

"Then why is it so hot in here?"

As if to answer the question, the radiator hissed maliciously. Abby untied the belt of her robe and shrugged out of it, then felt around for the desk chair and draped the heavy garment over the back.

"Great," she muttered. "We have no electricity, but plenty of steam heat."

"At least we won't freeze to death."

Oh, she'd been confident of that ever since she'd opened her eyes to find Joel Tandem wrapped in her blue throw. Somehow she knew she'd never wash the coverlet again, nor would she ever be able to sleep without it. She groaned aloud at the realization.

"What?" Joel asked, his voice full of concern now.

Before she had a chance to respond, he was beside her. His eyes obviously had adjusted to the darkness more fully than hers, because he deftly cupped his hand over her shoulder and brushed his thumb easily, affectionately, along the side of her neck.

"Are you okay?" he asked her.

Well, I was, Abby thought, *until you touched me like that.* "I'm fine," she lied, her voice a husky whisper. "Just a little, um, hot."

"Yeah, me too."

For some reason, she got the feeling that neither of them was talking about the way the radiator had taken on a life of its own. He continued the gentle, seemingly casual motion of his thumb along the line of her throat, a soft, rhythmic caress that mimicked the beating of her heart. Without questioning her actions, she removed her glasses and tossed them in the general direction of her desk, where they landed with a quiet sound. Then she turned her head toward Joel, and before she realized what was happening, he covered her mouth with his.

He kissed her as he had that first time, tenderly, experimentally, as if he still weren't sure what kind of reception she'd give him. Silly man, Abby thought vaguely as she surrendered to the shiver of delight that overcame her. How could he possibly think she wouldn't welcome such an overture?

Well, there was that small matter of his being a virtual stranger, she reminded herself halfheartedly. And of his thinking she was that sex kitten Candida, instead of a stuffy old medieval studies scholar. And of his being in no way the sort of man she normally found herself attracted to. And of his being an ex-con. But, hey, other than that . . .

Somehow, what little wedge of good sense she had left stepped to the fore, and Abby gently disengaged herself from his kiss. But she didn't go far. For some reason, she couldn't quite make herself release him completely, and she curled her palm tentatively over his jaw, scraping her fingertips lightly along the rough beard on his cheek and neck.

"I'm not Candida," she repeated emphatically.

"I know," he replied immediately. "And a good thing, too, I say."

When she'd pulled away from him, he'd dropped both hands to her waist, and now he toyed with the hem of her cropped pajama top, dipping the fingers of one hand to caress the bare skin below her rib cage. The soft touch set off a line of small explosions everywhere his fingers touched, muddling Abby's thoughts, compromising her intentions. For a moment his words didn't gel in her brain. Then, suddenly, their import struck her. Hard.

"You're glad I'm *not* Candida?" she asked a little breathlessly. "Why? Any man in his right mind would—"

"Hey, that woman scares me to death," Joel cut her off. "Maybe that means I'm not in my right mind, but I, for one, wouldn't have the first idea what to do with Candida. She'd eat me alive."

Abby hesitated a moment, certain she'd misunderstood. "But I thought that was what men wanted."

He chuckled low, then pulled her closer. "Only from women in glossy magazines," he told her. "In real life, real men like a woman who's . . . well . . . real."

"But—"

When he interrupted her this time, it was with a kiss. He pulled her body alongside his own, scooped both hands under her pajama top to splay them over her bare back, then covered her mouth insistently with his. And this time, weakened by the last kiss and his confession about Candida, Abby couldn't quite muster the strength—or the desire—to pull away. Instead she slid her hands over the hot satin of his naked shoulders and kissed him back. When he realized she was joining in, he uttered a rough, primal sound from the back of his throat and unleashed a power she could never have imagined.

It was quite an extraordinary kiss.

The darkness around Abby grew potent with an electricity she felt likely would consume them both. She sighed her delight at the gentle caress of his fingertips, murmured his name on a low whisper against his lips, scored her fingers through the silky curtain of his hair, and kissed him back. For long moments they only stood, so thoroughly entwined, their bodies rubbing together with an erotic friction that sparked a fire through them both.

She felt ... so many things. A completeness of spirit, a wholeness of body, a totality of soul. Something in Joel connected with all the things inside her that had existed alone for too long. It was as if the two of them connected at some elemental level, in a way that had been preordained aeons ago. And now that that union was fulfilled, there would be no separating them.

The realization of that—and the need for breath—made Abby pull away from him, in an effort to free herself of the hypnotic spell. When she tore her lips from his, however, Joel simply dipped his mouth lower, to the tender skin of her neck. He tasted the hollow at the base of her throat, then nudged open the collar of her pajama top with his lips and dragged the tip of his tongue along her collarbone.

She cried out at the explosion of heat that shot through her everywhere his mouth tasted her, then she curled her fingers more insistently into his hair. As if from a great distance, she sensed his fingers unfastening the buttons of her shirt, and she told herself she should stop him before they both went too far.

"Joel," she said, the word sounding soft and ragged and uncertain. "Please ..."

His fingers stilled on the third button, and she felt him smile against the tender flesh beneath her throat. His warm breath caressed her as he chuckled low.

"Please what?" he asked softly.

She inhaled a slow, ragged breath, tipped her head so that her cheek rested on the crown of his head, and wrapped her arms more snugly around his shoulders. Then, in direct contrast with her actions, she told him, "This is moving a little too fast for me."

He didn't move away, but he didn't carry their intimacy any further. "That's funny," he told her. "I was just thinking that it was about time we got around to this. It's taken forever."

She smiled, but for some reason she didn't feel exactly happy. "I just ... I mean ... " She sighed fitfully and tried again. "It's just that I don't really know you all that well, and—"

"My name," he interrupted her as he straightened, "is Joel William Tandem." He looped his arms around her waist, pulled her close, and settled his chin on her head. "I'm thirty-two years old and a Gemini. My parents are William and Andrea Tandem, and they make their home in Columbus, Indiana. I have a kid sister named Cathy in Boston who's getting married this summer to a guy who's not nearly good enough for her, but then I'm just the big brother, so what do I know? Let's see . . . what else? I have a BS and an MS from UMass, and I'm currently self-employed."

Abby smiled as he recited his curriculum vitae, thankful for the darkness masking her amazement that the man he described was the one holding her in his arms. Never in a million years would she have suspected even one of those things about him. His self-evaluation defined a man who sounded just so . . . so . . . so sweet. So nice. So safe. The man he described was exactly the kind of man she had always hoped to meet and fall in love with.

Except for his arrest record.

The thought materialized unexpectedly, and she felt herself stiffen in his arms. Joel obviously sensed her withdrawal, because he, too, grew a little rigid in response.

"What?" he asked. "What's wrong?"

She flattened her hands over his chest, not quite pushing him away but definitely erecting a barrier between them, however small and ineffectual. "I appreciate your introduction," she told him. "But I think there's one small thing you've neglected to mention."

He hesitated for a moment, and she wished the lights would come back on so that she could see his expression. "The part about self-employment, right?" he finally said, sounding strangely defensive. "Okay, I was deliberately vague there, because a lot of people react kind of funny when they find out what I do for a living. But it's really very rewarding, not to mention a lot of fun. I—"

"I wasn't talking about your job," Abby interjected, thinking that, too, was something they needed to discuss.

"Then what were you talking about?"

"I was talking about . . ." She might as well just spit it out, she told herself. After inhaling a deep breath, she licked her lips and said flat out, "I was talking about your . . . your arrest record."

Oh, *man,* Cupid thought. The guy was a criminal? How did that happen? He was never going to get back to Mt. Olympus now. He could just see Andromeda hanging all over Perseus at Zeus Junior High School's spring prom. This was like *so* not fair.

He sighed and shook his head, realizing he was going to have to start all over, from scratch. Wasn't no way a woman like Abby would settle for a felon. This was going to take some doing. Might as well can the darkness and steam heat. No need for ambiance anymore. . . .

CHAPTER EIGHT

*T*he power came back on just as Joel was opening his mouth to ask Abby what the hell she was talking about. Both of them blinked haphazardly as their eyes tried to adjust to the light, and the computer emitted an annoying beep as it rebooted. For a long moment, neither of them said anything. They only continued to hold each other tentatively as they tried to readjust to the awkwardness and enlightenment of their situation. Then Joel remembered he had been about to ask Abby a question, and he opened his mouth again.

But the words got stuck in his throat when he saw her. Her face was flushed from the room's temperature and the heat of their shared passion, her brown eyes had gone all soft and velvety, her pajama top was gaping open where he'd managed to free three buttons, and the creamy swell of her breasts was kissed with the blush of her desire. He swallowed hard and tried to remember what he'd been about to say.

"Joel?"

Her voice seemed to be coming from a million miles away, and he simply could not bring himself to avert his gaze from the soft ivory skin peeking out from beneath her pale pink pajama top.

"What?" he managed to murmur.

"What were you arrested for? And when?" She hesitated for a moment, then assured him, "It's okay. Really. You can tell me."

He shook his head, wondering where she'd gotten the idea that he had an arrest record. Although now that he thought about it, the ideas that were suddenly parading through his brain were anything but legal. "I've never been arrested," he finally said.

"But—"

With no small effort he forced his gaze upward, to her face. Her expression displayed total befuddlement, and he almost smiled at the way she was chewing her lip in confusion.

"Where did you get the idea that I had an arrest record?" he asked her, his amusement growing the more he thought about such a thing.

Her face changed again, this time reflecting complete embarrassment. "You, uh, you mentioned this afternoon that you, um, you don't like to be confined."

He narrowed his eyes at her, honestly unable to recall the episode she described. "Although that's certainly true, I don't remember saying that."

"You said that was why you liked riding a motorcycle." She swallowed with some difficulty. "After the part about, uh . . ." She glanced away for a moment, then met his gaze anxiously again. "The part about . . . liking something hot, shuddering, and wild between your legs."

He smiled both at the memory and at the fact that she was suddenly able to toss around sexual innuendos without blushing. It was a good sign. "Oh, yeah," he said softly. "That." He moved a little closer. "And you thought that when I said I didn't like being confined, it was because I'd been in prison."

She nodded.

He licked his lips and moved closer still. But for every inch he moved forward, Abby retreated two in reverse. They continued with the awkward dance until she bumped up against a bookcase full of literary texts that prevented her from going any farther. Joel smiled and began to feel much better about the way things were going. Somehow, they'd ended up in virtually the same position they'd been in earlier. Only they were on Abby's turf this time. How very convenient.

"I also recall telling you that I grew up on a farm," he said softly, noting the nervous way she squirmed against the bookcase. His heart grew lighter still.

"Yes," she said, meeting his gaze unflinchingly despite her obvious bout of nerves. "You did tell me that."

"That's because I *did* grow up on a farm. In Indiana. I'm used to wide-open spaces and having miles and miles of farmland to call my own. I spent ninety-nine percent of my childhood outdoors, in all seasons, in all weather. That's why I don't like being confined. I like the feel of the wind and rain on my body. I'm a very . . . elemental . . . person."

At his admission, Abby's pupils expanded to nearly eclipse her dark irises, and she licked her lips anxiously. "You . . . you are?"

"Oh, yeah."

"Oh."

"So you don't have to worry about my criminal record, sweetheart. 'Cause I don't have one."

"Oh. That's . . . that's good."

He nodded as he bent his arm and braced it against the bookcase, along the shelf above her head. He leaned in *very* close and smiled. "So now that we have *that* out of the way . . ."

"Yes?"

With his free hand, he fingered the lapel of her pajama top. "Maybe we could get these things out of the way, too?"

She stared at him for a moment with so much hunger and need in her eyes that he was certain the two of them were bound for glory. Then, very slowly, she shook her head in the negative.

"Even if you're not an ex-con," she told him quietly, "you're still not—" She sighed heavily as she broke off her statement.

"I'm still not what?" he demanded, running his fingers along the soft fabric of her shirt.

"You're still not . . . my type."

Her admonition did nothing to quell his desire or interrupt his advances. Because he was exactly her type. He knew he was, thanks to the epiphany he'd had the first time he'd kissed her. He was completely certain now about something he had suspected for a couple of months. He was in love with Abby Walden. And judging by the way she had reacted to him today, she was in love with him. Ergo, the two of them complemented each other perfectly. So why couldn't she see that as well as he could?

"And just what is your type, Abby?" he asked.

She licked her lips nervously, and he quickly dipped his head to touch the tip of his tongue to hers. She melted against the bookcase when he did and uttered a wanton little sound that made him smile.

"Oh," she murmured. "Oh, Joel."

"How can I not be your type?" he asked her. "The two of us generate magic when we're together."

She shook her head slowly again. "No, it's not magic. Not the right kind, anyway."

"What kind is it?"

"It's sexual magic. It's not—"

"What?"

"Love."

He smiled as he brushed his lips over hers. "You don't think it's love?"

"No," she whispered, her voice shaky and uncertain. "It can't be love."

"Why not?"

"Because you're not—"

"I'm not your type," he answered for her.

"Yes."

He chuckled smoothly, rubbed his open mouth over hers, reveled in the shudder that wound through her at his touch, and said, "Tell me what your type is, then."

He pulled back enough to look into her eyes, then watched them go all soft and dewy as she thought about her ideal man.

"My type is strong and confident, but also gentle and caring," she began softly, quickly, indicating that this was something to which she'd given a great deal of thought. "An intelligent, well-educated man, and one who has a wonderful sense of humor.''

"And I'm none of those things?" he asked dubiously.

She narrowed her eyes in confusion, hesitating a moment before admitting, ''Well, yes. Yes, you are. You're all of those things.''

"Sounds like I'd fit the bill nicely. So?"

"So that's not all my type is."

"What else, then?"

"My type is the kind of man who can make a commitment to something, to someone."

"Who says I can't make a commitment?"

"Well, nobody. Just . . . um . . . well . . .''

"Well, what?"

"I, uh . . . There's more.''

He smiled, then lifted his hand to skim the pad of his thumb along the swell of her lower lip. ''So get on with it already.''

Her eyes fluttered closed for a moment as she inhaled a quiet, erratic breath. When she opened them again, her gaze was only half-focused, as if she were more than a little preoccupied with something. Like maybe the way Joel had dipped his fingers into her pajama top and was skimming them over her warm flesh.

"I—I—I want a man who can build a home and family with me," she continued, her voice restless, her gaze fixed on his. "A man who would make a good father. Who likes and understands children, a man with whom children would feel comfortable and not be frightened.''

This time Joel laughed out loud, a bubble of pure, unadulterated delight fizzing up inside him. ''You think I'd frighten children?'' he asked.

She nodded but said nothing.

"Why?"

"Because . . . because . . .''

"Because?"

"Because . . . you frighten me.''

Oh, now *this* came as a real surprise. Naturally, he'd known all along that he made Abby nervous—there had been no mistaking that from the get-go. But frighten her? Joel Tandem? He'd never frightened anyone in his life.

He shoved himself away from the bookcase—and likewise from Abby—taking some small measure of comfort in the fact that she appeared to be so disappointed by his withdrawal. Then he moved to her desk and sat down, turning his attention to her computer.

He glanced over his shoulder to find her still plastered against the bookcase between volumes three and seven of Will and Ariel Durant's *The History of Civilization*. "How do you pull up the Internet on this thing?" he asked her, pretending he didn't notice her trepidation.

She hesitated only a moment before moving to join him. Then, silently, she skittered the mouse to the proper icon, typed in some instructions, and pulled up an Internet gateway.

"Great," he mumbled.

He typed in an "http://" address, and the two of them waited in silence while a Web page gradually appeared on the screen. The words "John Jacob Jellyroll" appeared in big, uneven, multicolored letters, followed by a full-color reproduction of a children's book called *Top Cat and Tales*. A goofy but lovable feline was on the cover, dancing hand in hand, toe to toe, with a big red book wearing purple high-top sneakers. Joel smiled, thinking the illustration was one of his better ones.

"What does this have to do with anything?" Abby asked.

She had moved to stand right behind him, her dark auburn hair falling over her shoulder and dangling right beside his face. The sweet smell of flowers surrounded him, and he wanted to tug softly on that hair until she tumbled into his lap. Instead he angled himself in the chair and gazed at her until she turned her attention to him.

"This is the Web site for John Jacob Jellyroll," he told her.

She smiled wryly. "I can see that. So?"

"So do you know who John Jacob Jellyroll is?"

She nodded. "My nieces and nephews love his books. I bought *Top Cat and Tales* for Jamie's fifth birthday last month. It's adorable."

Joel grinned. "Thanks."

"Why are you thanking me?"

He turned back to the screen and cupped his hand over the mouse, then scrolled down the page, past other book covers, a whole bunch of silly children's jokes, a half dozen interactive games, and a bibliography containing more than thirty titles.

"Look at that," he said as the titles whizzed past. "More than thirty books. Does that show *commitment* or what?"

"Commitment?" she echoed, her tone puzzled.

But Joel only smiled as he continued to scroll down more, slowing only when he neared John Jacob Jellyroll's bio. Then he halted completely when he reached the author's photo and turned to watch Abby's reaction.

The color drained from her face. "That's you," she said.

"That's me," he agreed amiably.

Her gaze darted from the photo of Joel on the screen to Joel in person, back to the screen, back to the person. "You're John Jacob Jellyroll?" she asked.

He nodded.

"That's what you go to do every night on your motorcycle?"

"I have a studio near the university." He shrugged. "I discovered some time ago that whether I like it or not, my most creative hours are from ten-thirty at night until about three-thirty in the morning. I've adapted."

Again Abby turned to the screen, and he could see by her expression that she really liked what she saw.

"Kids *love* me," he added unneccessarily in response to her earlier assertion about her ideal man. "I don't see how they—or anyone else, for that matter—could possibly be scared of me."

She nodded. "And I, uh . . . I'll bet you love kids, too, huh?"

"Oh, yeah. I'd even like to have a few of my own someday. Provided I find the right woman. One who is, of course, my type."

She had the decency to blush at that. "And, um, what type might that be?"

In one fluid gesture, he stood and swept Abby into his arms. "Auburn hair," he began easily. "Brown eyes. About five-feet . . . five?"

"And a half," she said with a smile as she circled his waist with her arms.

He nodded. "Five-five and a half," he confirmed. "She's slightly nearsighted, teaches medieval drama at a small Massachusetts college, and has an alter ego named Candida who is one hot mama. Oh, yeah," he added as an afterthought. "And she loves children's books and the men who write them."

She shook her head.

"No?" he asked.

"Not the *men* who write them. Just one man who writes them. The notorious John Jacob Jellyroll. Children's book author and illustrator by day, bad boy Mr. Leather Pants by night."

He smiled as one kind of tension unwound and dissolved inside him, while another, much more pleasant tension began to get strung tight. "You know, I bet Mr. Leather Pants and Candida would get along real well together."

"You think so?"

"Probably almost as well as you and I do."

She nodded as she gave the idea consideration. "I guess there's only one way to find out just how compatible they—and we—really are."

"Get them—and us—married?" he asked.

Her smile became absolutely dazzling, her expression incandescent. "Well, there's that, too," she agreed.

" 'That, *too'?*" He arched his brows suggestively. "Why, Abby. What other kinds of ideas do you have going on in that wily, beautiful head of yours?"

She skimmed her index finger slowly over his lower lip, then rose on tiptoe to whisper in his ear, "Maybe I should let Candida tell you all about it."

He nuzzled the warm, fragrant skin of her neck. "You

know, I think maybe this is something Mr. Leather Pants would like to hear, too.''

"Then by all means," she said with a throaty chuckle, "let's make it a foursome. We wouldn't want anybody to get short-changed, would we?"

With a final feline purr of contentment, Cupid turned his back on the couple and headed for the kitchen. He'd heard that mortal couplings could get kind of intense sometimes, and frankly, he didn't want to be around if that happened here. *When* that happened here, he amended quickly as the sounds in the other room started to become kind of . . . energetic.

Yo, Mom, he sent the silent thought skyward. *You better get me outta here, or I'm gonna be learning all kinds of things you told me I wouldn't find out about until I'm a full god.*

Immediately Abby's kitchen faded, and within seconds he was in his bedroom back on Mt. Olympus. His mother stood beside his computer, gazing at the picture of Joel Tandem, aka John Jacob Jellyroll, on the screen, her fingers tapping restlessly on the mouse.

"You know, I don't think he looks like a children's book author, either," she said as she turned toward her son.

"Yeah, but you wouldn't have been scared of him, like Abby was," Cupid said.

Aphrodite smiled. "Well, of course not."

He smiled back. All in all, his mom was pretty cool. Even if she was a total love goddess who was like way too strict.

"You did a good job, Cupid," she said softly. "You'll be a great god someday."

He blushed. "Thanks, Mom."

A moment of understanding passed between them, then she seemed to remember something. "Oh, I nearly forgot. Andromeda called while you were gone."

He brightened considerably. "Oh, yeah?"

Aphrodite nodded. "Seventeen times."

He brightened even more. "Cool."

"She said to tell you . . . let me see if I can remember her exact words . . ." She closed her eyes and pressed a finger to her temple in concentration. " 'Yo, Perseus is like *so* not with it. Me and Persephone will be at the mall looking for sandals. Get that hunky Icarus for her, and meet us at Orange Julius.' "

Aphrodite dropped her hand back to her side and smiled at her son once more. "Yes, I think that was it exactly."

"Thanks, Mom."

"But you have to do your geometry homework first."

"Mo-o-om!"

But she only crossed her arms over her midsection and adopted that posture that clearly stated she would *not* be messed with. "I mean it, Cupid. No work, no play. Do you want me to cast you back down to the twentieth century again?"

He smiled but moved to the desk where his geometry book was gathering dust. "Maybe some other time, Mom," he said as he sat down. "Maybe some other time."

Winning Ticket

MARGARET BROWNLEY

CHAPTER ONE

*W*inning the lottery was the pits! Of course, Paige Roberts had no way of knowing this—not until the day all six of her numbers came up and she was declared one of two *lucky* winners entitled to a three-million-dollar jackpot!

It was hard to believe. In the course of a single day, her entire life had been turned upside-down. Not only had every charitable organization in the Los Angeles area beaten a path to her doorstep, she and her mother were no longer on speaking terms, and Randall—the man she'd accused of not having a passionate bone in his body—had left her house in a passionate huff!

Randall Sacks was her fiancé—or would be if she ever got around to accepting the engagement ring he'd been waving in front of her nose for the last six months. Now it looked as if marriage were out of the question.

And all because of that damned lottery ticket!

This explained in part why Paige was in such a foul mood that Monday morning in early May.

Dressed in a crisp white chef's coat and black-and-white-checkered pants, her blond shoulder-length hair twisted into its usual French braid, she stormed into the Grand Occasions Catering Company, strode passed the cheering employees, the flowers, the balloons, and even the huge sheet cake bearing her name, and into her office, slamming the door shut behind her.

The nerve of her ex-husband!

Her loyal assistant, Lisa Maxwell, knocked before cracking the door open and showing her face. During the five years Paige and Lisa had worked together, they had become more than co-workers, they were friends.

A small-boned woman with shiny black curls and enough anxieties to keep at least one local psychiatrist occupied, Lisa wore thick glasses, silver braces, and perpetual worry lines. "Everything's okay, right? You won the lottery and you're happy as a clam." Lisa gave Paige a tentative smile. "Right?"

"Even a dead clam is happier than I am." Paige tossed the morning's newspaper onto her desk. "I just had a fight with Randall."

Lisa walked into the office, closing the door behind her. "You're a millionaire, for goodness' sakes. What's there to fight about?"

Paige ripped the obsolete pages off her daily calendar. After crushing each page into a ball, she tossed them one by one into the wastebasket. "Remember, I told you I'm one of two winners?"

"So what? Half of three million dollars is still nothing to sneeze about."

"I don't care a fig about the money." Strange as it seemed, that part was true. Paige's catering company had turned a handsome profit this past year, and she had more business than she could handle. "It's the nerve of someone else playing *my* lucky numbers."

Lisa looked confused. "I have no idea what you're talking about. Last month, seven people split the winnings. And remember the time an entire town won? You can't lay claim to numbers. Aren't you being a bit unreasonable?"

"You won't think I'm unreasonable when I tell you who the other winner is. Does the name Jeff Roberts ring a bell?"

Lisa's eyes widened. "Not *the*—?"

"The one and only. My ever-loving ex-husband."

Lisa was momentarily speechless. "But I—I don't understand," she stammered finally. "How could this possibly happen? You haven't even seen him in how long?"

"Two and a half years."

"You haven't seen him in all that time and suddenly, out of the clear blue sky, you both play the same numbers? That's amazing. It's gotta be fate or something."

Paige tossed her hands up in frustration. Not two hours ago her mother had voiced Lisa's same exact words. "Don't *you* start. Fate has nothing to do with this. He helped himself to *my* lucky numbers. Stole them! I can't believe he would do such a thing. It's like helping yourself to someone else's horoscope."

Lisa drew her brows together. "None of this makes sense. Why would he play *your* lucky numbers?"

"Who knows? Maybe he did it to spite me."

Lisa looked unconvinced. "But he hasn't seen you for years."

"Some people can hold a grudge for a long time. Besides, how else can you explain it? He knows I play my birthdate, his birthdate, and our now defunct anniversary date. I played those same numbers every week when we were married, and now *he's* playing them!"

"Holy sh— Do you realize that more than half of the men in America can't remember a birthday, let alone an anniversary date, and your ex remembers both? You don't suppose—"

Paige narrowed her eyes. *Please don't be thinking what I think you're thinking.* "Go on, say it. What don't I suppose?"

"You know . . . that maybe he still carries a torch for you." Paige shook her head vehemently, but Lisa persisted. "It's possible."

Paige couldn't believe that Lisa, of all people, would suggest such a thing. It was bad enough that her very own mother voiced the same opinion. And even Randall—Randall, the patron saint of logic—had the audacity to suggest much the same thought himself. What was wrong with everyone?

"No, I don't think he's carrying a torch. In fact, it's the most ridiculous thing I've ever heard. I'm going to tell you the same thing I told Randall and my mother—"

"Your mother!" Lisa blinked. "I can understand why

Randall might be suspicious of your ex's motivations. But your mother?''

''Mother thinks that my divorce reflects on her good character. She would do anything to see me and Jeff get back together. That's why she sees ulterior motives in everything we do. She honestly believes that our winning the lottery is a sign that we're destined to spend the rest of our lives together. Ever since she's been watching that angel program on television, she sees signs everywhere. It's ridiculous.''

''You mean she thinks you've been touched by an angel?''

''Something like that. Isn't that the most ridiculous thing you've ever heard?''

''Maybe it's not as ridiculous as you think,'' Lisa said. ''I'm not talking angels here. But it might be a sign you and your ex need to work on some unresolved issue.''

''Trust me. We have nothing to resolve.''

''Come on, Paige. Think about it. It would certainly explain why you two play each other's birthdates, not to mention your anniversary.''

Paige planted her hands on her desk and glared at her soon-to-be *ex*-friend. ''Now you're beginning to sound like Dr. What's-his-name.''

''Dr. Bonheiser, and he's a wonderful therapist. It might be a good idea for you to make an appointment to discuss this issue with him. It's the kind of problem he likes to sink his teeth into.''

''Trust me. There is no problem. My ex and I are through. Finis! Dr. Bonheiser will have to sink his teeth into somebody else's business.''

Paige ripped another page off her calendar before realizing she'd torn off the current date. She sat down and, in an effort to distract Lisa, abruptly changed the subject. ''Where's the Dunmiller contract?''

Lisa pulled the contract from a stack of papers on Paige's desk and, handing it to her, looked her square in the face. ''So how many divorced couples do you know who consider their anniversary date lucky?''

''It's just a habit,'' Paige said, and then repeated practically verbatim what she had told Randall earlier. "We played those numbers when we were married, and I continue to play them out of sheer habit. I buy lottery tickets to support our schools. I don't buy them to make a statement about my ex."

Lisa didn't look any more convinced than Randall or her mother had looked when she had used the same argument with them. "I didn't know that numbers were habit-forming."

"Everything is habit-forming."

"All right, let's suppose what you say is true and you play these numbers out of habit. What about your ex? Surely you're not suggesting he has the same habit."

"It's possible. Besides, knowing Jeff, he probably doesn't even know what the numbers represent."

Lisa looked unswayed. "Even so . . ."

"Jeff and I both agree that getting married was the biggest mistake we ever made. Why would he want to play our anniversary date?"

"The question is, why would you?"

Annoyed at Lisa's persistence, she studied the contract in her hands. "I told you why. Now can we please get to work?"

"You don't suppose your playing your anniversary date has something to do with why you're taking your own sweet time in accepting Randall's proposal?"

Paige tossed aside the contract. "That's ridiculous. I'm only twenty-seven years old and I've already been through one miserable divorce. Naturally, I don't want to go through anything like that again. Not ever. The next time I marry, it'll be for keeps."

Lisa stared at her nails. "I seem to recall Elizabeth Taylor saying those very same words."

"I mean it, Lisa."

"All right, I understand why you're taking your time with Randall. But that still doesn't explain why you and your ex play the lottery with your anniver—"

Her patience stretched to the limit, Paige lost her temper. "We're playing the same numbers because he is a low-down, number-stealing thief! Now, that's it. That's all I intend to say on the subject!"

Dismissing Lisa with a wave of her hand, Paige shuffled through the papers on her desk. The wedding season had started early this year, and the catering company was booked solid for the next six months, all the way till the end of September.

She handed Lisa the list of meat and produce that had to be ordered before noon. "Let's get to work."

Lisa studied the list, her lips pursed thoughtfully, but she made no move toward the door. "Paige . . . you're not going to sell the place, are you? Now that you've won the lottery?"

Paige's hands stilled. It surprised her that Lisa would ask such a question. "You know me better than that. I've built this business from the ground up." She glanced around her newly decorated office with a sense of pride.

No, she would never give up Grand Occasions. She'd started her catering business in her home, preparing food for literally hundreds of weddings, baby showers, and other private parties in her woefully inadequate kitchen before saving enough money to purchase this piece of property.

Conveniently located in Moorpark, California, her business was freeway-close to Los Angeles. Yet Paige had the luxury of looking out her office window at lush rolling hills, rich farmlands, and an abundance of sprawling oak trees.

The day she moved into her present location was one of the happiest of her life. "You're not getting rid of me that easy, if that's what you're afraid of."

Relief crossed Lisa's face, and the worry lines melted into a smile. "How about coming out and cutting the cake? I think we have a lot to celebrate. Besides, it's your favorite, chocolate raspberry."

"I'll be out in a jiff." Paige reached for the phone on her desk. "Just as soon as I call that two-timing, double-crossing ex-husband of mine."

CHAPTER TWO

*J*eff Roberts couldn't believe it. He'd won the lottery, won a cool million and a half smackaroos, and what did it get him? A proverbial slap in the face.

Worse, he was locked out of his own house dressed in nothing but his "Smile, I'm Irish" boxer shorts.

It was enough to make a man question his sanity. He pounded on the front door with his fists, his bare feet planted firmly on the doormat that read "A sane and rational man lives here."

At the moment, he was definitely more furious than sane. Not only had he been forced to endure odd looks from the *Arrowhead* Water delivery man, not to mention his nosy next-door neighbor, he was freezing his buns off. "Come on, Mary Beth. Open the door. This is no way to treat a millionaire!"

It took a whole lot of pounding and enough begging to do the entire canine population in Thousand Oaks proud before Mary Beth relented.

She opened the door, but obviously the twenty minutes or so he'd been freezing to death on the front porch hadn't cooled her temper in the least. Her green eyes were positively demonic. Never had he known her to be so unreasonable—or even mad. Not only were her eyes flashing, she was flanked by two suitcases.

"Move out of my way!" she demanded, scowling at him.

Without waiting for him to comply, she picked up her suit-cases and brushed by him.

"Wait!" He chased after her, ignoring old Mrs. Baumgarten next door, who had been watering the same rosebush during the entire time he'd stood pounding on his own front door.

The way she was staring at him, you'd think she'd never seen a man in his boxer shorts before.

"You can't just leave like this. We're millionaires."

"You and your ex are millionaires. I'm outta here!" Mary Beth shoved her suitcases into the backseat of her car, slammed the door shut, and marched around to the driver's side.

Jeff raced ahead of her to block the door. This was America, for chrissakes. He was innocent until the press said otherwise.

Mary Beth glared at him, her face dark with fury. "I want to know why you played *her* birthdate and *her* anniversary date."

"It was actually our anniversary—"

"Ohhhhhhhhhhh!"

"Now, calm down, Mary Beth. You knew I'd been married before. I never kept that from you."

"But you never remember *our* anniversary."

"That's because we don't have one," he said. Though Mary Beth had done all but set the wedding date, he hadn't gotten around to actually proposing. He'd already had one failed marriage. Who could blame him for not wanting to rush into another? For all he knew, he wasn't even husband material.

"We have *three* anniversaries," she said hotly. "The day we met, the day of our first date, and the day we officially became a couple."

Jeff slapped his hand palm down on the roof of her car. "How do you expect me to remember all that?"

"You didn't even remember my birthday!" she shouted. "But you remember *hers.*"

"I was married to her."

"And you could be married to me if you wanted to be."

"Ah, come on, honey. Let's not fight. I won the lottery. We should be celebrating."

"You won the lottery playing your ex-wife's birthdate."

Mary Beth had been singing this tiresome tune since the previous evening when he'd told her the name of the other winner. What else could he do but reveal the name? The way he figured it, Mary Beth was bound to find out sooner or later. It was better if she heard it from him—though, obviously, not much better.

"All right, all right. I made a mistake. No big deal. I won't ever play those numbers again. Okay? Now what do you say we go away for the weekend?"

"I'm not going anywhere with you—"

"Come on, baby. This is ridiculous. Surely you're not jealous of my ex-wife? We got divorced for good reason, believe me." And as soon as he remembered what that good reason was, he would tell her.

He lowered his voice so Mrs. Baumgarten couldn't hear. "Let's not fight. I said I was sorry. . . ." He gave an impassioned speech in his own defense, but judging by the stubborn look on Mary Beth's face, she wasn't buying a single word.

Finally he threw up his hands in an act of surrender. Desperate times called for desperate measures. "Okay, okay! If you want to get married, we'll get married."

Mary Beth narrowed her eyes and looked about to cave in to his pleas. Jeff congratulated himself silently. Proposing marriage while standing in his boxer shorts, freezing his buns off, might not be the wisest thing he'd ever done, but it sure as hell was a stroke of genius.

"Do you mean that?" she asked. "About us getting married?"

"Of course I mean it." Jeff tried to sound enthusiastic. "I wouldn't have said it if I didn't."

"Oh, all right," she said, showing amazing restraint for a woman who had just landed herself a prospective groom. "I'll marry you." Jeff couldn't believe his ears; she made it sound as though she were doing him a *favor*. "But only on one condition. You resolve your feelings for your ex."

"Feelings?" Surely he'd misunderstood. He hadn't seen his

ex-wife in two years, six months, and three weeks. "What feelings?"

"Don't act innocent with me," she snapped. "I'm talking about the unhealthy attachment you have for her."

"I most certainly do not have an unhealthy attachment for Paige!" he said with as much indignation as he could muster. It was the most ridiculous thing he'd ever heard in his life.

"You do, too. Last week, you told me that Gary Cooper was her favorite old-time actor."

"So?"

"So you made me watch a dreadful movie because *she* liked him."

"That had nothing to do with it. I happen to like that movie myself."

"And every time we order Chinese, you always think to mention that *she* liked Chinese."

"I'm just making conversation. It doesn't mean anything."

"Then prove it!"

"What?"

"I want you to prove to me that you're completely over your feelings for Paige."

"How am I supposed to do that?"

"That's your problem. You're a millionaire now. You can do anything you put your mind to. I'm sure you'll figure out a way. And when you do, you can reach me at my mother's."

She climbed into the driver's seat, started the car, and backed out of the driveway.

Hands on his waist, he watched her zoom away on screeching tires.

After she had driven out of sight, he turned and faced his house. Mrs. Baumgarten hadn't budged an inch. Come to think of it, she was still watering the same rosebush. He was tempted to snatch the hose out of her hands before she drowned the damned thing.

Caught in the act of staring at him, she gave him a tentative smile. "Good morning, Mr. Roberts," she called. She sounded all innocentlike, or at least as innocent as a woman caught staring at a man's boxer shorts could look.

"Didn't anyone ever tell you it's not polite to stare?" he asked irritably.

"I most certainly was not staring," she said in a huff. "I was just surprised. You and I have been living next door to each other for two years, and I had no idea you were Irish."

CHAPTER THREE

*J*ust before noon on Tuesday, Lisa poked her head through the open door of Paige's office. "You won't believe who's here to see you," she said, her voice hushed.

Her fingers skimming over the computer keyboard, Paige kept her eyes focused on the monitor. "Don't tell me it's Mrs. Dwyer." She groaned at the thought. The woman had married off three daughters in the last two years and had driven Paige crazy with her outrageous demands. During the last wedding, the executive chef had quit and the pastry chef had literally drunk himself into a stupor, but only after decorating the cake with miniature hatchets.

The woman had called last week to announce cheerfully that daughter number four was getting married. By last count, Mrs. Dwyer had two more daughters to marry off, but frankly Paige didn't think she could survive another Dwyer wedding. "Tell her we're booked through the year 2010."

"It's not Mrs. Dwyer," Lisa said.

"Then who?"

"Me."

At the sound of her ex-husband's deep, husky voice, Paige spun around in her chair to face him. Jeff Roberts greeted her with a sexy, heart-stopping smile that told her things hadn't changed much in the last two and a half years. He could still affect her as no other man ever could.

Some sort of greeting was called for, but Paige couldn't for the life of her think of anything to say. She was too busy trying not to drown in the depths of his piercing blue eyes.

Lisa blinked behind her eyeglasses. It was something she did out of habit whenever she was anxious or nervous or was faced with the prospect of dealing with a difficult client. "I'll leave you two alone."

"Wait—" Paige said, but it was too late. Already Lisa had disappeared—the chicken.

Paige resisted the urge to summon Lisa back to her office. She was quite capable of handling Jeff Roberts herself. She didn't need anyone running interference. To prove this, she crossed her arms in front of her and stared at him with narrowed eyes.

It irked her that the man who had broken her heart all those years ago looked so cool, so calm, so perfectly in control. Well, two could play the "cool" game. "What are you doing here?"

He leaned against the doorjamb, his hands in his pockets. "You left a message on my machine. Said you wanted to talk to me. Remember?"

"I also left my telephone number."

"That was mighty thoughtful of you. But under the circumstances, I thought I'd drive out here and see you in person. It's not every day you get to share three million dollars with an ex." His eyes clung to hers, as if he were monitoring her reaction. As an afterthought, he added, "You look great."

The unexpected compliment almost disarmed her. "So do you," she said. Not only did he make her pulse race, but he also managed to mess up her breathing. Something like a lump stuck in her throat.

Forcing herself to swallow, she lowered her eyes beneath his steady gaze and didn't look up again until he began to circle the room. He seemed intent upon checking out every painting on the wall and every magazine stacked upon the low table in front of the leather couch.

His handsome face seemed slightly leaner than it had in earlier years, but the dimple was intact, as was the cleft on his chin.

He wore his brown hair longer now, and it added a maturity to his good looks that didn't altogether coincide with the crooked grin that looked as boyish today as it had all those years ago, when she'd rear-ended his car.

She had fallen in love with him the minute he'd asked her for the name of her insurance company.

"You lost weight."

He shrugged casually. "Been working out."

She recognized his brown sports coat, and it looked every bit as stylish on his broad shoulders today as it had the day she had purchased it for his birthday, some seven or eight years ago.

He leveled his gaze at her. "You let your hair grow."

It was true. The longer style could be more readily brushed away from her face and confined. It was an important consideration when working around food.

"So did you," she said, feeling weak. Sooner or later they were bound to run out of mundane things to say. Then what?

He dimpled, as if it pleased him that she noticed. "Mary Beth says it makes me look older. I'm told looking older is a plus for an accountant."

"Who's Mary Beth?" She hated to ask, but her curiosity got the best of her and she couldn't seem to help herself.

"My . . . eh . . . girlfriend."

He continued to walk around the room. "I thought we could celebrate our winning the lottery by having lunch together." He turned to face her. "What do you say?"

"Lunch?" She could think of lots of ways to celebrate winning a million and a half dollars, but having lunch with her ex was not one of them. "I think you misunderstood why I called. I didn't call to congratulate you. . . ."

"Oh?" He glanced at his watch. "Sorry to change the subject, but it's a quarter of twelve. I made reservations for noon at that little steakhouse in the center of town. You remember the one? They refill your glass on the house every time a train passes by."

She glared at him. Not only had he stolen her numbers, he was now assuming she would drop everything to have lunch with him. Well, he assumed wrong! She had no intention of having lunch with him. She was in enough trouble with Randall already. "You'll have to cancel . . . I'm buried—"

"Ah, come on, Paige," he coaxed. "You're rich. You're also the boss. You can take an hour or two off. Unless"—he pursed his mouth thoughtfully—"you're afraid to have lunch with me."

His silky voice challenged her on some level, and though she resisted the urge to argue, she stiffened. Somehow he always knew what buttons to push. Well, let him so much as suggest they still had unresolved issues between them, and she would hit him on his handsome head with the gold-plated rolling pin she used as a paperweight. "Why would I be afraid to have lunch with you?"

He shrugged. "I never pretended to understand the way your mind works."

"My mind works fine, thank you very much."

"Good." He pulled her shoulder bag off the hook by the door and dangled it from his finger.

Watching her bag swing back and forth like a pendulum, she debated whether to give in and have lunch with him or boot him out of her office. Either way, he was likely to misunderstand her motives. She was just about to tell him where to go when she changed her mind.

Maybe it was the challenge in his eyes. Perhaps it was the desperate need to prove to herself—to everyone—that she was completely and unequivocally over her feelings for him. Whatever the reason, she walked around her desk, snatched her shoulder bag away from him, and marched out the door.

"My car or yours?" he called after her.

"It's only three blocks away," she said, and kept walking. She'd rather share the sidewalk with him than sit in the close confines of a car.

The restaurant was a two-story rustic building shaded by an enormous weeping willow. With its colorful Tiffany lamps, plank wood floors, player piano, and velvet draperies, it provided a temporary escape from the business world and was a favorite among locals.

It was still too early for the lunch crowd, and the restaurant was empty—intimately so. Wouldn't you know? On any other occasion the place would have been packed to the rafters and any sort of personal conversation all but impossible. Today Jeff could have whispered from across the room and she would have heard every word.

They were shown to a table for two by the window that overlooked Moorpark's quaint main street. Paige ate here at least once a month, but she'd never before noticed how small the tables were. She had to sit at an angle to keep her legs from touching his. Not only was Jeff tall, he required a lot of space. She remembered his taking up nearly the entire king-size bed they'd shared during their marriage.

Just the simple thought of sharing his bed quickened her pulse. Jeff raised a dark brow as if he sensed something, and she quickly lowered her gaze to the menu she clutched in her hand. It was a fine time for memories of their marital bed to pop into her head. Now she couldn't seem to think of anything else.

"So what will it be?" he asked when a waiter came to take their order.

Unable to concentrate on the menu, she ordered her ususal. "I'll have the garden salad, with dressing on the side."

Jeff ordered the prime rib and a bottle of champagne.

"Oh, no," she protested. "I never drink when I'm working."

"You're not working," he said. "You're celebrating." He turned to the waiter. "Make that Dom Pérignon."

Jeff leaned back in his chair and regarded her thoughtfully. "Your catering business has really grown," he said. The admiration in his voice surprised her. Even more surprising was how much his approval meant to her.

"I remember the first party you catered." His eyes took on a faraway look, as if he were mentally traveling back in time.

She laughed. "Mrs. Hampton's birthday party."

"That's the one. Remember how the cake flopped and you made me chase all over town looking for a bakery? Now you have how many people working for you?"

"Twenty full-time."

"That's amazing."

"What about you? How's the accounting business?"

"As fascinating as ever."

She couldn't help but laugh. "I swear you're the only person I know who thinks working with figures is fascinating."

He regarded her thoughtfully. "The way people spend their money *is* fascinating. Give me a checkbook and I'll tell you everything there is to know about its owner, including the person's age and philosophy of life. So tell me, how's your checkbook these days?"

"That's none of your business," she said, irritated. Just because her checkbook was unbalanced didn't mean *she* was.

His grin widened, and the lines around his eyes crinkled. "That bad, eh?"

"For your information, my checkbook is . . . semibalanced."

"Semi, eh? Well, if you ever need an expert to straighten out the mess, I'm at your beck and call."

"I'll keep that in mind."

The waiter brought their champagne, and after it had been poured, Jeff touched his flute to hers. "Here's to newfound wealth," he said.

She took a sip, and the bubbles tickled her nose.

He set down his glass and leaned back in his chair. "So why did you call me if not to congratulate me?"

She gazed at him over the rim of her glass. "To tell you that you had no right to play *my* lucky numbers."

"*Our* lucky numbers," he said, his voice gentle. "And I might add that since my birthdate makes up a third of the numbers, I have every right. The question is, why is it okay for you to play them and not okay for me?"

"You know how bad I am with numbers. I can't remember my own phone number. But I remember birthdates—"

"And anniversaries," he added.

She gritted her teeth. She was tired of having to defend herself, first to her mother and Randall, then to Lisa and now to Jeff. "Of course I remember our anniversary. It's not every day one makes a monumental mistake."

"Most people want to forget their mistakes," he pointed out.

"And that's why most people keep making the same mistakes," she said.

"But not you, right?" He studied her for a moment. "Is that why you haven't remarried?"

She eyed him warily, not sure that she wanted to talk about such personal matters with him. "How do you know I haven't remarried?"

"You're still using my name."

"Legally, it's my name, too." The waiter arrived with their order, and for a few moments they ate in silence, though she was acutely aware of his every move. She was grateful for the distraction of a passing train.

After the waiter had rushed over to refill their glasses, her curiosity finally got the best of her. "What about you? Why haven't *you* remarried?"

"I plan to. That's one of the reasons why I thought you and I should talk."

Now she really *was* curious. "Oh?"

"My . . . eh . . . girlfriend doesn't understand why you and I . . . you know . . . happened to play the same numbers. She thinks there's some sort of unfinished business between us." He set down his fork and lifted his glass. "Now isn't that the craziest thing you ever did hear?"

It *was* crazy. Of course it was crazy. "Randall suggested the same thing."

Jeff arched a dark brow. "Randall?"

She nodded. "Randall is the man I've been seeing for the last eighteen months, and he's asked me to marry him."

Jeff's face remained perfectly composed. "And he thinks you and I have unfinished business?"

"I told him the idea was ridiculous." She paused between bites. "You and I both know how ridiculous it is."

"That's exactly what I told Mary Beth."

"Did she believe you?"

"Not exactly. But she will."

Paige nodded. "So will Randall." She hesitated. "My mother's another story. . . ."

"Betty?" He raised his dark brows. "She thinks that you and I . . . ?" He motioned with his hand. "She thinks it odd that we played the same numbers?"

"She didn't say it was odd, she said it was significant."

"Significant in what way?"

"You know how Mother is. She suspects every human endeavor has a psychological motivation."

"Yeah, that's your mother all right. Remember when you misplaced the divorce papers and she got it into her head that you didn't want to divorce me?"

Paige laughed. It was annoying at the time, but now she could see the humor. "And remember when you got drunk and gave your designated driver my address instead of your own?"

Jeff laughed, and for a moment it was just like old times. "Yeah, and your mother was convinced it was because I was still emotionally married to you."

He laughed harder, and she frowned. It wasn't *that* funny.

"Mother said the same thing when I ordered new checks from the bank and forgot to remove your name," she said.

His face grew serious. "I didn't know you did that."

"There was no reason for you to know. I made a simple mistake. But Mother naturally made a big issue out of it."

"That's your mother all right," he said again, and she detected the fondness in his voice. Well, why shouldn't he like her mother? Her mother certainly liked him. She'd even taken his side during the divorce. For all Paige knew, her mother still took his side.

Without warning, a floodgate of memories opened up. "Do you remember the time you fell through the roof?" she said. Jeff had been trying to remove a bird nest from the chimney.

"Yeah, and I fell onto the bed right next to you and we made . . ." His eyes met hers, and a rush of warmth flooded her face.

She hadn't realized until that moment how clearly she remembered the day. It had been a Sunday morning and Jeff had served her breakfast in bed and had insisted she not move until he returned.

Suddenly he had dropped out of the ceiling and landed on the bed, next to her. Miraculously he hadn't been hurt—but oh, how they'd laughed, and the laughter had led to the most amazing and passionate . . .

"Come to think of it, I don't believe I ever did get that chimney working right," he said, and the tortured look on his face told her his memories were just as vivid as hers, though, judging by the dark look on his face, nowhere near as pleasurable.

"Plumbing was more your forte," she said, and she sensed a feeling of relief when he laughed, breaking the tension that had suddenly settled between them.

"Do you remember us spending an entire two days huddled under the sink and—" He stopped, and it wasn't hard to guess why. They'd made love under that sink, too, amid the monkey wrenches and leaking pipes. It was one of the reasons it had taken an entire weekend to do a relatively minor repair job.

"That wasn't quite as bad as the time you forgot to connect the hose behind the washing machine," she added, trying frantically to recall a "safe" memory. At least they'd had the good sense not to make love in the flooded garage.

"And remember the great VCR caper?" he asked.

"Was that the time you hired that ten-year-old to come and show you how to work it?" she asked.

"That's it." He smiled to himself. "Remember the time we got stuck in that elevator overnight? I'll never forget it. They finally pried open the door, but you couldn't squeeze through the opening because you were too fat."

"I was *not* too fat," she said, indignant. "I was nine months preg—" She quickly reached for her glass and took a sip.

Jeff's face grew tight as he watched her. "I'm sorry, I didn't mean to—"

"I know." She set down her glass and took a deep breath. With all the memories they'd shared, the one thing they hadn't talked about was their son, Joey. She stared down at her plate, willing herself not to give in to the tears that burned her eyes, waiting for release. Even now, all these years later, it still hurt like hell.

She considered the possibility that maybe Randall and her mother were right. Maybe she and Jeff really did have an unresolved issue between them. They had never discussed Joey, and maybe, just maybe, it was time they did.

CHAPTER FOUR

Paige looked up to find Jeff still watching her, long after she decided this wasn't the time to mention Joey's name. Their eyes locked for a moment before they looked away, he to reach for a roll and she to watch a woman walk by the window, pushing a stroller.

The restaurant was beginning to fill up with the noontime crowd, and the low murmur of voices from the next table broke the silence that had settled between them.

Jeff seemed to be tackling his steak with more than his usual gusto, though when she looked up at him, she found his eyes still on her. "I bet your mother would have a field day if she knew we were sitting in a restaurant sharing memories of the past."

Paige nodded. "Wouldn't she?" Especially if her mother knew that practically every memory had to do with their making love. Suddenly losing her appetite, she pushed her half-eaten salad to the side of her plate. "So what did you tell Mary Ann?"

"Mary Beth," he said, correcting her gently. "I told her the truth. That there's no deep, psychological meaning as to why we played the same numbers."

She smiled in relief. At last, someone who agreed with her. "That's what I told Randall."

"So what are you going to do with your half of the money?" he asked.

Grateful for the change of subject, she shrugged. She'd been so busy defending herself, she hadn't had time to think about the money. "I don't know. Maybe take a trip to Europe. Go on a cruise. What about you?"

"I was thinking about buying a motor home. Maybe take some time off work to see the country. Remember we talked about doing that one day?"

She remembered all right; she particularly remembered their goal of wanting to travel cross-country for the sole purpose of making love in every state.

"And I thought I'd give something to the SIDS foundation in memory of Joey," he said slowly.

She bit her lip and nodded. SIDS stood for sudden infant death syndrome. "That's a good idea," she said softly. "I'll donate money, too."

"Why don't we just make a single donation, in both our names?" he asked.

She felt a squeezing pain in her chest. "I'd like that," she said. "You don't think Mary Ann would mind, do you?"

"Mary Beth?" He shrugged. "Why should she?"

She watched him through the fringe of her lashes. "Jeff, you don't suppose . . . ?"

He met her eyes. "What?"

"That maybe . . . you know . . . What if everyone is right? Wh-what if . . . th-there really *is* a r-reason we played those s-same numbers?" It wasn't like her to stammer and stutter so, but she couldn't seem to help herself. She cleared her throat and tried again. "You don't suppose we really do have an unresolved issue between us?"

His eyes met hers. He looked confused, then skeptical. "Nah." He dabbed his mouth with his napkin before he laid it on the table next to his plate. "It's ridiculous. We re-solved our differences years ago." Frowning, he picked up his glass and swirled the bubbly contents. "Surely you don't think . . . ?"

"No, no, of course not," she said, and in her haste to assure him, she wondered if she hadn't sounded a bit too adamant.

She didn't want him to accuse her of protesting too much. "I just wondered what you thought."

He finished the champagne and set down his glass. After a moment he leaned forward and covered her hand with his own. "Do you want me to talk to this Randall fellow? I'll tell him the truth. I decided on the spur of the moment to buy a lottery ticket and I played those numbers without thinking."

"That won't be necessary." Her cheeks burning, she pulled her hand away. If Randall didn't believe her, he sure wouldn't believe Jeff.

She folded her hands on her lap so Jeff couldn't touch her again. She had enough things to worry about without having to control her galloping senses. Not that she couldn't handle her emotions, of course. Just because her pulse still leaped at Jeff's touch was no reason to think she was still attracted to him.

She was attracted to *Randall*. She *loved* Randall. He was smart and funny and easy to be with. He wasn't what she called passionate by nature, and he seldom showed any emotion. Sometimes she had to ask if he was happy or excited or depressed. She could never really tell. But that's what had attracted her to him in the first place.

Randall and Jeff were exact opposites, and not just in appearances. Jeff tended to rant if he was upset and laugh if he was happy. He'd even wept openly the day they'd found Joey dead in his crib.

In contrast, Randall pretty much kept his emotions to himself. For someone who was in constant battle with her own emotions, he was just what the doctor ordered. Never did he expect more from her than it was safe for her to give. That's why his unexpected reaction to her winning the lottery together with Jeff had come as such a complete shock.

"Once Randall has time to think about it, he'll see how ridiculous the notion is. Why, you're the last person—" Her eyes locked with his for a moment before her gaze dropped to her lap. "I mean, it's over between us." And it *was* over, she thought. *It was over the day I found out you were seeing another woman. . . .*

"I feel exactly the same way," he said.

She lifted her eyes to his. "Do you want me to talk to Mary . . . ?"

"Beth. No, that's quite all right. Once I tell her that we had lunch together and everything was cool between us, she'll realize she has nothing to worry about."

"Nothing," she reiterated.

"You're not mad at me, are you? For playing our lucky numbers?"

He looked so contrite, she couldn't help but laugh.

"Of course not," she said. "Just don't do it again."

They left the restaurant laughing over some ridiculous joke and walked the three blocks back to Paige's catering company.

Jeff leaned against his shiny red Blazer, parked at the curb in front of Paige's catering company. "It was great seeing you again."

"You too." She smiled up at him, and much to her surprise, he leaned over and kissed her on the cheek. It was a kiss between friends, but judging by the way her pulse soared and her heart pounded, no one would have guessed it.

Not trusting herself to speak, she watched him climb into the driver's seat with an odd combination of sadness and relief.

In all honesty, she'd enjoyed having lunch with him. They had been good together, once, and not just in bed. But he had hurt her, hurt her so profoundly and so deeply, it had almost killed her. She wondered if she would ever again trust a man as she had once trusted Jeff Roberts. Probably not. But odd as it seemed, she no longer felt angry or bitter toward him. Just sad and filled with a world of regret.

The important thing to remember was that her life with Jeff was over, and it was time to stop dwelling on the past.

CHAPTER FIVE

If Jeff lived to be a hundred, he would never understand the opposite sex. First Mary Beth insists he resolve his feelings with his ex, and then when he tries to do just that, she throws a fit.

They stood in the living room of her parents' modest home, facing each other, much as they had done three days earlier, in his driveway. The only difference was, he was fully dressed, his "Smile, I'm Irish" boxers at home in a mountain of wash.

"I did it for you," he persisted. "You were the one who insisted I was still hung up on her. So, against my better judgment, I asked her to have lunch with me to talk over old times. And it's just like I told you. We both agreed that the past is behind us and our playing the same numbers means nothing."

Mary Beth eyed him suspiciously. "You had lunch with your *ex-wife?*"

She made it sound as though he'd just admitted to having an affair. Sensing more trouble ahead, he heaved a sigh. "I'm telling you, Mary Beth. She's just as anxious to prove there's nothing between us as I am. Her boyfriend—"

"She's seeing someone?"

"Yeah," he said, feeling encouraged by the relieved look on her face when he mentioned Paige had a boyfriend. "You won't believe this, but her boyfriend thought it odd, too. You know, that Paige and I won the lottery together."

"I can't imagine why," she said, her voice heavy with sarcasm.

"Yes, well, you're both wrong. So what do you say we kiss and make up and go out somewhere and celebrate?"

"Well . . ." She gave a grudging nod. "If you're sure it's over."

"How many times do I have to tell you? It's over, and I swear to God I shall never play those blasted numbers again. Let's forget any of this ever happened."

"All right," she said at last, though she was still frowning. "I'll get my jacket."

Mary Beth left the room, returning a moment later wearing a light denim jacket that matched her blue jeans. She called to her mother, who had tactfully withdrawn to the kitchen upon his arrival, "I won't be late."

Obviously Mary Beth had no intention of moving back in with him, and he wondered how long she was going to cling to the ridiculous notion that he was still pining over his ex-wife.

The least she could do was drop the subject. But no such luck. No sooner had they climbed into the front seat of his Blazer than she started with the questions. He should have known. She was a lifestyle reporter for the *Daily News*. The drawback of dating a newspaper reporter was that she was always on the lookout for the newsworthy angle, even in her personal life. It wasn't enough that he'd won the damned lottery. No, she had to keep digging until she found the "real" story.

"Well?" she demanded when he didn't answer her question. "What *did* you and Paige talk about?"

"The usual stuff," he said, easing the car out of the driveway.

"You mean you talked about the weather?" she persisted.

"Not exactly. We talked about the chimney in our old bedroom. It never worked right. And our plumbing problems. We talked about the time I fixed the sink and . . ." What they had really talked about—or tried not to talk about—were the times they'd made love.

He shuddered to think what conclusions Mary Beth would jump to if he made *that* confession.

"What else?" she said stubbornly.

"You know," he said. "The usual stuff." *Like the time I fell through the ceiling and right into Paige's bed. . . .* Suddenly feeling warm, he turned the air conditioner on high.

Mary Beth pulled her jacket around her and hugged herself. "How come you never fixed our sink?"

"I'm not a very good plumber," he said. "That's what we talked about. What a terrible plumber I was."

"Is that all you talked about?" she asked, her voice edged in suspicion.

"Yeah." He glanced at her rigid profile and realized how different she and Paige were. They were complete opposites, not just in coloring and looks, but in other ways.

Mary Beth's idea of a home-cooked meal was popping a TV dinner into the microwave. But what she lacked in culinary skills, she more than made up for in other areas.

Unlike Paige, Mary Beth balanced her checkbook to the last penny. *Semibalanced indeed.* What the hell did that mean? "What do you say we get something to eat?"

"Okay," she agreed. "But will you please turn down the air conditioner?"

He adjusted the controls. He was just about to suggest a Chinese restaurant, then thought better of it.

Instead he stopped at an English pub. If his memory served him right, he had never eaten at a pub with Paige.

As they sat eating fish and chips and drinking ale from tall pewter steins, Mary Beth seemed more like her old self again. Much to his relief, she talked about work and didn't even mention Paige or the lottery. Maybe, just maybe, he had managed to put her mind to rest.

Suddenly she reached into her bag and pulled out her datebook. "What about September fifth?"

"What about it?" he asked.

"It's a Saturday. I thought it would be a good day to get married."

He almost choked on a French fry. "Married?"

"You asked me to marry you, remember?"

"Of course I remember. But I didn't mean so soon."

"It's four months away. We've been dating for two years. I don't see any reason to wait."

"But September? That's when Paige and I . . ."

"Oh, yes. How could I forget?" she said, her eyes flashing dangerously. "September sixteenth. The numbers nine and sixteen helped win the lottery for you."

Oh, boy, am I in big trouble this time. "I just think it would be better if you and I start out fresh," he said, choosing his words carefully. "What about . . . October?"

"It's too close to the holidays."

"All right, we'll wait until *after* the holidays. Come on, Paige, stop making this more difficult than it needs to be."

She glared at him, and he threw up his hands in frustration. "Now what's the matter?"

"You called me Paige," she said accusingly.

"What?"

"You called me by your *ex-wife's* name."

He groaned inwardly. Good God, what was the matter with him? "It was just a slip of the tongue."

"If you ask me, you have too many slips of the tongue lately. I'll tell you what." She shoved the datebook into her purse and stood. "Let's just put this whole marriage thing on hold, shall we? At least until you get Paige out of your system for good!"

"I'm telling you for the very last time, Paige *is* out of my system." He didn't realize he was shouting until the other diners turned to look at him.

Mary Beth narrowed her eyes. "Then prove it." She stalked out of the restaurant and drove off in *his* car. It wasn't until after she was long gone that he discovered his wallet was gone. He must have left it in the car.

Not only did Mary Beth not believe him when he said he was over Paige, but the owner of the restaurant didn't believe him when he said he was good for the money.

"Honest," Jeff said. "You've got to believe me. I won the lottery. I'm a millionaire."

The owner didn't look the least bit impressed. "That's what they all say."

It was after midnight by the time Jeff got home. Who would ever think that a little English pub could generate so many dirty dishes? Not only did his back ache from leaning over the sink all night, he had dishwasher hands.

He checked the messages on his answering machine. He recognized Mary Beth's voice immediately. "Jeff, I've decided for my own peace of mind to start seeing other men. If and when you resolve the problem with your ex, give me a call. Oh, yeah, I'll return your car in the morning."

Jeff stabbed the rewind button on the message machine. Wasn't this just nifty? Not only was he in the doghouse, he was out in the cold.

He took a quick shower and threw himself on the bed. How in hell was he going to straighten out the mess with Mary Beth? Not only wouldn't she listen, she wouldn't even talk to him.

If things weren't bad enough, he had the strangest feeling that maybe, just maybe, Mary Beth wasn't that far off. As much as he hated to admit it, he hadn't been able to get Paige out of his mind since they'd had lunch together.

Not that he thought there was anything between them, of course. But he did find himself thinking about her soft, curving mouth and wondering if it was still as sweet-tasting as it was in his memories. That wasn't the only thing gnawing at him; he couldn't stop thinking of the time he fell through that blasted ceiling. . . .

Not that his erotic thoughts should come as any surprise. Paige was a sexy lady. And the two of them had shared a great sex life—or at least for a while. It was only during the last year of their marriage that they had grown apart.

Actually, that wasn't exactly accurate. They hadn't *grown* apart; Joey's death had *ripped* them apart.

As for his obsessive thoughts, he supposed they were normal. Any healthy American male would want to take a sexy woman like Paige to bed. Not that *he* wanted to, of course.

If they spent any amount of time together, they would drive each other crazy, he was sure of it. They weren't the same people they'd been all those years back when Paige had rear-ended him and he'd fallen in love with her at first sight.

Now, he was certain, he would go bananas every time he opened the checkbook. She actually wrote IOUs to the bank, for chrissakes. As for Paige, she once tolerated his vast collection of musical instruments and CDs. But as people got older, they were less inclined to put up with another's bad habits. He doubted, for example, he would be quite so willing to sit through another ballet.

That was just for starters. Paige liked tearjerker movies, and he preferred his action-packed, the less dialogue the better. She liked classical music, and he liked country-western. Her dream vacation was the French Riviera. His was the rodeo championships in Las Vegas.

The simple truth was, he and Paige were as different as night and day. Had she not gotten pregnant all those years ago, they probably wouldn't have married in the first place.

So what in heaven's name was keeping him from marrying Mary Beth? That was the part that confused him. She was . . . well, sexy, in a sweet sort of way. And to his knowledge, she had never even seen a ballet.

She was intelligent and kind-hearted, and he would always be grateful to her for pulling him out of his shell. Following the divorce, he'd pretty much thrown himself into his work—until he'd met Mary Beth, who worked down the hall from him.

She'd kept badgering him to go to some action-packed movie, and he'd finally accepted her invitation. The movie, a real no-thinker, had provided a great escape; it was just what the doctor ordered. So, for that matter, was Mary Beth. At least she'd offered a sympathetic ear whenever he talked about his marriage to Paige, which in those early days was pretty much all the time.

She would make some man a great wife. Him, him! She would make *him* a great wife.

That's why he had to resolve this issue with Paige. He was tired of living in a vacuum.

Suddenly an idea occurred to him. He sat up in bed and switched on the lamp. Of course. Why hadn't he thought of it before?

He lowered his feet to the floor and reached for the phone book. He found Paige's number without any problem.

She answered on the third ring, her voice thick with sleep. He glanced at his alarm clock: it was four in the morning. Suddenly he remembered that Paige was a night person and he was a morning nut. It was one more reason why Mary Beth had nothing to worry about.

"Paige, it's me, Jeff."

It took her a full minute to respond. It was a good thing this wasn't an emergency. The house would burn down before she got her brain in gear. "Jeff? Have you any idea what time it is?"

"Yeah, I'm sorry about this. But it's important. Randall isn't there, by any chance, is he?"

"Randall and I are not speaking to each other."

"Still?" The problem was bigger than he thought. Convinced that she was as desperate as he was to resolve the issue, he plunged on. "I have an idea that will solve both our problems."

"The only problem I have at the moment is lack of sleep. I worked until midnight, and I've got to be at work by seven—"

"Hear me out, please," he pleaded. "You won't be sorry."

"All right, you have sixty seconds to tell me why you called at this ungodly hour."

He clenched his jaw. It seemed to him that she could give an ex-husband more than sixty seconds of her time. "All right. I called to ask you and Randall to have dinner with Mary Beth and me."

The silence stretched on so long, he thought she'd fallen asleep. "Why?" she asked at last.

"I thought the four of us could get to know each other and discuss the problem."

"We don't have a problem, Jeff."

"You and I know that. We're only doing this for Randall and Mary Beth. Come on, what do you say?"

"I say good night."

A click sounded in his ear, followed by a dial tone. Obviously she didn't think much of his idea.

Neither did he, actually, but it wasn't as if he had a lot of options. Mary Beth had threatened to date other men, and she was never one to make idle threats. If he didn't come up with a plan soon, he might very well lose her for good.

CHAPTER SIX

*T*hree hours later Jeff stood waiting for Paige outside her catering company. No one would ever guess from looking at her how little sleep she'd had; she looked magnificent. The early morning sun picked up the golden highlights of her soft, swinging ponytail. She had a long, graceful neck, delicate facial bones, and eyes the color of a blue Montana sky.

Not even the checkered pants and long chef's coat she wore could detract from her slender waist or rounded hips and breasts.

He knew the moment she spotted him by the flash of anger in her big blue eyes. "Leave me alone, Jeff. I don't have time for this."

"Before you say anything, let me explain." He followed her through the spotless kitchen and into her office, ignoring the curious stares of the employees they passed along the way. He closed the door behind them. "Mary Beth isn't talking to me and Randall isn't talking to you. And like I tried to explain to you on the phone, I have a solution to both our problems."

"Just what do you think our having dinner together will accomplish?"

"It'll prove to Mary Beth and Randall they have nothing to worry about," he said reasonably. "True, we had a really nice time at lunch the other day. But that's because we hadn't seen each other in years. After we spend an entire evening together, I guarantee we'll never want to see each other again."

She pulled her chair away from her desk and sat down. "Another four A.M. phone call and you'll accomplish the same thing at less cost."

"But Randall and Mary Beth need to see it with their own eyes. It's worth a try, isn't it? All we have to do is spend one evening together. Let them see how unfounded their fears really are."

Paige glared at him. "We're divorced. That should be proof enough how we feel toward each other."

"Well, you have to admit, our winning the lottery together kind of fuzzied up the picture a bit."

"It didn't for me."

"One dinner, Paige. That's all I'm asking."

"You're crazy."

"I'll tell you what's crazy. It's everyone thinking you and I are still carrying a torch for each other. We owe it to ourselves to prove them wrong. So what do you say?"

"Listen, Jeff, I don't have time for this. I'm leaving for Santa Barbara within the hour."

"Santa Barbara? Oh, that's right. Every year at this time, you attend some . . ." He snapped his finger, trying to refresh his memory. "Chefs' conference."

"That's right. Now if you'll excuse me, I have work to do." She picked up the phone and started punching numbers.

Since it was obvious she wasn't going to change her mind, he decided to reverse tactics. He waited for her to complete her call before trying again. "All right. Listen. What if our winning the lottery *is* a message of some sort?"

She gave him a look of warning. "If you dare to suggest we've been touched by an angel—"

"No, no, nothing like that. You know me, I'm not much for unworldly things. But what if our winning the lottery was a message from, say . . . Cupid?"

She rolled her eyes to the ceiling. "You don't believe in angels, but you believe in Cupid?"

He shrugged. "What can I say? I'm a romantic guy."

"And just what is it that you think Cupid is trying to tell us?"

"I think the message from Cupid is that it's time to get on with our lives. You're supposed to marry Randall and I'm supposed to marry Mary Beth. Obviously something is holding us back. Maybe *that's* why we won the lottery. Maybe Cupid wants us to take a long hard look at our marriage so we can put all this behind us and live happily ever after."

She looked at him, dumbfounded. "That's the most ridiculous—"

A tap sounded on the door and Lisa poked her head inside. "Someone to see you."

Paige waved her hand. "Tell them . . ." She fell silent when a thirty-something man walked into her office, wearing a suit and tie. "R-Randall," she stammered. "What are you doing here?"

Jeff frowned. So this was the famous Randall. Jeff disliked him instantly. Who wouldn't? The man made Mr. Clean look like a slob. To say his suit was impeccable hardly did it justice. The creases on his pants were razor sharp, the collar of his shirt starched to perfection. His tie was neither too bold nor too conservative, his hair neither too long nor too short. His mustache was so perfectly groomed, it could have been a paste-on.

"I think we should talk before you leave—" Randall stopped abruptly upon seeing Jeff.

"This is my ex-husband, Jeff," Paige said without apology. "Jeff, this is Randall."

Randall frowned as he looked him over from head to toe. He gazed pointedly at Jeff's scuffed sneakers, and Jeff returned the favor by staring at the brilliant shine on Randall's shoes.

"Oh, yes," Randall said archly. "Paige has told me all about you."

Jeff met Randall's hooded eyes with cool appraisal. "And it's all true. Even the good stuff."

"Jeff was just leaving," Paige said.

"As a matter of fact, I was," Jeff said, catching Paige's eye. "I just stopped by to invite you and Paige to have dinner with me and my girlfriend."

Randall glanced at Paige. "Dinner?"

Paige began stuffing papers into her attaché. "I told him it was out of the question."

"Maybe you can get her to change her mind," Jeff said. "You and my girlfriend, not to mention my former mother-in-law, think there's something odd about Paige and me playing the same numbers in the lottery. My idea is to spend some time together, just to prove to the lot of you that you're all mistaken."

Paige slammed the lid of her attaché shut. "I told him the idea is ridiculous."

"Have it your way," Jeff said amicably. "I just thought it would be a good idea to try to save our divorce."

Paige looked at him incredulously. "Our divorce doesn't need saving."

"It doesn't?" Randall looked confused, as if he weren't certain which side to take.

"No!" Paige said. "We are very happily divorced, and that's how it's going to stay."

"You know that and I know that, but Randall, Mary Beth, and your mother think otherwise." Jeff nudged Randall with his elbow. "Isn't that true?"

Randall looked about to agree with him, then apparently changed his mind. Or at least his eyebrow lifted a notch. "Your mother thinks there's something between you and your ex?"

"She's wrong," Paige said. "You're all wrong."

"Then why are you opposed to us having dinner together?" Jeff asked.

Paige straightened and glared at Jeff. "I have better things to do with my time."

Randall looked from Jeff to Paige. "Maybe we should think about this. I mean, the part about saving your divorce makes sense."

"Randall!"

The creases in Randall's forehead deepened. "Come on, Paige. Don't look at me like that. There has to be a reason you and Jeff played the same lottery numbers. We all agree on that, right?'' He looked to Jeff for support.

"I don't," Paige said.

"I don't, either," Jeff said, but only because he wasn't about to agree with anything Randall said, even if it suited his purpose to do so.

"Well, I do. And so does your mother and *his* girlfriend. It's three against two, so you're outnumbered." Randall looked so pleased with himself, Jeff was beginning to think he had missed something.

Paige shook her head. "I wish I'd never heard of the lottery."

"That makes two of us," Jeff muttered.

Randall glanced at his watch. "What do you say I make reservations for four at the Pierpont Inn for next Saturday?"

Paige sank onto her chair and grabbed the phone. "Do what you want!" She pressed a button and swung her chair around until her back was turned toward them. "Lisa, I'm getting ready to leave now. Did you confirm my reservations?"

Since everything was under control, Jeff couldn't think of a reason to stay. "I'll see you next week," he mouthed after catching her attention. He nodded to Randall and left her office, humming to himself. He had to admit that planning this dinner with the four of them was a brilliant strategy. He could hardly wait to break the news to Mary Beth.

CHAPTER SEVEN

*T*o say that Mary Beth was opposed to dining with Paige was an understatement. The truth was, she hated the idea.

"I don't understand you," Jeff said. "You're the one who insisted I still had feelings for my ex-wife."

"But I didn't mean for you to *see* her!"

"Then what did you want me to do?"

"I wanted you to see a counselor."

Had she told him to take a gun to his head, he wouldn't have been more shocked. "You're the one who came up with the ridiculous notion that I have feelings for my ex-wife and you want *me* to see a counselor?"

"All right, if you don't have feelings for your ex, then suppose you tell me why you two won the lottery together?"

"It's . . . a message," he said. "It's a message from Cupid that you and I need to put the past behind us and get married."

"A message from Cupid, eh?" Mary Beth didn't look any more impressed with his theory than Paige had. "That's the most ridiculous thing I've ever heard."

"Stranger things have happened."

"All right, have it your own way, Jeff. I don't care what you do. Just don't expect me to get all friendly-like with your ex!"

"All right, you want proof I'm over my feelings for her. I'll give you proof!"

Jeff slammed out of her house and drove straight home. He

spent the night tossing and turning until he finally made a decision. He didn't know if his plan would work, but it was worth a try. The next morning he packed his suitcase and drove to Santa Barbara, reaching the beach resort community in record time.

He exited the freeway and followed a narrow winding road toward the ocean, reaching the hotel by noon.

Maybe he was crazy, but if Mary Beth was right about him and Paige having some unresolved problems between them, he wanted to know about it.

The Spanish-designed inn was perched high on a cliff overlooking the Pacific Ocean. Scarlet bougainvillea covered the stucco walls, and tall, graceful palms swayed gently above the shiny red-tiled roof.

Paige, of course, had checked in a day earlier. He supposed she would be tied up for most of the weekend with the conference, but he was a patient man. He would wait.

He was a bit nervous about explaining himself. Paige had already agreed with him that there were no unresolved feelings between them. He wouldn't be surprised if she refused to talk to him altogether. Then he would have made the trip for nothing.

He signed his name to the register and was shown to a room right next door to Paige's, just as he'd requested. What could be more convenient?

As soon as the bell captain had left, Jeff stepped through the open French doors to his balcony and inhaled the fresh sea air. It was so clear, he could see the ghostly shapes of the Channel Islands in the distance.

That wasn't all he could see; directly beneath his balcony was Paige, her shapely body stretched out on a chaise longue by the pool, and she was wearing one hell of a sexy two-piece bathing suit.

Naturally he did what any full-blooded American male would do under the circumstances: he hastened inside to call Mary Beth.

*   *   *

Paige couldn't believe her eyes. She stood in front of her door, key in hand, staring at her ex-husband. Even more disconcerting was the fact that he was staring at her—or rather her two-piece bathing suit, which showed beneath her suddenly inadequate see-through cover-up. "What are you doing here?"

Jeff didn't have the good sense to look abashed or even apologetic. He just looked interested—*extremely* interested—in what she was wearing, or rather not wearing, beneath her cover-up. Heat crept up her neck to her cheeks.

"I told you we have to talk," he said.

"And I told you we have nothing to talk about. Now if you would kindly step aside . . ."

"Come on, Paige. Just a few minutes. That's all I ask. I know it sounds crazy, but I've not been able to marry Mary Beth and I need to know why. If, like she said, you and I still have some unresolved issues between us, then I need to know what they are."

Something in his voice touched her—or maybe he'd just caught her at a weak moment. He did seem sincere. Whatever it was, she found her resolve turning into putty. "This is important to you, isn't it?"

He gave a solemn nod. "Yeah, it's important."

"All right." She glanced at her watch. "I've got a full slate of workshops this afternoon."

"Let's talk now, then. The sooner we get this over with, the better. Please."

It was the "Please" that got to her. Or rather the slight desperation she heard in his voice. He obviously cared a lot for this other woman to go to so much trouble. Well, more power to him. She no longer harbored any ill will toward him. This revelation was as surprising as it was comforting. For it could only mean she was completely over her feelings for him. "I have to be at a lecture in a half hour," she said. "But I could squeeze you in tonight."

"That'll be great. How about dinner?"

"I don't know, I . . ." She hesitated. She had looked forward to hearing this year's banquet speaker. But the last thing she wanted was for Jeff to hang around all weekend. "All right,'' she said. "I'll meet you downstairs at seven.''

She turned and let herself into her room. Glancing over her shoulder, she wondered about the regret she saw on his face. He was still standing outside her room when she closed the door.

After a full afternoon of workshops and food demonstrations, Paige rushed back to her room to shower and change. She couldn't decide between the black dress or the blue one. The black crepe had a low neckline and a flared skirt. The blue dress was more modest on top, but its tight straight skirt showed off her shapely hips and long, tanned legs.

She knew how to dress to impress a man. The trouble was, she was having dinner with Jeff, and he was the last man she wanted to impress. Eenie, meenie, miny—the black dress won out. She studied it critically. Maybe if she wore it without the Wonderbra, it would pass for . . . semimodest.

She quickly finished dressing and then gave herself a critical eye in the mirror. Even without the deluxe bra that was guaranteed to push her bosom outward and upward, the neckline, while not daring, seemed a tad low. Funny how she'd never noticed. That did it, she was wearing the blue sheath.

But before she had a chance to change, Jeff knocked at her door. She should have known; during the time they were together, he had never once been late for anything. Promptness was yet another of his annoying habits.

"Ready?" he called.

She tugged on the scoop neckline and grabbed her evening purse. The dress worried her, but nothing prepared her for the look on Jeff's face when she opened the door.

His gaze swooped down to take in her neckline before he lifted his eyes to hers. "You look . . . great," he stammered.

"So do you." He was still the most handsome man she'd ever met. She hid her nervousness behind a bright smile. He was dressed in tan pants and a brown plaid sports jacket.

Knowing his aversion to ties, she was touched that he'd worn one, even if it was slightly askew. And his hair—that was askew, too, or at least a strand fell across his forehead.

She thought of the many times in the past she had straightened his tie for him, combed back his hair. It was all she could do to keep from doing so now.

As if to guess her thoughts, he reached up and fussed with the knot of his tie. "See? What did I tell you?" he asked, a humorous glint in his eyes. "You spend any time with me and I'll drive you crazy. You should see my room."

"I'd rather not," she said, grateful for the reality check. Her high-heeled shoes clicked across the tiled floor as she walked by his side toward the door leading to the hall.

"Stairs or elevator?" he said.

She raised her eyes to find him watching her. "The stairs," she said, and because she didn't want him to think she was afraid to be alone with him in the elevator, she added, "We need the exercise."

He looked skeptical. "We're only on the second floor."

She flipped her hair away from her face. "Every little bit helps."

The lobby was packed with people from the food industry. The noisy crowd waited for the doors of the banquet room to open.

Paige stopped to talk to a group of chefs from the San Francisco area. "Who's your new squeeze?" asked a redheaded woman wearing tight satin pants. Paige seemed to recall she was a pastry chef for some fancy hotel in the Bay Area.

"Oh, he's not new. He's . . . my ex-husband."

Jeff nodded his head as Paige introduced him. "I'm about as ex as you can get," he said.

The woman batted her eyelashes. "You can call me Monica," she said in a soft Texas drawl. "Why don't y'all join us?" She addressed them both, though clearly the invitation was meant for Jeff alone. "We have plenty of room."

"Thanks," Jeff said. "But we have other plans."

"Now don't tell me you're gonna miss that little ole speech." She ran her tongue over her bright red lips. "I hear tell Chef Fennessy is *very* entertaining."

"Maybe some other time," Paige said. The woman was beginning to get on her nerves. "Now, if you'll excuse us . . ."

CHAPTER EIGHT

*M*oments later she and Jeff walked into the hotel dining room and the maître d' showed them to a table on the terrace. Trees decorated with hundreds of little twinkle lights grew out of redwood containers. Each cozy table was bathed with the warm glow of flickering candles.

Jeff waited for her to be seated before taking his own seat. His eyes locked with hers before his gaze settled on her lips. Suddenly the muscle at his jaw twitched. He quickly glanced away, then reached in his pocket for his cellular phone. Keeping his eyes downcast, he began pushing buttons.

"Who are you calling?" she asked.

"Mary Beth." He finished dialing and lifted the phone to his ear. "I want to give her a full report so she doesn't worry." After a moment he spoke into the mouthpiece. "Hi, honey, I guess you're still not home. We're getting ready to eat dinner. You should have seen Paige's face when she saw my tie askew." Jeff winked at her, and, embarrassed to be caught staring at him, Paige quickly lowered her gaze to the menu.

Jeff continued his one-sided conversation. "Paige thinks I'm a slob. See? I told you. Everything is working out just like we planned. I'll talk to you later." He turned off the phone and slid it into his suit pocket.

"Did you call Randall?" he asked.

She studied the wine list. "No."

"Why not?"

She watched him through her thick lashes. "I don't have to report my every move to him."

He grinned. "So things still aren't right between you two, eh?"

She glowered at him. "I don't see Mary Beth falling all over herself to take your calls."

"But she will. Just as soon as I prove to her how much you and I hate each other's guts."

She folded her menu. "I don't hate you, Jeff."

Something flickered in the depths of his eyes. "I don't hate you, either. It's just a figure of speech." His lids came down swiftly over his eyes before he buried himself behind his menu.

She folded her hands beneath her chin and wondered why she suddenly felt so depressed. Even the lively atmosphere of the hotel failed to lift her spirits.

The waiter took their order, and the members of a four-piece band walked up on stage. After warming up, the band played "Fascination," and gradually several couples strolled over to the tiny dance floor.

Swaying her body to the haunting tune, Paige turned her head to find Jeff watching her.

Unarmed by the intense look in his eyes, she said the first thing that popped into her head. "Do you remember when we won that dance contest?" The trophy was still in her garage, though she had no idea why she held on to it.

"Yeah, I remember." They exchanged a look of amusement before she lowered her lashes against his steady gaze.

She felt strangely shy, out of her element, like a teen on her first date. It was ridiculous, of course. She was over her feelings for Jeff. And even if that weren't true, he was obviously smitten with Mary What's-her-name. "Want to see if we can still strut our stuff?"

"I don't know." He worked a finger between his neck and his collar and tugged. He looked like a man with a noose around his neck. "My dance skills are kind of rusty."

"So are mine," she admitted. Randall was perfectly at home in a suit and tie, but he didn't care much for dancing.

"I'm not sure it would be a good idea for us to dance," he said, frowning.

"Why not?"

"We're trying to recall all the bad things in our marriage, not the good."

"Is that what we're trying to do?" she said, surprised. Not that she had ever listed dancing among the many good things, though she supposed she could have. Still, they had so seldom gone dancing, and winning that contest had been a fluke.

"I suppose it wouldn't hurt to talk about some of the good times, too," he added.

"I don't suppose it would," she agreed. As long as they didn't talk about the times they made love.

"I mean, we don't have anything to worry about. It's over between us. We're just trying to tie up a few loose ends."

She smiled brightly. "That's all." She leaned against the table. "As I told my mother, you and I could climb into bed naked together, and nothing would happen." Something flickered in the depths of his eyes, and she drew back. Now why did she have to mention the word "naked"?

His gaze followed the full scoop of her neckline before his eyes met hers. "You told your mother that?"

"You know Mother. Once she sets her mind on something, it's almost impossible to get her to change it." She busily rearranged her silverware. "And as for unresolved issues . . . I don't think we have any."

"It doesn't hurt to check it out."

She moistened her lips but avoided his eyes. "I really would like to dance," she said. "But not if you think it's a problem."

"No, you're right. It's not a problem. Why would it be?" He jumped to his feet so quickly, he practically overturned his chair. Together they walked to the dance floor and turned to face each other like two wooden figures on a music box.

He planted his hand at her waist, holding her at arm's length. "See? I told you. It's not a problem."

She smiled nervously before placing a hand on his shoulder. "You're right," she said, her voice sounding a whole octave higher than usual. They kept their bodies perfectly rigid—and a mile apart—as they moved across the floor. "No problem."

It was awkward dancing with so much space between them, awkward and embarrassing. Ignoring the odd looks from the other couples, she tried to concentrate on the music, the twinkling lights—anything but her dance partner.

Finally he slid his arm around her waist and pressed his hand firmly against her back. He drew her so close, she could feel his hot breath in her ear. "It's easier to dance this way." His smooth, velvety voice sent a shiver of awareness rushing through her.

Easier? She lifted her lashes to find him gazing at her. *Easier for whom?*

"I hope you don't mind," he said.

"I . . . don't mind." She imagined she saw a glimmer of desire in the depths of his eyes, and feeling a terrible aching pain inside that brought a sob to her throat, she quickly looked away. She told herself it was the lights. That's all it was, the lights. Just to make certain, she met his eyes once again, only to find him frowning in concern.

"Are you okay?"

"Yes, of course I'm okay. Why wouldn't I be?"

"I thought I heard you make a choking sound."

Blushing, she laid her head on his chest so he couldn't see her flaming cheeks. "I was just . . . singing," she said. They both knew she couldn't carry a tune.

He chuckled, and her heart hammered against her ribs. God, she loved to hear him laugh. "Then you forgive me for taking you away from the banquet?"

For a moment she couldn't think what banquet he was talking about. Then she remembered her purpose for coming to Santa Barbara in the first place—and it sure wasn't to spend the night in Jeff's arms. She couldn't resist another glance at him, and that proved to be a grave mistake. This time their eyes locked and she found herself drowning in soft golden lights. "You're forgiven." She managed to sound halfway normal, with only the slightest tremor of her voice giving her away.

The band picked up the tempo with a hot Latin number,

and Jeff led her back to their table, his hand at her waist.

Nothing had been proven, except that winning that dance contest really had been a fluke.

That and the fact that she might have been overly optimistic in saying nothing would happen if the two of them fell on a bed naked. Fully dressed—now that wouldn't be a problem. Absolutely, positively not!

She glanced at him from beneath lowered lashes. Wouldn't you know? He chose that particular moment to give her one of his devastating smiles. She bit down on her lip and prayed to God she would never have to prove her bed theory.

All through dinner Jeff kept bringing up the subject of unresolved issues and she kept denying any existed. From time to time he'd give Mary Beth another call, leaving a message on her machine. Then he'd hang up and pick up the conversation right where they'd left it.

Finally she shook her head in exasperation. "Isn't it possible we played those numbers for no reason? Can't you just accept that?"

"I'm not the problem. Randall and Mary Beth are the ones who need convincing."

"Maybe we should just ignore them. They're bound to get over their suspicions eventually."

"Maybe," he said, though he sounded dubious. After a while he reached for his phone again. "Mary Beth should be home by now."

Paige grabbed her purse and stood. "I'm going to the ladies' room," she announced. If she had to listen to him leave one more message on Mary What's-her-name's answering machine, she would scream.

Later Jeff suggested they walk along the beach, and since it was such a beautiful, clear night, she agreed. Besides, she didn't feel the least bit sleepy or tired. A little exercise would do her good.

As if by mutual consent, they managed to keep a measured space between them, and if one accidentally breached that space, the other quickly moved away. For some reason her body felt oddly alert, as if something inside her sensed she was in a high danger zone.

Everything about him, from the smell of his aftershave to his swift, virile movements, commanded her full attention.

It surprised her that he still wore the same aftershave. She had chosen that particular scent for him shortly after they were married, and even now, all these years later, the woodsy smell of the great outdoors still complemented his rugged essence.

It was nearly midnight by the time they reached the door to her hotel room. She fully expected him to deposit her on the doorstep and leave. Instead he lingered, and not knowing what else to talk about, she told him about her afternoon workshops. "Tomorrow, there's a debate on strawberries."

He looked puzzled. "What's there to debate?"

She smiled. "You'd be amazed how passionate we chefs are over our strawberries." She told him more about strawberries than he probably ever wanted to know. "The Camarosa has a longer shelf life, but a Chandler tastes better."

Long after she fell silent, his gaze continued to linger on her lips. "Paige . . . I know we agreed that our playing those same numbers didn't mean a thing. But I want you to know, you're a very beautiful woman and I still find you . . . attractive."

Her breath caught in her throat. Though she had seen the unmistakable look of admiration in his eyes earlier, she'd tried her best to ignore it, telling herself it was nothing.

"Not that it means anything," he assured her hurriedly. "I'm attracted to a lot of women. Michelle Pfeiffer, for example. And I know for a fact you have a thing for Mel Gibson."

Yeah, but she wasn't within kissing distance of Mel Gibson. "Maybe we shouldn't be talking like this," she said nervously. She had a funny feeling this kind of talk could only lead to trouble. Key in hand, she turned toward the door.

He placed one hand on her shoulder. "Yes, we should," he said. "It's part of saving our divorce."

She glanced up at him. Dear God, if only he wasn't looking at her with such an open invitation in his eyes. If only his hand wasn't burning through the fabric of her dress. She pushed his hand away. "I told you, our divorce doesn't need saving."

"Maybe yours doesn't, but mine does."

It wasn't the kind of thing she wanted to hear. She pulled away, leaving as much space between them as she could manage without looking obvious. "You're right, we do need to talk."

He looked enormously relieved. "I can't tell you how much this means to me, Paige. You won't be sorry. I promise." He folded his arms across his chest and leaned against the wall. "All right. You go first."

"Me? You're the one who said your divorce was in trouble."

"I did, didn't I?" He thought for a moment. "All right. Let me think. Where should we begin?" He brightened. "I know. Let's start with our childhood. I read somewhere that we tend to marry the parent of the opposite sex."

"You mean I married you because you reminded me of my father?"

"That's it," he said eagerly. "Maybe you have unresolved issues with your father, and because of that, you're holding on to me. Maybe that's the problem."

She stared at him in disbelief. "For your information, I'm not holding on to you."

"How do you know you're not?"

Obviously he was serious about this. Maybe she should have Lisa introduce him to Dr. Bonheiser. "Maybe you're the one with the problem. Maybe you have unresolved issues with your mother."

"Maybe so." He looked delighted. "See how simple this is?"

"It's not simple," she said. "It's crazy. Besides, you don't remind me of my father. Not to mention he's dead."

"Dead doesn't matter."

"It matters to me."

"All right. Now think. What is there about me that reminds you of your father?"

She gazed into his face. "My dad had blue eyes."

"That's good. What else?"

"He was very intelligent. And bald. Yes, he was bald."

Jeff rubbed his hand over his full head of hair. "Well, two out of three isn't bad. Okay, now you resented him, right?"

"No, I didn't resent him." Her father had betrayed her trust, but she had never resented him.

"All right, forget that. Let's think about you and my mother. Let me see. Mother was short and kind of dumpy."

"Thanks a lot." Jeff's mother had died before they were married, so Paige never got to meet her. But from everything she'd heard, she was convinced they would have gotten along famously.

He shook his head. "You don't look anything like her. But she was an excellent cook, and she had a great sense of humor."

"Is that why you married me? Because I can cook and make you laugh?"

"You know better than that. I married you . . . because . . ."

"I was pregnant," she said.

"I was just going to say that." He studied her intently. "Would you have, I mean, if you hadn't been pregnant . . . ?"

"Would I have what?"

"Oh, never mind."

"You were going to ask me if I would have married you if I hadn't gotten pregnant, weren't you?"

"The thought did cross my mind."

It hurt her that he had to ask. "Of course I would have married you."

His eyes softened. "That's . . . nice to know." He gazed at her for a moment before seeming to catch himself. "Not that it changes anything, of course."

She tried to speak, but something was caught in her throat. She cleared her voice and tried again. "I guess it doesn't. That was a long time ago."

"And we're two different people."

"Two completely different people," she agreed.

They fell silent, and the faint sound of violins drifted

through the open French doors at the end of the hall.

He shifted his weight from one foot to the next. "I have a funny feeling we would both fail pop psychology."

"You're right," she said. "Maybe we're just on the wrong track. We're looking for answers that don't exist. Maybe there's no psychological reason for us playing the same numbers. Maybe everybody's making a big deal over nothing."

He thought for a moment. "You know what? I think you're right."

"I think so, too," she said, suddenly feeling tired. It had been a long day. She stifled a yawn.

"I can take a hint," he said.

"I think I'll read for a while."

"You still do that, do you? Read in bed?"

She nodded. "It used to drive you crazy."

"My playing the radio all night used to drive you crazy."

She smiled. He was right. She liked quiet and he liked noise. "Well, good night."

"Good night."

She unlocked the door and walked inside her room. She turned to find him still watching her. "I'm glad we figured out that we don't have a problem."

"Me too."

She closed the door behind her and took a deep breath. Jeff had admitted he was still attracted to her. Well, that made two of them. But just because they had the hots for each other didn't mean they still had feelings for each other. It was over, and it had been over for a very long time.

She tossed the keys on the bureau and slipped out of her dress. *It was over, with a capital O. Over!* After soaking in a hot bubble bath, she donned her favorite flannel nightshirt, then brushed her damp hair until it fell around her shoulders in a mass of golden waves. "It's over," she said to herself in the mirror.

Feeling better, she reached into her travel tote for the mystery novel she'd bought at the hotel gift shop.

Before climbing into bed, she glanced out her open French doors to the balcony next door. Jeff's light was off. Sighing to herself, she stepped back, leaving the doors ajar to let in the cool ocean air.

No sooner had she climbed into bed and opened her book to the bookmark than a knock sounded at her door. "Paige, it's me, Jeff."

She laid her book facedown on the bed and plodded barefoot across the room to open the door. "Jeff, what is it?"

He was dressed in the terrycloth robe provided by the hotel, and his hair was still damp from his shower. "I want you to know that what I'm about to do, I'm doing for Mary Beth and Randall. Just promise me you won't take this personally."

"I'll try not to," she said, though she hadn't the foggiest idea what he was talking about.

He raked his hair with his fingers and cleared his throat. "Ready?" he asked.

"I think so," she said. "But—" Before she could finish, he pulled her into his arms and kissed her. Actually it wasn't just a kiss, it was one of those knock-your-socks-off, Caesar-kissing-Cleopatra, death-at-dawn kisses that every girl dreams about.

The kiss couldn't have lasted for more than a few seconds, but by the time he released her, she was gasping for air and her senses were a mass of confusion.

"Remember," he said, his gaze steady. "You promised not to take it personally."

She swooned slightly, feeling utterly weak. "I always take kisses personally." Fearing her knees would buckle beneath her weight, she grabbed hold of the bedpost.

"That's what I was afraid of." He paced back and forth in front of her. "I know what you're thinking. But believe me, I wasn't trying to seduce you. I thought it would help."

Lord, if he wasn't trying to seduce her, what was he trying to do? She focused her eyes on him and tried with all her might to regain her wits. "Help?" she said, her voice hoarse. "In what way?"

"Obviously, we're both still attracted to each other. You have to admit it. There were times tonight when you felt ... when we ... On the dance floor, for example."

"Well . . . maybe," she admitted. If he was going to be honest about his feelings, the least she could do was be honest about hers. Besides, no one in their right mind could deny the magnetic attraction between them.

His hands behind his back, he continued to pace the floor. Meanwhile she held on to the bedpost for dear life and prayed for willpower.

"Anyway," Jeff was saying, "I figured out what the problem is. It's kind of like having a bowl of forbidden fruit. Worse, it's the Garden of Eden all over again. We always want what we can't have. So I thought if we allowed ourselves to take a bite of the fruit, the attraction between us . . ." He stopped pacing. "Would go away."

She was more confused than ever. She'd lost him somewhere between the fruit bowl and the garden. "So are you saying your kiss didn't mean anything?"

"Nothing, I swear. And it worked. Look at us. We're standing just a few feet from your . . . eh . . . bed and you're dressed in your . . . eh . . ." His gaze traveled the length of her. "Nightgown, and not one sexy thought is going through my head."

"I can't tell you what a comfort that is to me," she said, releasing the bedpost. She only wished *her* thoughts were as pure and innocent as he claimed his were.

Looking pleased with himself, he backed toward the door. "I'll let you get back to your book."

"My book? Oh, yes, my book."

"Good bed . . . I mean, good night," he stammered.

"Good night," she said, but already he was gone and she was left to try to figure out why Randall's kisses had never affected her like Jeff's.

CHAPTER NINE

*J*eff congratulated himself. Kissing Paige had been a stroke of genius. He just wished she hadn't been wearing that sexy nightgown of hers when he'd done it. Now it wasn't her lips that were driving him crazy, it was the vision of her in that blasted nightgown.

All right, so it was a plain flannel nightshirt, but it was cut to her thighs, and Paige just happened to own the longest and sexiest legs on planet Earth. No wonder he was beginning to think like a seventeen-year-old hormone machine.

What he needed to do was take a fast run and a cold shower. Then, if he knew what was good for him, he would call Mary Beth with a report, though naturally he would have to leave out a few details. Knowing her, she was bound to jump to all the wrong conclusions.

He jogged along the beach for an hour, plunged into the cold surf for good measure, then trotted up to his room to take a shower. A towel wrapped around his waist, he pushed the redial button on his cellular.

"Hello, honey," he said after the answering machine beeped. "Everything's going according to plan. We had a real breakthrough tonight. I'll be home sometime tomorrow."

He hung up. Things were going just as he'd planned. Once Mary Beth realized he thought to call her almost hourly while with his ex, she would have to believe what he told her was true: he was over any feelings he had for Paige.

Yes indeed, everything was under control. Actually, he felt pretty confident.

He walked out onto the balcony and froze in his tracks. Paige stood on the balcony next to his, her golden hair blowing in the light ocean breeze. The light from her room filtered through her nightgown, silhouetting the soft, luscious curves of her body.

One glimpse of her shapely body and he was ready to hit the icy ocean again. So much for confidence.

"I just called Mary Beth," he called, his voice strangely hoarse. Must be the night air, he thought.

She turned her head toward him. Her hair blew about her face. She looked rosy and pink and very, very desirable. "Oh," she said.

"She still isn't home. She must be away or something. I left a message saying I'll be home tomorrow."

It was a long time before she responded, and when she did her voice had a slight hollow ring to it. "She'll be relieved to hear that."

He leaned against the railing. He sure as hell hoped so. "Did . . . did you call Randall?"

"Not . . . yet. I will, though."

He stared out across the dark void that was the ocean. It was a moonless night, but the sky was filled with glittering stars, and he could hear the pounding of breakers against the nearby rocks. In the distance, the lights of a ship marked the horizon. It was a lonely sight, that ship, adrift on a dark and lonely sea.

"There's no hard feelings, is there?" he asked. "You know . . . what I did earlier. It was for a good cause."

"Oh, you mean when you kissed me?"

"Yeah."

"No, of course not. No hard feelings. What you said about forbidden fruit . . . it makes a lot of sense."

"You think so?"

"I think it was very generous of you to put yourself out like that . . . you know . . . for Randall and Mary Ann."

"Mary Beth," he said. After a while he added, "A lot of

women might have misunderstood my intentions.''

"You needn't worry," she said. "I know you were only trying to do what's right."

Several minutes passed during which neither one of them spoke. Finally he said, "Where'd you meet Randall?"

"I catered a party for his company," she replied.

"Is . . ." He felt foolish asking the next question, but he was truly concerned for her welfare. "Is his checkbook in good order?"

She laughed, and her laughter was like music to his ears. "I have no idea."

He was shocked. "You're going to marry him and you don't know about his finances?"

"I didn't say I didn't know about his finances. I said I didn't know about his checkbook."

"Same difference," he said.

They fell silent again, and finally she moved toward the open French doors leading to her room. "I think I'll go back to my book."

"Paige . . ."

She stopped, and he was momentarily mesmerized by the sight of her bare thigh. "Yes, Jeff? What is it?"

He inhaled deeply and shifted his legs against the low throb in his groin. "Would . . . would you have breakfast with me tomorrow morning? You know, before you go to your workshops? For old times' sake?"

"Sure," she said. "Why not?"

Later Paige lay in bed, listening to the waves crashing outside her window, and tried to figure out why she felt so restless of late.

She had everything she wanted in life. She was a successful businesswoman, and now that she'd won the lottery, she had more money than she'd ever dreamed of having. She had a boyfriend who wanted to marry her, friends who would do anything in the world for her, and a mother who loved her, even if they did have their disagreements. Life hadn't turned out how she'd planned it, but it was still a good life, a satisfying life.

So why did she feel so at odds with herself?

She turned over on her side. And why couldn't she stop thinking about Jeff's kiss?

Was she simply suffering the forbidden-fruit syndrome, as Jeff called it? His lips were off-limits, so she wanted them. It seemed rather simplistic, but in some weird way it made perfect sense. He had kissed her, but because he had caught her off-guard, she had been too much in shock to kiss him back. By the time she'd come to her senses, he'd already pulled away.

She sat up and hugged a pillow to her chest. No wonder she was obsessed with his kiss.

Well, she owed it to Randall to resolve this problem, whatever it was, and put it behind her so they could make plans for their future. Maybe . . . if she were to take just a tiny bite of the forbidden fruit herself, she could actually get around to calling Randall and telling him she was ready to set the wedding date.

Her heart skipped a beat. Kiss Jeff. Was that what she really wanted to do? Kiss him as he had kissed her? Would it really work?

Would she then be able to put him out of her mind for good? It was worth a try. Still, she didn't know if she could go through with it. Not even for Randall.

The following morning she found Jeff waiting for her on the terrace overlooking the ocean. Strolling casually to his table in a yellow sundress with spaghetti straps and a wide-brimmed straw hat, she was almost disarmed by the look of admiration on his face, but somehow she maintained perfect control.

He jumped to his feet and held her chair for her. "Did you sleep well?"

"I slept very well, thank you," she lied. She smoothed her skirt before sitting down and felt a jolt when his fingers briefly brushed her back.

A waiter poured champagne and filled their coffee cups. Breakfast was served buffet-style, but neither was in any particular hurry to eat.

Paige folded her hands on her lap. She had rehearsed her speech in bed, in the shower, and on the trip downstairs, but suddenly she felt embarrassed.

Still, she owed it to Randall—to herself—to find out if Jeff's theory on forbidden fruit was true.

"Shall we?" Jeff asked, standing.

Eager to take advantage of the delay, she followed him to the buffet table. The table was laden with large platters of shrimp, exotic cheeses, fresh-baked bread, and bowls of salads. The food looked tempting, but she couldn't seem to stop staring at the large basket of colorful fresh fruit.

After she had filled her plate, she returned to their table ahead of Jeff.

For the most part they ate in silence. She watched him through her lashes, trying hard not to stare. He, on the other hand, made no such effort. He hardly took his eyes off her. Trust him to make this more difficult than it already was.

The forbidden fruit was fast turning into a whole garden of temptation, and if she didn't do something soon, she was likely to jump across the table and attack him.

She cleared her throat and boldly lifted her head, meeting his eyes. She was a mature woman, and she would do what had to be done if it killed her.

"Remember what you said about forbidden fruit?"

He nodded. "I remember."

"Did it work?" she asked. "When you kissed . . . eh, tasted the fruit last night. Did it work?"

"Worked like a charm," he said, and nothing in his voice suggested he was being anything but honest. He smiled at her before going back to shelling his shrimp. He looked so utterly relaxed and unconcerned, she was torn between wanting to kiss him and wanting to wring his neck. If it hadn't been for his insistence that they had something to prove, she wouldn't be in this fix.

"I'm glad." She cast a glance across the ocean to the liner that was slowly moving along the distant horizon and wondered why she seemed to be growing more depressed by the hour.

"Any reason you asked?"

She glanced back at him to find him watching her with a speculative look. Forcing a smile, she shook her head. "No, none."

After breakfast they walked down to the beach. It was such a beautiful day. Far too beautiful to sit through a workshop on how the new federal laws affected the food industry.

They stood in the small circle of shade cast by a tall palm tree, and suddenly Paige couldn't help herself. Unable to think of a way to broach the subject, she simply decided to act. Without so much as a single warning, she flung her arms around his neck and kissed him squarely on the lips.

Jeff was obviously taken by surprise. He fell backward onto the sand, taking her with him.

His arm around her waist, he stared at her in astonishment. "What was that for?" he asked.

"Forbidden fruit," she replied.

His eyes darkened dangerously as he looked at her, and flames of desire flared within their depths. With a smooth swooping movement, he covered her lips with his own, crushing her body to his.

His lips ravished hers hungrily. Since he made it so easy for her, she wrapped her arms around his neck and pressed her mouth hard against his. Why settle for a mere bite when the fruit tasted so utterly delicious?

He released her eventually, but not until she was too weak to stand up. They sat side by side in the sand, both dazed. Jeff was the first to recover, or at least rise to his feet. Avoiding her eyes, he brushed the sand off his pants. Finally he caught her hand in his and pulled her upright, his eyes locking with hers.

In a desperate attempt to regain her balance, she pulled her hand away and tried to make light of the situation. "I hope you didn't take that seriously."

"Wouldn't think of it," he replied.

Well, then, it was done. She backed away. "I guess I better go to my workshop."

"I guess so."

She dug in her shoulder bag for her schedule and started across the terrace toward the conference rooms.

Jeff chased after her. "Paige, wait." When she kept going, he grabbed her by the arm, preventing her escape. "I was thinking. What happened back there—"

She feigned a look of innocence. "Back where?"

His brow furrowed. "You know perfectly well what I'm talking about. That wasn't just a kiss. That was a *kiss.* Come on, Paige, admit it."

"Why are you making such a big deal out of this? Why is it okay for you to kiss me, but when I return the favor, you choose to make something of it?"

"I know you, Paige. And I know you don't do anything without good reason."

"All right. I admit it, I'm still attracted to you. Just a little. And I thought . . . What you said about the forbidden fruit, it makes perfect sense. I thought if I kissed you, it would be over."

"And is it?" he asked.

"Yes," she lied. "You were absolutely right."

"You're a liar and you know it." He took her by the arm and practically dragged her through the lobby. He didn't even stop when Monica called to him.

"Where are you taking me?" she asked.

"To my room."

"I'm not going to your room."

"All right, we'll go to yours."

Moments later they stood just inside the door of her room, facing each other. "I lied, too," he said. "Sort of. I no longer want to kiss you, I want to make love to you."

She struggled to hold on to the smallest thread of control, but when she spoke, her voice was far too high. "I don't think Randall would approve."

"Maybe not," he said. "But if we have these feelings, we can't just ignore them."

"Yes, we can. And we will."

"So what are we supposed to do? Pretend that what happened outside never happened?"

"That's exactly what we're going to do. You're going to go back to What's-her-name, and I'm going back to Randall, and we are going to forget we ever spent this time together."

"Is that what you want?"

"That's exactly what I want."

He dragged her back against him. "Then you won't have any trouble proving it, will you?"

CHAPTER TEN

She was trembling even before his mouth covered hers. But once his lips made contact, there was no thought of pushing him away. Instead she flung her arms around his neck and, pressing her hands against the back of his head, deepened the kiss.

Without warning, Jeff broke away. Sighing deeply, he held her at arm's length. "I can't do this to Mary Beth," he said. "I can't cheat on her."

That's when Paige knew he was in love with his girlfriend, even if he didn't know it himself. Feeling foolish and ashamed, she pulled away. She wished with all her heart she loved Randall as much as Jeff loved that woman.

Knowing that she never would, no matter how hard she tried, she gave in to a moment of self-loathing. Randall was a good man, and he deserved better from her. He certainly deserved her faithfulness. The thought of how close she had come to cheating on him was depressing, but not as depressing as the thought of Jeff loving someone else.

She didn't want Jeff to see her cry, but Lord knew it wouldn't be the first time.

"I'm sorry, Paige. But I've never cheated on anyone in my life, and I don't want to start now."

That did it! She no longer felt foolish or ashamed; she was fit to be tied. How dare he lie to her! "No, you only cheat on wives, not girlfriends."

She stormed toward the bathroom, but he followed close at her heels. "And what exactly do you mean by that crack?"

She whirled to face him. "Don't act like Mr. Innocent with me. I know all about you and Barbara Hawkins."

"Barb . . ." He stared at her, looking positively dumbfounded. "You think I had an affair with my assistant?"

"You don't have to lie, Jeff. We're already divorced. Anything you say can't and won't be held against you."

"I'm not lying. I never had an affair with Barbara."

"Well, you had an affair with someone, and she was the likeliest candidate."

"Barbara Hawkins? A likely candidate? Are you out of your cotton-picking mind? What made you think I was having an affair?"

"The way you acted—so distant. And that day I showed up at your office, you and Barbara looked so guilty . . . like . . ."

"Yeah, I remember that day. I had just told Barbara I was afraid of losing you. I thought you'd be angry if you knew I had shared something so personal with my assistant. But I was desperate. I didn't know who to turn to."

"You mean . . . ?" She didn't know what to say. The fact that she'd been so willing to believe he was cheating on her with so little to go on could only mean that her state of mind after losing Joey must have been far worse than she'd thought.

"I never cheated on you—" His voice broke, but the huskiness remained. "I loved you."

She took a deep breath. She'd never thought to hear those words from him again—didn't want to hear them again. Her temper flared. Why was he doing this to her? Why? "You're the one who asked for a divorce."

"I was trying to shock you out of your depression. I lost you after Joey died. It was like I couldn't reach you, and I didn't know how to bring you back to me."

His words struck a chord, and the anger drained away. "You mean . . . you didn't really want a divorce?"

"Of course not. I wanted you. I wanted what we had together. I would have given anything to make our marriage work.''

"Oh, Jeff." The tears came fast and furious now. "When you asked me for a divorce, I thought I would die. But I didn't know how to get back to where we once were."

He took her in his arms. "I wanted to be there for you," he whispered. "But nothing I did, nothing I said . . ."

"I know." She laid her hand on his cheek. "I know."

He took her hand in his and kissed it tenderly. He brushed her brow with his lips, then dropped a kiss on her nose before angling his mouth to hers.

Locked in his arms, she buried her hands in his thick hair and kissed him back.

He fell on the bed, taking her with him, and they frantically tugged at each other's clothes. Her dress was the first to go. His shirt was next, followed by his belt.

Dressed only in her lace bra and panties, she moved against his body. His hands on her buttocks, he forced her closer until her aching breasts met his taut, muscular chest and his male hardness pressed into her thigh.

He let her have her way with him until she unzipped his pants and wrapped her hand around his pulsing manhood. He groaned at her touch and, taking full command, rolled her on her back.

Trailing a path of heated kisses down her torso, he unhooked her bra and worked her panties down the length of her, teasing her with the wonderful warm feel of his lips and tongue.

"You're beautiful," he whispered. He caught a pink nipple in his mouth, and she arched her back in ecstasy. He ran his hands up and down her body, his hands sliding smoothly over her velvet-soft skin until the pain of exquisite longing was too much for her to bear.

"Please," she begged. She pulled him on top of her, and their bodies fit together perfectly.

"Please what?" he teased, but he groaned as she moved her hips. "So that's how you want to play, eh?" After taking but a few seconds to reach into his wallet for protection, he eased into her slowly, as if to savor every precious moment they were together.

Slowly he increased his thrusts until she cried out for release. She felt herself spiral upward in a whirlwind of spinning sensations that exploded into wave after wave of pure ecstasy.

His body stiffened as he cried out her name and they rode out the final crest together. When at last he rolled off her, both were breathing hard.

Afterward they lay side by side on the bed, staring up at the ceiling. Paige was afraid to move, afraid to break the spell that still remained after their lovemaking, afraid that if she touched him, she would discover she had been dreaming and none of this was real.

She had no idea how long they'd lain there before Jeff spoke. "Dammit, now look what I've done. I've cheated on Mary Beth." He turned his head toward her. "She's been a good friend. She was there for me after the divorce." He sighed deeply. "She deserves better."

"So does Randall," she whispered.

Jeff's gaze settled on her lips for a brief time before he looked away. "I guess I should call her," he said, sounding miserable. "Tell her I'm going to be late."

She bit back the tears. "Are you going to tell her what happened?"

It took him a long time to answer. "I'm going to have to." After a moment he asked, "What about you? Are you going to tell Randall?"

"He has the right to know," she said. "But I swear nothing like this will ever happen again."

"I don't think we have to worry about that," he said, sounding strained. "It worked this time. My forbidden fruit theory worked. I no longer have this overpowering need to tear your clothes off."

Her heart skipped a beat. "That's because I'm not wearing any clothes," she said.

His gaze dropped to her bare shoulders before he quickly looked away. "You know what I mean." He sat up and reached for his pants.

"I'm not sure I do," she said, watching him. God, she loved his body. She was strangely comforted by the thought. Maybe these crazy feelings really were nothing more than lust. Lust was easy to cure. Or so she'd heard.

His hands stilled for a moment before he stepped into his jeans. "If we had gone back home without making love, we might have gone on thinking there was something more to those kisses than we intended."

"That would have been terrible," she agreed.

"But now we know it's just . . ."

"Lust," she said gently, and he grinned.

"I never could keep my hands off you."

She grinned back. And all these years she'd thought she'd been the one with that particular problem.

"That happens sometimes," he continued. "You know, a couple just clicks physically."

"I suppose you're right," she said.

"It doesn't necessarily mean anything. It could be a toxic relationship and they would still be good in bed."

"Do . . . do you think we had a toxic relationship?"

"Oh, no, nothing like that. We just ran into some tough times. . . ."

She bit her lip and nodded.

He looked at her from beneath an arched brow. "Now we can go home with a clear conscience."

"Nothing like a clear conscience," she said, trying to sound cheerful. She only hoped that Randall would appreciate just how clear her conscience was.

"Now that we have that settled, I guess I better pack." He glanced at his watch. "Checkout's at noon, and it's already eleven-thirty."

He reached for his shirt and grabbed his tennis shoes. "I'll let you get back to your conference."

Clutching the sheet to her breasts, she nodded. She'd never forgive herself if she missed the great strawberry debate.

Jeff stood in the hall, suitcase in hand, when she walked out of her room a short time later. He gave a curt nod, barely meeting her eyes. "I just wanted to say I'm glad we talked."

They had done a lot more than talk, but she thought it better not to mention it. "So am I," she said.

They gazed at each other for a long while, then he nodded toward the staircase. "I guess I better go."

"I'll walk down with you," she said. "It's on my way to the conference rooms."

She stood by the reception desk as he waited for the computer to print out his final statement.

Though the lobby was deserted and the desk clerk was on the phone, she lowered her voice.

"Jeff . . . you don't suppose . . ." Good heavens, now what was she doing? Looking for trouble, that's what! She bit her tongue and waved a hand. "Never mind, it's not important."

"Say it. What don't I suppose?"

She watched him sign his statement. "You don't suppose that we still have unfinished business between us, do you?"

His pen slipped. "I thought we settled this."

"I know, but I've been thinking . . ." She found herself blushing.

His eyes held hers. "What? What have you been thinking?"

"Will that be all, sir?"

Both Paige and Jeff stared at the desk clerk as if he had just landed from outer space.

"It looks like I'll be staying another day." Jeff grabbed the desk key, picked up the suitcases, and headed for the staircase.

Later, Jeff was waiting for her when she walked out of the great strawberry debate.

He fell in step beside her, matching her strides. "What you said earlier . . ." he began. "About us having unfinished business. You've been the one who kept saying the whole idea was crazy. Now all of a sudden you're having second thoughts. Why?"

She stopped. "I'm not having second thoughts. Everything you said about us clicking physically is absolutely right. It's just I feel . . . confused."

Jeff nodded in total agreement. "That's a very good word. I feel exactly the same way. I owe it to Mary Ann to straighten out the confusion before I go home.''

"Beth," she whispered. "Her name's Mary Beth."

He stopped in his tracks. "Now look what you've made me do. I can't even get her name straight."

"Blame me, why don't you? You're the one who couldn't leave well enough alone."

"You're the one who called."

"You didn't have to show up in my office and insist we have lunch. You didn't have to follow me here."

"All right, I admit it. Maybe I've overreacted."

"You?" She laughed. "Overreact?"

He gave her a lopsided grin, and her pulse raced. "Let's not argue," he said. "I'm just trying to figure out what's going on in my life. It seems like I had my life together, then one day everything spins out of control. Wham, just like that I lose my son, my wife . . . I lose everything I ever cared about."

"If Joey hadn't—"

"That's not the answer," he said. "Other couples make it through tough times. Why didn't we? Why did we turn away from each other when we needed each other the most?"

It was a good question and one she had asked herself many times over. "I don't know," she said honestly. "I think we were still so young."

"Maybe so," he said thoughtfully. He sighed. "So where do we go from here?"

She lifted her eyes to study his face. "All I know is that I can't face Randall until my conscience is perfectly clear."

He nodded. He felt the same way about facing Mary Beth. "Okay, so what's it going to take this time to give you a clear conscience? Do we make love or will a mere kiss suffice?"

CHAPTER ELEVEN

Lisa greeted Paige early that Monday morning with a "things to do" list a mile long. Paige took one look at the list of phone calls and vendor problems and shuddered. She wasn't ready to tackle work. She wished now that she'd stayed home.

Lisa followed her into her office. "Judging from the looks of you, I'd say that either you overpartied this weekend or you were hit by a ton of bricks."

Paige sank onto her chair. "How did you ever guess?"

Lisa's forehead wrinkled. "Don't tell me, you made a perfect fool of yourself."

"Totally."

"It sounds serious. I have an appointment with Dr. Bonheiser. Why don't you go in my place?"

"I'm afraid that even your shrink can't help me."

"All right, 'fess up. How bad is it?"

"I slept with my ex-husband."

Lisa let out a deep breath. "Is that all? You had me scared for a moment."

"For goodness' sakes, Lisa. Did you hear what I said? I slept—"

"I know, I know. You slept with your ex. Listen, don't be so hard on yourself. People do all sorts of strange things when they're drunk."

"I wasn't drinking."

"Oh." Lisa looked at a loss for words. "Does . . . does Randall know?"

"Not yet."

"Take my advice. Don't tell him. He'll kill you. Then again, this is Randall we're talking about. Maybe he won't."

No sooner had Lisa left her office, muttering to herself, than her mother called. "Did you read your horoscope?"

Paige rubbed her forehead. There ought to be a law forbidding mothers to call on Monday mornings. "No, Mother, I didn't."

"Then, listen to this. 'Leos hold the winning ticket.' Now isn't that interesting?"

"Yes, Mother, very."

"Wait till you hear the horoscope for Taurus."

"Why would I want to know about Taurus?"

."Because Jeff is a Taurus. Now listen. 'Look to Leo for guidance.' Mark my words, Paige. This is a sign."

Paige picked up a pencil and tapped it against her desk. Her mother wasn't going to give up on this ridiculous notion of hers that she and Jeff were meant for each other. "Do me a favor, Mother. Read Randall's horoscope. He's a Scorpio."

"Well . . . all right . . . if you insist. Let's see . . . Here we are. 'Curb your impulse to strangle those closest to you.' "

Paige inadvertently snapped the pencil in two. "Thanks a lot, Mother. You just made my day."

Randall arrived on Paige's doorstep at exactly five minutes before the appointed hour. Acting as if they had never argued or that she had never left town, he pecked her on the cheek and stooped to pet her ginger cat.

"I feel like Mexican food," he said casually. "And maybe we could take in that new Harrison Ford— Why are you looking at me like that?"

"Is this it?"

"What?"

"I told you on the phone I saw Jeff this weekend and you never said a word."

"What do you want me to say?"

"Nothing. Not a darn thing."

"What's the matter with you? You sounded strange on the phone, and now you're *acting* strange."

"My conscience is perfectly clear," she said.

He looked confused. "I never said it wasn't."

She looked him squarely in the face. "Just remember, it's against the law to strangle someone. What I did, I did for you."

He folded his arms across his chest. "Suppose you tell me what it is you did for me."

"All right. If you insist." She took a deep breath. "I slept with Jeff."

Randall was silent for a moment. "And you did this for me?"

"You're the one who insisted I had unfinished business with Jeff. It seemed only right that I wrap up a few loose ends."

"I've never heard it put quite that way before. So let me get this straight. The reason you played your ex-husband's birthday and your anniversary dates is because you wanted to sleep with him?"

"Yes . . . no! Oh, I don't know anymore. I just know I couldn't keep this from you. But it's over." She and Jeff had discussed this at length and had come to the same conclusion: they were two very different people from when they were husband and wife. It was crazy to think they could simply pick up where they'd left off. Too much had happened. "Whatever had us both playing those numbers, it's over. We dealt with it."

"So does that mean you're ready to set the wedding date?"

Her heart nearly stood still. "The w-w-wedding date?"

"Yeah, remember? I proposed to you."

"Are you saying you still want to marry me?"

"Sure. Why not?"

"After I slept with another man?"

"He's not another man . . . he's your ex."

"I cheated on you, do you hear? Cheated on you. And you

act like it's no big deal. Aren't you even tempted to strangle me?''

Randall looked at her oddly. "Strangling is against the law. You said so yourself.''

"What you're saying is you don't care that I slept with someone else.''

"What I'm saying is this is the nineties. No one's perfect. So you slept with your ex? It's no big deal.''

She stared at Randall as if seeing him for the first time. "It's a big deal to me.''

"Why are you making such an issue out of this?''

"Why? I'll tell you why! My father cheated on my mother and it nearly destroyed her. I left Jeff because I thought he cheated on me, and now it turns out I was wrong. You don't care a damn who I sleep with and . . .'' Her voice faded away as she burst into tears.

Randall hated it whenever she was in one of her emotional states. "I never said I didn't care. I said no one's perfect.''

"You make infidelity sound like a minor habit, like throwing dirty socks on the floor.''

"Would you stop putting words into my mouth?''

She took a deep breath. What was the matter with her? Randall was acting like . . . well, Randall. At one time she'd found his low-key personality a safe alternative to Jeff's more volatile one.

She had purposely picked someone as opposite Jeff as possible, even down to his body build and coloring. The reason was obvious: she never again wanted to lose control of her feelings. She never wanted to love as deeply or as completely as she had loved Jeff, and it had worked. For a time.

She and Randall had enjoyed a simple, uncomplicated relationship—one that was completely devoid of passion. She'd thought that was what she wanted, but after spending the weekend with Jeff, she knew she could never again settle for so little.

She knew now why she'd played those numbers: it was because she wanted to go back in time and find the part of herself that had somehow gotten lost along the way.

"I can't marry you, Randall," she said. "I just can't. I'm sorry."

Randall didn't say anything at first. He simply looked confused. When he finally spoke, his voice sounded slightly flat but otherwise normal. "I guess I always knew you wouldn't marry me."

Randall accepted her decision as easily as he had accepted the fact she'd slept with Jeff, and she realized she was doing him a favor. Maybe sometime in the future he would find someone who could reach the part of him that she was obviously unable to reach.

He kissed her on the cheek and she felt nothing, not even the sadness that one would normally expect after saying goodbye to a friend. "Feel free to play my birthdate," he said. As simply as that, he walked out of the door and out of her life.

Jeff was loaded down with two dozen red roses, a box of candy, and a gold bracelet. It had set him back a few bucks, but a man didn't confess to sleeping with another woman without showing proper remorse and bearing appropriate peace offerings. He was willing to bet that world peace could be negotiated for less than it had cost him for that bracelet.

He didn't have to knock on the door; Mary Beth was waiting for him. He could hear the TV in the other room, and assuming her parents were home, he lowered his voice. "Where have you been?" he asked. "I tried to call you all weekend."

"I have nothing to say to you."

"How can we make a life together if you won't even let me explain?"

"All right," she said, folding her arms across her chest. "Suppose you start by telling me why you spent the weekend with your ex."

"I did it for you. The reason it's taken me so long to marry you is that you were right. I did have some unresolved issues with my wife."

"Don't you mean *ex-wife?*" she said.

"Ex, ex, of course, ex," he stammered.

Her eyes narrowed. "So does this mean you're ready to marry me now?"

He looked her squarely in the face, and that's when it hit him. He'd kept telling himself that everything he had done that weekend, he'd done for Mary Beth. But now he knew differently. What happened in Santa Barbara had nothing whatsoever to do with Mary Beth, and knowing this, he could no longer pretend.

She shook her head. "Don't answer that. I can see it in your face."

"Wait! Let me explain."

"You don't have to, Jeff. I always knew it would come to this. I guess we were both kidding ourselves."

He tried to think what to say, what to do. He felt like such a heel. He'd never meant to hurt her. "I'm sorry. I really thought . . . things would work out between us." And because he didn't know what else to do, he handed her the gift-wrapped box. "Here's something to remember me by."

She opened the box. "It's beautiful," she said. "But under the circumstances—"

"Keep it," he said. "You were a good friend when I needed one, and for that, I shall always be grateful. I guess my mistake was trying to turn friendship into something more."

He took the bracelet from her and fastened it around her wrist. She smiled a faint smile. "We're both guilty of that. I guess Cupid was wrong, eh?"

He looked at her blankly. "Cupid?"

"Yeah, you know. You said Cupid was trying to send you a message through the lottery. I guess he was wrong."

"Yeah, I guess so," he said, feeling utterly depressed. Then suddenly something occurred to him. Maybe Cupid *wasn't* wrong; maybe he had simply *misread* the message. "You take care, you hear?"

"I will. And don't worry," she said. "Like I said, I always knew it would come to this." She looked resigned, maybe even relieved. "You know what? I'm really okay with this." She pushed him toward the door. "You better go. I have a funny feeling you've still got some unfinished business with your ex.''

This time he didn't argue with her. "I think you're right." He kissed her on the cheek and made a dash for his car.

She wasn't home. Paige wasn't home. Jeff tapped his fingers on his steering wheel. So where was she? At work? With Randall? His spirits sank. How could he possibly hope to convince Paige that marrying Randall would be the biggest mistake of her life, second only to their divorce?

He pulled away from the curb with some half-baked notion of driving to her catering company and making her face up to the truth. The two of them were meant to be together; that's all there was to it.

Suddenly he happened to notice her car in front of the minimart at the end of her block. He slammed on the brakes and was almost rear-ended from behind by a pickup truck.

Ignoring the horn-blowing driver, he made a quick turn into the driveway, parked his car in the first available space, and ran inside the store.

Paige stood at the counter, her back toward him.

The clerk, a big black man with a wide grin, stood behind the counter, watching her. "What's the matter with you today? I never knew you to take this long to choose your numbers."

"I know," Paige said. "I can't seem to decide what numbers to play."

The store clerk stood there, stroking his chin. "What's wrong with the numbers you always play? They were lucky for you once. Who says they won't be lucky for you again?"

"I can't play those numbers again," Paige said.

Jeff stepped toward the counter. "Sure you can."

Paige looked up, her eyes rounded in surprise. "Jeff! What are you doing here?"

"I came to tell you . . . it's not just lust," he said.

"What?"

"You know how I wanted to strip you naked?"

"Shhh," she said. Her face turning red, she glanced up at

the clerk, who seemed to be taking in the conversation with great interest.

Jeff lowered his voice. "I was right," he said. "Cupid was trying to send us a message. Only it wasn't the message I thought it was."

She opened her mouth to speak, but he stopped her. "What Cupid was trying to tell us is that we are meant to be together."

"Absolutely not." She pushed him away. "I'm not spending another weekend listening to you call your girlfriend—"

"That's not what I mean. I'm talking about you and me spending the rest of our lives together."

Her eyes widened in disbelief, and he nodded. "That's what I've been trying to tell you. It's not lust, it's love. I love you and I want to marry you."

She stared at him, speechless.

"What do you say?" he prodded.

"I . . . I don't know what to say."

"Say 'yes.' This is what Cupid has been trying to tell us all along."

"Maybe you're right," she whispered. "I mean, if it was just lust, I wouldn't have felt so miserable when you went back to your girlfriend."

His heart almost stopped. "You . . . you felt miserable?"

She nodded. "And every time you dialed her number—"

"The real reason I kept calling her was that I was afraid of what was going on inside me. Every time I looked into your eyes, saw you smile, I wanted to take you into my arms."

Her eyes swam with tears. "I wanted to *be* in your arms," she admitted.

He gazed into her face and never thought to see anything more beautiful or wondrous than the love that shone from her eyes at that moment. "It just so happens I have September sixteenth free."

Her hand flew to her mouth. "September sixteenth?"

"Our lucky number, nine sixteen. The date we were first wed. What better day to get remarried?"

Her mouth curved into the biggest possible smile. "Oh,

Jeff!'' She threw her arms around his neck. He kissed her right then and there, making it all but impossible for a customer to pay for his cigarettes.

"Would you two mind stepping aside?" the clerk asked.

Jeff didn't mind at all. He pulled Paige down one of the aisles and kissed her again.

"What about Mary Beth?" she asked.

"Mary who?" he said, nipping her ear. He then pulled away to gaze into her face. "What about Randall?"

She thought for a moment. "I can't even remember his birthday," she said softly.

It was all he needed to hear. He kissed her again, this time literally picking her up off the floor.

" 'Scuse me, miss," the clerk called. "You only have five minutes to buy your lottery ticket."

Paige gazed up at Jeff but made no move toward the counter.

"That's all right," Jeff called over to the clerk without taking his eyes off her. "We already have our winning ticket."

If you crave romance and can't resist chocolate, you'll adore this tantalizing assortment of unexpected encounters, witty flirtation, forbidden love, and tender rediscovered passion...

MARGARET BROWNLEY's straight-laced gray-suited insurance detective is a bull in a whimsical Los Angeles chocolate shop and its beautiful, nutty owner wants him out—until she discovers his surprisingly soft center.

RAINE CANTRELL carries you back to the Old West, where men were men and candy was scarce...and a cowboy with the devil's own good looks succumbs to a sassy and sensual lady's special confectionary.

In NADINE CRENSHAW's London of 1660, a reckless Puritan maid's life is changed forever by a decadent brew of frothy hot chocolate and the dashing owner of a sweetshop.

SANDRA KITT follows a Chicago child's search for a box of Sweet Dreams that brings together a tall, handsome engineer and a tough single mother with eyes like chocolate drops.

For The Love of Chocolate

YOU CAN'T RESIST IT!

Three breathtaking novellas by these acclaimed authors celebrate the warmth of family, the challenges of the frontier and the power of love...

ROSANNE BITTNER
DENISE DOMNING
VIVIAN VAUGHAN

CHERISHED LOVE

CHERISHED LOVE
Rosanne Bittner, Denise Domning, Vivian Vaughan
_____ 96171-5 $5.99 U.S./$7.99 CAN.

*Join three of your favorite storytellers
on a tender journey of the heart...*

Cherished Moments is an extraordinary collection of breath-taking novellas woven around the theme of motherhood. Before you turn the last page you will have been swept from the storm-tossed coast of a Scottish isle to the fury of the American frontier, and you will have lived the lives and loves of three indomitable women, as they experience their most passionate moments.

THE NATIONAL BESTSELLER

Cherished
Moments

Anita Mills   Arnette Lamb   Rosanne Bittner

CHERISHED MOMENTS
Anita Mills, Arnette Lamb, Rosanne Bittner
_____ 95473-5 $4.99 U.S./$5.99 Can.